Pinnacle Lust

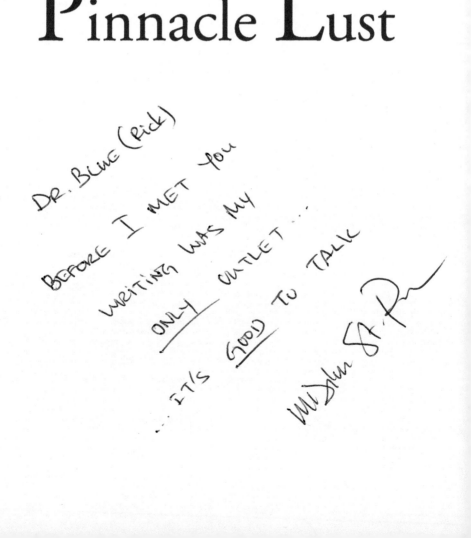

DR. BLUE (RICK)

BEFORE I MET YOU

WRITING WAS MY

ONLY OUTLET...

...IT'S GOOD TO TALK

WISDUM ST. PR

PINNACLE LUST

MICHELLE DIM-ST. PIERRE

BOOKLOGIX˙
Alpharetta, GA

Paperback ISBN: 978-1-61005-571-0
Hardcover ISBN: 978-1-61005-572-7
eISBN (ePub): 978-1-61005-573-4
eISBN (mobi): 978-1-61005-574-1

Library of Congress Control Number: 2015900552

Printed in the United States of America

♾ This paper meets the requirements of ANSI/NISO Z39.48-1992 (Permanence of Paper)

*For my mother who gave me
the wisdom and courage
to be who I am.*

*And in loving memory
of my father.*

With all my love, Michelle

Acknowledgments

First and foremost, to my husband Rick for standing beside me throughout my career, allowing me to follow my ambitions and live my dreams.

To Sherry Wilson, for pushing me further than what I believed I could ever achieve. It has been an honor to have you as an editor, a teacher and a mentor. Without you this book would have taken a different direction. I look forward to working with you on my next project.

To Linda Vega, for helping me in so many different ways, but mostly for keeping me reasonably sane throughout this project. Without you this book would have never been published.

To Kristen House at Kristen Corrects, for exceptional proofreading.

To J. Taylor Hays, MD, for the continuous care and support and for inspiring me with the word disjoin. I am grateful and honored to know you.

To George Foster, for a stunning book cover and other superb design work. You are a jewel in this world.

To Bill Adler, for displaying my beauty and personality through my photos.

To Richi Zane, MD, for keeping my OB/GYN scenes professionally correct and for believing in me. I am fortunate to have you as a friend.

To Dan Admon, MD, for reviewing my cardiac scenes. Your friendship means a lot to me.

To Scott Lorenz and the entire team at Westwind Communication for a proven record of superb marketing.

To Liz Jostes and Kristin Zaslavsky at Eli Rose for great social media.

To Mike Silverman and the entire team at Silver Web Solution for a captivating web site.

One

It was an early summer evening, around six-thirty, when the three paramedics pushed the narrow stretcher into the ambulance. Inquisitive people pressed close to see what was happening. There was no telling how bad the situation was—would the person survive?

The red lights of the ambulance blended with the colors of the sky. The gates of Heaven appeared to Leigh in a dramatic picture. It was a mixture of Heaven and Hell. Unique colors of the sunset dipped into the horizon—reds, blacks, golds, and pinks, changing their shades rapidly. A beauty that was distorted by the siren of the ambulance leaving.

Leigh drifted back into the past, reliving the day when she'd discovered that the man who had raised her was not her biological father—the day she'd turned eighteen—when she'd opened her birthday card.

Dear Leigh,

Best wishes on your eighteenth birthday. It is time for me to unveil the lie I live, and for you to face the truth. I wrapped up long pages from my life for you.

Love, Mom.

Leigh was uncomfortable. She looked at the large gift box and didn't want to think that her mother's journal was inside. *Would my mother really give me her journal for my birthday? Did she really believe that this was the gift I wanted?*

She ripped off the wrapping paper, thinking how the festive paper didn't suit the content. Leigh wondered what was buried in the box. *Does my mother really keep her secrets in here? What secrets can she have? Do I really want to know?*

But apparently, it was important to her mother that she read this. Her mother's words from her card played through her mind. *It's time for you to face the truth.* Leigh pulled the first page from the box. It looked new, not like the many timeworn, somewhat wrinkled, yellowish papers in the notebooks that were still in the box. She could smell the mustiness that the years had left behind.

Leigh recognized her mother's handwriting. With a black pen on white paper, her mother had written what she would not say.

My beloved daughter,

The first chapter of my life was relatively ordinary. Then, I entered colorful times. I was older, but probably not mature enough. It was, and still is, a beautiful part of my life—I was overloaded with excitement. Still, my happiness was diluted with loneliness and distress. My heart ached more often than it rejoiced and there were days when I couldn't distinguish between stupidity and courage.

What happened then turned into memories, some I buried deep inside me, and some I still live every day. Back then I had to keep it to myself, away from nosey people who craved gossip. I was faithful to my beliefs and to the man I loved. No doubt, some of this material gave the city something to talk about while the rest is still besieged within my heart and in my journal.

From the moment you were conceived, and throughout the past nineteen years, it never crossed my mind that my secret would be the evidence of who you are. I never thought that my lie could be your truth.

The pages you're about to read are my life, but more importantly they are YOU! Please be patient, read them all before you make up your mind.

Following my last entry is the third part of my life—the part that I will never regret.

I have to believe that you are old enough to understand how babies come into the world. I doubt you will argue about how easy and fun it is to make them. Yet, I question if you know how difficult it is to preserve them and how harsh it would be to lose them. I suspect that the thought of how you got into my world has never crossed your mind—certainly you never asked.

I'm wondering if the world I've provided for you compensated for the part I held away from you.

Love, Mom

Leigh was stunned. This was the last thing she expected to happen on her birthday. Reading her mother's journal? Facing the truth? What could she possibly find out?

She was overwhelmed—fear, anger, disappointment, and frustration mixed with curiosity—it was all there, churning inside her like a melting pot. The unknown scared her. She slipped off her shoes and dropped back onto her bed. She stared at the ceiling, holding her mother's letter close, before scooting up and nestling into her pillows to make herself comfortable. She read the letter one more time, trying to read between the lines. She loved the emotion and sensitivity. She admired her mother's attention to details and loved her sense of humor. While earlier Leigh was unsure whether she wanted to read about her mom's life, now she wondered what this journal could contain. Would it be about Leigh or would it be about her mother's life before her—Leigh's pre-life? Her hesitation didn't last long.

That night, on her eighteenth birthday and into the next day, her mother's voice played through her mind as she read those endless pages, learning about her mother, looking for answers, raising more questions and discovering who she was.

Her mother's journal was simply written in her elegant script. It revealed how back in November 1990, on a cold Friday night, on her way to work at a local religious Jewish hospital, she had no reason to think that her life was about to turn upside down.

Religious people? How bad can her secret be? Leigh thought and sank back into the journal.

Kol Israel Achim, the journal read, was a brand new facility built specifically to serve the Jewish religious community. It was a spacious building with endless corridors—finished with thousands of white marble slabs—located in a district where only the extreme religious Jews, the Hasidic, lived.

I was born a kosher and a graceful Jewish girl in Israel. Still, I was not one of them. I belonged to the other Jews—the secular ones. I had no interest in a religious life and sidestepped the radical Jews—especially those who wrapped themselves with a black capote and put on a *Shtreimel,* that beaver hat worn by a married Hasidic man.

As was my usual habit, I didn't use the *goy shel Sabbath* services. Instead, I drove myself to work. I parked within walking distance of the hospital but outside of the religious city's boundary. Only a busy highway separated the two distinctively different lives. Moving from one world to another was just a matter of using a flyover bridge above that highway. It was a bridge that allowed me to walk from my chaotic, secular world straight into the calm, religious one.

I walked through the religious silence that was disturbed only by the sound of prayers from countless local synagogues. In this holy atmosphere, I had to walk as many as ten to fifteen minutes to make it to the hospital on time.

The cold Friday night drew its holy atmosphere into the hospital. What should have been my comfort zone became disturbing. I felt like an outsider. Nothing could dim my non-religious attributes. I definitely stood out. I worried that my lifestyle, which was common and acceptable among single seculars, would seem cheap to those radicals around me. But when I read some detailed, intoxicating, erotic scenes written by several best-selling Orthodox writers, I worried that my own sex life was quite dull by comparison.

I tried to respect the owners of the building and those it served. I wanted to respect their lifestyle and customs, even to understand them. But their lifestyle was bizarre—way beyond my understanding. I dedicated myself to my job—but still, was astonished by some rules, many of which were strange to me—I was oblivious to some of the Jewish law, mostly to the allowable and forbidden.

I reached the labor and delivery lobby and stopped for a brief moment. I took a deep breath, making the effort to replace negative energies with positive ones. I entered my code into the keypad and stepped between the double doors as they swung open. Seconds before my night shift, moments before taking full responsibility for this hospital, I looked around, trying to gauge the atmosphere, figuring out who was about to go home and who would spend the night there with me. It looked calm. I expected a straightforward shift—nothing overwhelming.

Although my greeting was quiet and modest, everybody noticed me. They all stopped their work and acknowledged me with looks and words. Was it my appearance or my perfume? Was it my tone or my voice? Was it the authority or my personality? Were they happy or intimidated?—I never knew.

I continued on my way. And just then, right when I was about to step into the lounge, I noticed Dr. Katz—a senior member of the medical staff, another secular who had settled into the religious system for the benefit of heavenly pay. His presence that late in the evening was likely for a private delivery or an emergency requiring a senior member's skills on site.

"Hey, Sharon." I heard Dr. Katz's voice across the room.

I turned to find him and saw him with a stranger, making their way toward me.

"Hey," he repeated as soon as he got closer. "How are you?"

"I'm fine, thank you. And yourself?" I answered with a smile.

"Same. I'm glad you're here tonight!"

"Why, what's going on?" I asked.

"Well, this is Dr. Sloan." He gestured to the stranger. "He will cover some in-house calls," he said and turned to me to continue the introduction. "This is Sharon Lapidot, the house nurse supervisor. You couldn't ask for better on your first night here. She really knows the hospital and its politics."

I heard his voice but didn't register the words. I looked at him but could no longer see him. My mind was occupied with that stranger who suddenly had a name and a job. It was the physical part of me that reacted. I struggled to stay calm. I focused on my breathing, trying to maintain enough oxygen in my blood, making sure I would not hyperventilate. I couldn't remember when a man caused my heart to skip three consecutive beats—definitely not the man I was currently dating. My legs grew heavy and my knees shook. I stood there in front of that gorgeous new physician—an unusual and amazing creature—

and struggled to find something to say. I was speechless and couldn't remember what I was doing just a moment ago. I saw nothing but a six foot tall, well-built male, a pair of green-brown eyes, tanned olive skin, and silver highlighted hair that had possibly been brown at one time but had given in to the years. He looked to be in his late thirties.

I learned and memorized his intoxicating smell that enveloped me and captured my senses as if I was on the edge of addiction.

As we shook hands my body tingled with excitement, making it impossible to do anything more than just stand there. I don't remember how I greeted him or if I greeted him at all.

Dr. Katz continued, adding more speech to the air and still our hands could not separate. I couldn't tell if Dr. Sloan heard Dr. Katz or not. He seemed just as caught up in me. His eyes pierced mine, stirring something inside me. He perused every inch of me, like he could see through my modest scrubs. My heart quickened, extending both my jugular veins—did he notice? My reaction to him completely floored me. And thinking of it now, Joel, my boyfriend, never crossed my mind. Was I turned on or just fascinated by Dr. Sloan? I had to recover from the situation. I needed a diplomatic way out.

I reassured Dr. Katz that everything would be fine and that I would take good care of the new physician. I disengaged myself from the situation and walked toward the break room to meet with the evening nurse supervisor.

Her report was relatively short and light. I anticipated a painless night. "There is a new physician, Dr. Sloan. He seems to be okay. Did you see him? I think he's out there with Dr. Katz."

"I think I did." I avoided the subject.

"Anyway, here is the pager." She handed it to me. "I need to go." She collected her things and departed.

I was left to start my rounds in the hospital. Unlike other supervisors, my rounds were not structured—I didn't have a routine. I made my rounds based on the needs of the moment. I took action based on the problems that popped up during my shift. My priority list was dynamic, changing at a moment's notice, depending on what emergency might arise. However, I always managed to make at least two full rounds during my shift, each lasting around two hours.

But that night was different. I was systematic and determined not to let my interaction with the new physician affect me. I took the elevator to the upper floor and started my rounds there, making my way down, using the stairs and stopping on each subsequent floor. I completed the first round in one hour and ten minutes and found myself on my way back to L&D, as if there was a magnet pulling me back to the scene of a crime.

I obtained a verbal report from the charge nurse and completed a walkthrough of the unit with her. Nothing was unusual. I followed the same protocol as I would on any other shift and on any other floor. None of the staff members could see or tell that something had shifted in my mind and in my soul. They could not differentiate that night from any other. No one even knew that I had already finished with my first round.

While still in L&D, I received a personal phone call from Joel—my steady boyfriend—a career officer in one of the top-secret units of the IDF, the Israel Defense Forces. His occupation alone made him a good catch. He was educated, knowledgeable and well-mannered, with a clean background. God had blessed him with an impressive appearance—blue eyes, tanned skin, light brown hair, and a deep voice. Personality wise, he was an outgoing individual with a rich and colorful vocabulary. Bottom line, amazing features and qualities twisted into a five-foot-eight-inch man. In the culture where I lived, that was enough to make him a *keeper*. And still, he annoyed me.

I parked myself at the nurses' station, striving to be nice and respectful to the guy I was dating. I was painfully aware that this was not how I should feel when I sat down to talk to him.

"Hey sweetie," he said.

"Hey, how's it going?" I answered, trying not to let my emotions show in my voice.

"I'm fine, and you? Is everything okay?"

"Yes, why?"

"Nothing, just asking. Busy night?"

"Not particularly," I said.

"Good."

The momentary silence grew awkward. I was struck by the fact that after three months of dating we hadn't had sex. I was disturbed. *Do I really care about this guy? Am I wasting my time?* I asked myself and then returned to the conversation. "When will you be leaving?"

"Well, I'm not sure. There's a lot going on at the moment."

"Like what?" I asked.

"Different things—you know I can't go into the details."

"I understand—I hope it won't keep you there too late."

"Oh, I'm sure it will. I bet I'll spend the rest of the night here." He sounded cocky, which again reminded me what type of a person he was—someone who needed to impress others. Joel lived by tags and a detailed checklist. This behavior made it difficult to get to know him. He wasted endless energy to appear important. He made sure that everybody knew how high his security clearance was. He was obsessed with confidential information—he was all about security and secrecy. Many of our conversations ended before they began—everything seemed to be a top-secret matter that should not be discussed with anyone. So when he said that he couldn't talk about it, I respected him and gave him the benefit of the doubt.

But now, while on the phone with him, I grew tired of it. "I'm sorry." I lied—I really couldn't care less. All I cared about at that moment was my reaction toward the new physician on board.

"That's okay. Let me go. I have a lot to do. I'll see you sometime tomorrow." He tried hard to sound important.

"Sounds good," I said without thinking.

"Bye now."

"Bye." I let the receiver hang on my shoulder. I was struck by how boring our conversation had been—it was quite pathetic. And for a fraction of a second I had to admit that this conversation resembled our overall relationship.

"In love?" The masculine voice of a stranger cut into my thoughts.

Two

I looked up and saw Dr. Sloan. He was leaning on the counter at the nurses' station. There was less than two feet of laminated wood between us. His eyes locked on mine. We were so close I could see my reflection in his green-brown eyes. And beyond that I saw and sensed only temptation. I pulled my gaze away and placed the receiver back in its place. It took me a moment to remember that he'd asked me a question.

"That's what some people say." I didn't want to lie, but couldn't unveil the whole truth either. Let him think what he wished.

I collected my paperwork and was ready to continue my work, leaving the other nurses there to circle like sharks—they wouldn't let it go.

"Are you kidding?" one of the nurses said.

"Being in her shoes—it's impossible *not* to be in love," a different nurse said in a malicious voice.

"If you only knew who she's dating, you would understand," added another nurse, while passing Dr. Sloan.

I wanted to tell them a little bit about Joel, their hero—to share with them that he was basically good for nothing, that we'd yet to have sex. But how could I—and why should I? Instead, I made eye contact with Dr. Sloan and looked deep into his eyes—I could see the smile hidden there. *Does he sense mine?* I wondered.

That herd of horny women amused me. They really didn't care about me, or my love life—they were busy fighting for their own recognition, trying to seize Dr. Sloan's attention. I felt their jealousy. Their voices had a poisoned pitch. I was amazed at how important I was in their minds, at how much power they gave me, and the endless wasted energy they spent on me.

I focused on Sloan, debating how much attention, if any, he would offer them. But he didn't, he just asked who was available to assist him with stitching an episiotomy on a post partum woman. They all volunteered except one—"Why don't you ask the in-house supervisor," she suggested.

"Why wouldn't I?" he said with a smirk and turned to me. "Will you?"

My physical imbalance was no longer a brief crisis—I was attracted to him. "I guess I can," I said with a winning smile, as I stood and clipped the pager to my pocket. Sloan guided me to the delivery suite and kept his lips sealed.

As I stepped into the room, I saw an exhausted young woman in a gynecological position. Her lower extremities were stretched into cold stirrups—one to the right and one to the left. Her thighs shivered as her muscles grew weak. A green, sterile towel lay over her pubic area down to her perineum, like someone had made an effort to cover her privacy. It was hard to tell if the one who covered her intended to protect the patient from infection or embarrassment. My blood pressure went through the roof.

I was offended by the way the patient had been left. I felt humiliated for her. I assumed that Dr. Sloan was ultimately responsible for that crime and for that I was willing to strangle him. In exchange,

I was willing to place him nude in the same position and let him live to tell the tale.

I looked at Dr. Sloan for a split second and started gathering the supplies he needed for the stitching. By the time I passed by him I managed to work up enough anger to almost forget how gorgeous he was. Still, I had to avoid inhaling deeply so that I would not get dizzy from his inviting scent.

"How would you feel to be in her shoes?" I whispered loud enough so he could recognize the mean tone in my voice. I did not pause nor did I wait on his response. I didn't look at him again until I passed him the second time. "It's no wonder men cannot understand women and their feelings." And while passing him for the third time, I did my job and counseled him. "Next time, you should reposition the patient, not leave them in stirrups. I'm sure you know better."

He walked to the mayo stand, gowned and gloved himself. I tied his gown at the back and then carefully pulled the edge of the sterile cardboard that was attached to the waistline sterile string. While I was holding the cardboard, he circled around, letting the string wrap around his waist. He reached to the far end of the sterile string and pulled it back toward him, leaving me with the cardboard. He was well trained and in seconds tied himself without compromising the sterile field.

He stepped toward the patient and stopped in front of her pelvic area, waiting on me to bring the stool and immobilize it with my foot so that he wouldn't fall. It was not a gesture—it was part of my job. Finally, he sat, looking like a reprimanded child and didn't say a word—not to me nor to the patient. He had good skills and completed the stitching quickly. I couldn't fault him for that part.

After the last stitch, he stood up, stripped his gown and gloves, thanked me, and was ready to leave the room. I looked between him and the patient, hoping he would get the hint. When he didn't I asked, "Are you deaf or blind?"

He stepped back toward the bed and helped me remove the patient's legs from the stirrups and extended the bed, allowing her to rest her legs. Then he looked at the patient, reassured her with a smile, and left the room.

"Here is the call button," I said to the patient. "If you need anything, push it." I tied the cord to the bedside rail. "Try to get some rest."

I finished up my work, dimmed the lights, and exited the room.

Dr. Sloan was at the nurses' station, chatting with some of the nurses. My feet directed me to the lounge, but my ears were listening to their conversation. Clearly he had shared our incident with the nurses.

"She is tough," one of them said.

"But she's good," another nurse interrupted.

"And fair," someone chimed in.

Dr. Sloan did not argue. He didn't say much, though his eyes followed my steps. Disappointment fought relief. Obviously I wouldn't become one of his favorites. And maybe that was for the best.

It wasn't until I reached the lounge that I wondered whether I really needed a coffee break or whether I just hoped to end up in a cozy spot with Dr. Sloan.

The lounge was empty, leaving me to think in peace for a moment. But I couldn't expect it to stay empty for long. After all, the place served fifteen other individuals. It was only a matter of time before another staff member would walk in and interrupt my quiet. For whatever reason, it was Dr. Sloan who decided to take a break right at that moment. He stepped hesitantly into the lounge and lazed in one of the chairs, keeping his eyes away from mine.

"Are you making coffee?" he asked.

I couldn't tell if he was asking if I'd make him coffee, or just trying to start a conversation. However, since I resented the routine of nurses making coffee for physicians, secretaries for bosses, and female soldiers for commanders, I let sarcasm sharpen my words. "For you or for me?" And in seconds I continued, "How do you take your coffee?"

"Instant, two Sweet N Lows and milk." A winning smile stretched across his face.

"Just like me—hum—interesting," I said. "Well, why don't you make one for me?"

Sloan didn't respond. He probably wasn't impressed with my immature and grouchy attitude—who would be?

He looked at me intensely, as though he was seeing right through me. I felt naked under his gaze. After his short silence, he shook his head and stepped toward the beverage counter. "Why not?" he said.

My ego was boosted. I felt as if I'd won. *Won? Who in the world am I fighting with?* I tried to understand where I was going with this. *Why am I aggravating this man? What's the big deal if I make him a cup of coffee?* I did serve coffee to some other physicians. I'd really taken this too far. But, by then it was too late. I could not take back my words or my aggression. My pride wouldn't allow it. I had to stand my ground. But I filed away the thought that I could tone it down next time.

I scanned the room and noticed the door was partially closed. I walked over and made a point of opening it wide. "I hope you don't mind, but we have to keep this door open—you don't want us to commit *yichud*—seclusion—you know what I mean, right?" He gave me a puzzled look so I continued, "Seclusion of a man and a woman is forbidden—unless you're married," I said and quickly added, "to each other, I mean—otherwise it's prohibited to be in a closed room together." I shared my newfound knowledge of all the intricacies of Jewish law.

He looked at me like I was out of my mind, and I couldn't blame him. It did sound like a ridiculous rule in this day and age. Or maybe what I said made him wonder if he was flirting with the right person—a secular Jew or a religious one. Honestly, I hadn't given him a fair shot—I had gone from being friendly to reprimanding to refusing to make his coffee. And now, I was lecturing him about seclusion. He probably thought I was trying to make him look foolish. Still, he had to know the rules. "Seriously, I'm not kidding. Don't look at me like that. Trust me, it's different here—a world of religious fanatics. Everything here has a sexual implication—you can lose your job for that."

Sloan had a blank expression on his face. Was he rethinking his decision to accept the job here?

"Don't worry. You'll get use to it—like the rest of us." I tried to soften it up a little bit.

"You know," he said, "my wife's name is also Sharon."

Where did this come from? What is he trying to say? Who cares if his wife and I have the same name? Besides, I bet he calls her Sharoni and not Sharon or maybe he even calls her baby or honey or darling—who knows? And what exactly was I supposed to say to that?

Honestly, I had no interest discussing his married life. Luckily, I didn't get a chance to say anything before he spoke again. "I heard you are getting married soon."

Was he looking for conversation topics? Maybe he sensed that I had no interest in discussing his marriage. But my personal life was not up for discussion either. True, my life wasn't as perfect as everyone thought. They all thought I'd be crazy not to marry Joel. Well, they could have him. I was sick of everyone else deciding what was best for me. Besides, what would this stranger think about me if he knew that I was in a sexless relationship?

"I'm glad you're advising me," I said, putting all the scorn that I felt for everyone into my voice—the other nurses, Joel, and even this new physician who made me feel things I had no business feeling. "Thank God everybody is managing my life, otherwise I would get lost."

"I didn't mean it that way—you're probably right, it's really none of my business."

Well, I thought, *a man who knows how to admit his faults—incredible. Maybe I should give him some credit for that—even a second chance.*

"Any children?" I asked and cringed. *Why am I doing this? Didn't I just say I had no interest talking about his married life?*

"Two," he answered.

"Where do you live?" I continued so that I could determine if he met my criteria.

"Between Tel-Aviv and Jerusalem, and you?" He countered as if we were playing Ping-Pong.

"I'll be more specific than you—Ramat'sharon." I contracted my hometown's name as only those who originated there would do—just so that he would have proof that I was born there. His eyes opened wide as if it was the first time he came across a real Ramat'sharoni, the residential community of the known military and political figures.

"So, your boyfriend, what does he do?"

"I really don't know," I said and laughed. "It's secret, hush-hush."

"Career military or *Shu-Shu?*" He used the slang version for the Israeli Mossad.

"Look at you—on the ball, aren't you?" I said sarcastically. *Hell,* I thought, *why am I so hard on him? He doesn't seem to be looking for a fight. Why can't I simply be nice? Maybe even feel flattered? Why am I so aggressive?*

Our high-speed exchange of personal data seemed suspicious. It made me think that Dr. Sloan was just another womanizer, rambling in town free without a leash. The truth was that he had the looks, the charm, and a sense of comfort with himself to be one of those. However, I did not play prohibited games with married men who were desperate for quickies. They weren't worth the trouble. *Although now when I'm in a sexless relationship, it might taste different, but who needs the headache?* I thought. Was he interested in having an affair with me or did I want him to be interested in me? The way he looked at me made me think he was.

The temptation was so strong—right there, in front of me. I was concerned that I would not be able to hold back against the attraction. I saw it, smelled it, and understood it. I wanted to be brave enough and ask him not to test me—to tell him that there was no place in my life for this.

Luckily, thanks to my good judgment, I left the room before I made a complete fool of myself. "Thanks for the coffee," I said. "I have to get going."

"Wait a second, I need to go to the GYN floor," he said.

Three

We left L&D and walked toward the elevators. It was pretty dark, as the lights were dimmed for the night. Sloan and I along with the darkness were a dangerous combination. The silence shouted at me to think twice—but I disregarded its message.

The few long seconds while waiting on the elevator seemed forever. And in the elevator, after the cold, stainless steel door shut, it didn't get any easier.

In that cold metal box, where no one could see us, I didn't fight the physical attraction I felt—I enjoyed it. I was tempted to push the stop button and see where it might lead. But he didn't give me the chance as he said, "Hopefully this is not considered seclusion" with a wide smile that revealed a set of white teeth.

"Of course it is—but during night shifts we are less careful." I laughed but, at the same time, thought to myself that maybe there was something to this *yichud*. Otherwise why was there so much physical tension between us once the metal doors closed?

I didn't want him to think that I was hitting on him, so I tried to amuse him with some other rules related with *yichud*.

"You know," I told him, "when we—I mean the secular nurses—started to work here, we couldn't figure out why a Hasidic man would escape out of the elevator in a panic when we walked in. Not to mention how he would not join us and would wait for the next elevator, or just take the stairs."

"Are you serious? That's hard to believe," he said.

"Wait, it gets better," I said. "So, we approached the hospital's rabbi and asked him if such a thing is *yichud*."

"Did you really? What did he say?"

"He was sort of confused and said that he had to further investigate it. Then he ran it by some respectable, municipal rabbis."

"And?" He raised his eyebrow.

"His final answer was that as long as the two are not behind a closed door longer than the time it takes to boil an egg it is not *yichud*."

"So, we only have three minutes." He shook his head and laughed.

"Right, I thought the same thing, so I made the rabbi's life even more difficult."

"How?"

"I asked him what if the elevator gets stuck?"

"Did he give you an answer?"

"Nope, I guess all lines to God were busy." I laughed.

"You are funny."

"I almost told the rabbi that if he knew how much I could do in three minutes he probably would recommend changing the rule, but I didn't want to lose my job."

"That's hilarious, unbelievable." He laughed.

"I bet you'll come across lots of surprises here." I laughed with him.

As we entered the GYN floor, I rushed to introduce him to the staff.

"Finally, it's been almost two hours since we paged you," they accused Dr. Sloan.

Sloan took a deep breath and said, "I did answer the page—I called right away."

"Yes but…" the charge nurse said.

"You told me your concerns and I made the call." He was apologetic but firm.

He looked at me with a defensive expression. I had to jump in to rescue him. I felt like it was time to balance our battle, to make up for the way I criticized him in L&D. Besides, I had to justify what the nurses told him about me earlier—that I was fair.

From that moment until the end of that shift, Sloan became my shadow. Wherever I went and whatever I did, he was right there next to me. His excuse that this was his first night at work sounded legit, though I wondered if there was more to it.

At six-thirty a.m., on his way out to his full-time job, he found me in my office. He handed me a piece of paper with all his contact numbers, including his home number. I smiled and he left to return to his other world. I continued with my work, but not before I filed his contact numbers in the office's phone book as well in my personal one.

Over time Joel showed more of his ugly qualities—he became more arrogant. He was obsessed with his military clearance and often played the secrecy issue. It all contributed to our empty relationship.

By the time I had to deal with the sad reality of not getting laid, I was ready to pretend to be Eve and offer him the apple or to just rape him. My voice and my body language reflected my feelings and my needs but did not elicit a response. I didn't know if he was deaf or blind. I was worried that perhaps the problem was with me and not him.

I quickly put a plan in place. I went on an aggressive crash diet and joined an aerobics class, hoping to get rid of the few extra pounds I had put on. I invested in a new expensive perfume, shopped for new clothes, dyed my hair one shade redder, as some said it was sexier, and made an appointment for a facial. I changed the housekeeper's schedule from once a week to twice a week so my place would always look perfect.

I increased my grocery expenses and found myself shopping in a deli instead of a supermarket. The food I selected was more expensive and included selected wines on a regular basis—things that I could not afford. I ran over my budget long before I realized it, but still continued with this marathon as if it would bring sex into my relationship with Joel. On the intellectual side, I did everything possible to make my house look educational and stylish. I purchased new books and signed up for the morning paper. It was important to me that Joel found me knowledgeable, smart, and sophisticated.

Two weeks later, on a twelve-hour night shift, I walked in the L&D and smelled Dr. Sloan in the air.

I leaned on the counter at the nurses' station and reviewed the white board on the wall, trying to get the sense of how busy my night would be.

"Hey there." I heard a familiar voice speaking into my left ear.

Oh my God! I could feel his breath on my neck. The voice sounded so close. I turned my head and pulled back. As my eyes engaged with his, I realized that Dr. Sloan was closer than I'd thought.

"Hey," I said.

"I thought you would have called me by now."

"Seriously? What made you think that?"

"I don't know."

"Well, neither do I." I was doing it again. Why did I feel the need to snap his head off? I took a deep breath and adjusted my attitude. "So how are you?"

"I'm fine."

"I need to go. Maybe we can catch up later." I turned my back to him, hoping that he wasn't staring at me. I accelerated my pace and quickly entered the empty lounge.

But Sloan, as before, had his own agenda, and in matter of seconds he joined me. "Well," he said.

"Well what?" I replied.

"So why didn't you call?"

"Wow, that's how it works? You hand out your contact information and wait to be called?"

"Not at all. But I think that you wanted to call."

"And what if you're wrong?"

"Why are you so angry?" he asked.

"Are you flirting with me or what?"

"I'm not sure. I'm certainly not ignoring you." His voice was smooth.

"I thought we already straightened this out. Didn't we?"

"Coffee?" he asked.

"Please."

"Sugar?"

"Sweet N Low, please."

"Of course, how could I forget?"

I sat at the table, letting my eyes focus on his pants. I could swear that his package grew. I quickly looked away although my eyes were still level with his hips. And then, when he got closer, only a few inches away, placing the coffee on the table in front of me, I dug my nails into my palms. I tried not to think about any possible physical interaction with him, but my body disagreed with my logic and I found myself squeezing my vagina.

My pager went off. I looked at the displayed message and reached for the phone. I called the hospital operator and let them know where I was so they could transfer the call to me. It was Joel. I listened to his regular bullshit and looked straight into Dr. Sloan's eyes, hoping he would rescue me. I could no longer stand the forged importance Joel was trying to fertilize our conversation with. His long calls were seasoned with refined words and sophisticated phrases. The fake love that he offered dragged me into conversations where I sounded enamored with him. He knew how to orchestrate those calls so everybody would believe that we were in love. But the truth was different, and in our truth there was no love—it was all left behind with the fairytales. What we had was a pseudo affair. It was time to deliberate my options. *I really should move on.*

"Are you okay?" Sloan asked as soon as I hung up.

"Yes. I am."

"Are you sure? You look sort of confused."

"No, not at all. I'm fine."

My pager went off again. This time I was called to the OR. "I need to run. Sorry," I said as I rushed out the door.

"We can catch up later."

"Maybe."

Four

Once I entered the OR I no longer thought about Joel or Dr. Sloan—other things occupied me. The OR had its own life as if it was a separate unit from the entire hospital. The intensity of the place made it powerful. The surgical team's high level of adrenaline let them do and say things that would not be heard or seen outside of those oversized, heavy double doors. Not everybody loved it, but I did. Again and again I was fascinated by the blade, the incision, the blood, the drama, the stress, the unknown, the crisis, the solution, the resolution, and the correction—the saving and loss of life, the success and the failure. It was a place like no other.

As soon as I was done in the OR, I left and started my rounds. I dealt mostly with the routine. Everything went along as usual until I heard the overhead pager announcement. "Code 99—fifth floor—bay 6—code 99—fifth floor—bay 6."

"Shit," I said and rushed to the fifth floor—the neonatal department. By the time I entered the place the entire team was working, the pediatrician and the anesthesiologist along with two nurses. It was so hectic that I could not see the victim. The four adults and their four pairs of hands hid the tiny little newborn. I looked at the monitor, listened to their talk, and determined that I was not needed. Still, I did not leave but made myself available in the event that they would need help. It was my job to attend and stay for any emergency until resolved. Not to mention the amount of paperwork that I was required to complete after the fact.

"Come on, little man. Don't die on me now." I talked to myself when I saw the monitor displaying a long straight line. And I prayed, and I hoped, but it didn't seem to help.

"Call it," the anesthesiologist said to the pediatrician and everybody lifted their eyes from the preemie and looked at the monitor. It took a few long seconds before the verdict was heard.

"Time of death, twelve-twenty three," the pediatrician said and the team of four stepped back.

"Damn it," the pediatrician said in a frustrated voice while he ungloved himself. He grabbed the chart and sat in the chair at the nurses' station, holding his head in his hands.

"Let's see," he said as he opened the chart. "Is Sloan here today?" he asked.

"Yes, he is," I answered.

"Can you page him for me? He delivered this baby."

"Sure," I said as I picked up the phone.

Losing a patient was never an easy thing. You always questioned yourself—did you really do it all, did you do something wrong? It is this kind of thing that you cannot get immune to. No matter how many patients you lose or how long you have been in practice. It is one of those things that will bother you for a long time, maybe forever—an incident that will continue to come back and haunt you, almost as if it is your shadow.

"So what happened?" I asked the pediatrician.

"I have no clue. I guess we'll have to wait for the autopsy."

"Are you kidding me? Did you forget where we are? There's no way you will get consent for an autopsy. Not in this place."

"You're right. How could I forget? Sometimes I wonder if I'm a real Jew. There are so many things I don't agree with. Are you sure these people don't make up all these rules?" he said with a chuckle and went back to his charting. "And by the way," he continued as I was on my way out, "next time, don't ask me the cause of death—I'm not God—how would I know?"

The rest of my night was consumed by that incident. There was a lot to deal with—a family that, until two hours earlier, had no reason to worry about their newborn baby, but now had to deal with his death, a mother to be transferred from the L&D floor to the Gynecology floor, and endless paperwork to complete. And the worst part was dealing with the body.

Since Sloan was the one who had delivered this baby, we had a lot in common that night. But it remained professional, no tricky answers and no double messages.

He stopped by my office a few minutes before seven, on his way out. "Are you okay?"

"I'm fine. Thank you for asking."

"Hang in there. I'll see you soon." He gave me that penetrating look and left.

From that morning on, not one day went by that I didn't think about Dr. Sloan. His name didn't cross my lips, though it did glide through my thoughts all too often.

A few days later, on a Friday night, Joel and I were playing out our boring routine—a movie and dinner. I was determined that this would be the night. I was tired of his games and could not take any more of the sexual frustration.

Joel was quick to set the ambiance—a select bottle of wine and classical music, more in particular, opera—Luciano Pavarotti. Not that

I didn't appreciate Pavarotti, but I would have preferred something lighter—a different ambiance, a sensual one. I had no interest in clever conversation, listening to opera, or being mentally observed by Joel. I wanted to take his clothes off and smell his body. I was starving to explore his body and to discover his sexual skills and abilities.

But Joel, as always, was calm and in control. He sat on the couch in my living room and I found a spot on the love seat. He stood up to pour more wine and joined me on the love seat. That was unexpected—maybe he wasn't as oblivious as he seemed. He leaned back, pulled me closer to him and stretched his legs. Was he reading my mind? I became paralyzed as my heart raced, thinking what to expect next. *Perhaps I should let him make the next move*, I thought, or maybe now it was my turn? I let my hand travel to his thigh and stopped right there. I tried to manipulate the situation. But even then, when he was turned on and hard, I could not trap him—he was smart, careful and vigilant. My efforts were in vain—it seemed as if he wouldn't give in, while I was desperate and close to giving up. Clearly he was not sexless. *Is he gay?* I became terrified. The room was saturated with tension. I felt like I was competing with Luciano Pavarotti and couldn't win.

After a while, I realized that this was all there would be. But then, when I'd finally given up, Joel grabbed my hand and led me to bed. His touch and look didn't turn me on—he was so technical. My dreams were dashed to pieces. I prayed that our bodies would merge by their needs and not in conjunction with Joel's sophistication and restraint. Only God knew how much I was waiting for this moment. I felt as if I was about to give away my virginity.

Joel delayed it all—he left to get another bottle of wine, insisting we leave his classical music on. I could not envision making love to the sound of Pavarotti. But by that point, I didn't care—I just wanted it to happen. I wanted to feel the passion. I wanted my relationship to be real. I lay in my bed, waiting on Joel to come back and make love to me.

Perhaps the wine took over my dreams. I woke up the next day in the early morning hours. The bright light came in through the window and filled the entire room with the energy of a new day. I was spinning from the night's memories. I worried that I might be hallucinating and looked around. Once I saw that the linens were all straight and in place, I assumed that nothing had happened. We were both dressed as if we'd just gotten into the bed a minute ago. I felt like I was trapped in a revolving door with no opening. The spinning feeling was evidently not from riding a carousel in the park, and not from the climax that I hadn't reached.

I carried myself out of my bed and headed toward the bathroom. I turned back to look at what was lying in my bed, snuggling with my linen. I wanted to be mad—to hate him—to ask him what the problem was, but I didn't have the courage.

It took me a few minutes to recoup before I stepped into the shower.

My shower took forever but didn't last nearly long enough. The stream of the water washed away the sleepiness, though it couldn't wash away the nightmare that I was living. I was comfortable as the water trickled down my body. The touch of the water soothed and secured me, like I was back in my mother's womb. I wondered if I still wanted Joel to be there by the time I finished my shower. Part of me wished that he would just disappear—maybe indefinitely.

While I continued to survive my daily mental battle, preserving my relationship with Joel, destiny created interesting interactions for me with Dr. Sloan. Whether God intended it or not, most of our schedules overlapped and circumstances allowed us many hours together, especially during the night shifts—we became each other's shadow. We kept our relationship work related, away from personal channels. Sloan played by my rules, avoiding opportunities that might invite us to make mistakes. It would be a lie to say that I didn't sense the hidden intensity between us—we stimulated each other physically and mentally. How funny was it to think that the Jewish law, which had so often been a source of humor, actually turned out to be the truth as it saved us from committing a sin. Evidently, there was something brilliant about the Jewish law.

As time passed, Joel introduced me to more of his friends, most of whom were involved in some organization called "Quintessence." Soon I learned how deeply engrossed he was with this mysterious society. I was left out, but not passive. I investigated and learned that this institute offered intensive workshops, helping people to find themselves or their integrity—targeting individuals who could not accept their imperfections, training people to keep their power without being takers. They convinced people that they were what they were and that it was okay—as though there was no such thing as free will, to change and grow. I felt sorry for him and his friends. They struck me as spineless—I wanted to vomit. I couldn't believe someone actually believed that there is no room for improvement.

Over time, Joel frequently mentioned "Quintessence" and said that attending this workshop would improve our communication. He believed that the problems we were having would vanish. He sounded as if this could bring sex closer to our bed. I took this as an ultimatum and hoped for the best. I put some serious thought into giving in and registering for the workshop.

Then came the day when I felt relieved to see Sloan at the hospital. I suspected that my workplace was no longer just a source of income but rather something that I looked forward to. It was that day when I realized that Dr. Sloan brought joy and excitement into my life. I had second thoughts about registering for the workshop.

"Hey, how are you?" I said once I saw Sloan stretched out on the sofa in the lounge.

"Hey, kiddo, glad you're here," he said.

"Coffee?"

"No, I just had some."

"Do you know anything about 'Quintessence'?" I asked and walked to the beverage counter.

"I'm not into this nonsense—why are you asking? Are you planning on going?"

"I'm not sure."

"Come on, are you kidding me? Why would you put yourself through that bullshit? There is nothing but bad reviews about it. What's wrong with you? Haven't you read how many couples are getting divorced after participating in this?"

"I didn't say I'm going to attend this crap…"

"But you didn't say that you were *not* going to—and you better not. Anyway, how is your boyfriend doing?" he said with a teasing voice.

"He's doing fine—and how is your wife doing?" I teased him back.

"I guess she's still there."

Obviously, she is, I thought.

"Hey, I'm scheduled to do a C-section. I'll catch up with you later," he said as he left the lounge.

An hour later my pager went off and displayed the OR extension number. I picked up the phone and dialed.

"OR," a strange voice answered.

"This is the house supervisor. Did someone page me?"

"Let me check," the stranger said and right after asked in a loud voice, "Did anyone page the house supervisor?" After a brief moment he continued, "Yes, Dr. Sloan is looking for you. Hold on."

"Hey, it's me. I'm done. I'm going to order something to eat, are you in?" I heard Sloan's voice.

"No, I'll pass. But thank you for asking."

"Aren't you hungry?"

"Not really," I lied but didn't feel the need to explain that I was watching every single calorie that went into my mouth and how hard I was working to burn it off.

"Are you busy?" he continued.

"Not really. I'm in my office."

"I'll see you in a few."

Five

Shortly after, Sloan showed up in my office. My heart did a little flip as he sat on my desk, leaving only a hair's breadth between us. The thought of touching him aroused me. I pulled my chair back, trying to avoid any physical contact with him. He pulled off his green disposable cap and the surgical mask from around his neck, and folded them together into the size of a golf ball.

"So, what's going on? Are you sure you don't want some dinner?"

"I'm positive," I said and grabbed my pager as it went off. I stood and bent over my desk to grab the phone on my colleague's desk, so as not to get too close to him. Once I figured out who needed me and why, I turned back to Sloan, wondering if he'd detected my thong while I was bent over. "I need to go," I said as I straightened my scrubs.

He squeezed the cap and mask in his hand and lobbed it into the trashcan. He didn't get off my desk, though—leaving me very limited space to pass.

Tension boiled inside me. I doubted I could pass by him without brushing against him. I hoped he would get off my desk and move. His body was a magnet for me. My desire to introduce him to my secular life was boundless and intense. Yet, it wouldn't be in my best interest to become involved with someone like that, or even to have one-time incredible sex with him. The room was charged with sexual energy that overwhelmed me. Still, I managed to remain modest and strictly professional. Yet, in the eyes of the Hasidic we were two criminals who'd already sinned.

The daily news slightly diverted my boring routine with Joel and I spent less time with him, as he was hardly ever released from his base. The media reported, in its full capacity, information about the Iran-Iraq war. The US president, President George H.W. Bush, was worried that Iraq would control half the world's oil reserves. The US threatened to attack Iraq. Consequently, Iraq revealed its ability to use chemical and biological warhead missiles to retaliate. The Israeli government, along with the public, got the hint.

The year 1991 started with the media speculating on any possible war—conventional, biological, or chemical. Each reporter and anchor analyzed the political situation and gave his own opinion, like he was some expert holding a crystal ball. High-ranking individuals from the military were interviewed daily but did not reveal a thing. The spokesman from the Israeli Defense Forces, IDF, advised the citizens that they must prepare for a possible war.

Three days later, I stood in line to get fitted for my gas mask and pick up my biological-chemical kit. Fear and panic were clear in the eyes of the people waiting. I watched mothers being trained on how to set up special tent-like safety carriers called MAMAT for newborns and toddlers. The feeling of fear was palpable and I hated being there alone. Joel didn't bother going with me, as he'd collected his mask and kit at his military base. Not to mention how he reminded me daily that this was nonsense. He despised any authority that discussed the topic and refused any instructions given. Sadly, as comfortable as he seemed, he didn't provide me with security or comfort. I was on my own, following the instructions as they came.

I carried my personal rescue supplies everywhere, exactly as instructed. I rushed to get rolls of tape, hoping that Joel would help me apply strips of tape to the windows, but he refused any preparation. While he thought he was brave and smart, I was convinced that he was an asshole. He claimed that nothing would happen. He was so sure of himself to the point of being full of himself—determining that even if Iraq attacked Israel, it wouldn't be significant. And to make matters worse, he was not shy to accuse me of panicking.

Discouraged and emotionally exhausted, I dropped the tape next to the TV and left for the hospital.

At work, things weren't much better. I witnessed the orthodox praying to God, asking for help and mercy, but besides praying, they did nothing. Just like Joel, they ignored the instructions from the authorities.

That evening, I participated in a mandatory in-service, learning what to do during any possible attack. Each one of us was assigned to a different area and had different responsibilities.

Two hours later the entire hospital conducted a major drill. Anxiety and dread made my stomach ache and threatened to turn into a full-blown panic attack. I tried to stay in control, but couldn't seem to calm my jagged nerves. I looked for Dr. Sloan, not for advice, but for comfort.

Ten days later, on January 17, 1991, Operation Desert Storm began with the US Apache helicopters attacking Iraqi air-defense sites near the Iraqi border with Iran. From that moment on, it was quick. With no time for adjustment, less than twenty hours later, the sirens went off—Iraq responded by attacking Israel, the coalition's most vulnerable point.

I was at the hospital, exercising what I had learned only a few days earlier. My actions were confident. It was much easier to deal with the fear when I had duties to perform.

While in the Neonatal Intensive Care Unit, I took the newborn babies off the ventilator and attached the little endotracheal tubes, which were inserted in their mouths, to the Ambu bag. I delivered the first two breaths, making sure enough oxygen was delivered to these little ones. Only then did I shut off any valves to the exterior lines, while continuing to deliver oxygen through the Ambu bag—all for the sake of eliminating any potential contact with outside air if missiles damaged the lines. I continued to deliver breath after breath, while making sure not to hyperventilate these newborns. Their lives were literally in my hands.

I watched my colleagues and realized that none of us were wearing the nuclear-biological-chemical masks. It hit me hard when I realized that no one had bothered to place the newborns in the MAMATs. It all happened too fast. I wondered what my co-workers were thinking about. I wondered what would happen if a missile landed close to the building. Would it shatter the windows that no one had taped? Would a million pieces of glass fly into this big open space? How many of us would get hurt? I was upset with the hospital administration for their ignorance. How could they leave these huge windows like that? My thoughts were disturbed by a loud whistle.

Seconds later, a huge fireball flashed by the window. A scud missile, the first one I'd ever seen. It looked as if the sun was falling from the sky. The bomb blast followed just a few seconds later. I looked around and saw these babies, lying in their own, individual cradles and incubators. They didn't seem bothered. Their future was questionable regardless of the war. Right after the all-clear siren sounded, I made sure each newborn was secured back on his or her vent and that the equipment was functioning properly.

My drive home from work was uncomfortable. It felt like driving through a ghost town. No one was on the street. Coffee shops and restaurants had closed their doors and switched off the lights. Only a few other cars shared the road with me. I ignored the traffic signals and ran red lights. There were no rules at the moment—not for me, anyway. It was quiet—like everyone knew there was more to come. And it did.

Bombing became part of life. I no longer counted how many scuds fell. The alarm sounded at least once a day, if not twice. The only unknown variable was which city would be targeted. The Iraqis knew which sites they wanted to destroy. Israel is a very small country and most of the targeted sites were inside cities or nearby, thus all attacks would be directed to urban areas.

The military, like the civilians, adjusted to the situation and finally Joel was released for the night.

I arrived at Joel's place earlier than he did. As soon as I entered the condo, the siren sounded. Fear gripped my chest. His windows weren't taped and I couldn't think of any spot that might be safe. Dread clouded my judgment. I grabbed my mask and my kit, and ran to the first neighbor's door, praying that someone would be there. Every second seemed to last forever. I was impatient. In retrospect, I should have stayed in the hallway—it was probably the safest spot.

Finally, a man opened the door for me. His face was completely hidden under the mask. I wanted to explain who I was, that my boyfriend was his neighbor and wasn't home, and that I was afraid. But before I could say anything, he ushered me inside.

"Hurry. Get in." His voice sounded muffled through his mask. I followed him to the safe room. "Put on your mask." His tone was extremely authoritative.

I did not argue and pulled the mask out of its case. Two other people sat on the floor, wearing their masks and holding on to their rescue kits. In seconds I looked like one of them—as though we were aliens from a sci-fi movie.

Seconds later a loud whistle sounded—it seemed louder than ever. Then, the bomb hit. It was so strong that it felt like it had hit the building. Before I knew what was happening, the blast threw us all from one side of the room to the other. I was short of breath and needed more air. I wondered if we were under a chemical attack.

All I wanted was to take off the mask and get out of there. But I couldn't—I had to follow the instructions—I had to stay in the room and wait patiently for the all-clear siren and the IDF spokesman's announcement. The room started to spin as the neighbor extended his hand toward my face.

"Your air filter is capped, let me open it," he said. And all of a sudden there was so much air passing through and I started to feel better.

The all-clear siren sounded.

The radio played gloomy songs. There were no commercials, no interviews, no breaking news, and no hope. I was terrified by the thought that the spokesman would announce that it was now necessary to inject ourselves with the Atropine syringe from the kit. Would I really be able to do that? Would I also act as a nurse and inject everybody else? What if it was too late? Would I die? And how long would it take? Would I suffer?

Finally it was over—the calming voice of the IDF spokesman was heard. He was the only authority that could release the civilians back to their lives.

The neighbor opened the door and we all walked to the balcony. We leaned over the side rail to look outside. Ambulances, fire trucks, and police cars were all over the place. The missile had hit the building next to us. That explained why we were thrown from one side of the room to the other. We looked at each other but said nothing. Only then could I see the faces of those who had given me shelter.

This is scary, Leigh thought. She wondered just how well she really knew the woman who had raised her. It was like meeting a whole other person with a life she knew nothing about.

Six

As the war dragged on and we all started to live normal lives in between the missile attacks, Joel revisited the "Quintessence" subject. This time he was pushy about it. I had to decide whether I was willing to go through this experience or if I wanted to move on with my life without Joel.

I wanted to believe that the "Quintessence" certification would guarantee me wild sex with him.

Winning Joel's body had become a challenge and, sure enough, I made the call and registered for the next workshop. Getting time off from work was tricky. By the time my request was approved, I truly regretted agreeing to participate in the workshop.

While I was making all the effort, Joel remained passive. He did nothing to show his support. I thought that maybe I was a victim of a sick relationship. Maybe my Apollo boyfriend was the real problem.

But I still wondered if there was something wrong with me. It only took one phone call to my very special friend, Dave, to test the notion. Dave was a relatively high-ranking career officer in the IDF. I'd met him a few years earlier. There was nothing bad that I could say about him. He was nice, funny, and single. Actually, he was the exact opposite of Joel—always laughing and fun to be with. I really liked him, but didn't want to lose him as a friend, so we never dated—I hadn't even considered it.

"Commander's office," a female clerk answered.

"May I speak with the commander?" I asked for Dave in a common fashion.

"Who is asking?"

"Sharon Lapidot."

"Regarding...?"

"It's personal."

"Hold, please."

"Yes?" Dave finally came on the line, drawing out the word in his special way.

"Dave?"

"It's still me," he answered and laughed, bringing a smile to my face. "What have you been up to?"

"Nothing special," I answered as a wave of tears choked my throat.

"What's going on?"

"I'm not sure."

Dave had many questions. He was direct and didn't play games. He put me on the spot. The less I answered, the more he probed. I felt like he was cross-examining me, although he didn't expect any answers.

"Give me three and a half hours and I'll be there." He sounded so decisive.

"Are you out of your mind?" I panicked.

"What's the problem? Are you expecting Joel?"

"Oh, no, he's not coming home tonight. He's at the base, but it's getting late. It's already after nine and the weather is really bad. It's kind of crazy to drive all the way from the Golan Heights," I said, although the truth was that I did want to see him. I needed him to hug me tight and let me rest my head on his shoulder, where it was safe.

"I won't be driving. I have a driver. It's not crazy—I don't do crazy things. So, I'll see you after midnight." He laughed his unique laugh and didn't leave me any time to answer.

The fact that Dave knew Joel from the military made me nervous. Dave was higher ranking than Joel and I assumed that he knew things that I did not.

The next three hours were long. My brain was exhausted, but my body was fresh and alert.

The buzz of the intercom interrupted the silence surrounding me. I reached for the intercom and pushed the button to open the electrical gate. I watched Dave's image through the spacious windows. Something in Dave's confident steps relaxed me. He didn't knock, but walked straight in as if he was a closer friend than I'd thought.

"This is insane," I said.

"Well, you sounded like shit," he said and followed me to the kitchen. "I know that you're not happy with Joel. You're a good friend and, as you know, I don't care much for Joel. Are these good enough reasons? Because I can give you more." He put his arm around my neck and looked into my eyes. I looked down at the floor. Endless tears that wouldn't come, nor vanish, sliced my throat. He wrapped my shoulder with one arm and my waist with the other. I let my head rest on his shoulder and leaned against the cold, granite counter.

My tears, my life, my past and my future were mixed up in my head and jammed in my throat. I felt as if I was choking. I had no clue what Dave's thoughts or plans were.

I took a long, deep breath and begged him, "Please, tell me—tell me the truth."

"You know the truth. You really don't need my help to see it," he whispered into my ear.

Obviously, I was not about to get any information from Dave. He'd never made a secret of his disapproval of Joel for me.

I poured some coffee and devoted myself to the conversation with Dave. I let it all out, rehashing my life and defending myself for staying in a relationship with Joel. I wasted so much energy trying to justify myself. Dave just sat there and listened to me. Was he tired of my stories or was he worried about my pain and sorrow? Or was he just physically exhausted?

Eventually he headed to my bedroom. He was truly tired.

"Can you set the alarm for five o'clock?" he asked while disappearing behind the wall.

"Of course," I said and followed him to the bedroom.

Dave took his shoes off and stretched out on the bed. I took my jeans off and was left with only my underwear and sweatshirt on. Then I made my way to the bathroom.

"The special forces that Joel is in," he said abruptly from the bedroom and paused.

"Yes?" I let him know that I heard him.

"There is really no such thing. It's just a small trailer—an office space that was invented for Joel."

What? That was enough to get my attention. I gave up brushing my teeth and traced my steps back to my bedroom. I stopped by the door, looked at Dave and waited for him to continue.

"It's nothing, really. They didn't know what to do with him so they gave him an office. Whatever he claims to be doing, he isn't. It's bullshit."

I felt as if my boyfriend, the hero, was melting away. I didn't know if I should try to preserve him or let him go and be relieved. I didn't say a word. I looked in Dave's eyes and lay next to him.

Dave did not say a word, nor did he make a move.

He looked exhausted and was about to fall asleep. I did not want to disturb him, but thought he might be more at ease if he slept in his undershirt. I unbuttoned his shirt and lost it right there. I looked at his white undershirt and let my mind imagine his chest and six-pack underneath. My hand wanted to take the next step, but instead I rolled over him and sat on his lap. I took another long look at his face, moved down to his chest and stopped at his groin. I did not pause for another thought and gently unbuckled his belt. His brown eyes were slightly open. He looked at me with a tired gaze as if he did not care what I did next. I took a deep breath, crossed my arms around my waist and pulled off my sweatshirt.

There, between the linen and the blanket, while having sex for the sake of my sanity, I did not think of Joel. I left him and our relationship far away from my bedroom. I wasn't worried if I was cheating on him or not—didn't even care why he had never been interested in having sex with me.

I couldn't tell if Dave was a variable in my moment of happening. I dedicated myself to the sex that was played on my bed. My body celebrated while my mind was disabled. Except for the physical excitement that evolved around our bodies, nothing really happened. My emotions and intellect froze as if they were disconnected from my body or my spirit. I let it go. Dave seemed to be in control and to have a similar attitude. He didn't say a word. And after the fact, he was quiet and relaxed—not a lover, but a comfort.

Obviously, I was desirable. I felt relieved. Clearly, Joel was the problem—not me.

Seven

I spent the rest of the night in Dave's arms, almost as if it would change our experience from a one-night stand into something more meaningful. And maybe there was more to that night.

At five a.m., when the alarm went off, I sensed the victory but not the freedom.

I wished I could stay in bed and let Dave do me one more time—maybe even let him love me in a way, but I had to consider the circumstances—he couldn't run late and I didn't know if he could ever really love me. He was the kind of guy who easily stayed detached.

I drew myself out of bed, put on a thong, grabbed a T-shirt, and went to the kitchen. There, in front of the counter, waiting on the water to boil, I closed my eyes and let the evidence of last night drip out of me into my thong. The morning after was just as comfortable as the night before. Dave's presence didn't make it stressful or awkward—everything felt safe and secure. Knowing that life might never summon us to meet again did not concern me at that moment—there was something unique in our relationship that I could never figure out.

"Are you okay?" Dave asked.

"Are *you*?" I handed him a cup of coffee.

"You know I am. I'm always okay," he said. "Are *we* okay? No regrets? Just making sure that you're fine with last night." He lit a cigarette.

There was no need to discuss how I felt about last night or about tomorrow—it was irrelevant. Dave was a butterfly who needed his freedom. Any regrets that I might have had would stress him and put our friendship at risk. I wanted him to hug me one last time, but I thought it might be too much to ask from a one-night stand who I might never see again.

"By the way," he continued with a grin, "I used Joel's razor blade and shaving cream. I hope he doesn't mind. The toothbrush, I used the red one, assuming it was yours—is it?"

"I'll ask him and let you know." I looked at him and smiled while he laughed.

He walked toward me, embraced me and said, "This is your wake up call, girl. Make up your mind. It's never too late."

Despite the episode with Dave, which I buried between my linens, my life resumed its routine. My relationship with Joel continued with doubtful qualities. Apparently, my night with Dave didn't seem a good enough reason to break up with Joel. I accepted my melancholy lifestyle, refusing to believe that I deserved better.

I prepared for my journey to the workshop. The loneliness gnawed at me as I packed a small bag. Joel made no effort to recognize my upcoming experience, but his audacity reached its peak when he neglected to walk me to the car.

"Good luck, sweetie," he said and left the house minutes before me.

Hesitation hit me again. I wanted to take my little suitcase and change my plans—maybe disappear completely and start a new chapter in my life. I threw my bag in the trunk and hit the road. There was an hour-and-a-half drive ahead of me.

Driving north along the Mediterranean at sunset was peaceful. The sky was colored in rainbows of reds, oranges, and yellows while the sun appeared as a golden ball ready to turn its back and travel to the other side of the globe.

By the time I entered downtown Haifa it was shortly after seven-thirty. I was on my way to the upper city when the mountain slope appeared on my right and the whole bay was positioned in my sight to the left. The bay emerged in its night beauty, nestled within the curve of the shoreline. The Mediterranean showed its dark color, decorated with boat and vessel lights. My thoughts glided to those who were spending the night on the water—fishermen in small fishing boats, soldiers and armed forces in navy vessels, sailors on supply vessels, and vacationers on cruise liners. Some were docking while others were en route. I could see them all. Right at the shoreline more lights blazed in a mixture of various hues.

The lights on top of the refinery towers caught my attention. The beauty of the bay with the shimmering lights was replaced with pictures from the war. Everyone anticipated the Iraqis targeting this refinery. Hell, who didn't know the value of this plant? I pictured being under attack far away from home or from my workplace. The threat seemed stronger here, away from the security of the familiar. Would I survive? Would I know what to do? Who would be next to me?

My drive ended at my friend's house. I found the key to his flat in the unlocked mailbox, exactly as he'd promised. Yet, I left it there and went back to my car. I wanted to be alone for a while and not be part of a place or a thing. I thought about the friend I would be staying with, Ron. He was more of an acquaintance than a true friend. I didn't think he would expect me to explain why I was there or ask a lot of questions.

As time passed, the night started to show its features and the cold air settled in. I put on my jacket and huddled in my seat, shivering slightly as I stared at the bright full moon.

Finally, when Ron's car approached the driveway I stepped out and waved.

"Hey," I greeted him, "long time no see. How's it going?"

"The usual—tired—had a long day." He sounded worn out. "How about dinner, did you eat?" he asked while still in his car.

"Not yet."

"Good. Let's go grab something."

I joined Ron in his warm car and we headed downtown. This time the bay was on my right and I could pay more attention to its beauty without having to watch the road.

"So what brings you here?" he asked.

"Oh, nothing too important. There's a conference at one of the hospitals—not a big deal," I lied.

"It must be nice to get away from work for a few days, isn't it?"

"At times—and you? Is life good? Anything new?" I asked, trying to shift the focus of the conversation to him.

"Nothing really," he said. "Getting tired of this city, looking at moving. Not sure where." He paused as if searching for a topic, then asked, "So, how does it feel to be near the front line and getting hit by all these missiles?"

"I can't wait for it to be over—I don't like it—and I'm afraid..." I said and locked my eyes on those towers. "Don't you think that this refinery is a prime target?"

"I wouldn't be surprised. I think it's just a matter of time." He hesitated a moment before continuing, "However, I hope that these won't get hit—that would not be fun. It seems like they know exactly where the important sites are. Fortunately, they don't have precision hits," he said and parked, parallel to the sidewalk, in the part of the city where Jews and Christian Arabs lived side-by-side with no animosity.

We crossed the street and entered a local restaurant owned by an Israeli Arab. The place was busy with mostly Jewish Israeli guests—not an unusual phenomenon.

The Arabic table had its own culture with a colorful, savory menu. It was a cuisine that was easy to be passionate about. What in other cultures looked uncultivated was mannerly here. Using pita bread instead of silverware was the norm.

Once we were seated, a waiter served us fresh, warm pita bread, a plate of homemade green olives, and pickled vegetables.

"Are you going to start with some salads?" the Arabic Israeli waiter asked in proper Hebrew with an Arabic accent. Clearly, he knew we were not Arabs.

"Yes. Please," Ron said.

"And for the main course, what would you like?" He looked at me.

"I'll pass. Thank you."

"Are you sure?" Ron asked.

"I'm sure."

"Okay then. I'll have the lamb shish kebab."

In minutes our table was covered with different salads. Simple presentation on small size plates—humus, tahini, fried eggplant, broiled eggplant, tabouli, stuffed grape leaves, labneh, mujadara, falafel, and more.

We devoured these salads passionately. We used the right etiquette, skipped the silverware, and wiped the plates with pita bread—so when it came to table manners, we fit in.

While Ron had his main course, I continued enjoying the salads. And by the time he was finished, I was stuffed but couldn't resist the coffee and assortment of baklava—things that I always had room for.

Our dinner was perfect—good food and not much conversation. It was comfortable and convenient. I probably could handle this kind of relationship for a while—no stress—nothing too intense—no need to explain and no reason to ask—no clever conversation and no need to impress. *God, what an ideal setting.*

"What time do you need to get up tomorrow morning?" Ron asked as we arrived back at his place.

"No later than six."

"Do you have the key or is it still in the mailbox?"

"It's still there. I didn't take it out," I said as we were walking from his car to the entrance of his condo.

Ron's place was in a nice, contemporary duplex with a spectacular view—a place that many could appreciate.

"Hey, a glass of wine?" he asked.

"Sure. Are you going to have one too?"

"Why not?" he laughed mischievously.

I could smell the wine from a distance and thought it would be good to let it breathe a little bit. But Ron seemed to have a different opinion. He handed me the glass, touched his glass with mine, and said, "*L'chaim.*" He settled into his armchair and elevated his legs on the ottoman. I got comfortable on the corner of the sofa next to a small end table—an easy spot to keep my glass of wine.

Ron switched on the TV and flipped through the few available channels, and I went through a neglected magazine that was on the table.

"Nice evening…." He broke the silence. "I really enjoyed it."

"I'm glad you did—so did I," I answered carefully.

I looked at Ron and replayed that evening years ago when he'd been my patient, in the Post Anesthesia Care Unit, after his major surgery.

Ron had been a top gun pilot who had been taken hostage by the Syrian enemy right after he had to eject from his fighter. I remembered that evening with the hospital corridor congested with reporters and media people—obnoxious people starved for updates concerning the hero who was just released in exchange for 460 terrorists. Any news that could possibly give them a chance to be the first one to release some information would have been good enough for them. And, that young lady outside the crowd that spoke with the surgeon right after surgery—I recalled how cold she'd seemed, like the whole deal was not part of her life, like she'd already moved on. And she sure had.

She walked toward me right after speaking with the surgeon and handed me an envelope.

"Will you please give it to him?" she asked. "I'm about to leave and I won't be coming back."

"I can't do this," I said and handed the envelope back to her.

"Please, do this for me," she begged.

"Who are you?" I asked. "Are you related to him?"

"Just give it to him," she said. "I can't deal with it. This is way too much." She left without taking the envelope back and disappeared into the crowd.

I stuck the envelope in my pocket and went back to my patient. Ron was still unresponsive, but was breathing on his own. I was disturbed by that woman and the envelope she had given me. I could not imagine what it held. I thought of giving it to one of Ron's family members, but since she didn't do it herself, I felt it would be wrong. I thought to stick it under his pillow, but was worried it would get lost when he was transferred from the OR stretcher to his own bed. I knew I had to give it to him in person. But in PACU there was no right moment for these kinds of things. Patients didn't reach the level of consciousness that might allow doing such. I debated asking the nurse in the Intensive Care Unit where Ron would spend the night to give it to him later, or keeping it and handing it to him myself during my next shift. I assumed this envelope was important and I could not ethically take it home with me.

Shortly after Ron was responsive and stable, I transferred him to the ICU. After giving the nurse a detailed report, I looked one more time at him and assessed how alert he was. *Not enough*, I thought. *Not enough to give him this envelope.* I returned to PACU with the envelope still in my possession. I did not take the envelope home with me, but left it in my locker with the intention of delivering it to him the next day, and I truly tried.

At the end of my next shift, I went to see Ron. Less than twenty-four hours since he had been under my care in PACU, Ron looked better but still in pain. I had to introduce myself again, as nobody remembers a PACU nurse. After that I didn't have to say much. Once I held the envelope in my hand and he could see the handwriting, he asked, "Did you see her?"

I wanted to lie but I could not. "I did."

"Did she step in to see me?"

"She didn't."

"Did she say anything?"

"Not much." I lied, though it was true in a way. She didn't say a lot of words, but what she had said, that she wasn't coming back, was huge.

He looked at me and said, "I don't need it. You can throw it away."

"No, I cannot," I said. It wasn't that I was afraid, but ethically, I felt I had to give it to him. If he chose to throw it out, that was up to him.

"I said I don't want the envelope," he repeated with a raised voice.

"Are you sure?" I tried to confirm.

"Your name again?" he asked.

"Sharon. Maybe I'll keep it for you in case you change your mind. You're going through a lot right now," I offered kindly and placed the envelope back in my pocket.

"Whatever," he agreed.

"I'll stop by later on this week," I said while leaving his room.

This was where the envelope episode ended and where our friendship began. I continued to visit Ron at the hospital and after, at the rehabilitation facility. Ron was no longer eligible to be a fighter pilot in the air force or to fly for a commercial airline. His career was over and he had to accept all his losses—a leg, a woman, and a career. He had a long way to go—a tough road. I was committed to be there for him even though we never really talked or spent much time together. I'd felt that, as long as I'd had the envelope, I'd been the only link to that young lady, and I had never been sure about her role in Ron's life.

Pulling my thoughts back to the present, back in his living room, I looked at Ron from a different perspective. I recapped all that he had accomplished. I had to go through a long list—there was a lot to recognize. He looked comfortable, sitting in his armchair, sipping his wine. To me he still looked bitter and in pain, like his journey had never come to an end. I saw things that he did not talk about, things that I'd never asked. Ron was a strong person. He didn't talk about his emotions. Some, at first, might find him cold and arrogant, like that day when I attempted to hand him that envelope. But once you knew him, you saw his other side.

Eight

I must have fallen asleep on the sofa and spent the night there. I woke to the aroma of fresh coffee. I was still in my clothes, covered with a blanket, with a big fluffy pillow under my head. I was embarrassed and uncomfortable. *Why am I here and not in the guest room?* Was he fed up with me or just being considerate? Had I turned into a pathetic guest or what?

"Good morning." Ron greeted me with a smile. "Did you sleep well?" he asked without looking at me.

"I guess I did. What happened?" I answered.

"Nothing happened," he said. "Coffee?"

"Let me jump into the shower first." I couldn't believe he was seeing me like that, first thing in the morning, after an unclear night, with smudged makeup. For God's sake, I hoped this would never happen again. I took a quick shower, cleaned up, and refreshed in less than fifteen minutes.

"That was quick," he said. "You smell good and look like you're ready to start the day."

"Thanks," I said and joined him in the kitchen. "So what happened last night?" I asked again in a worried tone.

"Stop worrying so much—nothing happened," he insisted without making eye contact with me. "You fell asleep on the sofa. You looked comfortable and I didn't want to disturb you, so I got you a pillow and a blanket—not a big deal." His voice was quiet and calm as he scanned the morning paper.

"I'm sorry. I didn't mean to cause you trouble."

"Trouble?" He laughed. "You are no trouble. Don't worry about it." He sounded like he'd already moved on. "What time do you think you'll be back?" he asked.

"I'm not sure. What about you?"

"I should be home early. If not…I'll leave the key in the mailbox."

"Sounds good. Thanks." I wrapped up our conversation and left.

On my way to the workshop, anxiety pushed me close to hysterics. It was too late to change my mind. I tried to stay calm and be in control. Time went by faster than the ride itself. My thoughts vacillated between the people I would meet and the assignments I might have to complete. By the time I arrived, I was near panic.

I parked and double-checked the address on the registration form before entering the building. The lobby was noisy and crowded in contrast to the empty, gloomy street. It felt like two different worlds—the outdoor one that reflected the day-to-day reality of war, versus the lively one inside.

I looked around to see if I recognized anyone, or if someone might know me. I signed in and stepped aside, as if subconsciously attempting to isolate myself. Scanning the crowd, it looked like about twenty-five percent of the people were trainers—people who'd probably become damaged and addicted after participating in this crap. They reminded me of Joel and his friends. Their lives revolved around this organization. It was a bit unsettling.

I tried to blend in without getting too involved, being careful not to reveal anything about my life. I was alert to the potential risks of getting in too deep. I just wanted to save my relationship with Joel—a relationship that I resented.

The first day's assignments were not too intimidating. But even the simple task of searching the room for a buddy—someone who we would stick with for the entire workshop—became daunting. If I chose wrong, I might be stuck with some monster or devil. How pathetic!

I tried to get a grip of the overall concept, but I was busy thinking about Dr. Sloan's comments about this workshop and the fact that I never told him that I'd decided to come here.

The only person I spoke with was someone I believed was at low risk of getting damaged from the workshop. Later she became a very close friend of mine, Lori Rosin.

Returning to Ron's place was the best part of the day, elating in a way. I was overwhelmed with excitement—my stomach was fluttering with butterflies. I wondered if Ron would be home when I arrived. I wanted him to be there. I needed him.

That envelope from years ago crossed my mind. I wondered if that was the only link between us or if there was something else that kept us in touch over the years—it was uncommon that I would establish any relationship with my patients outside of the professional boundaries. I was curious if he was ever bothered with the envelope that he'd dismissed a long time ago. I doubted he'd forgotten about it. Did he ever regret his response? Had he reacted impulsively or had it been well thought out?

I could see Ron's car way before I hit the driveway. I was surprised at the relief I felt. I parked just behind his vehicle and quickly stepped out, locked my car, and rushed to the front door. My hand reached the doorknob to open the door and walk in, but instead I paused and knocked.

Ron opened the door with his phone to his ear. He looked at me but didn't say a word, didn't even place the person he was talking with on hold. All he did was stand there, waiting for me to step in so he could close the door and get back to his chair. His movements were robotic. He treated me as if I was just a deliveryman who had brought some merchandise.

It didn't take me long to figure out that Ron was casually chatting with a female. I got completely worked up and headed to the guest room, reminding myself that I was only a friend, and at the moment, a guest. I wanted to rule out the option that I was jealous. Was I?

I was in the shower when I heard Ron's voice. "Sharon, are you there?"

"I'll be out in a few minutes," I said loud enough so he could hear me.

By the time I was out of the shower and dressed, I found Ron in the kitchen and off the phone. Finally, he gave me his attention. "There you are. How was it?"

"Okay," I lied. "Nothing special."

"Did you run into anyone you know?" he asked.

"Yep, as usual." I made no effort to sound interested in this conversation. "And how was your day?"

"Just another day—nothing exciting."

"What time did you get in?"

"Well, I cut the day short. I thought you might be done early."

"Hmmm, that was nice of you."

"I hope you're hungry. I'm making this thing that calls for two."

"What is it?"

"Cheese fondue, have you had it before?

"I have. Do you need any help?"

"Not really, unless you don't mind setting the table."

"Not at all. Dining table or kitchen counter?"

"Dining table."

"Do you have a tablecloth?" I asked.

"Getting fancy, ha...." He smiled.

"Not really—but nice people—nice table." I was on the defensive.

I pulled a tablecloth from the cabinet and set the table, making sure that Ron's seat had the easiest access. I seated myself closest to the kitchen so he wouldn't have to take extra steps. And I was careful to seat us not close enough to each other to give him the wrong idea, but close enough to share the fondue without spilling. I wondered about candles, but decided it best not to ask.

"Red or white?" He interrupted my thoughts.

"Red or white what?"

"Wine," he answered with his back to me.

"White."

"Great, works for me."

"Are you celebrating something?"

"Well, I'm about to have dinner in my house with a delightful person like you." He turned to face me and continued in an angry tone. "Do you have any idea when I last fixed dinner for someone? When was the last time I had dinner with a woman in my home? Did you ever think how lonely I am or how I'm navigating my life? That I'm a hero who might fall apart? Can you see me through my own eyes and my own heart? Or, do you always look at me through your eyes?" He took a deep breath, and grabbed a bottle of white wine from the refrigerator. "Your hero might not be made out of iron as you think he is."

Well, how should I answer? That was definitely a lot to take in. Was he expecting me to say something? Did he have more to say? I wanted to hold his hand, maybe even hug him for a long moment, but I thought he might be mad. I felt like he didn't trust me. I felt that I was shifting away from my nursing role and wasn't sure what direction I was heading in. I worried that our relationship had gone off track. He was no longer my former patient—he now meant something different to me. I felt out of control and helpless in a way.

I watched him uncork the bottle of wine and hoped to get a glass of it now. I didn't know if Ron was a real hero. He never told me a thing about his plane crash. I didn't know anything about the moment he ejected from the plane or the time he was in the Syrian prison. I didn't even know when he'd injured his leg—while ejecting from the plane or during his time in captivity. Had he been mistreated? Had the cruel enemy tortured him? He never shared his suffering, fears, nightmares, pain, dreams, or hopes. I really knew nothing about him.

What made Ron a hero in my eyes was the way he rehabbed after his surgery. He kept it all to himself. He never complained about his loss, never said a word about pain, was never seen without wearing his prosthesis and never limped, not even a bit. For all of these reasons Ron was my hero.

"Are you angry?"

Ron shook his head in response.

"Are you upset?" I tried.

"Not at all," He handed me a glass of wine and turned back to the stove to check on his melting cheese mixture.

The air was saturated with the aroma of the melting cheese fondue. The windows fogged up and started to sweat. The cold, stormy weather outside conflicted with the cozy ambiance inside the house. The wind whistled and I could hear the rain pouring down, hitting the roof and gutters. I had second thoughts about the table I set—was it too formal?

"So, when was the last time you were involved in a relationship with a woman?" I finally responded to his earlier confession.

"It was a long time ago." He laughed.

"Are you gay?" I asked.

"Hell no!"

"Thank God." I laughed and walked toward him. I leaned with my back to the counter, went up on my toes, pushed with my palms and lifted myself up on top of it, next to the stove. Now I could see his face and I could try to hold a conversation with him, forcing him to look straight into my eyes.

"You sound so relieved. Why do you care if I'm involved with someone and whether I'm gay or not?"

"Obviously, I do." *Did I just admit that I have an interest in him?* I thought and watched him stick a skewer into one of the bread cubes.

"You want a bite?" he asked while dipping the skewer in the cheese mixture. "Here." He pulled the skewer from the pot and directed it to my mouth. "Be carful—it's hot."

No, no, no. You are not feeding me. This is way too romantic. I was uncomfortable. "I'll hold it for a minute," I said in effort to save the situation.

I studied every move he made. He had so much charm, his presence made a statement, and he was very charismatic.

"Can I ask why you aren't involved in a relationship?" I quizzed him while blowing on the hot cheese-covered bread.

"I'm not sure. I never thought about it like that." He looked at me as if he had to think more about it. "You know…I really don't ask women out—I'm not sure if they are interested in me. I'd rather not take the chance of being turned down."

"You're not sure if they are interested in you? You're kidding, right? Who wouldn't want to date you?" I said strongly and laughed.

"Someone like you, I guess." He looked at me with a smile and refilled my wine glass.

"Ha-ha-ha," I said with an insulted voice.

"Here, let's go. Come dance with me." He lifted me up from the counter.

"Dance?"

"Yes, dance with me—here."

Before I understood what Ron was saying, I found myself sharing one floor tile with him—a slow dance with my hero in his own living room.

"How about moving our dinner to the living room?" he whispered in my ear.

"Sounds cozy," I said and wasn't sure how we would manage that fondue over there.

But Ron made it happen and created a lovely evening. The fondue was a perfect meal for a non-formal, light dinner. The wine blended well with the cheese pot. The lights were dimmed and the music penetrated our souls. Ron was a perfect partner and I wanted to believe that he was benefiting from this evening too.

I was tired but didn't want to end the evening with Ron. I stretched out on the sofa and made myself comfortable.

"Do you mind if I close my eyes for a minute?" I asked him.

"Of course not. Let me get you a blanket," he said.

A few seconds later as he covered me, I opened my eyes and looked at him. I wondered if he was just the perfect friend or maybe there was something that I didn't see. I wasn't drunk, but a bit tipsy. Maybe the wine was controlling me. "Hey, are we about to get in trouble?" I asked, half conscious.

"Not unless you insist." He laughed.

"Good, because I'm way too tired to insist."

"That is a pity."

"No it's not. You couldn't possibly want to have sex with me." The room felt like it was spinning. "Oops, I think I might have had too much wine." I grabbed his hand.

"That's okay. Come here, close your eyes, and try to forget about it. I promise you that we won't have sex." And I believed him and let myself drift off.

Nine

I woke up at six. It was quiet enough to assume that Ron was still asleep. I jumped off the sofa, rushed to get ready, and went to the kitchen. I looked around and couldn't find any evidence from last night. Everything was back in its place and all cleaned up. I wondered what would have happened if we'd had sex, and why we hadn't—I don't think I would have objected. But what if I'd conceived a child? I couldn't decide if I wanted Ron to be interested in my body or in me. I felt pretty cheap and wanted to believe that it was all a consequence of my sexless relationship with Joel. With these thoughts buzzing through my mind, I left to continue the workshop.

That cold morning, I drove with an open window, trying to appreciate some fresh air and to absorb as much oxygen as possible. I wanted to be free from commitment, not involved with anything and able to enjoy life. The drive was shorter than expected. I arrived thirty minutes early and waited in my car.

Back at the workshop my head was congested with my everyday matters and I could not let myself go. I didn't pay much attention to the workshop and had no interest in understanding it. I robotically participated in the assignments and was tuned into pleasing the trainers—to say and do what I thought they might want to hear and see. I was completely disengaged during the assignment of leadership, so when we were divided into groups of six, pretending we were left in a boat somewhere far from shore, I was the first one voted out—they didn't need me to survive. *Come on guys, are you crazy? You are committing suicide without me. Me, a loser?* This definitely didn't reflect who I was in my actual life—still it hurt. But at least I was left out with good company—Lori, was voted out right after me.

Lori turned into my pal. The more we talked, the more we found we had in common. She appeared honest and fun. I found her very direct but personable. She was married to a successful man. The two of them, along with their three children, were living in a town only fifteen minutes away from mine. I thought I'd keep her as a friend.

At the end of that day I found Joel waiting on me outside. I saw him from across the street. He was not far from where I'd parked my car—in his uniform, leaning on his car, smiling. His unannounced visit was an unpleasant surprise.

"I thought you might need some company for the night," he said.

"You know, I'm staying at a friend's house...I don't know if it's appropriate to impose another guest on him." I hated his spontaneous visit.

"I thought we would check into a hotel."

"I guess we can." I surrendered to his plan, visualizing the upcoming night. It seemed like I was better off with Ron than with Joel—less conflicts, a less patronizing attitude, and a better chance for being held by strong arms. I kept quiet. My mind rehearsed the call I was going to make to Ron, telling him that I wouldn't be there that night, but when I finally called his house there was no answer. I was hoping that I could talk to him face to face when I stopped by to pick up my stuff.

I rushed to my car and was on my way to Ron's to pick up my hand luggage. *And what if he's waiting on me? Then what? How will I tell him that I'm spending the night with Joel?* Though I had nothing to hide. He knew about Joel—so why did it bother me?

My fear and anxiety were in vain. Ron did get home first, but left before I made it there. He left me a short note saying, *Hey kiddo, I headed out. I'll be back late. Ron.* His note was so abrupt that it hurt.

I got my stuff and stopped to look at his note again. I could not let him have the last word. I definitely could not let him think that he left me alone in pain. I ripped off a piece of a paper towel and wrote him, *Sorry we missed each other. Hope you had a great evening. Have a glass of wine for me. I will not stay the night, I don't like empty houses, and I guess you don't like them full. I will call you tomorrow. Me.*

I pulled a bottle of wine from the cabinet, placed it along with two empty wine glasses next to my note, and left.

That night and the next day I called Ron obsessively every few minutes, like a psychopath. His phone rang over and over again, but no one answered my calls.

I never spoke to, nor saw Ron again. I lost him before being held by his strong arms. I didn't even have the opportunity to thank him for the hospitality. The very last chance I had was at his funeral and ever after in my heart. Ron's life ended in a fatal car accident on that night when we'd left each other notes. I never knew if he'd read my note, and I never was told if his tragedy happened before he drank that glass of wine for me or after. His death was announced across the country. The media took time to pause and talk about the hero who'd lost it all—a leg and a whole life.

There, at the cemetery, I was one among thousands of individuals who came to say goodbye. I was one among thousands who thought they knew Ron. I was the only one there, among so many people, who knew that the envelope I was to deliver to Ron had never been accepted. Therefore, the woman next to me buried, with anger, the father of her child, and the little girl next to her buried the man who never knew he had a daughter. I buried the man who had strong arms, a man who never knew how much I wanted him to hold me tight. I buried my hero who I'd failed to tell.

The workshop came to its end—I concluded it had been completely worthless. As I settled back into my routine, my life revolved around Joel, Lori, and her husband Jonathan. From the initial introductions, it quickly turned into a close friendship. It all appeared to be perfect, everybody got along with one other. But, for me, it wasn't real.

Soon after, on February 27, Kuwait City was declared liberated, and with allied forces having driven well into Iraq, President Bush and his advisors decided to halt the war. A cease-fire took effect at eight the following morning. During the war, approximately thirty-eight Scud missiles showered Israel. Most hit the greater Tel Aviv region and Haifa.

With the war now over, I had fewer things to worry about. I could now place my personal life on the front burner.

While soul-searching, my gut was telling me to move on. It was a hard decision. I didn't share my thoughts or concerns. I kept it all to myself. I even kept Lori out of the loop—was it because I didn't trust her? Or maybe because she was not that close of a friend—maybe she was only a visitor, passing through my life.

Time did not promote a thing in my relationship with Joel. Still we put on a good show. We looked like Romeo and Juliet, but felt like shit. Surviving became my focus, and I developed a special technique of wearing different masks at different times.

In early March, I made my way to work with my smiling clown mask firmly in place. It was a special mask that made me look as if I had it all, like God had been really generous with me. But the truth, my truth, did not resemble my appearance or other people's perceptions.

By ten-thirty p.m., I walked through that ghastly, silent corridor. I was on my way to receive a report from the evening supervisor, but not before checking to see who was on call. I was disappointed to see that Dr. Sloan was not on the schedule. I wanted to tell him about the stupid workshop and the tragedy of Ron. I was ready to share with him everything except the sad legacy of Joel.

I turned around and stepped into the lounge. For many different reasons, which I never bothered to agree with or oppose, the nurse supervisors exchanged their shifts in the L&D lounge.

Minutes later, I left the floor almost ready to start my rounds. I got off the elevator on the first floor and went to the administration offices where I could find the entire call list for the month. I found Dr. Sloan's name on the tenth and, checking it against my schedule, was disappointed to discover that I was off that day. In fact, our schedules didn't overlap for the next few weeks.

By the morning, after my shift ended, my frustration with the schedule had reached a point where I called one of my colleagues.

"Hey, Noemi, it's me."

"Hey. What's going on?"

"I was wondering if you could possibly switch shifts with me on the week of the tenth?"

"That night of the tenth or the entire week?"

"Just that night...or, whatever works for you. I'm scheduled to work two evenings but have some conflicts."

"Let me check," she said.

"Take your time."

"I don't see a problem—that will work."

"Thank you so much—I owe you one."

"I'll hold you to that." She laughed.

What a relief, I thought and counted the days left before the tenth.

Ten

Sunday the tenth finally arrived. I spent more time than usual getting ready for work. I considered going in early, but eliminated this option right away. I forced myself to keep my normal routine.

As I entered L&D I could smell Dr. Sloan's cologne in the air but didn't see him. I bit my tongue so as not to ask about him.

I continued to the lounge to meet with the evening nurse supervisor. She mentioned an emergency C-section in the OR.

"Who's doing it?"

"Sloan and Rappaport," she said.

The hospital was busy and I had a lot on my plate. I picked up my clipboard and notebook and started my first round, assessing the work and setting my priorities. I had a crazy night ahead of me—I wouldn't be able to spend much time with Dr. Sloan.

I was almost done with my first round when I got paged to the fifth floor, and from there to the second floor, and then back to the fifth floor. Then I had to go to my office to get some forms and run them to L&D. But not before rushing to the lab to pick up four units of packed cells and deliver them to the fourth floor. Finally, I took the elevator and was on my way down to the ground level.

The elevator stopped on the third floor and once the doors opened I saw Dr. Sloan standing in front of me. He walked in with a big smile. "Hey—long time, no see," he said. "How are you?"

"I'm fine. How about yourself? Busy night?"

"Sort of—not too bad."

"It's been pretty busy for me. I haven't had a chance to stop," I said as the elevator doors opened at my final destination.

"Ready for a break?" he asked as we stepped out of the elevator. "Let's have a smoke."

"Actually…." I paused and looked at him. "Will you go to the second floor with me for a minute?"

"The second floor? You mean the lab?"

"No, the other side, the north wing."

"There's nothing there."

"I just heard something that I'd like to check out."

"Right now?" His eyebrows rose with his voice.

"Do you mind? I'm not sure that I want to go there alone."

"Sure, why not? Let's go," he said and started back toward the elevator.

I hesitated to tell Sloan the real reason why I needed to go there. If what I suspected was true, he'd find out soon enough.

"Are you sure that's where you need to go?" he asked as we walked out of the elevator and turned right. "It's so dark. It looks like a ghost town. I didn't know that they'd already put something here."

"I didn't either." I hesitated to volunteer too much information.

"Are you certain you know where you're going?"

"Yes, I do. Trust me," I said, while trying to find the light switch.

"Be careful," he said. "It's very tempting. I may rape you."

"I'm not sure it would be rape. Do you have a light?"

"Here," he said as he flicked his lighter.

"Good, let me try my master key."

"What the heck is this? Are you about to seduce me?" he asked and laughed.

"Wishful thinking...ha?" I said and successfully unlocked the door. "Where is the light switch?" I whispered, as if I was a thief.

"Hurry up! My finger is on fire.... There, on the right wall." He walked over and switched on the light. "Is this what you were looking for? It looks like a storage area."

"Not really."

"So, what is it?"

"You don't want to know," I said.

"Listen, we can't spend the whole night up here, so why don't you just tell me what is going on."

"Look," I said. "You see these mattresses? That's where that son of a bitch is doing all the *britot*—the circumcision ceremonies. Here on the floor, like a butcher."

"What are you talking about?"

"You know all these Russian immigrants—the ones that nobody knows whether they're Jewish or not?"

"Yes." He dragged the word out.

"Well, evidently someone is circumcising these people so that they can be considered Jews. I'm not saying all of them, but certainly some of these are done here by the hospital CEO."

"You mean here, on the floor? No way. What is his specialty? Don't you need to be a surgeon for this? Does he get paid for this?"

"That's what I heard."

"Seriously? Who told you about it? How did you find out?"

"You know how everyone tells me everything."

"This is insane."

"No kidding. You can't talk about it, or mention that I told you about it."

"Are you sure that this is what's going on here? Don't you need to be a *mohel* to perform the ceremony?"

"No—you can do these too—I guess you just need to recite the right blessing. Look what they have here."

"Not much," he said.

"Mattresses, alcohol swabs, Betadine, 2cc syringes, needles, Xeroform gauze, four-by-four gauze and two-inch bandages—and some Lidocaine." I spat out what I saw and walked to a box full of unprocessed packs. I picked one up, looked at it, opened it, and handed it to Dr. Sloan. "Scalpel handle, scissors, hemostat, forceps, needle holder, and a guard. I guess that's all you need. And to make matters worse, none of these are sterile." I looked at him.

"This is unreal," he said.

"Look there," I continued, "there is the sweet wine for the ceremony and printed cards with the blessing." I grabbed a card and handed it to him.

"I wish you hadn't shown me this. This is unethical—scandalous even."

"I agree."

"Let's get out of here." He headed toward the door.

In the elevator, as the doors closed, I turned to him and said, "I ended up going to 'Quintessence.'"

He turned toward me and said, "You did, huh?" And after a long moment, he added, "I hope you're not going to end up doing something stupid."

"Like what?"

"I don't know, people make bad decisions after this workshop."

I wondered what he meant, but he didn't elaborate.

Spring was around the corner. The days turned longer and warmer while the nights stayed cold. The universe was brighter and more inviting. Endless blooms decorated the landscape in a wide rainbow of colors. The air was saturated with a scent that called the bees to start their work. The birds sang in the early morning and the late afternoon, as if they scheduled their singing by the sunrise and sunset.

My friendship with Lori tightened. I shared my pain and my dreams with her. And, in turn, I knew everything about her. She was the type of woman who had a career, a husband, children, and a life—a person who lived for the day. She would not intentionally hurt someone, but made sure no one got in her way. She came first most of all. On one hand she was family oriented, but on the other hand, she never gave up her single life. That was the part of Lori's lifestyle that suited mine—the single life. And for that I could tell her secrets. Once that happened, she disapproved of Joel and revealed her excitement over Dr. Sloan.

"Why didn't you say anything?" she asked.

"I wasn't sure which side you would take."

"Oh my God, do you really doubt it? Anyway, you're wasting your time. You have to kick Joel out of your life—the sooner the better."

"But everyone thinks that he's Mr. Perfect."

"Who cares what people think? You need a good lay. How long will you last without sex? I bet one day he will come out of the closet. Are you naive or what? Move on—hit on that Dr. Sloan."

"He's married," I said.

"So what?"

"It's a headache that I don't need."

"You don't know what you need."

"You might be right. Time will tell." I sat back and I let her orchestrate my split from Joel.

Two days later, I secretly gathered my belongings from Joel's condo and went back to my place. When he arrived, I rushed to confront him.

"Hey there." My stomach churned, thinking of what I was about to say. "We need to talk." I sat stiffly on the couch.

Joel took off his sunglasses and looked at me. "What's going on?" he asked.

"We really need to end this relationship. It's not working for you or me." My voice shook. I had to gasp for air to keep my tears deep down in my throat.

"Fine. I need an hour." He stared out the window for a moment, not showing any emotions. "Why don't you leave and give me time to pack and get myself out of here?" He sounded so blunt but looked in pain—his lip twitched. He reached for his head, running his palm over his short hair. And then he relaxed his shoulders as if a weight had been lifted from him.

I stood and made for the door. Joel blocked my way. He put his arms around me, forced my head on his shoulder, and whispered, "You're right. We need to end it. Take care. I'll leave the keys on the counter."

"Let me give you yours," I said while disengaging from him and walking away.

"What about your things at my place?"

"I already picked it up."

"Well planned."

"I'm sorry."

Within a few minutes and with minimal talking, I ended my relationship with Joel. I didn't place blame and he didn't ask questions. As Lori had assumed, it was quick and painless.

I jumped in my car, drove to the corner, and parked in the first available spot—close to where I'd agreed to meet Lori. I searched for her in my mirrors. My heart raced as though I'd just finished a long jog. I couldn't imagine going back to the house by myself. I needed Lori to hold my hand.

I gave Joel thirty minutes longer than he'd asked for before returning home.

I looked around to see if he might have left something behind. It had been less than two hours since I'd stood in my boyfriend's arms, asking him to leave, and I was already feeling lonely. The emptiness slammed into me and I fought back the tears—my throat spasmed. My eyes surveyed the room in detail as my brain put Joel in the past and my heart closed on that chapter of my life. My body ached. I was detached from reality and didn't know what to expect next. Suddenly, my life was on hold.

Two days later I thought about calling Dr. Sloan and asking him to take our relationship outside the hospital. I looked at the numbers he'd left me on the first day we'd met and started dialing. My fingers trembled and froze. I put the phone down.

Later that day, I was trapped in the same quandary. Repeatedly, I initiated that call that I never actually made. I had the desire to hear Dr. Sloan's voice but not the courage to follow through. My desire turned into a craving and then into a need. I became anxious—afraid to take the chance of being rejected by him.

I decided to talk to him at work, hoping it would be easier. *Yes, face to face would be better—I should skip the phone call.* But for whatever reasons, our shifts didn't overlap and I had yet to see him. The thought of calling him followed me every day. The temptation was always there.

Eleven

It was about two weeks after Joel and I broke up—a day shift. I walked into my office and sat at the desk. I was still disturbed by the hospital's involvement with the Russian immigrants' circumcisions. The fact that it was done secretly in the back corridor led me to believe that this was a scandal. I tried to imagine how the hospital CEO was performing these procedures in that awful room. I tried to put aside my clinical knowledge and look at the brighter side of it, but I really couldn't find one.

My morals were higher than the CEO's greed. Clinically, I believed in circumcision and could not agree more with the authority's requirement to have the procedure done regardless of age. But I resented the way it was done—I agreed with Dr. Sloan that this procedure should be done under general anesthesia in a sterile environment like the OR. Needless to say that I believed all fees should be collected from governmental health insurance—not from the patients.

I wanted to believe that the CEO didn't collect fees for the procedure itself, but accepted some sort of *tzedaka*—charity. I didn't know much about his morals, but I had to assume that he accepted cash only and that it went directly into his pocket as tax-free earnings—or, as some would say, cash under the table.

The only person I could talk to about this issue was Dr. Sloan. I glanced through my telephone book and left it open at the letter S. Dr. Sloan's phone numbers were in front of me.

Calling him from work made it seem that I was not committing a sin. I sounded confident while asking for him.

"Sloan speaking," he said as soon as he got on the phone.

"Hey, this is Sharon Lapidot, the house supervisor at Kol Israel Achim."

"Oh yes. How are you?" he asked, obviously making the connection.

"Great, and you?" I sounded short.

"As always...." He paused.

"Listen."

"Yes!" His tone was terse.

"I need to talk to you," I said rapidly and took a deep breath, delaying the tears that were about to flood me.

"I'm listening. What's going on?" He still sounded tense and businesslike. I didn't know how to tell him that this was a personal call without being too direct.

"It's personal." I paused, hoping that he would pick up the conversation from there.

"I'll be there tonight—will you?"

"No. Besides, I don't think it's a good idea to talk about it in the hospital."

"Is that about those circumcisions? I really don't want to get involved with that."

"No. I said it's personal."

"Are you pregnant?'

"Hell no!" I said.

"What's so personal that can't be discussed over the phone?"

"Just forget about it." He was the one who gave me his number and waited for me to call him. Could he not figure this out? Was he trying to torture me?

"No. Just tell me where and when you want to meet."

"You tell me. I'm pretty flexible. You're probably busier than I am."

"What time do you get off work?"

"Three."

"Can you make it by three-thirty—do you know where Café Landau is?"

"A coffee shop?" I tried not to let my voice raise an octave, but probably failed. *Half of this town still thinks I'm marrying Joel this summer and this married player asks me to meet him in a coffee shop? Is he crazy?* "No, not in a public place," I said. *Did I just invite him to meet in a private place?*

"Okay," he agreed. "So what's left, maybe your house?"

"That would be fine." I could only imagine just how fine it could be.

"Give me your address." He was so practical.

He repeated my address and my directions, and reconfirmed the time. "I might be a few minutes late. It all depends on how the day goes."

I was not sure if this was reality or a dream. I didn't want to think of him as prohibited game or as a wild player. I told myself he was only a friend. *Did I really believe it?*

By three-thirty sharp, Dr. Sloan was at my house only a few steps away from me. There was no doubt that this was real. My head was crowded with partial thoughts. I couldn't spit out a word, certainly not a complete sentence. I contemplated why I wanted him there, but couldn't come up with a comfortable answer. Finally, he interrupted the tension between us.

"Do you have anything to drink?" he asked.

"Sure, what would you like?" I headed to the kitchen.

"What do you have?"

"Pretty much anything you want."

"Something cold and wet." He smiled.

"Like what?" I ignored his play on words.

"Beer." He laughed.

"Sure, which one?"

"Whatever you have—Goldstar?"

"Coming up." I opened the refrigerator and memorized his favorite beer, making it a permanent item on my shopping list—anticipating that this would not be his last visit.

I handed him the beer and sat on the other sofa, far away from him.

"So, what's going on?" he asked.

"Well, we broke up," I said.

"You mean you and your perfect boyfriend, the one everybody was envious about?"

"Yes," I answered and grabbed a box of tissues, just in case.

Dr. Sloan was quiet, though he seemed comfortable enough.

"Who initiated it, you or him?" he finally asked.

"Me," I said as big tears poured down my face.

"So why are you crying? I don't get it. You should be relieved."

I tried to tell him about Joel, our messed-up relationship and how we'd broken up, but my crying was louder than my words. I was an incoherent mess.

The phone rang, grabbing my attention.

"Hello," I answered. "Hello?"

The call ended.

"Damn it." I slammed the phone down.

Dr. Sloan sat silently, not moving from his spot on the couch.

Before I could say anything the phone rang again and the anonymous caller hung up on me just like before.

I was aggravated and badmouthed Joel as if he was the caller. I couldn't stop crying. My eyes felt puffy and so wet that I lost my contact lenses and most likely, my makeup too. I grabbed more tissues, trying to wipe away my misery. I hated that Sloan was seeing me like this. I wanted to rewind the drama and have another chance.

Suddenly, the radio station played Joel's favorite song—I wanted to scream, but instead I cried some more.

"Do you mind changing the radio station?"

"What's wrong with this one?" He did not bother to get out of his seat.

"Bad memories," I said and walked toward the stereo.

"Come on, kiddo." He stood up, blocking my way. "You're a basket case. You need to let it go." He grabbed my arms and held me back from changing the music. He was strong, but I fought him like a determined child. It was pretty silly, maybe even funny. Eventually I laughed. But when I found myself locked in his arms, I didn't move and hardly dared to breathe. I gave up fighting, and didn't object to his arm around my waist.

"How about we turn this song into a new memory," he sounded positive but more like a shrink than a potential sex partner. Still, I believed him—and trusted him and put my arms around him. He pulled me closer and looked straight into my eyes.

"You have to move on," he said.

"Eventually, I will," I smiled, trying to avoid the temptation we offered each other.

I don't remember if we were moving or just standing there in each other's arms. But, as soon as the song was over, Sloan took his hands from my waist and grabbed his bottle of beer.

We sat on the sofa next to each other and let our knees touch.

"Let me answer it," he said when the phone rang again.

I wondered if he was trying to protect me or if he wanted to be in charge.

"Hello," he answered with a confident voice. "Sure, hold on." He passed me the phone.

"Hello," I said and, once I heard the voice at the other end, I stood up and stepped toward the dining table.

"That was my mom." I told him as I hung up the phone.

"Sounds like she's abroad."

"She is."

"You never mentioned it before."

"You never asked. Besides, we never talked about personal things. We always kept it work related."

"So, I guess I should change the subject."

"Not anymore, not after I was trapped in your arms," I said.

"I guess you're right."

"I'm taking some time off and going to visit her."

"When?"

"Tonight."

"Are you really?" He opened his eyes wide.

"Yes."

"Where does she live?"

"In the US."

"When will you be back?"

"Next Wednesday."

"Are you packed?"

"There's not much to take for such a short trip. But yes, I'm ready—well, almost ready."

"How are you getting to the airport?"

"My friend Lori will give me a ride."

"You're on top of everything, aren't you? You really don't need a boyfriend." He smiled.

Time flew by. Sloan needed to be at the hospital by seven. I couldn't stop the clock nor change his shift.

He looked at his watch. "I need to get moving."

"I know."

He collected his keys and sunglasses and was ready to leave. He glanced at his watch and walked back over to me. "Cheer up. Soon this will be behind you—I promise you it will pass." He gave me a partial hug and left.

Only an hour had elapsed and the telephone rang. I answered the phone, expecting to hear Lori.

"Hello." The voice sounded familiar.

"Yes?" I was surprised to hear Dr. Sloan's voice.

"Are you okay?" he asked.

"Yes, why?" I answered quickly, trying to take a deep breath to slow down my heart so it would not shatter inside my chest. I was touched by his call and was on the verge of crying.

"So, are you ready?"

"I am—nothing has really changed since you left."

"Just checking."

"That's really nice of you."

"When did you say you'd be back?"

"Next Wednesday, early morning—I think the flight comes in at five."

"Well, have a safe trip. I'll call you when you get back."

"I'll be waiting," I said and thought, *You'd better call me once I'm back.*

"I'll be waiting too—I have to get back to work."

"Bye," I said.

A few minutes later, while still standing next to the phone, Lori buzzed the intercom and shook me out of my thoughts.

"Hey there, what's going on? Are you packed?" she asked.

"I'm ready, but it's still early, isn't it?"

I had to be at the airport by one a.m. I had plenty of time to fill Lori in with the latest.

Lori took her time, she asked a zillion questions—just like Lori. She put it all together and then responded, "Don't you want to stop by the hospital and say goodbye? It's on the way."

I would probably have objected to the idea, but any suggestion from Lori was worth considering.

"You know what, I never thought of that. Let me call him." I rushed to pick up the phone. But a second before I dialed I stopped and asked Lori, "Are you sure?"

"I'm positive, call him."

And I did.

"Hey, can I ask you something?" I asked Sloan once I got him on the line.

"Sure," he said.

"Will you meet me in the parking lot on my way to the airport?"

"Of course."

"Are you sure?"

"Why not?"

"So, eleven-thirty sharp." I hurried to finalize the time, hoping he wouldn't change his mind.

"Unless there's an emergency, I'll be there."

"Oh my God," I shared with Lori, "talking with him is like being in Heaven."

Our drive to the hospital was fun and noisy. Still under the influence of the "Quintessence" brainwashing, we listened to a bunch of songs that "Quintessence" brought into our lives. I liked them in a way, although they were different from one another. Some made me happy, some made me sad, and some brought up lots of junk that I didn't want to remember. Lori could listen to those over and over again. Sometimes, I felt like those songs replicated what her mind and heart would not share.

She lit a cigarette and became engrossed in the music. I knew that her offer to stop by the hospital was not only because of her friendship and kindness but more to fulfill her curiosity—she wanted to meet my forbidden friend.

Twelve

Lori knew her way to the hospital and didn't need my help with directions. All she needed was my badge once we hit the parking lot.

I could see Sloan from a distance. He was wearing a long, white lab coat over green scrubs. He looked so hot. As soon as I stepped out of the car, he strode toward me with a smile.

"Hey, this is Lori—this is Dr. Sloan." I introduced them.

"Nice meeting you. I heard a lot about you," Sloan said.

"No, you didn't." I cut him off.

"Nice meeting you too. I heard a lot about you, too," she said.

"I bet you did," he said and we all laughed.

While Sloan and I got back in the car, Lori stepped out and made herself scarce. She was sensitive to our privacy.

The forty-five minutes when Sloan and I were left unattended were intense. Out there, in the dark, we were like strangers, like we were on our first date, maybe even a blind date. It was as if we'd forgotten that right there, in the building next to us, we'd already met and spent hours, walking side-by-side throughout endless corridors and chatting for hours in the lounge. The memories we'd built next door were gone—rushing to the OR, scrubbing for surgery, delivering babies, and administering blood. And, most of all, holding ourselves back from getting involved with each other.

Out there, in the dark, fearless of getting caught, we could let our lust illustrate some memories for tomorrow. But we didn't. Was it because we were afraid to admit, or because we didn't dare to challenge the circumstances?

Time flew by. I was willing to rebook my flight for a later departure time just so I could extend my time with Sloan.

Lori, the responsible chauffeur, cut our stolen time short. "The time is midnight and sixteen minutes! The time is midnight and sixteen minutes!" She sounded like an automatic wake up call. Lori sat back behind the wheel, and we stepped out of the car, hoping to steal a few more seconds of joyful sin.

We stood very close to each other, maybe too close. I was able to hear and feel his breath. His intoxicating smell overwhelmed me. The full moon was enough to let me see his face and to watch his eyes looking into mine.

"Have fun. Make the best of it. Don't think about anything, not even about me." The stillness of the chilled night made his whisper loud and exciting. And when I was ready to answer him, he gently held my neck and pulled me toward him. By the time I thought to ask him to slow down, his lips were sealing mine. It was a short moment, not an erotic one. It was something I'd never experienced before—like magic. I wondered if my world was falling apart or if I'd been given the chance to be born again. His voice reached through my dazed senses. "Did you wonder why I didn't try to seduce you earlier today?"

"What makes you ask that?"

"I didn't want to take the chance that I might lose you."

"You're right. You would have."

"And I'm not planning to," he said but never finished his sentence, leaving me wondering if his plan was not to tempt me or not to lose me.

"The time is twelve thirty-two! The time is twelve thirty-two," we heard Lori in her automatic voice while she stuck her head through the window.

I could disregard the clock but couldn't ignore Lori.

I turned to get back in the car. I reached for the passenger door and stopped, stealing one last look at Sloan. It was a long moment before I climbed in the car and when I was ready to shut the door Sloan blocked it with his arm.

"I'll see you next Wednesday," he said and closed the door for me.

The drive to the airport was intense. While I remained mute for the most part, Lori never stopped—she talked and talked until I couldn't listen anymore. She was completely overwhelmed by Dr. Sloan. Whether it was his appearance, his manner, or something else, she couldn't stop talking about him.

"What are you so excited about?" I finally responded to her. "The most we are talking about is a quickie." I strived to convince her and to remind myself that I shouldn't get involved with something that was prohibited and had no future.

"Yeah right, when was the last time you had that kind of a hookup?" she said with a loud laugh.

"Ha-ha-ha, very funny. I don't need this headache now."

"It's not a headache—it's a lower head with no brain. Get it? That's what you need."

"I don't need this type of affair."

"What the hell is wrong with you? If you are not planning to jump him then I'm taking over. I'm telling you he's a keeper."

Lori meant every single word she said. When it came to sex, affairs, and men, she didn't care who her friends were. She played whenever the opportunity arose but was careful not to hurt her family. So if I were to give up on Dr. Sloan, I had no doubt she would jump right in.

"Hold your horses, Lori. Don't push your luck," I said what I really meant. I would hate to see it happen. I would never forgive her.

We entered the terminal with just a few minutes to spare. There was a lot to do—completing a thorough security check, getting a boarding pass, riding the slow escalator, and passing the police checkpoint. But there was only so far that Lori could accompany me. Right before the escalator we stopped and skipped a dramatic farewell, as I would be back in a week.

"I need to go," I said.

"Call me when you get there," she said.

"I will."

"I'll pick you up next Wednesday," she yelled while I disappeared up the escalator.

My journey of one international and two domestic flights ended in a very small airport in the United States. It was a warm day with blue skies. I walked into Southern hospitality and my mother's arms.

My mother and I had a special bond. I could dissect my life with her without censoring any of the details. She was not selective of my tales but made sure I knew her opinion about each one of them.

This time, she obviously had every right to reprimand me. She could remind me of my recent mistakes—months of wasting expensive time with Joel, inappropriate financial decisions, a wasteful lifestyle that was borderline scandalous, and a checking account that indicated a continually overdrawn balance. But she didn't. My tale about Joel's drama made her laugh. And when I revealed the potential affair that I was about to enter into, I expected a powerful attack, but instead she gave me her advice. "Keep in mind that good men don't leave their home or their family," she said. "Not even for the true love they may find. You will be chewing nothing but stones. Think twice before you take the next step."

The spring was at its peak. The flowers and trees were in full bloom—azaleas, daffodils, and tulips along with the magnolia, dogwood, and weeping cherry trees—all in a wide range of colors. The air was immersed with a powerful floral scent and the pollen floated in the air. The entire landscape was covered with a thick, yellow, powdery blanket. It was a picture that captured my heart as if it was my first spring in the south. I let its power take over and, with each breath, my addiction grew. What nature created for me made me think I was in paradise. I tried to enjoy every bit of it, exactly as Sloan had advised me before I left. I fashioned a new agenda that contained nothing but comfort and a loose timetable—a lifestyle that would no doubt bore me in the long term was perfectly welcome during my short visit.

It was joy mixed with distilled relaxation. Maybe I could live here, if I found a suitable job. I started to doubt my life back home in Israel. But, my vacation came to its end before I reached any conclusions about my life and my options.

I arrived back in Israel at Ben-Gurion airport—it was my birthday. Lori waited for me right outside of the baggage claim area, exactly as she'd promised.

I didn't have any spicy stories to feed her—my trip had been short and uneventful. But she quickly showered me with anything and everything she'd heard and seen in my absence.

"Coffee?" Lori asked as soon as we entered my house.

"Sure," I said and started going through the mail.

"Are you looking for something in particular?" Lori inquired.

"Not really," I answered and pushed the play button on the answering machine, letting it spit out never-ending messages from noble-minded people who were busy updating the gossipers. Other messages were from those who truly had an interest in my well-being. Several were from people who were unable to talk to an answering machine and hung up. And one very special message that came in the night before at eight-twelve p.m. I listened to it until I memorized all the words.

"Hey, welcome back! Hope you had a great vacation. It's Tuesday, I'm about to leave the hospital, heading home. I'll call you tomorrow morning." He did not identify himself but his voice did. I had the feeling that Dr. Sloan was waiting on my return as much as I was, if not more.

I fell into a deep conversation with Lori. I questioned this potential affair. I could not make up my mind and was trying to decide if I wanted this adventure or not. The sound of the ringing telephone cut me off before I told Lori all of the pros and cons.

"Hey, it's me. How are you? I'm finishing up my rounds at the hospital and will head to your place...around nine, I guess." He sounded decisive, short and to the point, as though he might have been in a hurry. He didn't really give me a chance to talk.

Evidently, I had no say. Sloan had his own plan, and his mind was set and clear, unlike mine. He knew exactly what he wanted and made my plans as well.

My emotional world conflicted with my rational one. I was happy and excited but confused.

Lori was in a hurry to go to work. She couldn't stay and fiddle with my spinning.

"Hey, have fun, no plans for the evening, huh? We will pick you up around six-thirty. Make sure you're ready on time. It's your birthday—relax," she said on her way out.

I checked the time. There was not much left before Sloan showed up. I rushed to the shower and commenced my polish and wax protocol. I paid a lot of attention to my makeup and struggled with my hair. I wished I could tell Sloan to come an hour later so that I could run to the hairdresser for a quick fix. But I didn't. I took care of it myself—and it took time. I had to make sure it was evenly spiked, not too much gel. I added a few shots of hairspray and finished up by infusing some of my perfume. Lastly, I squeezed into the sundress that I'd just purchased during my vacation. I performed a swivel dance in front of the mirror and paused for a few seconds, looking at my reflection in different poses. I summarized my findings with a final grade of A minus. It was hard to admit, but I was happy with the result. God, I looked good, actually very good.

By eight-fifty I was ready but the clock kept its leisurely pace.

Thirteen

Minutes after nine Sloan walked into my fortress. I fell straight into his arms, sinking into his hug. "I couldn't stop thinking about you," I admitted.

He squeezed me tight but didn't say a word. I presumed he didn't like to talk about his feelings—men were exempt from anything that might put them at risk. Exposing their feelings didn't fit the macho image they strived to project. For them, actions were stronger than words. Perhaps I should slap my hand for being honest with him.

I looked deep into his eyes for a brief second before he touched his lips to mine. What I could not see in his eyes I felt in his lips—a long, soft kiss that set me on fire. And from there to my bedroom we took a shortcut. Every minute outside of bed would be counted as lost time.

In bed with Sloan, words had no place. Talking was not necessary. The dynamics of our moves took us to perfection. Most of what happened occurred in a horizontal position. We both knew our passion shouldn't be executed. Yet, neither of us was willing to miss the opportunity. Our bodies had their own language. It was as if they'd known each other for a long time, as if they belonged to each other. The room was saturated with a sensuality that could not fulfill our lust. We were mentally and physically devoted to each other. We could not resist the sin. His instrument played an erotic song in my vagina and hit my G-spot on each entry. His movements were slow and correlated with mine. I wanted this to last forever, to be able to learn his body and read his mind.

I could no longer play the game or resist the situation. My body took over my brain. I let him know how close I was to coming, that I couldn't hold off any longer. I asked him to hold me tight as if I was afraid to lose the power of my satisfaction. His breathing accelerated along with his movements. I reached the climax right at the same time with him. What a moment! I was in heaven.

The only guests at our party were he and I, coffee and cigarettes, music and silence, sex, desire, passion, needs and cravings for each other. We left out the clever conversation, the promises, the decisions, and the pointless trials to understand what was happening.

We emerged from our cocoon when I looked at the clock and discovered that it was time to get ready for the evening. I didn't urge Sloan to leave nor did I ask him to stay. I let him decide. I wanted to see how far he would go. Would he wait to see Lori again and meet her husband or would he disappear and avoid the exposure?

Sloan stayed. The official introduction between him and the Rosins lasted only a few seconds—then, he became an integral part of the gang.

By seven-thirty Sloan went back to work and Lori, Jonathan, and I were on our way out to dinner.

"Are you duck walking?" Jonathan asked as we made our way to the car.

"Ha-ha-ha," I answered.

"You'd better take that smile off your face. You look like you've been working out for hours." He showed his playful side and made me laugh.

"Your wife said that I'm out of shape—I guess she was right."

"She is always right."

"So what's on the agenda? Where are we heading?" I asked.

"Why do you always ask so many questions?" Lori asked.

"I don't have that many questions. Maybe you don't have the answers or just don't want to give them to me," I said.

"Aren't you the smarty pants?" She made us laugh.

"That's fine," I said and sank back into Sloan's smell that still revolved around me. I was thinking how to put the day and Sloan in the past. I needed to move on, but Lori and Jonathan disagreed. They both liked him. They strongly believed that he didn't fall into the one night stand category.

We entered the place—a restaurant I'd never been to before. A stiff waiter welcomed us. He politely conversed with Jonathan and figured out our reservation. I peeked over his shoulder at the room, trying to decide if I wanted to celebrate my birthday there. I was hit by surprise and felt dizzy. The place was filled with familiar faces, though I couldn't put names to them. I tried to focus. Before I realized what was happening, they all stood up and shouted, "Surprise!"

"You guys are too much—this is crazy." I told Lori and Jonathan.

I walked toward the crowd, appreciating how careful Lori had been when she put together the guest list. The combination of friends, kindness, warmth, love, joy, and fun touched my heart.

My face mirrored my inner excitement but didn't divulge that I was thinking about Sloan—I missed him.

By the end of the party, Lori became impatient. As soon as we got in the car she asked, "Which one first, your mom or Sloan?" She passed me the car phone.

"Neither one. Maybe later."

"Come on. Let's call Sloan," she said.

"Are you nuts? It's one o'clock in the morning. I'm not calling him. He's probably asleep by now. And why call him? Leave him alone. He's not part of this and probably doesn't care. Move on." My aggression bubbled over and I wasn't sure who I was trying to convince more—them or myself.

"What's wrong with you?" she said.

"What's wrong with you?" I fired back.

"Nothing. I just think he's waiting on your call."

"Why would he?"

"Because. Just call him."

"Stop it. I'm not calling him, " I said.

"Trust me, he's waiting—he knows about the party," Jonathan said.

"How?" I asked.

"We told him," he said.

"When?"

"When you were in the shower, getting ready," Lori said.

"Seriously?" I couldn't believe the three of them had entered into this conspiracy.

"Seriously," she said.

"But he didn't say a word to me."

"Did you forget whose side he's on?" Jonathan said with a smile.

"Okay, you win." I dialed the hospital number, hoping the operator would not recognize my voice.

"Hello," I roared in a happy high-pitched voice.

"Happy birthday, kiddo. How was it?"

"Did I wake you?"

"No, just reading. Actually, I was waiting on your call."

"Why didn't you tell me anything?"

"What exactly was I supposed to tell you? That there's a surprise party for you?"

I was surprised how quickly the Rosins had made Sloan part of my present life and probably part of theirs too.

It was almost two in the morning when Lori and Jonathan walked me into my house, helping me carry my gifts in.

My bedroom was just as I'd left it a few hours ago. Its disarray was evidence of an unforgettable afternoon. A heavy marbled ashtray filled with cigarette butts was next to an empty pack of cigarettes on the floor. Coffee cups lay scattered around. Clothes were strewn all over, insinuating that they had been taken off starved bodies. And two damp towels were still at the corner of the bed, reminding me of the shower that we had shared. The linens gave off mixed smells of my perfume, his cologne, and our sex. I crashed in my bed and wrapped myself with the sheets.

I had to believe that I was at a turning point in my life. There was nothing for me to complain about—I was surrounded by close friends, almost in love, messing around with a hot married man, and I'd just had amazing sex.

My limbs felt as if they weren't connected to my body. Fatigue overcame my desire to dive into deep thoughts and I fell asleep.

The stubborn and annoying sound of the phone woke me, bringing me back to that chaotic room.

"Good morning," I heard Sloan's tender voice. "Hey. How are you?"

"Recovering...."

"Any plans for today?"

"Not really," I said.

"I can stop by around one. Will that work for you?"

"I can hardly wait," I said and drifted back into my dreams.

Later I replayed his call and thought about his upcoming visit. I was surprised he'd initiated a visit back so soon. It seemed a little intense, but not something that I couldn't handle. *What's wrong with you, don't you have some work to do, or a home to go back to?* I thought, sarcastically.

But after he walked in I melted, leaving the sarcasm aside. His presence and apparent comfort threw me off.

"Do you mind if I take a shower?" he asked.

Wow, I thought, *isn't our relationship a bit premature for that?* Wasn't he pushing it a little bit too far? How could he be so comfortable and sure of himself?

"Sure, why not? Make yourself at home," I answered. "Just don't forget that this is my home," I added quietly enough that he wouldn't hear.

I was uncertain where my place was in his life but thought it was better not to go there. It really wasn't necessary to make it more complicated than it already was. So he made himself at home and asked to take a shower—*so what?*—*what's the big deal?* Besides, I appreciated his desire to shower before making any direct contact with my body. As for the shower after, I couldn't care less—he could take my smell, wrap it in a gift box with a bow, and take it home to his wife. Not that I knew a thing about her, but I already had a lot against her. I was angry with her just for being his wife.

"Hey, do you mind getting me a towel?" I heard his voice from the bathroom.

"I guess I can." *Holy shit!* I thought. *How am I going to bring him a towel? Should I open the door wide, or just a little bit? Should I hand it to him or place it on the countertop?* I'd obviously already seen his body but still felt as if we were new to each other. I hesitated, but had to make up my mind quickly.

Bashfully, I opened the bathroom door just enough to let my hand sneak in a towel and place it at the very end of the countertop. I was about to close the door but Sloan didn't like the way I acted.

"Hey, the floor is going to get wet," he said.

Is he trying to convince me to hand him the towel? I stepped back in the bathroom, grabbed the towel, looked straight in his eyes, not glancing down, and threw it toward him.

"Good catch," I said once the towel was in his hands.

"Don't you want to get wet?" he asked mischievously.

"I'm already wet," I said with an inviting smile.

"Let me see," he wrapped the towel around his waist and stepped out of the shower.

"See what?" I asked.

"How wet you are," he said as he lifted me up and set me on the counter, keeping his arms around me. I bet the tight jeans I had on didn't leave much to his imagination. His lips skimmed over my neck. He studied my smell, inhaling me deep into his lungs and his memory. I took the next step and wrapped my legs around him. It didn't take long before his hands traveled under my loose, sleeveless shirt. I wiggled closer to him.

"You are hot," he whispered.

"So are you," I said.

"I missed you." He looked at me. I had no choice but to believe him. I felt secure and protected. I had to trust my feelings but still needed reassurance.

"Did you really?"

"I honestly did," he said.

"Is that good or bad?"

"It's bad," he said and picked me up with his strong arms and carried me to the bedroom. He gently put me on the bed. I looked at him and saw nothing but lust. I let him take the rest of my clothes off and explore my body. I was wet by all means. His touch was magical, the most sensual I'd ever felt. He was ready to glide into me and to take me back to the same places we visited the day before. My body grew heavy and my legs shivered. I looked straight into his eyes, trying to find some assurance that he was going to make love to me and not just have sex. He leaned toward me, gently kissed my knees, and let his lips travel north. By the time he reached my nipples we were ready to engage our bodies. I kept my legs around him and turned him on his back. I wanted to be on top this time, to control the pace of our erotic motions. I felt that it was my turn to lead. And I did.

Fourteen

My new routine with Sloan turned out to be the most intense part of my life. We developed a schedule of ongoing calls throughout each day. Outside of work we spent at least two days a week together—mostly having sex. This relationship didn't offer much more—what else could I expect from a married man? Yet, the physical attraction with Sloan brought something different into my life—something I had never experienced before. The duet between us seemed flawless.

Over time, when this grew into a refined relationship, I started to fear losing what I'd never truly had. I continually reminded myself that he wasn't mine—that I might end up with nothing but pain. But how important was it? Was I willing to act in prevention and send him out of my life before we became even more entangled? I couldn't decide.

At the scene of the crime, we became physically, emotionally, and mentally closer. It was a place where no one could possibly interrupt us. What we created in our small world was forever ours.

As time passed, we worked our schedules so they overlapped. Whenever Sloan took in-house calls I worked double shifts, sixteen consecutive hours. And he took it one step further and showed up at work before his shift. We took advantage of anything that would allow us more time together. Still, we kept the affair to ourselves. Our daily sin played out as if it was a crime.

My affair with Sloan took a lot of my attention and I'd almost forgotten about what was happening on the second floor of the hospital until I came in for my shift one Tuesday.

"Hey." I greeted the chief of nursing as I entered the office.

"I was about to page you," she said.

"I guess I saved you a phone call."

"I need to make some changes to the schedule. Do you have a minute?"

"Of course."

"I need you to work next Wednesday at the *britot*."

"Huh? What are you talking about?" I tried to play it as if I knew nothing about it.

"What, you don't know that the crazy man is circumcising the Russian immigrants here?"

"I heard something about it but preferred not to get involved with it."

"So now you are."

"I didn't know that you are providing staff for this."

"Well, I am. I need my job. Usually it is myself or Ester."

"Hum…." I nodded.

"Well, I need you to cover for me next Wednesday morning."

"I don't know if I can do this," I said.

"What's the problem?"

"I don't know. Let me think about it."

"There's nothing to think about. We can talk about it again tomorrow morning after your double shift."

"Sure," I said, but deep in my heart I knew that I couldn't be part of this.

And two hours later when I told Sloan about it, his eyes opened wide and he said, "I don't know what to tell you. Like she said, she can't afford to lose her job, but I know you and your ethics.... Just remember, this is a private hospital. There is no union here...I don't know...I need to think about this one."

At the end of my shift, neither my boss nor I brought it up. I rushed home and, after three hours of sleep, jumped in the shower and left to meet Sloan at the beach.

"So what did she say?" he asked.

"She didn't—she didn't bring it up."

"Did you say anything?"

"No. I needed more time to think about it. What should I do?"

"I can't tell you what to do, but remember you might lose your job."

"I also might lose my job if the Health Ministry pops in for an inspection."

"This is true too," he said.

"But, if I work there on Wednesday, at least I'd have proof and could file a complaint."

"You're right. However, filing a complaint would not secure your job. That's how it works."

"You know it all. Don't you?"

"No, I don't. I'm just older than you are." He smiled and grabbed my hand and we set off for a walk.

I took my chances and lost my job. Some things were more important than my income. Being part of this unprofessional environment was something I could not live with. Yet, losing my job was not pleasant—not even Sloan could sweeten it.

With this said, our relationship took on new aspects. We faced new facets that were not linked to sex or lust. Sloan became more involved in my personal life. His opinion was important to me. I let him take over the open position I had for a significant other, allowing him to step into my life. Yet, in his life, there was very limited space for outsiders like me. The rules of our affair played in his favor. I was there for him in good days and bad, but at the end of each day, he went back home—to his wife and family. I wanted to believe that he took our memories and me with him wherever he went. I hoped that he was losing sleep and that he no longer made love to his wife.

I have no plans to get divorced at this time in my life, he said often. While on other occasions he confessed, *My marriage could be better. If I could choose a wife again, I guess it would be a different woman. But, my two sons are my privileged obligation, and I'm not going to leave them right now.*

Things became complicated. I was now officially a mistress. Nothing was easy on me. Life was a bitch. The lies and the alibis we wove were difficult to keep track of. I realized that I was only passing through his life—so why keep track of all these fabrications?—sooner or later it would end.

Well, I had to admit that I couldn't compete with two kids and certainly didn't see them being part of my life. His words were loud and clear, but the unspoken ones were even louder. I heard him but didn't want to listen to what he had to say. My intellect and my emotions were waging a war. But I let the emotions win. I couldn't resist Sloan's voice or charm. His smell and his body were intoxicating. It felt like a moving train that was impossible to stop, despite the wreck that might come.

Each time Sloan left and went home, a feeling of emptiness overcame my joy. I loathed that feeling of being left behind and falling into melancholic thoughts after committing our sin—so I usually headed to my confidants, the Rosins.

It was one of these times, after Sloan left, that I arrived at the Rosins. While Jonathan preformed his incredible skills in the kitchen, putting together a mouthwatering dinner, Lori made the effort to cheer me up. She set up a table for four and I had to convince myself that Sloan was running behind at work. It was a game that didn't last long, but it did cheer me up. I knew I deserved better and didn't argue the privilege of having the whole cake. In the back of my mind, I knew that my relationship with Sloan had limited options. Still, I couldn't reject the crumbs.

When we finished discussing my relationship with Sloan, we turned the conversation to other serious matters—my income, for instance. The reality of prolonged unemployment had turned my checking account into an emergency situation. The bank manager called me daily, threatening to close the account. I lived on a budget and cut costs. My grocery shopping was limited. Coffee, milk, cigarettes, and Goldstar beer for Sloan were the core items on my list. I had to let the housekeeper go. And still it wasn't enough. I mailed out my resume for every opening, even if it only partially suited my skills and qualifications. I contacted and used my considerable network. The responses I received were all the same—*Sorry, you are overqualified for the job.*

I remember sitting in front of one chief of nursing at a local hospital. I begged her, "Forget my accomplishments. Put my resume aside. Look at me. I'm an RN. Please let me work as a staff nurse, even as a nurse assistant—I really don't care—just let me work so I can pay my bills. I don't need a title—just a job."

"I'm sorry, but I cannot. I wouldn't hire you for anything less than a charge nurse and I do not have any openings like that at the moment," she said, her voice cold and unyielding.

Feeling completely frustrated, I left her office. I thought about one of my former bosses—that chief of nursing who'd taken me under her wing, promoted me, and made me a superstar within a few short months. Years later she betrayed and destroyed me in a heartbeat. She sold me out to the CEO just to cover her own ass. In my eyes she'd committed a brutal murder. Since then it had been impossible for me to find a job—almost as if I no longer had the right to live. I would never forgive her. I considered putting together a resume that would not reflect my extensive experience or achievements, hoping that someone would take the bait.

I attempted to mange my crisis, but any light at the end of the tunnel turned out to be another train that could run me over. *Wait, hold on a moment—I need some mercy!* I wanted to tell the world, but no one was there to listen.

Along with the emotional defeat, I emptied all my bank accounts and accumulated debts.

Lori and Jonathan stepped in and handed me a personal check for three thousand shekels. "Here, take it. Pay us back when you can." I was embarrassed and uncomfortable but didn't refuse their offer.

Sloan's sympathy and empathy toward me and my situation touched my heart but didn't solve the problem. I loved him more than before, though my patience dwindled. His presence began to annoy me. I lost interest in my love affair. My nerves were fried.

A few weeks later, I came home and rushed to answer the phone but missed it. The caller didn't bother to leave a message but immediately called again.

"Hello," I answered.

"Thank God you're home. Where have you been? I've been calling you the whole day." It was my hysterical friend, Rachel.

"I just walked in," I said.

"I can tell, but where have you been?"

"I had to run some errands. What difference does it make where I was? I'm here now."

"Fine, you don't want to tell me. That's okay. Anyway listen, my blood pressure is sky high, one hundred forty-five over ninety-five. Do you think I'm about to have a stroke? Do you think I should go to the hospital? Did you ever have a systolic that high? Maybe I should call Dr. Gilman. What do you think?"

"I think that your blood pressure is fine, maybe slightly elevated but nothing to worry about."

"Are you sure?"

"I'm very sure," I said with a confident voice.

"What is your blood pressure?"

"Right now? Talking to you? It's probably two hundred over a hundred and fifty. Calm down. You're crazy. There's nothing wrong with you. Stop checking your blood pressure every five minutes."

"But you don't understand..." she said.

"Listen," I interrupted her, but she cut me off hysterically.

"Also, I have tons of palpitations. Do you think I'm in a v-tach, or am I having a heart attack?"

"Let me tell you something. Effective today I'm charging one hundred shekels for each telephone consult," I told her.

"Come on, don't be a bitch. Can you be serious for a moment? I need your advice." She sounded panicked.

Rachel was the craziest person I knew, but without a doubt, the most connected in the entire world. She knew everybody in detail, including people's home, work, and fax numbers, addresses, work places, and working hours. She knew everybody's spouses, ex-spouses, mistresses, friends, zodiac signs, pets, and kids. You name it, she knew it. Of course she had an opinion about everyone. She could be rude and annoying. Sometimes she was diplomatic, but most of the time she was not. She was sensitive to herself but not to others. Her connection to the medical sector was in three ways—one, she exclusively imported needed medical supplies, two, she believed she invented the stethoscope but had no related background, and three, she was the biggest hypochondriac on Earth.

Above all else, she was obsessed with prophesying the future. She could have a master's degree in fortune telling if such a major was offered. She maintained a separate and special telephone book just for psychics—coffee readers, tarot card readers, even tealeaf readers. And yes, also a handful of astrologers, numerologists, and graphologists—there were mystic ones, crazy ones, and crooked ones. All you had to do was tell Rachel what you were looking for.

So, once I answered all of her medical questions and put her health back on track, I asked her if she knew a good fortune-teller—a very good one. Funny to say how asking her for a fortune-teller was better than my aspirin consultation—she became lively right away. And for the price of knowing what my future held, I was willing to listen to her.

Fifteen

The next afternoon I met Rachel at a shady corner in the south of Tel-Aviv—a place I'd never visited before—a habit I wasn't about to change in this lifetime. She walked me to a dark entrance of an old building. The walls were congested with notes and ads for private tutors, cleaning services, babysitters, and people selling stuff next to big, printed bereavement ads. The rusted, broken mailboxes dangled there as if they were asking if someone would kindly secure them back to the wall. The smell of mold hung in the air, making me nauseous. I focused on breathing in and out so that I wouldn't throw up. I tried to ignore the dejection and filth around us.

When I was convinced that this was real and not a nightmare, it was too late to run away. Before I knew it, Rachel had already knocked on the door. A few seconds later, a middle-aged woman answered, "Coming." Immediately after opening the door, Ms. Know-It-All welcomed Rachel merrily. I wondered if it was Rachel she was so happy to see or the potential income.

While the witch was busy cooking the black coffee, my eyes searched the place. I abstained from jumping to the conclusion that the place was a sanitary hazard. However, I had to convince myself that I would not get some fatal disease just by sitting there. I could not believe that people lived this way. A few minutes passed and the fortune-teller served us the thick, black coffee. I studied the cup and noticed some leftover red lipstick on the rim. I pictured the witch rinsing the cups between clients using only water, doubting they ever saw soap or a sponge. I prayed for a miracle of somehow finding a straw just to avoid direct contact with that cup. But no miracles happened. I wanted to point out the dirty cup to the hostess but was afraid of pissing her off. I had to drink my coffee mouth-to-cup or more precisely mouth-to-mouth, hoping that the person with the red lipstick was a healthy one. I bravely finished the coffee and turned the cup upside down, letting the coffee dregs drip onto the saucer—exactly as I was instructed. I had to wait patiently for the cup to dry out before hearing the verdict.

"I see a man," she determined once she started analyzing the cup.

Well, this is a very impressive start, I thought.

"He is tall and has a beard," she continued.

"But he has no beard." I cut her off.

"So, he will grow a beard, or maybe he knows someone with a beard," she quickly corrected herself and continued, "He's in work clothes."

Yeah, right! I thought. *Did you really think he might be naked? What type of work clothes exactly? These days any clothes could be counted as a work clothes, even the rags you have on are "work clothes," aren't they?* But I kept the thought to myself.

"I see tears! Did you cry?" She was trying to change the subject.

"Me, crying—absolutely not—why would I cry?"

"Oh, you didn't cry? Okay, so you will, or you may see someone who is crying," she said in one breath without mixing up the words. Her style aggravated me. I felt as if she was disrespecting my intelligence.

"Your man is a Pisces." She continued as if the collection of her mistakes did not bother her.

"Sorry, but there is no way he is Pisces," I said to her impatiently. "And by the way, I'm not even sure that he's mine."

"What do you mean he is not a Pisces? I am sure he has a horizon in Pisces, you just don't know it," she insisted stubbornly and swiveled the cup, continuing to study it.

"I see a change in your workplace. You will be moving to a new job—in a building."

I couldn't keep my mind from responding to her, although I held my tongue. *What kind of a change—from unemployed seven days a week to unemployed twenty-four hours around the clock? Did you say a building? Of course my new job will be in a building. What do I look like to you? A farmer? A construction worker? Come on, get serious!*

"You have nothing to worry about. I see it in the cup. Everything is going to be fine. You have to have more patience.... I see a child," she said out of the blue, giving me a chill.

"His child?" I wanted her to be more specific.

"I don't see any other men in the cup," she said vaguely.

"But what about that child?" I asked.

"What about it?" she replied.

"Has the child been born yet?" I asked her. *Is she talking about his child with his wife or a child with me?* I asked myself.

"Maybe you should ask will he be born? Maybe you have the answer," she said and put the cup away. "Put the money here, wait two years, and come back to tell me that I was right. I'm never wrong." She finished up the session.

I paid her a sum that would be enough for at least one week's worth of gasoline or two weeks of groceries with some change, and left.

"Where were you when God dispensed intelligence?" I asked Rachel as soon as we were out of the building.

"Calm down, so she's not the best—so what? Don't make a big deal out of it," she said and then, in an effort to save the day, she continued, "But I do have someone that I heard is the best. Seriously. Do you want me to call her?"

I was stunned at Rachel's lack of concern. She had no limits. Was she rude or just totally dumb? "Tell me, are you nuts or what? I wouldn't go to this show again even if it was free," I yelled. "I've got to go. I'll talk to you later," I said and made my way to my car.

"Call me," she shouted and went on her way.

I headed home. The twilight did not add sparkle to my overall mood. The air, saturated with the heavy scent of spring blooms, did not create magic or capture my heart. Sloan crossed my mind and my soul in every possible direction. I missed him but, at this time of the day, I couldn't reach him or even leave him a message. It was a time when I had no place in his world—a time when he returned to his own family, his wife and kids. And me? I could not compete with this bonded group that made up such a nice family. So I fought. I fought him but not them. A virtual fight. I argued with him in my mind.

Tears filled my eyes, rolling down my face and neck. I had no tissues and no Sloan, not his shoulder or even his voice.

Back home, I found two new messages from Sloan. He called me gorgeous in both messages and asked where I was, letting me know that I had missed his visit. In both messages, he admitted his love to me and promised he would see me tomorrow.

His messages couldn't make up for his absence. It was a brief second before I returned to my virtual fight with him.

"Don't call me gorgeous. I have a name," I said as if he was standing there next to me. "And why are you asking me where I was? Since when do I need to provide you with my agenda?" My voice became louder as I continued my attack. "And let me tell you something, I did not miss anything. Maybe you missed something. And what are we really talking about—an afternoon quickie? Come on, let's put things in perspective. Stop playing that music. If you really missed me, you'd be here, with me, now."

I made my way into the kitchen, looking for some food to cheer me up and continued my monologue. "You'll be here tomorrow?" I let my anger out and slammed the cabinet door. "That's great! Thanks for letting me know—maybe I won't be in the mood to wait for you—just a possibility—have you ever thought about that?"

My ranting just seemed to feed my frustration. I was pissed. I felt as if I was sacrificing so much for him and our relationship. I realized that I was no longer just involved with a married man. I was completely in love with an unavailable man who had become an integral part of my life. I wanted to disjoin myself from him, but at the same time I wanted more of him. More than what he was willing to give.

One-sided conversations weren't unusual in this relationship. They were pointless and foolish, yet they provided me with some outlet for my anger and gave me some relief.

As I was immersed in that monologue with Sloan, in the core of a war, another message from my answering machine caught my attention.

"Hi Sharon, this is Ruth Hofmann. If you could please call me back tonight—you can call as late as midnight. Thanks."

Ruth was a successful person who owned a midsized corporation providing lab services. She was honest and respectful, and never got involved with gossip. I met her about two years earlier through work. Coincidently, she resided only a few streets away from me and yet I had minimal contact with her. I was clueless to what she might need from me. Curiosity had me dialing right away.

"Hey, Ruth, it's Sharon. I got your message."

"Hey, thanks for calling back. How are you?"

"I'm fine. How about you?"

"Same old, same old. I heard you're looking for a job. Is that right?"

"Desperately," I said.

"Well, maybe this will work for you. I'm taking eight weeks off—and I'm looking for someone to fill in for me—at least part time, if possible—would you be interested?"

"Of course," I said without asking her about working hours, location, or pay.

"Great, could you come meet me tomorrow in my office, so we can go over the details?"

"What time?"

"Would eleven-thirty work for you?"

"Sure, I'll be there at eleven-thirty."

Before I had time to digest the news, the phone rang loudly and interrupted my glorious moment. It was Rachel, hysterical as always. I promised myself that if she dumped her usual hypochondria on me, telling me about severe migraines or premature heartbeats with palpitations, I would advise her to go to the emergency room. Alternatively, I considered suggesting she take five milligrams of Valium and go to bed. But this time she had no migraine and no chest pain. She was not short of breath and didn't have any unexplained diarrhea. It was not about unexpected vaginal bleeding or heartburn. She was feeling great except she was desperate to share one piece of gossip.

"Tell me," she started like always. "I heard that there is a new physician at Kol Israel Achim hospital who takes in-house calls, someone from Tel-Hashomer hospital."

"Uh huh," I said.

"What 'uh huh'? Do you know him?"

"I have no clue who you're talking about. I'm no longer working there, remember?" I tried to get out of the conversation, although I knew exactly who she was talking about.

"Stop pretending—his name is Dr. Sloan. I'm not sure about his first name—good looking, some say he's a lady killer," she said in a tone that told me that she'd gotten her information from someone who knew all the details.

"What do you mean by a lady killer?" I asked, trying to buy some time until I figured out how to answer or how to change the subject.

"Are you stupid or what? They say he's good looking and a good physician. Did you have a chance to see him before you left?"

"Yes, I did," I said and bit my tongue, not telling her that I'd already seen him naked. Besides, the wiser part of me knew that whatever I told Rachel would be broadcast wide and far in a matter of hours.

"Yes, what?" she continued, with a high-pitched tone of excitement.

"What, what? He didn't examine me, but he definitely gives the impression that he's okay. I didn't have the chance to spend much time with him before I left."

"How does he look?" she insisted.

"He looks good—maybe too good."

"Really? That's what I heard. Tell me, is he married?"

"Are you kidding? Married with two children." I provided more information than she needed. *But who knows? Maybe she can arrange for him to get divorced,* I thought.

"Who is he married to?" she asked.

"How would I know?" I said and hoped that maybe one day I would know.

"Are you telling me that you haven't talked to him?"

"Not on a personal level."

"What are you waiting for?"

"What exactly do you want me to do?" I replied.

"Go after him." She advocated as if I wouldn't know what to do on my own.

"Will you please stop it? He's married and I have enough drama in my life without him."

"For God's sake, when are you going to get married?"

"After the holidays…." I answered her sarcastically without saying which year. But Rachel continued on and on until I cut her off. "Listen," I told her.

"What?"

"Ruth Hofmann called me…" I said and gave her the whole spiel. Telling Rachel about this temporary job was my only way out. It would take only a few seconds and she'd forget about Sloan and I'd be able to stop lying to her. *If only it was that easy for me to forget.*

Once she found out about my upcoming temporary position, she had a whole new set of questions—how many hours, when will you start, where, why, how much does it pay, who else is working there? Her questions went on and on in a style that was unique only to Rachel.

Sixteen

Ultimately, I had to add the alarm clock back to my routine. The box with that special ring that would normally annoy me was welcomed that early morning. I was charged with positive energy and was ready to jump back into the workforce. I hesitated in front of my closet, trying to decide how I should dress. I wanted to call my hairstylist, but it was still too early, so I took my chances and popped over to his salon as soon as it opened.

Sam was a top hairstylist and the owner of a very trendy salon. I was totally dependent on him and would go ballistic whenever he took time off or called in sick. Needless to say that over the years he'd become involved with more than my hairstyle. So of course he squeezed me in and quickly styled my hair.

The heavy morning traffic could not aggravate me that day. Any comments made by annoyed drivers escaped my attention, and the heat of the summer day didn't even feel oppressive. Even the dull dunes along the way were exciting. Nothing could bring me down. Life was great—I appreciated what I had.

I followed the directions I'd been given and arrived fifteen minutes earlier than my scheduled meeting with Ruth.

The building I was about to enter was simply designed. Its exterior didn't provide a hint about what lay inside. And when I walked in, its interior didn't carry the typical smell of a hospital. The style of the place gave the impression of a high-end facility, more like an American medical center. Things that were hard to find in standard hospitals around the country were now easily within my grasp—cleanliness and a pleasant scent of sanitizer wound through long, wide corridors, double doors employed automatic mechanisms, and detailed signs welcomed visitors.

Finally I reached my destination, the laboratories.

"Hey Ruth," I said as soon as I was shown into her office.

"Hey there," she smiled and put aside her paperwork.

I listened carefully to Ruth's instructions and explanations, trying not to miss a thing. I recognized how articulate and professional she was and wanted to make sure that I wouldn't disappoint her.

By the end of the day, I looked at my notes, realizing that Ruth left me with more than I'd expected. I was confident that I could do the job and assured her that she could count on me. I was aware that this temporary job could be a great opportunity and could open other doors for me.

I expected changes in my daily routine and foresaw less time available to see Sloan. I wondered if our relationship would be put in jeopardy and survive this new reality.

It didn't take long before Sloan and I missed the hours that we could no longer spend together. He sounded lonely and wasn't shy about saying so. It felt good to be loved. I melted from his words and let his voice travel down my spine all the way to my pelvic area.

"I miss you too," I assured him.

"I can't wait to see you," he continued.

I felt a spasm in my throat. On top of seeing each other less, we also spent less time talking on the phone—I had to limit the number of personal calls during work. I called him each day, and at the same time, left him a message through the pager service when he was not available, using the codes we'd agreed upon.

As much as I wanted him to be only mine, I was careful not to expose our affair. Maybe I didn't believe that broadcasting our love affair would break his marriage. Perhaps deep in my heart I knew that he would never leave his family. Needless to say, there was no point in leaving a message with my name—how would he know which one of his Sharons was calling, me or his wife?

Sloan on the other hand was less careful, calling me as often as he could, not using any codes or taking any precautions. I often questioned if he was subconsciously asking, maybe even begging, that someone would do him a favor and reveal our secret.

With time our affair became predictable. I knew when he would call and when we would meet. I quickly adopted the characteristics of a mistress, losing the flavor of a growing relationship—almost as if ours had reached its pinnacle.

My emotions were in a constant war with the cognitive part of me. For the sake of my sanity I needed to try going one day without him or his voice. I had to assess life without him. I called the hospital, but he'd left for the day. I paged him but he didn't answer. I was surprised that Sloan had left to go home without calling me. Maybe he was reading my mind, or even feeling the same way. What if he wanted to end this relationship? I panicked at the thought that he might be having another affair.

It had been almost thirty-five minutes since I'd paged him when the intercom buzzed unexpectedly. I walked to pick up the receiver. "Hello?"

"Hey, gorgeous." I heard Sloan's voice and pushed the button to release the gate.

He walked into the house, wearing a big smile and holding a single flower—something that looked suspiciously like one of the plants on my porch.

"Guess what?" he said happily while squeezing me around my waist, passing the flower across my cheek and down my neck.

"You got an order for service," I said, hoping to celebrate a few nights with him at my house.

"Nope," he said, "better than that. I was approved for the continuing education program at the medical school." He looked deep in my eyes.

"Tel-Aviv University?" I asked.

"Hu-huh," he answered. "Mondays, afternoons."

"Every Monday—you mean every week?"

"You got it. Six months—two-thirty to eight."

"Seriously? How many of these will you really have to attend?" I was excited, hoping that he would use this as an excuse to spend more time together in our little nest, rather than rushing home.

"I'm not sure. We'll see after the first class."

"When does it start?" I asked, bearing in mind that it might clash with my working hours.

"I think five weeks from now."

Lucky me! I thought while I was still twisted in his arms. *The more time with him the better.*

Sloan spun me around and let his one hand rest under my shirt on my flat, tight stomach. His other hand was around my chest and his lips whispered words of love into my ear. "It feels empty when you're not around. I'm going crazy." His lips gently touched my neck. "This has gone way beyond an affair." His words traveled through my heart, touched my G-spot and aroused me. It was enough to provoke my id to do things that might be in conflict with my super ego. *What happened to my earlier thought of trying a day without him?*

"Do you really think so?" I let my id bait him before my super ego would control it.

"I don't think so, I know so," he answered in a very soft voice.

My super ego took over. I swiveled out of his arms, eager to change the subject. "Do you want something to drink?"

"Not right now." He took his shirt off.

In the war between passion and logic, there was no winner. As much time as we spent together, it wasn't enough. Our affair turned into a commitment.

Gradually, we removed more and more boundaries from our relationship. Sloan found ways to allow us more time together. He turned every possible thing in his life into an excuse—medical conferences were no longer interesting enough to keep his attention, and once he signed in he was ready to leave. When he received his order for reserve duty, he would stop by on his way back and stay late. Soon after, he began spending nights at my place while telling his wife that he would not be released until the morning. I memorized his daily agenda along with his entire life. I marked all his in-house calls on my calendar—marks that eventually turned into long hours of celebration on a single, narrow bed next to him, in a small on-call physician room.

Soon, this room became our second home. It was a place where we did it all, made love and had wild sex, recovered and reset, agreed and disagreed, snacked on food and watched TV—a place where fears and consequences didn't exist. Often I thought that if the walls in the room could ever talk and tell the legend of our love, maybe my life would be different. But sadly, later, when a colleague told the story of what the walls witnessed, my life turned upside down.

My temporary job at the lab was interesting and convenient. I met a lot of new people—though I made none of them my friend. I kept myself in a safe zone, developing a formal and corrective rapport with them. I collected information and avoided any confrontations. I kept my lips sealed and did not volunteer anything of my personal life. Still, my overall life created its own stress and I lived a hectic, demanding schedule that required me to tell more lies than I could keep track of.

Despite my efforts, one woman in her late thirties commanded my attention—Dalia. She was extremely attractive and always appeared fashionable and fresh, but never extraordinary or extravagant. Notably, she never wore a piece of jewelry, not even a watch or a wedding band. I found it interesting. It definitely suited her. I could see how decorating herself with all sorts of accessories would take away from her uniqueness. She was sharp, intelligent, vital, and fun. I loved her sense of humor and could easily relate to it. Still, I was careful and limited our friendship.

I quickly learned that her boss, Dr. Shelton, and his business were dependent on Dalia. She controlled his life completely, but was never overbearing. She had lots of power over his practice but never seemed to abuse it. I was quite fascinated by her. The ugly gossips in town talked about an affair between the two of them, but it was all just talk—there was no proof. I liked the duet they played and was willing to be a fan of any affair they had, if they truly had one.

Eventually, Dalia and Dr. Shelton became my friends. I trusted them and was comfortable enough sharing my situation with them. When I told them the specifics, that the man in my life was married with two children, they didn't ask questions. The gossipy part of my love life wasn't important to them. Their sympathy made me think that they could relate to my own personal experience. They had their own elegance—they had a different style.

Seventeen

Sloan's visits to the lab never raised questions. Everyone assumed he was more than just a visitor but no one suspected that we might be committing a sin. On the few occasions when comments were made I managed not to volunteer unnecessary information. I had to believe that God was navigating the traffic at the center otherwise Dalia or Shelton would have run into Sloan at least once. Not that I put any effort into showing him off, but I certainly hoped to introduce them to one another.

It was three-thirty in the afternoon on a hot summer day. The air-conditioning caused me to forget the outside temperature of 102 degrees. I was sitting at Ruth's desk, doing my work when the man I truly loved walked in.

Sloan paced slowly in the quiet, chilled room. His smile captured my heart as if I'd never witnessed it before. His eyes were filled with joy and softness, although he seemed to be fatigued. He leaned toward me for a kiss and looked into my eyes. I could feel the summer temperature radiating from his body.

"Why do you torture yourself in that old piece of junk, leaving the air-conditioned car for your wife?" I asked, hoping to bring to his attention the thoughtless action of his wife. I wanted him to finally realize that his wife was a nasty piece of work—a real bitch—what else would it take?

"She runs lots of errands and drives the kids from one place to another," he said, leaving me a little hurt at his defense of her.

"I see." I let it go.

A few minutes later, when he recovered from the road and the heat, we walked to the break room. Sloan leaned on the cool, stainless steel counter, looking at the employees' parking lot through the oversized tinted window.

"Hey!" he said. "Is there someone from my neighborhood who works here?"

"Huh?" His question seemed to come from nowhere.

"Do you know if any of the staff here might be my neighbor?"

"What are you talking about?"

"Do you see that car over there—that one, the second from the left." He pointed to a blue Toyota.

I stepped toward the window, stood on my tippy toes and leaned over the counter. "Yes," I said once I recognized the car he was talking about. "That's Dalia's, the one who works with Dr. Shelton, the plastic surgeon. What makes you think she lives in your neighborhood?"

"Do you see the sticker on the windshield?"

"What sticker?"

"The white one in the lower corner, with the yellow fig leaf."

"Yes?"

"If you're a resident, you get one for each vehicle."

"Seriously, I didn't know. Kind of snobbish, don't you think?"

"It makes it easy for security, when the gates are closed," he tried to explain. Anyway who is this Dalia?" he asked. "What does she look like?"

"Dalia Kolman. A very nice person…"

"Rami's wife?"

"How would I know?"

"What does she look like?" He asked but cut me off before I finished, putting the pieces together. He didn't seem stressed but his laugh conveyed how uncomfortable he was.

"Do you know if she has something going on with Shelton?"

"Some say they do, but honestly, I've never discussed this with her." I turned my head toward him and smiled. "And by the way, since when are you representing the department of morals?"

My thoughts of making Dalia my confidant vanished. I was disappointed. Everything in my life aggravated me at that moment—Sloan the lover, me the mistress, the little settlement where he lived, a place where everybody knew everyone. My antagonism for that neighborhood maxed out. I wanted to change Dalia's home address so that she wouldn't live near him.

I looked at Sloan, thinking about the long, upcoming weekend—how long would it be before we would see each other again? The thoughts of being apart got to me and I wanted him to leave.

"I have to go back to work." I pushed it, trying to expedite his departure. I reached his lips for a soft sensual kiss, leaving him craving more.

My next day was busy. I was overwhelmed with work, managing to work systematically and stay on top of everything. Nothing disturbed me except Sloan.

"Hey gorgeous."

"What's wrong?" I asked, worried, knowing it was his Friday off and it wasn't his regular time to call.

"Nothing."

"Where are you?"

"At home."

"Home? What's going on?" I hoped to hear that he'd had a massive fight with his bitchy wife and was ready to move on.

"Nothing—Sharon is running errands so I'm calling you."

"So that's it? No particular reason—just missing me a bit?" *What a stupid question on my part. Of course he misses me, otherwise he wouldn't call.* Was I trying to provoke him? I spun the chair and looked through the window.

"No!" He paused. "I guess it's that I love you."

Wow, that sounds different, I thought and I approached him in a voice that suggested a fight. "That's great, but not enough." I stood up from my chair.

"Are you having a bad day or something?"

"Me? Of course not."

"Why you are so aggressive—are you stressed?"

"Why would I be stressed? No reason. I'm ecstatic that I'm here and you're there." I obsessively dusted the air-conditioning vent with my finger.

"What are your plans for tonight?" he continued.

"Why? Do you have anything tempting to offer?"

"You don't have to make my life more difficult than it is," he answered with an uncomfortable laugh.

"Do me a favor, get off my case. It's about time you understand that I'm not the one who is making your life difficult. You're actually doing it to yourself."

"So, what are you doing tonight?" he insisted, ignoring my comments.

"Let's see, one blind date in the afternoon, then dinner with someone who can see me on Fridays, and after that I might consider someone for a one night stand. So let's see, what are we talking about, three different guys? That's not a big deal, is it? You have nothing to worry about." I barked at him in a spiteful voice.

"What's wrong with you?"

"Tell me, is it really that important what my plans are for the evening? Suppose I have no plans, or at least not the kind that might worry you. Why does it make any difference to you? Are you trying to be funny or are you trying to aggravate me? I don't need you to remind me that my next forty-eight hours will not involve you."

"I'm sorry. Just forget about it. I didn't mean to piss you off."

"Stop it." I sat back down in the chair, clumsily dropping the telephone on the floor.

"I guess you're still mad."

"No, I'm not. I'm in pain, that's all. Wouldn't you think that I would love to spend Friday night with you?" I choked back the tears and placed the phone back on the desk.

"But I do love you." He sounded so honest.

"And a few others." I refused to make up with him. Though, he was close to neutralizing my combative mood. Somehow, I felt as if he was not sure if I still had a place for him in my life.

"Am I going to see you after the weekend?" he asked.

"Are you asking or saying?" I made it more difficult.

"Saying," he said.

"Well, I guess."

We ended that dramatic phone call with soft words, stormed emotions, and defeated lust. I could swear that my lover's mood was no better than mine. I still felt some hostility in the air and wondered how far this relationship would roll. I could not deny the joy of Sloan courting me—it was delightful. The idea of him being jealous turned me on. Moreover, the fact that he was calling me from home on Friday morning added a new element to our relationship. We were hostages to each other.

I wished that Dalia would step into the lab and I would have the courage to ask her about her neighbors, particularly about Mrs. Sharon Sloan. My curiosity had no boundaries. I was willing to give a lot for some information about the woman who put my life on hold, Mrs. Sloan. I wanted to know my enemy—what she looked like and how she dressed, if she was smart or stupid, what her style was and if she had any class. I wondered who her friends were, what she bought at the grocery store and anything else that could complete the puzzle.

But deep in my heart, I prayed that Dalia would never step into the lab and that I would never make her my friend. After all, I had no guarantee what I would hear. It was possible that Sharon Sloan was a very nice lady, good looking, smart and sexy, someone with class and style. It didn't make sense that someone like Sloan would share his life with an ugly bitch. Besides, there was a chance that Dalia and Mrs. Sharon Sloan were close friends, maybe even confidants. *So, for God's sake, why should I take any chances?*

Eighteen

The weekend was long and lonely, leaving me without much hope. Minutes before seven, twenty minutes before I had to leave for work, the intercom buzzed. And before I reached it, it buzzed again.

"Coming, damn it," I shouted impatiently and picked up the receiver. "Yes."

"It's me." Sloan was at my door. I was surprised and didn't want to think that he might have dropped by for early morning sex.

He stepped in and stopped beside me, wrapping his arm around my shoulders. He gently lifted my chin and kissed me.

"Good morning," he said and handed me a few jasmines that he'd picked near the fence in my yard. He continued straight to the kitchen without waiting for my response. "Coffee?" he asked while I went back to getting ready.

"Sure," I answered and bit my tongue so as not to say something that might provoke him or start an unnecessary argument about his call to me last Friday.

"Are you still on call tonight?" I sipped the fresh coffee he served me.

"Yep," he answered.

"Are we still on schedule?" I wanted to make sure that his morning visit was not replacing the afternoon one.

"Of course," he said, while following my steps out of the house.

"I might be a few minutes late," I told him before jumping in my car.

"No problem. I'll be waiting for you right here—in my car."

I looked at him and wanted to tell him how much I loved him, but instead I ran back into the house. "Wait one sec."

I ran back inside, grabbed a spare set of keys, and rushed back outside. I shut the wooden gate behind me and tossed him the two keys twined on a simple ring.

"The gold key is for the gate and the silver one is for the entrance door. I have to run—I'm late—I love you," I said while jumping into my car.

Within seconds I left and was on my way to another day at work.

My day was long, busy, and tiring, cutting short my precious time with Sloan. Finally, I parked in front of my house, right behind Sloan's car. He wasn't waiting in his car as he'd promised. I assumed he'd used the keys and was already inside.

The house was quiet as I entered. His sunglasses and keychain were next to the telephone in the spot he always used. I noted the two keys I'd given him, blending with his other keys on one chain, like he'd officially adopted them. I wondered whether he would give me the keys back before he left that night or if he would hold on to them. Maybe he'd even consider changing his address. *Wishful thinking.*

I put my stuff away, looking for Sloan. He was in my bed in a deep sleep. His clothes were organized on the stand and the jasmines he'd brought that morning were now in a wine glass with water on my nightstand. I glanced at the room, studied everything that was happening in my life—it could make me believe that the man in my bed was mine. I was worried how comfortable I felt. Allowing someone to enter my life had never really happened before. Until then I had let people into my house, but not into my life.

I quietly entered the bathroom, passing a wet towel, thinking that my lover had made himself at home.

I let the water relax me, allowing the soapy bubbles to dissolve the summer's sweat and stickiness away. My spa was disturbed when the bathroom door opened. Sloan had a smile as if he'd just woken up from a sweet dream. His eyelids were half open as if the bright light disturbed his pupils.

"Hey," he said, softly.

"Hey, what time did you get in?" I asked.

"Two-thirty, I think."

"So you really got some sleep, didn't you?"

"I did, I guess I was exhausted. Thirteen nights on call in one month is a lot." He left the bathroom and continued talking but I couldn't really hear him. The distance, along with the sound of the water, kept me isolated until he returned.

"Come on, turn off the water.... Let's refresh in a bath," he offered and threw the stopper into the bathtub.

By the time I readied the bath, he'd arranged two tall glasses filled with iced coffee. I was impressed and touched.

I watched him take off his boxers. He dipped into the water, crushing the bubbles. The water and its fresh scent were enough to give us a second wind.

Between the smoke, the talk, and the iced coffee, we let our bodies touch. It didn't take much for us both to get aroused. I added more bath oils to the water. Our bodies were saturated and slippery. He rubbed his toes over my thighs while I was letting mine check how hard he was. Sloan was ready. I could see his head popping out from the water. Sloan was quiet. It was erotic, very tempting and inviting. I could not resist the next move. I got on my knees and let my lips glide over his head. He gently pushed himself in and out. I could feel his joy and wished he would last forever. But he had other things in mind. He pulled me up on top of him. My clitoris rubbed against him on each stroke and he let me ride as much as I could. I was on my third climax when he exploded in me.

We ignored the sound of the phone ringing, letting the answering machine pick up. "Hey there, we'll stop by later—around six," Lori's voice blasted from the speaker in the machine.

I picked up the call before she hung up. "Hey," I said.

"So, you are home."

"I am—with Sloan."

"That explains why you didn't answer the phone and why you're short of breath," she said with a big laugh.

"Very funny—anyway, seven will be better."

"Sure." She laughed.

"I'll see you later."

Sloan and I didn't deny the sin we were living or fight the verdict of ending this affair someday. We hoped that some miracle would save us. Sloan pleaded guilty, confessing that right after we met, he wanted to bring this affair to an end, except he could not give it up. He looked deep into my eyes and said, "I always respected you and what was between us. I loved you long before I touched your body. It was your brain that I first fell in love with. However, exploring you was what made this relationship real. I would never have thought that it would go this far."

I listened to every word he said and could hear the pain in his voice. And when he added that he would be happier living his life with me, I believed him and felt his hopelessness. I became discouraged and wondered about the future.

Days later, after exhausting each other's bodies, we snuggled on the couch. The open windows let the breeze waft through and caress our nude bodies. The sad truth we lived failed to reflect the endless love we had for each other.

Painful brief moments like that pushed us to place our sweet dreams on hold.

"There is nothing I can do right now," he said for the third time.

"I'm not sure that this relationship has a future," I said.

"You know it does." He pulled me closer and let my head rest on his chest. "I know it's not fair of me to ask, but you have to give me some time. You have to trust me."

"You're right, it's not fair." A tear rolled out the corner of my eye. "If you love me then let me go."

However difficult and strange it was, we agreed to break our bubble of a fairy tale.

It was difficult to think or to believe that this would be the very last time that I would see and smell his body here in my house. How difficult would it be not to be touched by his hands?

"It's your choice," he said.

My stomach ached and tears burned the back of my throat. "Please," I begged him, "please, don't ever call me again. You must be strong. Don't even call to check on me."

"But I love you," he said.

"I love you too," I said. "I love you more than I have ever loved anyone else." I let him hold me tight.

We opened a bottle of wine and let our bodies touch one more time. I let him love me on the kitchen counter. I seduced him when I served dinner and he let me love him one last time instead of having dinner.

Two hours after Sloan left, I was shattered. All I heard was his voice echoing through my mind, shadowing me. "I love you—but I love you" and, "I love you" I heard again.

The decision to bring this affair to an end became my new reality. Sloan respected my request and skipped my next day wake up call. The daily visit when he used to check on me, kiss me softly, wishing me a special day was now gone. My entire world collapsed. Though the separation from Sloan was a gift for my own good—still I couldn't accept it. I wanted my soul mate back. I put the blame on myself. I could not forgive myself for pushing him away. My body ached all over. I felt like an addict going through withdrawals after the use of street drugs. I was clueless how to struggle through this and could not see myself surviving it. I tried to hold on to the thought that if I could stay away from Sloan, I might settle down and start a family with the right guy. But it was in vain. The feeling of loss and regret was overwhelming. I wanted to spin back the wheel and give up all those heroic power games that I'd played the night before.

By midmorning I was so restless that I put my sweats and my running shoes on. I left the house and walked through a few small streets until I reached the avenue. I made a right turn and gradually started running down the road, west, all the way to the open fields at the edge of town. The Mediterranean Sea was in my horizon. The sun was burning. Another hot summer day.

By the time I returned back home I was worn out, thirsty, and sweaty. I was glad that I'd kept the shutters down so the house would stay cool. I pulled a bottle of chilled water from the refrigerator and rested on the cold, tile floor.

I fully regretted my decision. I couldn't stand the separation and was ready to call Sloan. By noon I was a wreck and dialed the hospital's main number.

"How can I help you?" I heard the operator. I delayed my response to her as my attention was diverted to the pager that went off. The same number which I dialed only a few seconds ago was now displayed on my pager. I assumed it was Sloan. My tongue stuck to the roof of my mouth. It took me a few seconds before I continued. My heart raced, butterflies moved into my stomach, and my head searched for answers. I wanted to know why he was looking for me—did he have something to say—did he forget something at my house—or was he just checking on me? But the one thing I really wanted to find out was if he was suffering just like me—was that why he called?

"May I speak with Dr. Sloan?" I finally heard myself asking in an important tone.

"Who is calling?" the inquisitive operator asked, like she really needed to know.

"Lori," I said, confidently.

"Of course. Please hold for a minute," she said as if she knew who I was, or was it in my mind that she sounded that way?

"Hello," Sloan's voice melted me.

"Can I change my mind?" I said quickly, sounding like a child.

Sloan laughed and I smiled at the sound. Was it my imagination that he sounded relieved? Finally he said, "I should be done here by two and I have to be at my practice by five—so sometime around two-thirty," he said in one long breath, the excitement clear in his voice.

"Try to make it earlier if you can," I told him.

"I will," he said in a relieved voice and hung up.

The drama that had unfolded during the last twenty-four hours was history. Instantly my entire world turned from black to bright white.

At two-fifteen Sloan stepped back into my life. I realized that he'd kept the keys. I thought we should rehash all the drama we had just created, but Sloan had different ideas. He walked in and passed me with a smile. He didn't bother to stop beside me, just continued on to the kitchen. He grabbed a bottle of water from the refrigerator and turned back to me. I was still at the entrance hall, leaning on the waist-high wall, at least twenty steps away from him. He looked me in the eyes, sipped more of the water, smiled and took off his shirt. I watched him and examined his body as if it was the first time. I trusted the situation, but hoped that he would open up a conversation. My mind was captivated. I was held by my strong need to touch and feel his body. Obviously his needs were stronger than mine. He walked toward me until he reached the closest distance possible without touching me.

"We're not going to talk. I have to love you here and now," he said and let his body rub against mine. "I don't want any clever conversation. I really don't care why and when. All I want is you."

The choice was mine. I could refuse him or give in. But I couldn't resist him.

After a long, slow sexual encounter, Sloan whispered into my ear, "I don't know when, but I know it will happen."

I bit my tongue and tried not to ask any questions. Instead, I turned my body to him and started all over again.

But when he had to leave, I could not hold it in and had to ask him one little thing, just one. "Hey, when you paged me earlier, were you sure that I would return your page?"

"Of course," he said confidently and continued on toward the heavy wooden gate.

I watched his back, wondering if what I felt was love or lust. I saw him extend his hand, ready to grab the gate knob. He turned around and looked at me for a long second. He made his way back from the gate, nailed my eyes and said, "It's too late to separate. We cannot spin back time. I guess I live a double life but I love only one woman." He didn't wait for my response but turned his back and left.

Nineteen

I busied myself around the house, letting my thoughts and feelings fade while trying to put the place back in order. For some reason Sloan's short visits created a complete mess, almost as if the house had been redesigned. The kitchen turned into a bedroom, the bedroom became a lounge and the bathroom was left with traces of water that needed to be dried out.

Finally, I was on my way out the door. I had to drop some keys and paperwork off at Ruth's house as she had returned from her vacation. My temporary job had ended and was replaced with the worry of being unemployed again.

Ruth invited me in. I turned over my notes and keys to her, and she thanked me. "Oh no, thank you," I said.

"By the way," Ruth went on. "Yesterday, one of my employees turned in her resignation as she will be relocating to another city." Ruth sounded somewhat annoyed.

I could only imagine how stressful it was to have your own company, but I didn't know what to say. Should I offer my help, show my sympathy, or say nothing and just wait for her to continue?

Before I made up my mind, she spoke again. "She didn't give much notice. Her last day is going to be this coming Friday."

"Wow, what a nuisance," I said.

"Would you be interested in filling in for her?" she asked in a pleading tone. "I know it's only part time, but I'll try to get you more hours." She tried to make the offer sound more attractive.

"Sure, why not?" I answered quickly. "However, I need to tell you that I just found out that the PACU director position at the center is available. I would like to give it a shot."

"That's great." She sounded honestly happy for me. "When are you planning on turning in your application?"

"Tomorrow."

"Good. I'll make sure I talk with Mark for you," she said.

"Really?"

"Of course, I know him well. I don't see a reason why he wouldn't offer you the position."

"Don't be so sure. You know how it is—too much politics. Besides, I don't have much luck."

"I'll do my best."

"Thank you. I really appreciate it."

Ruth went back to the part-time job she was looking to fill and I made it clear that if and when I found a suitable full-time job elsewhere, I might or might not continue to work for her. We finalized the pay and agreed that I would start right away.

The next day, I turned in my application for the PACU director position. Only a few hours later I received a call to schedule an interview. I wanted to believe that it was fate but I knew that Ruth had probably talked with Mark as she'd promised.

I was excited as I arrived for my interview. I walked through a quiet, wide, threatening corridor that led to the administrative offices, the one area of the building that I'd never visited before.

After being interviewed by Mark Liberman, the CEO of the center, I made my way to see the chief of nursing. She was the one person that I had to establish and maintain a good relationship with—even if that required being overly gracious with her. She was the person who I would report to. I would be at her mercy and would have to convince her that I liked her.

Evidently my interview went well—I was offered the position before I left. I accepted with no hesitation and hurried to human resources to deal with the paperwork.

I looked for a pay phone so that I could catch Sloan, hoping to update him. I intended to meet him somewhere in town, maybe a coffee shop, to steal a few more minutes from his family for an instant celebration.

"Sorry, I can't. I have to run home." He hesitated for a second and continued, "Sharon is in bed with back pain and I have to look after the kids."

Disappointment flooded me. *She can go to hell. And you too,* I thought. *What do I care about your wife's back pain?* All that I cared about was me. *And what about me?* I wanted to ask him. But my phone conversation with him was already history. He was still on the line, but not there for me.

I didn't let Sloan's obligations bring me down and celebrated on my own. I ran from one place to another, shopped and spent money from the paycheck I had yet to earn or receive. I stopped to visit different friends and ended my day at Lori's.

By the time I returned home it was late, way past midnight. I was surprised to find three messages from Sloan.

"Hey baby. Where are you? Free bird—ha...." I could hear how disappointed he was that he wasn't able to talk to me. He sounded caring and loving, but he had nothing special to say. His messages were pointless, like he'd just called to remind me of him. He spoke quietly and had some hesitation in his voice. I assumed he called from home.

My conscience worked overtime. I blamed myself for the life he lived. I was bothered by the potential damage to his family and to his marriage. And in the same breath, I had insurmountable anger toward him. I could not forgive him for being so selfish.

I gazed at the answering machine, thinking about the tapes I'd kept—tapes that held messages I didn't want to erase—special, endless messages from Sloan. Whenever he called, he talked and talked, never hanging up the phone. The sound of his voice made him alive and present. Normally, his voice comforted me. I could listen to his messages again and again. They all meant a lot to me, but some of them were truly special.

That night, I listened to all of his messages. From the very first one he'd left me almost a year ago to the one he left earlier that day. I listened to them in the sequence they were recorded. Each one was different. Some of them were sarcastic, and some were funny. A few were painful, but others were encouraging. Other ones were special and recaptured my heart—the sort of messages that only mistresses get. They all floated along with our affair—like a fairy-tale. The sound of his love could be the testimony to our stolen affair. It was happiness mixed with sorrow.

The new job and the pressure of meeting a deadline were a good source of energy for my creativity. Setting up the PACU was a challenge that revived my abilities and inspiration. I stepped into my new job in full capacity and worked out my plan systematically and analytically. I was motivated and fulfilled. Nothing could possibly get in my way. I was entirely geared toward that upcoming inspection by the Department of Health. I inspected, cleaned, and organized every inch of the place. I went through each cubical, cart, and piece of equipment. I completed a meticulous inventory, created par levels, and submitted a list of items that had to be purchased. I met regularly with the chief of anesthesia, studied him, and made sure I became familiar with all of his protocols. I accepted the allocated staff and did not argue about its qualities. I created and posted signs and logs, established and implemented policies and procedures. By the day of the inspection, the place was completely me. I had no worries and was confident that the inspection would result with no deficiencies or findings. And that was how it was. Perfect. I reaped nothing but compliments.

Soon I knew all the physicians who were running around, and in no time I could determine who was good, who was very good, and who I wouldn't even let to care for my dog. But I had to work with all of them, and for that reason, I was better off keeping my mouth shut.

Some of them were easygoing, some were difficult and, no matter what I said, they had to fight me. I placed and categorized every one of them, but was nice to them and tried to keep a low profile. And for me, that was not an easy task.

With time Sloan and I became inseparable. Our lives were entwined. He was present and nothing could make him fade away. It seemed as if we were living like a couple. My house changed—revealing the lives of two people sharing a home. Two sets of towels hung on the towel rack and a second toothbrush took up space in the ceramic cup next to the sink. The bathroom sported his razor blade, shaving cream, and aftershave.

Day after day, week after week, I was busy with my career while Sloan progressed through and neared the end of his residency. There were only six months left before the exam. I imagined myself keeping the house quiet while he studied for long hours. The thought that he might choose to study elsewhere never crossed my mind. Yet, there were other things that I looked forward to, mostly the twenty days of service that he was called to order for the military. Sloan was ready to take advantage of the situation, lie to his wife and family, and to spend most of the nights at my place. My excitement had no boundaries. I challenged my imagination, using its skills to create a collage of pictures of me and Sloan sharing one sink late at night, enjoying candlelit dinners, consuming each other's bodies, and arguing over nonsense. I wondered if he might forget I was his mistress and fall asleep in front of the TV. I visualized us hanging out in public places alone or with Lori and Jonathan. In the meantime, until the big day arrived, I crossed one day off at a time on my calendar.

Twenty

"Hey, still around?" A feminine voice interrupted my dull moment at the lab.

"Hey there." I looked up and saw Dalia at the door.

"I wasn't sure if you'd already left for the day. It's late."

"Actually, it's my last day here." I pushed my chair away from the desk and leaned back.

"Really?"

"Yes. It's kind of quiet here in the afternoons. Besides, it's hard for me to make it on time. I get stuck in the Recovery Room most days. It's really not working that well for me."

"I can see how that would be a problem." She sat in the chair next to my desk. "How is it going up there? I hear they love you."

"I like it," I said. "Kind of what I expected."

"Are you sure? You don't sound very excited."

"I don't know. It's okay. It just seems like I've accomplished my mission. There isn't much more for me to do. I don't like the routine." I could hear the worry in my own voice.

"Are you disappointed?"

"No, not at all. It's a job. I have to make a living."

"How is your love life—still hanging in there?"

"Oh, yes, definitely," I answered with a big smile. "It's the one thing that adds excitement to my life. It keeps me alive. Maybe it's the excitement of being a mistress—I don't know." I laughed.

"I hear you," she said but didn't go into detail.

My friendship with Dalia had become tighter but was still limited. Although she was fun and I truly enjoyed our time together at the center, we never socialized outside of work. I trusted her but restricted the information I gave her. I didn't know what the consequences would be if she discovered that I was making love to her neighbor.

My pager went off and interrupted our conversation. I looked at its small screen. I didn't recognize the phone number but returned the call.

"Hello," I heard an unfamiliar voice.

"This is Sharon Lapidot. Did anyone from this number page me?"

"Yes. My name is Yael and I work for Dr. Kaminski." She identified herself but still didn't tell me the reason for her call.

"Yes?"

"Dr. Kaminski got your name and number from Dr. Lotan and he is asking to meet with you at your earliest convenience," she explained.

"What is it about, if I may ask?" I answered without much interest.

"A job opening."

"I see," I said in a reluctant tone. I was ready to tell her that this isn't practical, that I have a job and am comfortable with my career at the moment. Then I thought, *Why not? Maybe for once I will be the one to decline. Maybe it's my turn to look into the interviewer's eyes and say, "Thanks, but no thanks," or "Thanks, but this is not what I'm looking for."*

"When would you be available to meet with him?" She sounded pushy.

"How about next Thursday?"

"Anything earlier? Dr. Kaminski did ask to give this priority."

"The best I can do…" I said, thinking through my agenda, "…is Sunday." I couldn't find another opening.

"That will work." She rushed to confirm.

I asked her for the address, reconfirmed the date and time, and wrapped up the call.

Dalia didn't ask any questions. She continued where we'd left off. "So, I guess I'll see you less often since you won't be at the lab," she said.

"I'll still be around. I'm not going anywhere."

"Anyway, here is my phone number in case we don't run into each other." She handed me a scrap of paper with her number.

"Thanks."

"Okay, I need to get moving. I had a long day."

"I can only imagine. Get some rest," I said as she left.

As Dalia said, it was late—a few minutes before seven. Eight weeks from the time I'd started my job as the director of PACU, and my last day at the lab. I picked up my things and looked around. I paged Sloan and left him a message that I was on my way home.

"Hey gorgeous, I miss you." I heard Sloan on the answering machine an hour later as I walked into the house. "Take your time but hurry up. Call me before you leave. I cannot wait to see you."

I jumped in the shower, letting the water rid me of the stress I'd brought with me from work. I shaved my legs, my armpits and my tutti, cleaned up and got ready to drive to the hospital to see Sloan.

On my way, after picking up some takeout, I drifted into the secret sin I had committed with Sloan. I loved those nights when he was the on-call physician and spent the night in the hospital—when he was all mine. Nights when I didn't have to compete with his wife or family, but with his patients—when we survived in a small call-room, eating dinner out of a takeout box and sharing one cot—when the nights were too short for our love but long enough for our lusts. Nights when the walls witnessed our truth and lies, but remained mute and faithful to our sin. Nights that ended with painful mornings when I had to sneak out, making sure that no one saw or heard me.

My life continued its fast pace. Even after quitting the part-time job at the lab, I still didn't have enough time. There were many things that I wanted to do but could not fit into my agenda.

It was Sunday when my sprint started. I drove home from work, took a shower, got in business attire, refreshed my appearance, spiked my hair, rushed out of the house, and tried to beat the clock. I was supposed to meet Sloan at four-thirty at a coffee shop somewhere in the northern part of Tel-Aviv. At six I was scheduled to meet Kaminski at his office. Only God knew how I could make it all happen, so I prayed.

The drive to Tel-Aviv was the easy part. What I was worried about was the parking. I simulated the upcoming parking drama and could only assume that I would not find a spot near the coffee shop at that time of day. I rehashed the scenario that had yet to happen, willing to accept the possibility of a parking ticket, but my worries ended when I easily found a spot nearby. I was left with a short forty-five minutes with Sloan. *Well, better than nothing*, I thought.

"Good luck. You'll do fine." Sloan said right before I jumped in my car and went back to my mad rush.

By five fifty-five p.m., I was outside Kaminski's office, but still in my car. *Damn it, just another parking drama*. I drove around the block one more time, resigned to the fact that this time I might end up with a ticket, when I spotted a parking space—a tiny parallel spot that I managed in nine maneuvers. I grabbed my purse, touched up my lipstick and ran, and I mean ran.

Seconds before six, out of breath and wearing a fake smile, I was in Dr. Kaminski's office. It was a nice place, clean but small—very small. It looked like someone did an incredible job utilizing every little inch of the space.

"Hi," I said to the clerk, who looked to be in her twenties.

"Can I help you?" she asked.

"My name is Sharon Lapidot. I am here to meet Dr. Kaminski."

"Of course." She suddenly sounded friendlier. "Have a seat. He will be with you shortly." I saw how the rest of the office staff turned their heads to get a better look at me. It was clear that each one of those young chickens knew about me and my interview. *I guess my interview is already in progress,* I thought.

While sitting in that small office, waiting on Dr. Kaminski, I tried to ignore those inquisitive looks. I glanced through a magazine and strained to listen to the conversations around me. I tried to figure out what type of services the place offered. The number of incoming calls was astonishing—very unusual for an average office, unless services were provided by phone. There were five girls, all on the phone, talking non-stop. Simultaneously, they were checking me out. From the little I heard, it sounded as if they were talking about physical exams, something I wasn't overly familiar with. Listening to the one-sided conversations, it was obvious that the place offered some sort of medical services—though, I wasn't sure what kind. *There is no way I can do this for a living. I should probably leave now, before meeting with Kaminski.*

Fifteen minutes elapsed and I was still seated on the same sofa. No one said a word to me and I hadn't seen or heard Dr. Kaminski. Three times I was offered something to drink, but not once did I hear a word about Kaminski or the delay.

I became impatient. I was trying to decide whether to ask her to reschedule or to have her boss call me, when she interrupted my thoughts.

"Excuse me," she said. "Dr. Kaminski just called from his car and apologized for being late. He is stuck in traffic and will be here in a little bit, maybe fifteen minutes." The lie was obvious. I'd been in this business too long not to recognize it.

"Listen, young lady," I wanted to tell her, "your boss is not stuck in traffic, he is late—that's all. Don't lie to me and don't cover his ass." But I did not.

At six-fifty, almost an hour later than my scheduled interview time, Dr. Kaminski walked through, straight to his office, ignoring me and everybody else. He immediately closed the door. The young lady who had welcomed me joined him in his office for a brief second.

"Please come in," she said on her way back.

Kaminski's office, like the rest of the place, was small, well-designed, and functional. He picked up the phone and invited another person to join us.

"This is my wife, Shirley." He gestured to the lady who had just walked in. "We work together and I would like her to join us. I hope you don't mind."

"Not at all," I agreed. *Like I have a choice*, I thought.

I wasn't sure about any of them. I couldn't put my finger on anything specific, but remained reserved. They appeared conjoined, but I couldn't relate to them. The situation, along with my gut feelings, made it difficult to get excited. They didn't provide much information—at least not enough for me.

"It is a private medical center that will offer executive checkups and medical services to a very select clientele. It will serve mainly tourists, executives, and contracted groups. We would like to open it to the public but aren't sure what response to expect. It will be located in the Bait-Asia building." I listened to him explain the business and its potential. It sounded to me as if the medical services provided there would serve individuals in the top ten percent income bracket and employees of established corporations.

"We are looking for a manager," he said and talked briefly about his expectations.

Neither of them mentioned anything about compensation and I felt it was inappropriate to bring up the subject during the first interview. I was cold, careful, and suspicious. I did not express my thoughts or feelings. I remained hard to read—just like them.

"So how does it sound? Would you be interested?" he asked.

"Well, I would like to see the place before any further discussion."

"That's a good idea." They both agreed with me.

"Generally speaking, is this something that you would like to be part of?" He tried again.

"I don't know. We'll see." I left him in the dark. I didn't want to make any commitment before discovering more about the business and about him.

"How about Friday?" He was ready to meet me at the actual construction site.

"This Friday?" I verified.

"Yes. Are you available?"

"Not in the morning," I said. "Maybe late in the afternoon, around five."

"Sounds good. I'll meet you in the lobby."

"Okay." I said and left with incomplete information. I wanted to know who I would be reporting to, how much his wife was involved in the business and if she was a bitch. I definitely was wondering what pay rate he had in mind. But I played by the rules and didn't show too much interest.

I was positive that they liked me. I was confident that the job was mine but was not sure if I wanted to work for that man and his wife—I could tell that she definitely was part of the deal. The one thing that motivated me was the idea of starting something new and the assumption of a high-paying job. Projects like that were my favorite thing and my forte. I was good at planning, designing, and executing. I was extremely resourceful, competent, and knowledgeable.

I was enthusiastic when I got back to my car. I carefully checked under the wipers and felt fortunate that I hadn't received a parking ticket. I thanked the driver that had left ahead of me so that I didn't have to struggle to get out of that tiny parking place.

What a day? Life is good. It's about time.

I had roughly twenty minutes to drive before I made it to Lori's. The drive on the highway was fast with light traffic. Once off the highway, I caught all the green lights and the drive was quick.

"Well?" Jonathan said once he opened the door for me.

"Too good to be true."

"So it's bad. Can you give some details?"

"Where's Lori?" I walked into the kitchen. "Let me call Sloan first."

Sloan was busy at work and could not talk at the moment. I had to wait for him to call back.

Meanwhile, I shared the details from my odd meeting with the Kaminskis with the Rosins. I didn't skip a thing, repeating everything I'd heard, observed, and interpreted. Lori and Jonathan were excited but cautious in their enthusiasm. They knew that I would be tempted to take the job even though I had no guarantees. They believed that this was a wishy-washy situation and could not really advise me.

Two hours later Sloan called, eager to hear about my interview.

"So, how did it go?" he asked.

"It was okay. I'm not sure about it."

"What did you find out?"

Unlike the Rosins, Sloan was optimistic. He found the job attractive, different, and challenging. He thought that it would be a great opportunity that could open many doors for me in the future. "I think you should keep the Friday meeting and go see the place," he said in a firm voice.

Eventually the Rosins were convinced and agreed with him.

As Sloan suggested, I kept the Friday meeting but tended to believe that this was not going be a good prospect. I didn't want to miss this opportunity but couldn't take the chance of more drama in my life. True, meeting with Kaminski on site was not a commitment but would promote my engagement with him.

Twenty-One

Three days later I saw Dalia and Dr. Shelton. I conveyed the scope of the story to them and asked them never-ending questions. I hoped that they had heard about Dr. Kaminski, maybe even knew him. I needed them to say something bad about him—that he was not trustworthy, that he was sneaky, a bad physician or an unsuccessful individual—something that would stop me from going forward with Kaminski's plan.

But they said none of those things. In fact, all that they could add was that he was an anesthesiologist who was no longer practicing in his specialty. They also said that he'd deferred his work to the business side of medicine and he was known as a shark—a proven businessman.

"He knows how to make money," Shelton said but could not add anything beyond that.

"I don't think you have anything to lose," Dalia said.

"I have to agree." Shelton sided with her.

"I hate to see you leave, but if you're planning to keep your door open here, make sure you are honest with them about it. You probably should tell them that this is an opportunity that you cannot turn down," Dalia said.

"That doesn't mean they'll rehire me," I said.

"You're right, but at least they will respect you. It's not less valuable."

"I hear you, but first let's see whether I take the job," I said and went back to work.

The stressful part of the week ended. By Wednesday, on Sloan's first day of active duty, I had an extreme feeling of joy.

I went straight from work to the grocery store and shopped for all of Sloan's favorites. I went wild and added some strawberries and lots of whipping cream to the shopping cart. I pictured us covered with whipped cream, trying to consume each other's body through white, glossy temptation. To make it a perfect night, I picked up a few candles scented with ocean breeze.

Arriving home, I took a deep breath, inhaling the scent of cleanliness. I unpacked the groceries and rushed to my bedroom to place one of the candles I'd just bought. I smiled at the properly made bed with fresh linen. The thought of my housekeeper's role in my love affair made me laugh. My bedroom was staged as if she wished me a heavenly, sensual night. Often I wondered about her special attention to Sloan and his things. It was all done as if she approved of our romance.

It appeared that Sloan was of a similar mind and did not let the excitement and wonder pass him by. The look on his face, when he arrived, was one that I hadn't seen before. He was dressed in a pair of blue jeans, a pullover, and tennis shoes. I had to take a moment to get used to his casual appearance. Until then, I'd only seen him in scrubs, business attire, or naked. I had never seen my man in casual clothes. He looked sexy.

"So what do you do with a mistress in the evening, when you don't have to rush home?" he asked aloud and continued, "Do we watch TV first or have sex?" He smiled sheepishly.

"Maybe you should ask what's for dinner first," I suggested sarcastically.

"Let me take care of my family obligation before I devour you," he said, squeezing me to his side.

He grabbed the phone, took a seat, and stretched out while dialing.

"Hey, Eric. It's Sloan," he said and then he paused. "I made it. I'm here…." I overhead him talking with Eric, his best friend and the only person in his circle who knew about our affair. I could only assume that Sloan wanted Eric to be his alibi.

"I'm at the number I left with you." He wrapped up the call.

I could only imagine how Eric answered him. Did Eric owe Sloan this kind of favor? I didn't know.

Sloan was not ready to give me his attention—he had one more call to make. "Hey, it's me, Dad. What are you doing?" he said and swiveled the chair so that his back was to me. "Where's your mom?" he asked. And then after a short pause I overheard his side of his conversation with his wife.

"How is it going? Is everything okay?" He swiveled the chair back and forth. "We just finished up…I'll call you tomorrow." He shook his wrist and allowed his watch to twist so he could look at the time. "I don't think we'll be released tomorrow." And that was it. He was so blunt.

I registered every word of what he said to his wife. My heart raced as if I was the one who lied. I was annoyed but amused. I thought of the way he referred to her as "your mom." I found it pretty appalling. The way he ended the call sounded discordant. "Bye" was all he said—nothing more. It was cold and rude. *He could show more kindness,* I thought and then laughed at the duality of my own inner monologue. It wasn't long ago that I'd wished the woman would just drop off the face of the earth and here I was defending her in my mind. Was it because I could see myself in her place? When Sloan was done with me would he be that cold?

"What's about dinner? Should we order some takeout?" He shook me from my thoughts, but his back was still turned to me.

"Well, I was thinking of putting something together, but if you'd rather have takeout that's fine with me." I suddenly felt unsure of the situation.

"Come here," he said and spun his chair so that he was now facing me.

For once I didn't respond and made myself busy in the kitchen, and then he left his seat and made his way in my direction.

"Preparing dinner is a marital thing." He tried to tease me.

"Is it really?" I asked, showing no interest in listening to him.

"Yes, it is, unless I cook for you," he said while lifting me up and sitting me on the counter.

"Sure," I agreed. "So, what's on the menu?"

"Let's see?" he said, ducking into the fridge to see what was available.

He grabbed a few fresh artichokes and rinsed them under the stream of water. He trimmed them like a chef, filled a pot with water, added some salt, lemon juice, a few drops of olive oil and put it on the stove.

By the time the water boiled he'd already opened a bottle of white wine and was ready to let go and to enjoy life. He added the artichokes to the boiling water and let them cook.

"Is pink sauce going to work for you—or would you rather have a mustard sauce, or curry sauce?" he asked and opened the refrigerator.

"Pink is good."

"Okay, let's see." He gathered the necessary ingredients and started to prepare the sauce. He mixed the ketchup with some mayonnaise and some whipping cream in a bowl. He added salt and pepper and whisked it until it became foamy, not too thick. Then, he stuck his finger in it and tasted it.

"Pretty good, I think." He stuck his finger in the sauce again.

"Here, taste it," he said, moving closer to me. He put his finger in my mouth and allowed me to lick his creation from him. "God, you are irresistible," he said and took me in his arms.

"Watch the stove," I reminded him.

"I can be fast. You want to see?" he asked but didn't wait for my answer.

There, on the counter, next to the pot with the boiling water and fresh artichokes, I let Sloan illustrate his love to me.

The rest of the evening and night were similar to the cooking. I let Sloan take charge, bringing me to a wonderland of love, sex, lust, and passion. Thoroughly spent, we crashed and fell asleep.

Returning back from wonderland into reality found us together in my bed.

"Good morning." He spoke softly into my ear.

Waking up in Sloan's arms in my house was new. Unlike at the hospital, we could take our time. We were safe, not worrying about being disturbed by those who might see us.

He didn't ask to make love to me one more time, nor did he start a conversation. He did not need my attention. It was easy and smooth. We didn't bump into each other, nor did we fight over the shower or the sink. It was a quiet, peaceful morning without stress or tension.

"Have a nice one. I'll see you tonight." He held me in his arms and gently kissed the tip of my nose so my lipstick would not get messed up.

Sloan left in one direction, back to the base, and I went the other way, to work.

It was only the second day of Sloan's active duty and we had already established a routine. Sloan made it earlier and walked in around six p.m. He squeezed me to his side, picked up the phone, sat on the couch, and called Eric, repeating his sentences from the day before. He spun his seat around and called his home and spoke with his wife in a shorter version than the day before: "I'll be home tomorrow night, not sure what time."

Like the day before, I was in the kitchen. Sloan, like the night before, walked toward me and asked, "So, how was your day?"

"Nothing special—just another day."

"Well, are you still on for tomorrow? Are you going to meet with Kaminski?" He leaned against the counter.

"I guess." I handed him a cup of coffee. "Are you tired?"

"Not at all. Why?" he asked.

"Well, Lori called earlier and asked if we would come for dinner."

"Sounds good, why not?" He sounded comfortable with the idea.

"I hoped you wouldn't mind."

"So, let's go. I want to meet their kids before they go to bed." He sounded like he already had a plan on how to introduce himself to them.

"Hey, did you ever think that we would go out, together, in your car, that late in the day?" I tried to share my excitement and get his feelings and thoughts.

But Sloan had no words. He just smiled.

"What if we end up at a traffic light next to someone we know?"

"I didn't think about it," he admitted.

"The last few days feel as if we are married." I turned my head to the left and looked at him.

"I know. It does feel that way sometimes," he said.

"Are you anxious?"

"Yes and no. I really don't care." He reached over and rested his hand on my leg.

And from that moment on, I didn't really care either.

It was the next day, early in the afternoon, when Sloan found me at work. He was released earlier than expected and hoped to see me before he went back to his other life.

"Can you leave work early?" he asked.

"What's going on? Where are you?"

"I was done early and thought we might meet before I go home, I mean…"

"Where are you?" I cut him off.

"At your place. I stopped by, thought to wait for you. But I guess it won't work." He sounded disappointed.

"I wish I could, but I really can't. You know how Fridays are," I told him and hated everything about the rest of my day. It was only one-fifteen. I thought about all that I had to do and what I was missing. "I'm sorry. I just can't." I was sure my disappointment showed in my voice as well.

"I know. I was just checking." His voice was tender.

"I wish you would have called earlier," I said but knew that it probably wouldn't have made any difference.

"That's fine. I guess I'll see you tomorrow night, right?"

"Of course, I'll be waiting. I love you."

"I love you too."

The rest of the day played out as planned.

By five I was in the lobby of Beit-Asia, sitting across from Dr. Kaminski. This time he was by himself. It was a one-on-one meeting. I felt as if I had more power than before—as if I was already in a winning position. After gaining more information about the future center and seeing the actual place, we discussed the compensation. I was uncomfortable, willing to skip this part or have someone else negotiate it for me. In retrospect, if I would have known how big this job was and all that was involved with it, I probably would have declined the offer or asked for double the salary he offered.

Two hours had elapsed since meeting with Dr. Kaminski. I was totally overwhelmed from the arrangement I'd just made with him. I agreed to start working for him on the first of the following month, about three weeks from that day.

The pay sounded good. The other miscellaneous bonuses such as an expense account and an unconditional year-end bonus of ten percent that Kaminski had mentioned were attractive as well. The challenge that came with this job was the ideal match for my personality—enough to recharge my batteries. I was eager and wanted to start right away. But I didn't. I stayed loyal to my present employer and gave them appropriate notice, following Dalia's advice.

It was premature to have an opinion about Dr. Kaminski. Yet, I could say that something about this man stimulated my intellect. I was captured by his vision and his never-ending enthusiasm. I was overwhelmed but inspired by his elaborate contact list and the sense of business he demonstrated.

There was nothing about him that aroused the womanly part of me. I couldn't find anything attractive in his appearance. He seemed like he'd be the classic boss who could regularly supply me with intellectual stimulus. More likely, my new job would spare me from my everyday routine.

I still needed my entire army of counsels to approve Kaminski's offer. Not that they would have changed my mind, but I needed them to confirm that I chose right. I wanted to talk with Sloan, but couldn't. He was in his other world, with his wife and kids. I had to wait until the next day, Saturday, when he would pretend to return back to his duty at the base, but would actually return to my world.

The weekend played out as planned except that around three my pager went off and interrupted my waiting. It said, "Five at the beach." And nothing more. *Five at the beach? Who the hell is sending me this message, and what beach?* I tried to break the code. If it had said six, I would've suspected it was Sloan, as that was the time that he was supposed to show up. *But five o'clock? And why at the beach? Could Sloan have sent it? And which beach? How obscure.*

The first thing I did was call Lori. "Hey," I said. "Listen to this." I relayed the odd message to her and my list of concerns.

"Well, I bet it's Sloan, but I can see how you might think it's someone else."

"Well, that really doesn't help me much."

"Let's see, if you are at the beach by five and it's not him, then you still have enough time to make it back home by six."

"Maybe. But what if this is someone else and I'm in trouble? Besides, what beach should I go to? It could be any beach."

"Do you have Eric's number?" she asked.

"No, I don't. And if I did, would I really call him?"

"Of course you would—and you do have his number."

"No, I don't," I insisted.

"Didn't you tell me that Sloan called him the other day from your home phone?"

"Yes, he did."

"So trace his number from the phone." She sounded as if she could be a private investigator.

"Let's see, hold on a minute," I said to her and tried my luck.

Sure enough, Lori was right. On that day, when Sloan called Eric, there was only one unfamiliar number. The time of the call was appropriate to think that this was Eric's number.

"I think I got it, but wait a sec, let me see if that's the same number from the next day—Sloan called him again on Thursday, remember?" I felt as if I was a member of her PI team.

I was right. That number appeared again on the next day's log at six-twenty, right after Sloan walked in the house.

"So what now?" I asked her

"Call him."

"Call him and what?" I asked her in a helpless voice.

"Tell him who you are and that you need his help verifying if this message is from Sloan."

"Are you crazy? I can't do that."

"Of course you can. That's your only option."

"And what if he's not home?" I assessed my odds.

"Then we'll see. But call him before it gets too late."

"No, I don't think it's a good idea." I started panicking.

"Listen, call Eric. It's not like you're calling Sloan's home. Obviously, Eric knows about you. There's nothing for you to worry about."

"How about if you call him?"

"Are you nuts? Call him and let me know," she said.

I hung up the phone, took a deep breath, and dialed the number.

"Yes?" I heard an unfamiliar voice on the other line.

"May I speak with Eric please?"

"Speaking."

"This is Sharon Lapidot. I'm assuming you've heard my name before."

"Yes, I have."

"I'm sorry to bother you, but I need your help."

"Sure. What's going on?"

I gave him the scoop, trying not to sound hysterical.

"Can you please find out for me?" I asked him.

"I don't need to—I know it's him."

"How do you know?"

"Because I'll be jogging with him on the beach at four."

"Are you really?"

"Yes," he said, clearly at ease.

"I'm still puzzled." I doodled on the scratch pad next to the phone.

"Trust me. Just be at the beach by five."

"What beach?" I asked.

"Dabush, of course."

"How was I supposed to know that?"

"You're right, how would you know? Anyway, be there at five. He'll be there. I promise."

"What's happening there?"

"Nothing in particular. It's Saturday. That's all. Just relax."

"Are we staying there?" I was inquisitive.

"I guess."

"Well, I guess I'll see you at five."

"Okay. I have to run. It's getting late," he said.

Eric sounded like a nice, easygoing guy, exactly as Sloan had described him. He seemed comfortable with me, as if my affair with his married friend didn't bother him.

The clock was ticking and I was running out of time. I had to clean up and put on my best before heading to the beach. But before that, I called Lori back.

"Hey, listen, you were right."

"You see?" She responded and listened while I told her about my conversation with Eric.

"I told you," she said and laughed.

"Anyway, I was thinking that since Eric is planning to be there, then you and Jonathan should be there too. What do you think?

"I don't see why not. Let me talk with Jonathan."

"Great. Sounds like a plan."

"So, I guess we'll see you then. What time again?"

"Five. I have to run. Hey, call me if your other half says no." I confirmed and hung up the phone.

That afternoon on the beach created a few memories for me. Memories of a peaceful picture of white chairs on powdery sand, Eric and his friendship with Sloan, happy voices, and Sloan's testimony, "This is the life I want." But most, I remember the sunset in the form of a big golden ball surrounded by a red and orange sky—a sun that was getting ready to be buried in the sea. Nothing else was there for me until we were leaving—when Sloan wrapped his arm around my shoulders and nobody made a comment or gave a second look—as if they all approved it, as if there was no other life for Sloan but this one with me.

But I—I did have another life, an empty one—a life of long hours without him. I lived long hours of loneliness that could not be dimmed by the short, happy moments with him. I felt the pain of getting old by myself without the chance to have a family of my own.

It was hard to ignore the lie I lived.

Sloan's life was staged before me—a life that became more complicated by the day. There were times when I could see and feel his pain and confusion, when I wanted to send him away, back to his family, as if I was the one who'd jailed him in my cage. At times, I could feel his conscience calling him to go back to his wife and kids. But when he was there, at home, my mind replayed his voice from our stolen calls, as if he could no longer stand his situation, as if he was begging to move on and start a new life—a life with me.

What saved me from that exhausting and tedious routine was my upcoming new job. My resignation from the medical center was handled professionally. Nobody rushed me out and no one exhibited hostility toward me. They all hated to see me leave, but they all wished me well.

I said goodbye to all of them but one, Dalia. To her I said, "See you later." The persistence of our relationship was not dependent on our physical location. It was clear that our friendship would continue and deepen.

Twenty-Two

S hortly after I started working for Kaminski, I realized that learning and knowing my new boss was going to be a long, tough mission—not an impossible one, but without a doubt, no less difficult than the job itself. In a matter of days, I clearly understood that Kaminski and his life were part of my job description. He dealt with at least ten different things at the same time, working with thousands of people. While Kaminski considered many of them friends, I wondered what his definition of a friend was.

I worked with an extensive contact list that barely fit into three phone books. I omitted the option of memorizing any of the numbers and preserved the space in my brain for other tasks.

Kaminski's lifestyle was interesting but extravagant. He drove a brand new vehicle, imported from the United States, used a cell phone, and wore expensive clothes. Everything he had, except his pager, was a luxury that not many could afford.

It appeared, with all the gadgets he had, he would be available at all times, but the truth of the matter was that he was accessible only when he wanted to be. His concept of time was unique. I never witnessed him arriving anywhere on time. He was an expert in excuses. The word *late* was replaced in Kaminski's vocabulary with the phrase *running behind.* And for him, running behind was the norm. Only those close to him knew that his apologies were empty and held no validity—actually he didn't give a shit about anybody but himself. Sometimes I wondered if these acquired traits were the satisfaction of a careless and overbearing person.

Soon I met countless people who Kaminski knew—people in public and political positions, CEOs, chairmen, members of the parliament, and ministers. Within a short time, I knew most of them. It seemed as if he worked hard to show off with his entourage. But the more new figures he exposed me to, the less impressed I was. Kaminski and his lifestyle didn't trigger my curiosity or make me feel important. My indifference aggravated him. He couldn't find a way to capture my curiosity. Intentionally, I avoided any confrontation with him. I kept my background and my personal network to myself so that he wouldn't try to use me as a link to new, influential contacts. If he only knew my connections, he probably wouldn't try so hard to impress me with his. But he was clueless. I held those cards close to me as if they were my jokers. I kept them for a better moment.

Though, there were a few things that I gave Kaminski credit for. He was double board certified—definitely an achievement. Furthermore, he knew how to make money from medicine, and I mean lots of money.

Kaminski's other activities, the political ones, were really in conflict with my beliefs. I didn't mind any of the things he did unless he tried to involve me. Scheduling his related meetings or coordinating affiliated events didn't bother me. What stirred me up was when Kaminski brought me a mailing to be folded and put in envelopes, thousands of them.

"I need you to mail these out by the end of the day," he said, while placing three huge boxes on my desk. "Call Naomi for the address list."

"Well," I said, "regardless of your political interests, I really don't think that this mailing project is part of my job. Why don't you ask one of your secretaries?"

"Well, young lady, let me remind you that the one to pay is the one to say." His hard stare indicated that he was serious.

"Really?" I looked straight into his eyes.

"Really," he said.

"Well, I guess you hired the wrong person. I'm not mailing these. And for your information, I don't have any interest in your political activities. As a matter of fact, I hate politics and am not going to be part of it." I could hardly believe my own words.

"I understand." He responded in an undetermined voice.

"I guess I'm not the right person for you," I said and started to pick up my stuff.

"Actually, you're the perfect one. I couldn't have done any better." He turned to leave the office.

"Meaning what?" I asked while his back was to me.

"Meaning that I'm leaving now," he said without turning around.

"I'm not taking care of this mailing."

Kaminski didn't answer nor turn to face me. He rushed into the elevator and disappeared behind the closing doors.

I sat behind my desk, trying to figure out if I was in the right place. The telephone rang and cut into my thoughts.

"I need you to call a courier, have him pick up those boxes, and deliver them to my office." Kaminski's voice was brusque on the phone.

"Sure," I answered.

"Listen, you're the best person I've ever hired. Just make sure you don't disappoint me. I'll see you tomorrow." He hung up without waiting for a reply.

I'd clearly won the first battle but was not sure how to win the war. In fact, I didn't want to get into a war. I questioned my decision to take it in the first place.

My boss' workday started at seven and continued late into the night, sometimes until after midnight. He never stopped and expected his employees to keep the same schedule and pace. At times it felt like slavery and I made a note to put some boundaries around my private life. I reminded myself that there was a fine line between a workaholic and a dedicated employee. I strived to keep myself away from Kaminski, to make sure he didn't control me or my working hours.

I truly enjoyed the freedom and autonomy I had. There was no doubt that Kaminski trusted me and my decisions. His comments were proof of how satisfied he was.

It had been almost three months since I'd started working for Kaminski and about two and a half months since I'd made myself clear about my job responsibilities. Not only did I have the freedom to speak and act, I rarely saw Kaminski. Most of our interactions were over the phone. We spoke numerous times throughout the day. During these calls, I reported, updated, questioned, advised, and consulted with him—and he answered, agreed, fumed, resolved, created, and refused.

The entire project of setting up the center was on my shoulders. My plate was full. I worked all day, every day. I planned, created, wrote protocols, put together bilingual forms, argued, confronted, and decided. I had to be flexible, creative, and mobile. My office was still under construction so I used the business lounge, coffee shops, and the floor of the future center.

I worked six days a week, putting in an average of seventy hours each week. I was entirely captured by creation. Any challenge that I came across amplified my motivation. Any problem that I resolved contributed to my ego and my satisfaction. I interviewed secretaries, techs, and others, having the liberty to pick and choose who to hire. But when it came to physicians, things were quite different. Kaminski didn't give me much leeway and voiced his opinion as well as showed his domineering side.

He was not shy to show his ugly side. At times he could be vulgar, like that day after he interviewed an acquaintance of mine, a dermatologist.

"Where did you get this clown?" he barked as he entered my office.

"Why a clown? What don't you like about him?" I stopped my work and looked up at him.

"Well, I don't think there is a need to see any more candidates. I think I've nailed it down."

"There is nothing wrong with these people. You don't even know them. Actually, you know nothing about them. Maybe we should give it a second thought." I was determined to get some of my people in the door.

"As a matter of fact, I know more than you think. Some of them will not work here or for me. Some of them I won't meet."

"Like which ones exactly?"

"Like your friend Dr. Mayer."

"What do you have against him?"

"Let's put it this way, I have nothing for him."

"Give him a chance. He's a great doctor."

"Listen, young lady, we're not in negotiation. I said I'm not going to meet with him." He turned his back to me and was ready to leave my office.

"But you're going to meet with Ruth, right?"

"Ruth?" He turned back and faced me.

"Yes, Ruth, from the lab."

"Only if she will beat Arie's offer."

"Why do you think that your people are better than mine?"

"Because I know they are. I'm older than you and know this business very well." His face and neck turned red and he left.

As Kaminski promised, he didn't meet with Dr. Mayer, the orthopedic surgeon, but met with Ruth. And as he said, he signed a contract with her because, financially, she was more attractive than Arie—the one he considered his friend. Still, he left himself room for other options, so he gave Ruth a monopoly on seventy-five percent of the entire lab work that the center would generate.

Surprisingly, I made Kaminski commit that once Sloan passed the boards he would give him some work. It was an expensive deal. I had to reveal a major portion of my private life and make Kaminski a partner to my sin.

Kaminski's empathy toward my situation caused me to raise my eyebrows. At the moment his reaction didn't make much sense and I found it suspicious. But later, when I became Kaminski's pal, I realized that he was guilty of having an affair with a lady who lived in another town—a place he visited regularly.

With that much in common, Kaminski had an understanding that my mood and productivity could often be subject to one thing— Sloan. For that reason he guarded my affair with Sloan as if it benefited him, which it did.

"Make sure Sloan is nice to you," he teased me often.

"And if not?"

"I'll have to take care of him." He sounded so stupid, but assured me that he supported the circumstances. And I sort of enjoyed it.

By the time the center was developed, all that was left was to bring in patients. Kaminski relocated his office, his personal secretary, and his wife to the center. I had no expectation that these two women would do anything for me or for the place. It was clear that they were Kaminski's personal belongings.

As I watched Kaminski and his secretary, I noticed how dependent she was on him. It was pathetic to see how she gave into him instead of fighting for her rights. The blunt tone he used with her annoyed me. I was disgusted with her devotion. I pledged that I would never pander to anyone that way. I wanted to believe that I had more to offer. After all, I had a strong background and hoped that my knowledge and qualifications would save me from such situations.

However, I trained his secretary to answer the phone, coordinate my calendar, manage the mail, and explained to her that when I was out of the office she was in.

Although at first Kaminski didn't object to me using his secretary, after a while he disapproved of it. He brought up the subject during one of our lunch meetings.

"We are not sharing my secretary," he said in a calm voice.

"I cannot be here all day every day."

"Hire someone," he ordered me.

"Hire someone for what?" I asked.

"Hire yourself a secretary. Someone who will work for you eight to five, nine to six—I don't care."

"And do what?"

"Be your secretary, your assistant! Find someone who will do what you ask my secretary to do."

"Simple as that?" I asked.

"Yes, simple as that."

So I did. Having a secretary changed my working style but didn't reduce my working hours. My crazy schedule, the business meetings and dinners became longer. The rush home to see Sloan, my boss' lifestyle, and the enforced involvement with the politics turned into a routine that became tiresome, but not dull. I trusted that my hectic schedule would change once the center was opened.

Kaminski was ready to determine the opening date, putting me under a great deal of pressure with a deadline.

It was mid-morning when he walked into my office, running his fingers through his hair, pacing back and forth. Finally he stood at my desk, next to my chair, glancing over my shoulder at my calendar.

"Let's see. I think the seventeenth of next month," he mumbled.

"For what?"

"The grand opening." He was short. "Make sure you get at least ten signed contracts from giant businesses for checkups before the opening. I'm planning on a first-class launch. You are in charge." He tapped his pen on my shoulder.

"That's only forty-one days away." I clasped my ten fingers together close to my face and bit the knuckle of my index finger.

"I'm glad you can count. Don't waste time. There's a lot to do," he said and headed to the door.

"No kidding. Tell me about it."

He stopped for a second and added, "I am expecting a guest list of three hundred people." And he left.

In all fairness to Kaminski, he was involved and helped with the business part of the center. In no time he'd signed exclusive contracts and launched the scheduling department. I was amazed with the number of calls and how the schedule filled with appointments.

"What about Visa?" I asked him.

"What about them?"

"Well, they are the biggest credit card company in the country. They have hundreds of executives and they also could offer the check-ups to their card members as a benefit. That could bring us thousands of exams."

"There's no chance we will gain their business."

"Why?"

"Because I said so. Trust me." He was so blunt.

"Do you mind if I try?"

"Good luck." He continued on his way.

Twenty-Three

It was obvious that Kaminski knew the business. I had nothing to offer to Visa but an attractive price. The market was saturated with similar centers offering various packages. Our odds of winning their business were slim if any.

"Here is my proposal. Please let's try." I handed him a folder.

"I told you, you have no chance," he repeated, while briefly reviewing it.

"I have nothing to lose. I know that the profit margin is very low, but you should think about the publicity, we could get free publicity quickly and benefit from free advertising through their monthly mailer.

"Fine. You win." He handed the folder back to me.

"Not yet, but I'll try."

"I doubt you'll get a meeting, or even a response."

A week later, in a meeting at the business center of Beit-Asia around a huge elegant conference table, I presented our center, along with our proposal to Visa.

"Can I get a copy of the proposal?" the vice president of marketing asked.

"Of course," I said and handed the proposal to him.

"Thank you. We'll get back with you." He ended the meeting, and stood up.

That's all? Kaminski was right. "Thank you for your time. Let me know if there is anything else you might need."

"Thank you," he shook my hand kindly.

I watched him step out of the room, followed by the two other individuals who'd accompanied him to the meeting. I looked at Kaminski and prayed that he wouldn't say anything.

"Well, do you feel any better?" Kaminski rubbed it in.

"I'm not going to tell you that you were right. I'll wait to hear *no* first."

"And you will hear it. They will decline the offer. You know they will." He was pissed.

"I'm going back to the office," I said, while picking up my papers.

Kaminski and I didn't exchange one word in the elevator, nor over the next few hours. And if not for the unexpected visit from Sloan at the office, I guess it would have been a few more days before Kaminski would forgive me for the embarrassment.

I survived the formal face-to-face introduction between Sloan and Kaminski. *What a moment.* It was the crossroad of my professional life with my personal one and my forbidden affair. I tried not to freak out. Although the two were technically not strangers to each other, they shook hands and went through the motions. I felt uncomfortable.

"Finally," Kaminski said to Sloan.

"Same here."

"I started to worry that she was having a virtual affair," Kaminski said with a smile.

"It sometimes feels that way," Sloan said with a grimace.

"Well, I understand that you are about to take the boards, aren't you?"

"Yes, I am," Sloan said.

"I'll be sure to keep an opening for a fresh OBGYN."

"That would be nice."

"Nice meeting you. I have to run. Make sure you keep her happy," Kaminski said and left.

Sloan followed me to my office and shut the door behind him, stepping close to me. "You look beautiful," he said in an inviting voice.

"I look the same."

"True. That's because you always look beautiful," he said while grabbing my love handles.

"We are in my office," I reminded him.

"Are you going to put off a quickie?" he asked, mischief clear in his voice as well as in his eyes.

"Yes. But, I'll take a rain check." I looked into his eyes.

"How long before you can go home?"

"I could leave now."

"Could you really?" he whispered in my ear and let his body rub against mine so that I could feel how hard and ready he was.

"What's wrong with you? I'm not going to have sex with you in my office." I pushed him away.

Sloan didn't give up. He set his lips on mine, while his hands found their way under my skirt. Once he touched my clitoris I gave up, let him pull down my underwear, and took my rain check.

I never thought that I would be that wild at my place of work, or that I would be able to fulfill my sexual needs on my desk. On second thought, this was no different than having sex in the on-call physician room—his place of work.

With this on my mind I made my way home. I stepped in the shower, erasing the evidence of our earlier sex and got ready for the upcoming one. I could never have enough with Sloan. I looked forward to hearing him enter the house and join me in the shower.

The next day Kaminski was still pissed. He would not forget the embarrassment with VISA. He acted juvenile. I didn't play his game. I planned on going home on time, refreshing, and making my way to the hospital to see Sloan.

It was right after six when my plans changed—the fax rang, receiving a letter to my attention. It was short. Very short.

Dear Ms. Sharon Lapidot,

After reviewing your proposal, I am pleased to confirm our sincere interest in signing a contract with CheckMed for the medical services offered in your proposal.

Please forward a draft of the contract to my attention for review.

Job well done.

Good luck.

Sincerely, Joe Melnick

Vice President of Marketing, Visa, Israel

I tried to read between the lines. It sounded somewhat personal but absolutely professional. I was not sure what to think and walked into Kaminski's office.

"Hey, look at this." I placed the fax carefully on his desk.

"What is it?" he asked and grabbed the paper. In seconds he was done reading the fax and said, "Interesting that he addressed it to you." Kaminski refused to let me get the credit for the deal and was not ready to give up.

"Well, I was the one who initiated the contact and the one who gave the presentation the other day." I paused for a brief second. "You didn't even give him your business card. He probably doesn't even know your name."

"Are you kidding or what? Everybody knows me. I don't have to hand out business cards." He sounded offended and let his aggression surface.

"Does it really matter?"

"Of course it does."

"There's nothing wrong with me getting some business in the door. It's not about who got the deal. It's about how much money you're going to make." I leaned against the exam table in his office. *Why am I trying to rationalize with him?* I thought, *After all, the one who's going to benefit from it is him, not me. I'm on salary. I don't own the business. So if I can't enjoy the money, at least give me the credit.*

"So I guess you want me to put together the contract for you, but you want to be the one to make the call to Melnick. Correct?" He swiveled his executive chair around and finally looked at me.

"Well, I could try to work on the contract with the attorneys, but I assume you want to stay in the loop. Besides, I don't see you spending the money." My tone displayed how aggravated I was with him.

"I just want to make sure you understand that you could not make this deal happen without me," he said.

The phone rang and put an end to our wrestling match. Kaminski answered the call.

"Who is asking?" I heard Kaminski say. "Sure. Can you hold?" Kaminski placed the call on hold and said to me, "I guess you win again. It's Melnick, asking for you." He handed the receiver to me and got out of his chair. "You might want my chair as well." He sounded like a petulant child and then stormed out of his office.

I made the effort to maintain a professional conversation with Mr. Joe Melnick, but couldn't avoid his flirting. I didn't like his kiss-ass voice along with the endless compliments he threw at me. I could no longer see Melnick as the VP of marketing. He was just another horny male, looking for adventure. I wondered if we won the contract because of my skirt or because of my brain, but I didn't ask—I didn't want to know.

"I appreciate the business opportunity," I said, hoping he would get the clue that I'd be keeping my skirt on.

"I can't wait to see the final contract," he said.

"I'll have it faxed to you as soon as it's ready so that you can review it."

"Maybe we can look it over together, at lunch," he said.

"Sounds like a plan," I said, thinking that this would be a great opportunity to make up with Kaminski, as I wasn't going to meet with Melnick by myself.

I hung up the phone and turned to Kaminski. "He wants to meet once we have the contract. He was thinking about lunch."

"Sure. Get the attorneys to draft a contract and call Melnick to set up the lunch. Also, tell him about the opening. Make sure he gets invited," he said happily as the only thing that would attract him was prestige.

I thought about the card I still held—the one I had kept for the right moment. The only way that I could possibly get back in good standing with him was to make him feel more important—now was the time. I supposed that revealing that joker about my background and network would open the door back to Kaminski.

"By the way, I know you're upset with me, but I need to talk with you about the guest list."

"There is nothing to talk about. Don't think of revising my list."

"Of course not. I wouldn't dare. However, I was wondering if it would be okay if I invite a few additional people."

"A few people—like whom? More of your married lovers?" he said, insolently.

"No, but speaking of which, what about your mistress? Is she on the list?" I stabbed him back. Shifting back to my original question, I mentioned three people that I wanted to invite. People that were all known for what they did and who they were. A combination of one celebrity and two VIPs, maybe even VVVIPs. I stated their names.

"Are you crazy or what? Don't make a fool of yourself! None of these people will come. They have nothing to do with the place."

"That's true. But they have something to do with me. I'm sure they'll be happy to see what I put together and to meet my boss. What do you think?"

"Do you know them personally?" he asked.

"Obviously. But that wasn't the question. Can I invite them or not—yes or no?"

"I guess I don't know you or your friends…. What the heck, that's fine," he said with a defeated look. Perhaps he was finally piecing together why I'd never been sufficiently impressed with his friends. It was more humility than I'd ever seen from him.

Time flew by—one day after another. The clock was ticking and everybody was in line with the timetable and the deadline. Kaminski grew bossier and more overbearing by the day. He was short and blunt with everyone. Everybody heard him yelling at his wife and being rude to his mistress. Nothing was good enough for him and he was hard to please. He had no sense of humor left and I started to realize who he really was.

On the day of the opening, I didn't have much say. I walked on eggshells. The entire day consisted of loud voices and arguments. There wasn't one person around who seemed happy. One crisis after another was followed by poor troubleshooting and tears. The center was tremendously chaotic and I wondered how this place would operate with patients but no leadership. I questioned my patience as well as my future, and by lunchtime I was ready to resign without giving notice. I considered leaving Kaminski a note on his desk saying, "Sorry, I'm moving on. Good luck." I thought it would be my best shot since he was too busy to be approached. He probably wouldn't have the time to read that note, which was still in my mind.

I looked around. The flower arrangements looked cheap. *Maybe I should tell Kaminski,* I thought, but quickly changed my mind. What if he'd been the one who selected them? I'd probably be better off discussing this directly with the florist, but didn't know if he was one of Kaminski's selections as well—how could I take the chance? So I gave in. I took a deep breath and convinced myself that attacking the flowers might not be the best thing to do at the moment—neither would resigning from my job. I would be better off waiting for a later day.

I had enough reasons not to miss the opening. I had personally invited a few people who'd never met Kaminski and had likely never heard his name. The event was well planned and, in the last two weeks, it had become the talk of the city. Kaminski played his cards well and was careful to use his public relations. He arranged for the media to be present at the event. So how could I miss this? I couldn't! No way! I'd worked too hard putting this center together.

Today I am going to be the first lady, maybe even the bride, and if anyone is planning to compete with me, then they should expect a tough race. I gave myself a pep talk while tying up loose ends. I was not willing to give up the position of hostess. It really didn't matter how Kaminski behaved or what he said. He couldn't take from me what I'd worked so hard for. *So let him get pissed. Let him be rude and mean. Who cares?*

I pushed the stress out of my mind. I traveled into an imaginary picture of Sloan walking into the event, finding a safe spot, and watching me from a distance. Then, when it was safe enough, he would walk toward me with a glass of wine and say, "You look exquisite tonight."

I let my thoughts reach far-away places where Sloan would announce our relationship. But I knew he would not. Nothing like that would happen that night.

I distinguished between my dreams and my truth. My heart ached when I thought about Sloan, calling it an evening once the first few guests left. "I love you but I have to go," he would whisper and then leave, going back to his home to that woman who was the mother of his two children.

I floated back to the present and thought about my current situation. I went through my position, my job, my boss, the upcoming grand opening, my married lover, his wife and his kids. They were all a burden to me. The dynamics of my life and the people around me were suffocating me.

Early in the afternoon, when everything was moving at a frenzied pace, when nothing fell into place and the stress was at its peak, my boss revealed his big balls.

"I'm out of here. I'm heading home and will be back around five thirty," Kaminski said as if his audacity had no limits.

Is he brave or stupid? I thought and wanted to tell him that if anybody needed beauty time it was me, not him! I wondered why he was so worried about his appearance tonight. I wondered if he was concerned that his wrinkles would be more noticeable than usual, or if someone would say he looked tired. *Of course he looks tired—he is starting a new business.* He'd better look worn out. And since when did he give a shit about what people said or thought about him? I was the one who needed the time to get ready. However, Kaminski had a different opinion, and on his way out he shared it with me.

"Make sure you don't leave before everything is one hundred and ten percent," and before I had a chance to respond, he continued, "I really need the extra mile from you today."

He dared to challenge me, like until today I hadn't given him one hundred and ten percent. Obviously, there was no room for me to come back to him with an answer—for one he had no interest in hearing me, and two, his words sounded like an order rather than a request.

As soon as the elevator swallowed Kaminski, I reached for the phone and dialed my hairdresser. "Hello, is Sam around?"

"Yes, but he is busy right now. He's with a client." The receptionist's voice sounded as if she was his personal protective device.

"God, could you please tell him that Sharon Lapidot is on the line?" I asked and hoped that she would switch from a bitch mode to a more helpful one.

"Sure, can you hold?"

"Yes, I can." I was short with her.

"What's up?" I heard Sam's voice.

"Well, I'm not sure. My life is falling apart. My boss is nothing but a son of a bitch. I have no clue what time I can leave here and when I'll hit your place. I'm literally living and breathing against the clock. Please don't make it more difficult for me. Will you please wait on me?" I begged him.

"Calm down. Take it easy. I'm here—I'm not going anywhere," he said.

"And don't make me wait."

"I won't," he promised.

"And be nice to me."

"I would not have it any other way." He laughed.

"Thanks. I have to run. I'll see you later," I said and hung up.

Twenty-Four

I finally made it home by four-thirty and was left with only a short time before I had to be back. *Well, I definitely won't make it by five-thirty, maybe by six,* I thought and prepared myself for Kaminski, who would no doubt have something to say.

I hurried inside and dropped my bag on the floor. I undressed while rushing to the shower, throwing my clothes all over the place. I tossed one shoe into the living room, almost hitting the TV while the other shoe landed with my pants and underwear next to the dining table. My shirt and my bra were left on the floor in the bathroom. Within seconds it looked like a cyclone had blown through my house.

My quick shower took me back to my initial training in the military—a traumatic schedule with no time for myself. By the time I was out of the shower I wasn't sure if I'd ever gone in. Luckily, my new custom-made dress was hanging on the door of my closet. My high-heeled shoes and a pair of silky pantyhose were ready next to the couch.

I smeared my entire body with my perfume and its matching lotion, giving my skin a soft look, a velvet feel, and an attractive scent. I was efficient and skilled with my make-up, and quickly let my cosmetics erase my stress and give me that finishing touch. I took a quick look at my reflection in the mirror, making sure that my entire look was perfect. My foundation blended well with my skin and neck. My eyeliner was straight and clean and did not reach more than half way to the inner side of my eye. My eyes looked big and bright. My mascara was perfectly brushed on my eyelashes and no trace of it was found under my eyes or above my eyelids. My lip liner was not too dark and looked as if a professional tattoo artist had designed it, thin and straight. It appeared as if my makeup did its job as well, removing any evidence of tiredness and frustration. I approved of what I saw, grabbed the phone, and called Sam's salon.

"Hey, this is Sharon calling. Will you please let Sam know that I'll be there in fifteen minutes?" I said, while continuing with my preparation.

"Of course."

"Thanks." I hung up and rushed to finish getting dressed.

I slid into a clean thong, skipped the bra, and wrapped my legs in a new pair of black silk pantyhose. Finally, I packed my entire body in that special one-piece dress that was custom made just for me—a production of a known designer who got overpaid for not duplicating the dress. I selected some jewelry and decorated myself. I sprayed a few more shots of perfume in my deep cleavage, and one shot between my legs at my pubic area. I collected my purse, put on my shoes, locked the door and left.

I looked at the clock—three minutes before five. *Good timing, but not good enough.* I took the back road and drove fast, trying to avoid the traffic and the traffic lights. Six minutes later, I parked in a spot that God had reserved especially for me, right in front of the salon. Who would believe that I would find a parking spot in the Champs-Élysées of Ramat'sharon at that time of the day?

I gathered my long dress in my hands and carefully stepped out of the car. A few short steps and I was in the hair salon. Those who knew me didn't hesitate to share their thoughts and those who I never met before could not take their eyes off of me.

"Wow," Sam said and walked toward me, leaving his client and guiding me to another chair. "Are you alright?"

"I will be," I said with a stressed voice.

"You look amazing," he said while spraying my hair with water.

"Thank you."

"How much time do I have?"

"As much as you need, but be quick." I made him laugh.

In less than twenty minutes, Sam styled my hair, spiked it, trimmed a few millimeters in one spot, brushed it again, reworked the spiky look, gelled it, and sprayed it.

To be honest, I looked stunning and loved every little bit of me. I could not wait to hear what Sloan had to say. I stood up and let Sam check that every single hair was in the right spot and at the right angle.

"You are the most beautiful thing I've ever seen. I must take a picture of you. Hold on a minute."

"Come on, let's keep it in perspective." I felt that he was exaggerating to put me in the same lineup as a model.

"Hold on, I said," he insisted.

How could I disappoint Sam? I couldn't refuse his request. I had to wait for him to shoot some photos. If not for the weather that divulged its rudeness and brought the rain, I could almost beat the clock. But now, every second turned into a minute delay. I looked at Sam as he grabbed two umbrellas and nudged one of his employees. "Come on. Let's go."

I pulled my dress up above my knees and walked between the two of them and under two umbrellas. Sam was careful and didn't move his umbrella before I sat I the car and shut the door. I was amazed that I didn't get wet, not even one drop.

The heavy rain slowed the traffic and the windshield wipers were not fast enough to clear the view. My drive was extended by over fifteen minutes. I had plenty of time to think about where I would park my car and how I would make it into the building. I rehearsed my upcoming dialogue with Kaminski and heard him saying, "It would have been nice if you'd been here earlier...."

As I got closer to my workplace, I decided to use the expensive valet parking. *I'll pay, dammit, who cares,* I thought. But as I arrived at the main entrance, my worries faded. The two valet guys welcomed me warmly. One opened the door for me while the other one said, "Don't worry, sweetie. I got you covered. It's a special day for you, huh? Don't worry. We'll take good care of you."

The free valet parking that I was offered was enough to make me feel important, almost like I was the big boss.

I entered the building and rushed to the elevators, absorbing every little word that was thrown toward me by complete strangers.

As I expected, Kaminski was already there. His gave me the cold shoulder, but couldn't hide his reaction to my appearance. His body language said it all. I was about to ask him to keep his eyes off me, but I couldn't take the chance of getting in a confrontation with him. Instead, I approached him in a polite way and asked, "Is there anything you want me to do?"

Kaminski didn't say much—not even complimenting me on my appearance or the work I'd done. All he could put together was a list of mannerly behavioral orders—where to stand, how to smile, how much I should drink, what and who required special attention, and what I should say. I literally could not take his crap anymore. I was willing to put my pride before my income. It was enough to pull the trigger. I opened my eyes wide, took a deep breath, and told him, "Did you ever think that I might have attended similar events in the past? Stop talking down to me as if you found me in the gutter. This is neither a Cinderella story nor *My Fair Lady*. You're not about to teach me finishing school tonight." I turned my back and disappeared from his sight, thinking he should look at his wife's dress, which was too short, and put his opinion there before lecturing me.

Twenty-Five

U pon the first guest's arrival, Kaminski transformed from surly to charming. He started his PR right away. He knew his job. He was sharp, diplomatic, and careful with his words, absolutely not making any commitments. Not one of the guests snagged my attention, not even the VIPs who swarmed the place. I looked into their faces with a forced smile. I used the same small talk and phony attitude with each of them while I impatiently waited for Sloan and the Rosins.

Aggression crept into my chest. I felt irritable. Sloan's tardiness disturbed me. I felt insulted. The desire to get into a virtual fight with Sloan boiled inside me, but I managed to shift my anger toward Lori and Jonathan—who also had yet to arrive. I was worried that someone might recognize my stress. I avoided talking to people and escaped to the bar to get a drink, hoping it would help me to control my central and my peripheral nervous systems.

"Where is Sloan? I thought you said he was coming." I heard my secretary's voice over my shoulder.

"He's coming. He's seeing patients—he's probably running late," I said carefully, so as not to reveal my irritation or provide information that might invite her to dig into my life.

I looked around, hoping to find someone who I could use as an excuse to get away from my inquisitive secretary. "Excuse me, but I have to work on some PR," I said once I saw Melnick, the VP of VISA.

"Good evening," I said to Melnick.

"Hello, hello. Look at you." His eyes roamed my body as if he was on a mission to collect every possible detail of my appearance.

I could tell that Melnick's imagination had already settled under my dress. I tried to navigate our small talk so it would not contain any personal flavor. Our chat was continuously interrupted by Melnick's PR. It seemed as if he was well-admired. I watched those approaching him to shake his hand and exchange a few words with him. Some of them knew him well while others were looking for the opportunity to be able to say that they had met him. I had to accept that this was the nature of the business world. That's how people were—*life is not about what you know, but who you know.* I wasn't sure if I suited Melnick and wondered if he would rather not be seen next to me. Regardless, I enjoyed the situation and the attention. I loved the way he introduced me to each and all of those who passed by. He made me feel important—vital.

Finally, Sloan arrived along with Lori and Jonathan. I wondered if they'd met earlier at a coffee shop and came together, or if they'd run into one another in the lobby or the elevator. My curiosity and anger wanted me to quiz them. But sagely, I transferred my energy to introducing them to Melnick, who kept me on a tight leash beside him.

"Joe Melnick, VP of Visa, this is Dr. Sloan, Jonathan Rosin, VP of IBM Israel and his wife, Lori, an attorney." I played the role of the polite hostess.

I looked at Sloan and sank into his green-brown eyes. All I wanted was to be seen with him without being disturbed. I needed him to tell me something personal and sexy. But Melnick trapped me. He was smart and charismatic, but also manipulative and controlling at times.

He overruled any excuse I had tried to use to get away. I sensed his jealously, thinking that he didn't want me to be alone with Sloan.

Just when I was about to come up with another creative excuse, someone from Kaminski's VIP list came to rescue me. It was the minister of foreign affairs shadowed by two professional bodyguards.

"May I steal the young lady for a minute?" He was upfront yet sophisticated. Nobody could refuse him, not even Melnick.

"Of course," I said.

"Please." He offered me his arm.

"Do I need to go through a security check first?" I asked while entwining my arm in his.

"I'll take my chances." He smiled.

"I hope you are not planning on letting her make any political decisions." Melnick tried to be funny. They all laughed and we stepped away.

"Let me get you a drink," he said as we walked arm in arm.

"That can't hurt," I said and turned my head back, glancing at the group I'd just left.

Sloan watched me with jealousy in his eyes and frustration written all over his face. He was not happy and neither was I. But there was nothing I could do about it. I couldn't break away from the minister.

My past interactions with the minister were limited to his hypochondria. Kaminski had introduced me to him soon after I started working for him and turned me into his private nurse. I provided free medical services to the minister at almost any time, but had refused to support or be associated with his political beliefs and campaigns. Often, I had been forced to bring some medications and other medical supplies to him. I had run his EKG each time that he thought he was having chest pain, and had taken his blood pressure every time he had one of his headaches.

Quite frankly, as someone who knew so much of the minister's medical history and needs, I felt pretty close to him. Definitely closer than many others who thought they knew him.

He habitually stopped by my office once or twice a week, asking for some medical services—it could be something as minor as a band-aid, but it was always something. He needed a lot of attention. For the most part I really didn't care, but at times, it was borderline suspicious, much like this moment, with my arm entwined with his. I felt no less trapped than I had a few minutes earlier while I was next to Melnick. I started to worry that I might be the one who needed the help.

I hoped to calm myself and stay in control—to believe that someone who was a minister and my boss' friend must be a kind man and a gentleman.

"Well done," the minister said and we both raised our glasses for a toast. "*L'chaim.*"

"Thank you. That's very kind of you. I wish Kaminski would think the same," I answered.

"Are you kidding? I don't think you need more credit with him. He admires you."

"Not really."

"What are you talking about?"

"I don't really think that Kaminski appreciates anybody but himself."

"I think you are wrong about that."

"Well, I guess we have differing opinions," I said.

"Anyway, I meant to tell you—you look very nice."

"Thank you," I said in a monotone.

"I actually mean exquisite." He used a different vocabulary and moved one step closer to me.

I didn't like what I heard or saw—I became uncomfortable with the direction this conversation was taking. He stood so close to me, I wanted to ask him if we were making small talk or if he was flirting with me. But I remained professional and polite. Moving slightly away from him, I glanced across the room, searching for Sloan—he was drinking his wine—watching me from a distance. *How nice it would be to stand next to him instead of the asshole beside me,* I thought. I was annoyed. Something inside me, maybe a sixth sense, warned me that despite everything, the minister was no different than any other male—just another womanizer with imbalanced hormones. Evidently, he was trying to get as close to me as possible. Obviously, it wasn't about his blood pressure or his headaches—it wasn't even about politics. It was about me. I drifted in my thoughts, ignoring him.

Naturally, I could have enjoyed being so close to a public figure like the minister. Seriously, who doesn't like celebrities? But once my imagination took over and I pictured the minister trying to find his way under my skirt, I became nauseated.

I looked for a way out of the situation that I was jammed into.

Finally a member of parliament approached the minister and started conversing with him. Luckily, I was exempt from the politics and excluded from the conversation. I took advantage of the political gathering, and took my leave without making any excuses, and disappeared.

I locked Sloan in my sight and walked toward him. A few guests pulled me aside for a brief chats while others wanted to steal longer moments. The twenty feet between Sloan and I seemed farther.

I was ready to go home, to get away from the crowd and the nonsense. The sophistication, the celebrities, the stress, and the drama lost their powerful intoxication—I was tired of the flashy lifestyle but was far from willing to give up the glory. I needed a break.

While still making my way to Sloan, Kaminski, stressed as tight as a tampon, approached me. He drew me aside and whispered a new assignment he hoped I would agree to. I was surprised he would ask me to do something that I thought he would love to do by himself. It was weird but I didn't care. I was simply glad to move away from him as his breath was laced heavily with garlic. I gagged from the smell and was aggravated that he hadn't taken my advice concerning the menu. He had refused to listen to me, thinking he knew better.

"Not a problem," I said and parted from him.

So, here I was, still away from Sloan walking through the crowd, looking for the minister who I'd escaped from less than ten minutes ago.

As expected, he was occupied with others. But I'd been given my assignment and had to interrupt the VIP conversation.

I walked up to him and his company with confident steps flavored with formality and finished up with a sexy move. How did I put all these ingredients into one dish? I don't know, but it worked.

"Excuse us for a minute," I said with a smile, while threading my arm through the minister's.

"Yaron." I approached him for the first time on a first name basis, watching his guards following us. "I'm sorry to pull you away from your conversation, but shortly we'll commence with the formal part of the evening. Kaminski is asking if you will be the guest of honor and cut the ribbon."

"Well," he said as his eyes detected my deep cleavage, "I will be glad to with one condition."

"And what would that be?"

"You will stand next to me," he said in a victorious tone.

"Meaning what?" I tried to gain a better understanding.

"Meaning that you'll stand beside me while I make the toast and you'll cut the ribbon with me."

Well, that didn't sound too difficult, but I wondered what was on the minister's mind. I had the feeling that there was more to his request than met the eye. He seemed a little too friendly. So all I said to him was, "I don't think that's a good idea."

"I disagree. You have to trust me."

"Of course," I answered as I turned away and he walked back into his public relations business. But first, I had to find Kaminski.

"I spoke with Yaron and he agreed," I told Kaminski.

"Good."

"But...." I paused, thinking how to convey the minister's condition to him.

Kaminski loosened his tie a bit. It was hard to say if he was pissed or jealous. He kept his emotions to himself. His body language revealed that he was disappointed, maybe even hurt in a way. He would do anything to keep his friend happy, but to watch him pay the high price of being left out during the formal opening of his own business was not easy. I felt sorry for him.

While Kaminski didn't stand in the minister's way, the minister sure made it special by putting me in the spotlight. I was the one he mentioned in his speech, the one he requested cut the cake, and the one he joked with during the ribbon cutting. It was pathetic. I doubted the minister's jovial mood was due to the alcohol. I suspected that his excitement was tied to his thought of getting under my skirt. I truly felt as if I'd taken Kaminski's spot and didn't cooperate with the minister or his comments.

Sloan stood next to the Rosins, gaping. He looked sad and lonely. I tried to figure out what was on his mind. I wanted to hug him and hold him tight, but I couldn't—I was confined between the minister's efforts to woo me and Kaminski's anger.

Ultimately, the formal part was over and I landed in front of Sloan, who was grouped with several other physicians. I sought his attention, but he ignored me and continued his conversation as if I wasn't there.

I needed him to tell me what was on his mind and in his heart. What did he think about my dress and if he liked my look. I expected a compliment, something, anything, but he kept his lips sealed. Disappointment triggered my craving to fight with him for not rescuing me earlier—for not becoming my knight in shining armor. But he did not appear willing to do battle. That night, nothing happened the way I'd wanted it to.

On his terms and on his watch, he entered into a dialogue with me and isolated us from the crowd. He walked me to the bar and got himself vodka and a gin and tonic for me. He looked into my eyes—I was surprised to see how comfortable he was.

"Look around," I said once I realized how far we were from prying ears, but close enough to be seen. "Look how many pairs of eyes are watching us."

"I don't really care." His words seemed honest.

"Do you think they suspect?"

"No. I think they know. Actually, I know they know."

"What do you mean you know they know?"

"I mean…"

"You mean what?"

"People already made some comments to me about us."

"Seriously?" I snapped my head back. "In a nasty way or just being nosey?"

"Actually, they were pretty kind."

"Can you be more specific?"

"I'll tell you later." He wrapped his arm around my shoulder. "Let's walk to your office," he said.

In my office, out of sight, Sloan finally said the things I'd been waiting to hear. He showered me with congratulations for the event I'd put together and flattered me for my appearance. He swore that I was the classiest and sexiest woman out there and that I drove the men crazy. Lastly, he spoke about the guests who mentioned us.

"So what did you say?" I asked him.

"I said, 'It is what it is.'"

"Just like that?"

"Yes, just like that. What did you want me to say?"

"I don't know. I thought that maybe you would deny it."

We got comfortable, each in our own chair. It was as if our relationship had grown to the next level. I took my shoes off and rested my feet on Sloan's lap.

"Did you see that minister of foreign affairs?" I asked.

"How could I miss it?" He smiled.

"I didn't like it at all."

"Neither did I," he said and rubbed my feet gently. "You are exhausted, aren't you?"

"Sort of." I leaned back in the chair and stretched, staring at the ceiling. "I wish you didn't have to leave."

"But I do," he said right before someone knocked at the door.

"Come in," I called and didn't bother to move my feet off Sloan's lap—I guess the alcohol I'd consumed had loosened me up and I enjoyed its benefits.

"Oh, I wasn't aware of my competitors." The minister stumbled over his words and kept his hand on the doorknob.

"Competitors?" I asked and after a long silence continued, "This is Dr. Sloan, and I guess we all know who you are." I watched Sloan to make sure he wasn't troubled by the situation. But he looked more relaxed than I was and replaced his jealousy with amusement. The minister, on the other hand, looked totally stupid trying to woo me.

"Do you have a minute?" he asked. "I need to talk to you in private."

"Sure," I answered, thinking that he might need some aspirin.

I tried to move my feet but Sloan held on to them as if I was his hostage. I made eye contact with him, recognized his boyish grin, and said with a giggle, "Stop it. Let me go."

He gently moved my feet from his lap. I slid my shoes back on and walked out of my office, following the minister.

"Do you have any plans for the night?" the minister asked as I shut the door behind me and we were left alone in the hallway.

"Excuse me?" I was totally taken off guard. Had he completely forgotten that he was my boss' friend, a member of the parliament, and married? Had he not just seen my feet resting on another man's lap?

"What I'm asking is what are you doing after this event? Do you have plans with that friend in the office?

"Why are you asking?" I said instead of simply refusing the conversation.

"I thought we could meet later on."

"For what?" I asked.

"I need to talk to you."

"About what?'

"Stop quizzing me. I'll tell you later, when we meet." He was turning into quite the mystery.

"Where do you want to meet?" I asked him. *What did I just say—am I really going to get involved in this shit?*

"I'll pick you up at ten by the lobby's entrance." He rushed to answer.

"I will see you then," I answered quickly, wanting to backtrack and bail out of my earlier blunder.

The minister's face stretched wide with a smile and he left as if he'd just closed an important deal. I wanted to ask him to come back for a minute—to advise him to erase the smile along with any hopes he might have in his pants. But I was more interested in getting back to Sloan.

I contemplated whether to share my plans with Sloan or to keep it to myself. I was nervous that Sloan might be upset if he knew that I was going to meet with the minister. Or, would it make him jealous? There was a lot on my mind. I was congested with thoughts. Sloan was already checking the time—ready to go back to his other life while leaving me to the wolves. In minutes he was gone.

I sat behind my desk, still stunned from the interaction I'd had with the minister and from the idea of meeting him later that night. Suddenly, Kaminski stepped in and sat in the chair across from me.

"Well done. I have to admit, it was perfect!" He rubbed his hands together and stretched in his seat. "Don't you agree?"

"I agree. I want to see what they put in tomorrow's paper."

"I'm not so worried about that. I'm sure it will be fine."

"So what are you worried about?"

"That you're getting into trouble." He bit his nail.

"What are you talking about?"

"I'm talking about our friend, the minister, Yaron," he said.

"It sounds like you know more than I do—don't you?" I opened my eyes and had the feeling that I'd finally figured it all out.

"It's not my fault." He sounded defensive.

"Really? How come? I bet you told him to go for it, didn't you?" My voice, tight with stress, was much higher than normal.

"It wasn't like that." He pushed his glasses higher up on the bridge of his nose.

"Of course not! You probably planned the formal part of the evening with him. You were willing to give up the spotlight for a friendship with a crooked VIP, to support his stupid fantasy of maybe winning a blowjob. Well, let me tell you something, he is not going to get a blowjob, not even a lay. And once I tell everyone what a wonderful friend you are, I'm sure you will get back the glory!" I said with tears and anger in my voice.

"Calm down, don't take things out of proportion."

"Don't tell me what to do." I cut him off. "You need to call him and tell him that he can't pick me up."

"Are you insane?"

"No, you are. Get me his personal assistant's pager number, his car number—something. Just get me a number so I can call and cancel this pitiful date…"

"I have to stay out of it."

"But you're already in it." I started to pack up my things. "Instead, you could walk me to my car so I can go home alone. Maybe you should wait for him up there at the lobby and relay the message to him."

"Are you afraid of what he might do to you?"

"Of course not. I know he wouldn't get involved with misconduct. I just want to eliminate the possibility of running into him by myself. So please walk me to my car." I was already waiting by the door.

"Alright, I'll give you his pager number."

I returned to my desk, grabbed a scratch pad, and jotted the number down. I looked at Kaminski and was hoping that he would do something—maybe even make the call eventually. But he didn't. He remained silent and seated. His eyes followed my index finger as I dialed.

Once I heard the tone, I punched in my office number and hung up. Seconds later, the phone on my desk rang.

"Hello?"

"Did you page me?" Yaron's voice was on the other end.

"Yes, I did."

"What's going on?"

"Listen." I paused and put my lies together. "I'm really exhausted. It was a very long week and a long day for me. I have to go home." I stood and turned my back to Kaminski, leaning against my desk—I just couldn't look at him anymore—I wished I'd never met him. "Maybe we can catch up some other time." I made the effort to soften the blow.

"If you're tired, I could come to your place. We could talk there," he said after a few seconds of silence.

"I don't think that's a good idea. I'm very tired. I need to get some rest."

"How about lunch tomorrow?" His voice had lost its arrogant tone and was almost pleading, making me feel guilty and angry all at once. *How did I get myself into this situation?*

"Maybe next week," I said.

"Are you by yourself or with that doctor friend of yours?"

"No, actually, I'm here with Kaminski."

"Really?" He sounded surprised.

"Really."

"Interesting…. Did he give you my number?"

"Why is it important? A minute ago you hoped to come to my house and now you seem upset that I have your pager number—wow, this is hard to believe."

"I don't see your point."

"Well, I can't explain it any better except to say that I'm not interested. I need to go. You need to leave me alone."

"Can I call you tomorrow?"

"Please don't," I said and started to feel relieved.

Twenty-Six

In a matter of days, the excitement at work had vanished and a routine had yet to be established. I felt a little let down, as anticipated after a big project like that. I thrived on the bustle of activity—on having so many things to occupy my attention. It was always disappointing to settle back into a calm routine. I needed a lifestyle that would be saturated with excitement and challenges, something that could stimulate my intellect.

I left the office and stopped for the daily paper. I continued to a small, cozy bistro in the building next door for lunch. I sat down at a table by myself and glanced at the paper. My thoughts drifted to all that I had just accomplished. There was a lot I could be proud of and I'd earned the right to hold my head high. Kaminski was satisfied with my work as well, but still would not adjust my work hours. Clearly, he'd taken advantage of my workaholic nature. I was tired of him and my job. I had the urge to make a change, to break the monotony in my life.

I added two new stubborn figures to my stable of men—Yaron, the minister, and Melnick, the VP. I needed more time to pinpoint what exactly they were looking for, or what they were up to. I was irritated by the mystery behind their behavior, yet I couldn't blame them for a thing.

With time I believed that Melnick saw me as a friend. I'd tested him at every opportunity. I felt that he had no thoughts or intentions of depravity—but still, I tread carefully.

On the other hand, Yaron seemed as though he didn't care about his marital status, his position, and his public obligations. He called me continuously, early in the morning and late at night. He looked for reasons and made excuses to stop by my office whenever he could. Visibly, his hormones controlled him. He seemed willing to take any chance and pay any price for the poor odds of winning sex with me. But me? I had no need for any sexual adventures and I definitely didn't find him attractive. I couldn't imagine having sex with him, nor did I want to be in a position to have to say no. Not to mention that I'd bet he'd be a lousy lover. I wagered that his penis was probably the size of a peanut and visualized him being quick and selfish in bed. Still, I was fair enough to treat his effort with respect. I rejected him with kindness, tried to avoid confrontation, and was diplomatic with my answers.

I sipped my coffee, realizing how hectic my life had become. My finances didn't suggest a vacation, but certainly indicated that I was far from financial crisis. The man who was present in my life was not available, but certainly fulfilled most of my needs. My work situation seemed to be secure, even if it was annoying.

With this in mind, I paid the check, left the restaurant, and went back to work.

I didn't wait long to approach Kaminski and ask for some time off. And just as I'd thought, he was unhappy with the idea, but smart enough to approve my request.

A few days later, I left to visit my mother—more than six thousand miles away, where no one would bother me. I needed to be alone for a while—to be able to put things into perspective from a distance.

I intended to disconnect myself from what I'd left back home—particularly those four intense figures who wanted my attention daily—Sloan, Kaminski, Yaron, and Melnick. But them? They sought my attention regardless of how far away I was.

My dear boss was the first one to call without any reason. Just to interrupt my vacation. Our conversation was short and painless.

The next call came a few hours later. It was my fan, Melnick. All he asked was if I was enjoying my time off. But the tone of his voice led me to believe that he wanted to say more. Nevertheless, I remained composed and kept the conversation business-like. I limited our talk to the point when I felt as if I was no longer being polite.

Two days later, Yaron's voice disturbed my vacation. He really didn't have anything to say. He sounded confused and uncomfortable— more like an inexperienced womanizer who wasn't sure of his actions. Thus, I made it easy for both of us—I didn't drag the conversation out and ended the call quickly. *My God, with this kind of character, no wonder politics are so bad—how embarrassing.*

Yet, Sloan, the only man I wanted to hear from, didn't call. It drove me crazy. I wanted to bitch at him and tell him about my new fans and their phone calls—anything that would give him a twinge of jealousy.

Sloan was in my thoughts day after day, hour after hour. He was present the entire time. I missed him greatly.

It was mid-morning the very next day. I soaked in the tub, inhaling the aroma of soft oils in the water. The ringing phone didn't get my attention, until a few seconds later when my mother entered the room and handed me the phone.

"Hello?" I said, and watched my mom close the door behind her.

"Hey, how are you?"

"Sloan?" My voice reflected my excitement and my body lost it as I slid further down into the tub.

"Why are you so surprised? Were you expecting someone else?"

"Where are you calling from?" I ignored his question.

"Your place—where else would I be?"

"It would be better if you were here in the tub with me. You're missing out on a lot of fun."

"I can only imagine. Anyway, how's it going?"

"It's fine, but I miss you."

"I miss you too. Are you still coming back as planned?"

"Of course I am. Why?"

"My call schedule had changed. I won't be able to pick you up at the airport. I spoke with Lori. She'll pick you up and I'll see you later. I'll come straight from the hospital to the house, right after the morning rounds—do you mind?

"That's fine. Is everything else okay?" I continued in an effort to draw a few more affectionate statements from him.

"Yes, more or less. It's pretty quiet and strange without you around."

"I'll make it up to you when I get back."

"I can't wait," he said.

"Neither can I."

The vacation came to its end. I rested, I shopped, I shared, and I missed Sloan. I loved him, and I hated him. It was time to get back to the life that was waiting for me on the other side of the globe. It all played out as it was planned—the drive to the airport, the connection to New York, the non-stop flight to Tel-Aviv, and Lori at the Ben-Gurion airport, meeting me and driving me back home.

There was not much for me to tell Lori—I'd only been gone a week and hadn't traveled anywhere exciting. I'd pretty much focused on rejuvenating and recharging my batteries. The only exciting thing that I could tell her about was those three phone calls I had received. But

Lori didn't show much interest in my tale—not even when I raised the question of how these clowns obtained my phone number. All she wanted to hear about was Sloan.

"Did he call you? What did he say?"—but it was not enough, she wanted to know more. "When exactly did he call? Where did he call from? What did you say?" Lori was intense and dragged me into a conversation about him, his efforts, his wife, and his neighbor. It was a conversation that never seemed to end—it went on and on, even after we arrived home.

If Sloan hadn't told me that he'd stopped by the house, I would never have known that he was there—everything looked the same. He hadn't even bothered to bring the mail in.

An hour later, Sloan walked in, holding a bouquet of yellow roses. He set the flowers on the white stone counter near the entrance. "Here you are." He took off his sunglasses and placed them next to his keys.

I wanted to stay calm and hide my emotions. But the cloud of energy and rainfall of desire that he brought into the house took over my plan. He looked at me with a big smile, showing how excited and happy he was.

"Come on, Lori. It's time for you to go," he said while he stuck his left hand in his right palm and popped his knuckles. Finally he moved closer to me. "Damn it, I missed you." He pulled me out of the chair and enveloped me, squeezing me close to him.

We took our time as if Lori wasn't there. Her presence didn't bother us but apparently inconvenienced her. "Okay, that's enough. What happened to your modesty?"

"I said you should go. Didn't I?" Sloan said with a smile, took my seat, and rested me on his lap.

"Why yellow?" Lori teased Sloan.

"Why not?" he answered her.

"Yellow means jealousy," she continued in her own way.

"Not that I'm not jealous, but why does it make any difference?"

"It doesn't. But still, I wanted to make sure you are aware of it."

"Lori darling, no matter what color I picked, you would find something to say, wouldn't you?"

"You're probably right. Besides, you don't mind if I stir Sharon up a little bit, right?" she said.

"Will you guys stop it? What's wrong with you? You sound like children in daycare."

"Just kidding, you don't have to get so serious." Lori laughed.

Finally, the conversation changed direction and, after a short chat, Sloan approached Lori again. "Do you mind leaving us alone? I haven't seen the lady for a week."

"What's the rush? Are you on call tonight?"

"No, I'm not."

"Oh sure, how could I forget? You have to go home," she said.

Lori was smart and often came across as brash. She had no filter and never held back her thoughts. She spit it all out, not worrying if her words might hurt someone or how they might respond. She was a straightforward person who I liked a lot. Sloan avoided confrontation with her—he kept it to himself.

When Lori left, Sloan and I caught up with what we'd missed. Nothing had changed. I loved him and loved the way our bodies conversed. I was addicted to his touch and could never have enough of him. And like before, he left to return to his family and I was left alone, frustrated and disappointed. It hit me again. I was fed up with being number two.

My body was struck by the craving for a child, reminding me of my strong desire to fulfill my maternal needs. I wondered how old I'd be when I could finally get pregnant. *Should I wait for my married man to become mine before giving birth to my child? By then I would already be an old lady.* My thirtieth birthday was approaching and I felt as if I was about to miss the train. Until this moment, I truly didn't realize what I was sacrificing for Sloan. But he was the first one who made me think about a child. Our love gave me that urge to see what the product of it would be. What would our child look like? How would we make it work?

The thought of being a single mom was frightening. Again, I contemplated my affair with Sloan—I tried a virtual dialogue where I would give him the ultimatum of making up his mind within a month. Alternatively, I could discuss the option of having a child with him and ask him if he would recognize the child as his. I refused to let him control my life or direct my future. I had to persuade myself that all I needed was one sperm—better if it was his, but I really didn't need him. My love for Sloan was thinned by anger and resentment.

The winter was in full force and displayed its intensity. It was cold, wet, windy, and gray. Empty, quiet streets appeared neglected with broken branches and puddles. Dry leaves mixed with light trash swirled in the air. It was a classic picture of winter that came along with its typical disruptions—water leaks, power outages, and slow traffic. The common statements were, "…this bad of a winter?" and "This is the worst winter ever…." But the truth was that all winters were the same. Each winter brought in the same disruptions, same temperatures, same rainfall, same winds, and same colors. It was the people who didn't remember. It was we who couldn't admit that we had poor infrastructure for winter. And it was we who did nothing to correct the situation before the next winter came.

It was an unusually cold day in December. The dry wind howled angrily. It would be best to fill your pockets with rocks to remain anchored to the globe—definitely not a day to leave your coat at home.

I was busy with paperwork, trying to design a new package that might beat other offers in the market. My secretary's voice came through the intercom and pulled me from my work.

"There is a courier here, insisting on delivering a package only to you," she said in a frustrated voice.

"Who is it from?" I asked.

"He won't say."

Interrogating my secretary would not affect the courier's attitude. I stepped out of my office to the lobby where I found this stranger.

Twenty-Seven

"How can I help you?" I approached him.

"I'm looking for Sharon Lapidot," he said, abruptly.

"That would be me."

"I have a package for you. Please sign here." He placed the package on the table and pointed to where he needed my signature.

"Who is it from?" I asked while he handed me his pen, rushing me to sign.

"This is for you." He ripped off my copy and handed it to me. "The instructions are inside the box."

"Instructions?" I asked but he didn't answer and rushed to leave.

Well, that was odd, but not something to call security about. It was a light package about the size of a small TV. I glanced toward my secretary and saw how lost she was—just like me.

"Any ideas?" I asked her.

"Are you expecting any equipment?"

"No." I unfolded the top of the box, which wasn't taped shut. *That's odd*, I thought.

"Well, let's see..." I said and my secretary came to assist me. She held the box down while I pulled out a metal cage. Fortunately, I hadn't tilted the box or turned it upside down. A small red canary with an identifying golden bracelet tied to his ankle sat in the middle of a brand new cage. He looked terrified—a vagrant creature, fascinating in his beauty and disappointing with his silence. His orange feathers were bright and shiny.

Wow, I thought and looked back inside the box and pulled out a package of seeds—the sender obviously didn't want my new roommate to experience starvation or humiliation. The other things that I found in the box, I wasn't sure about—a plastic dish, a small bottle of red liquid, a clear bag with black seeds labeled "poppy seeds," and a letter.

My knowledge of ornithology or bird keeping needed improvement. Anything I knew about birds was associated with my profession and from textbooks—eyelash lice comes from doves, and asthma patients are better off away from parrots. But that little canary really didn't look like a dove or a parrot. Besides, I wasn't asthmatic and didn't have respiratory distress. I couldn't find a good reason why I shouldn't adopt this canary.

I had no choice but to open the last item in the box—the letter.

It read, *Dear Sharon, I hope that you will love him as much as you do NOT love me. Please name him Alon after me.*

"Kiss my ass," I said, as if Alon was standing there next to me.

Call me for more instructions, he'd added below.

And me? I was not sure if I should bite my tongue or call him and chew his ass out.

I picked up the cage and the box, and looked for a secure spot in my office for it. I assumed that Kaminski would not say a word, if only for the fact that the crazy sender was a very close friend of his. *Oh my God*, I thought, *working for you, Dr. Kaminski, has been more than a challenge. You are really exposing me to strange people.*

I had no choice but to call Alon, who was a certified, professional ornithologist, not just a birdwatcher. Someone who would bring down the moon for me if I asked him to. I thanked him for the gift but skipped his request to name the canary after him.

The entire situation annoyed me. *For God's sake, what do I need a canary for? Why did he drop this shit on me? What will I tell Sloan and why in the world do I need to deal with bird poop? Do I not get enough of this as a nurse?*

I sat in my chair, staring at the mute canary. *Aren't you supposed to sing?* My mind drifted, contemplating my life at the moment. How had it become so complicated? I'd started out in what I'd thought was a serious relationship, moved into an affair with a married man and now, I'm lonely and surrounded by four men who are trying to win my attention—a physician, a VP, a politician, and an ornithologist. And the crux of it was that every last one of them was married.

I made an effort to understand the subconscious in me, the one that prevented me from dealing with stability and commitment. Was it my subconscious that didn't allow any man to step fully into my life? Or was I the one who didn't welcome any potential relationship? I guess it was convenience. *Leave me alone,* I wanted to tell the entire world. Let me live my life.

Complicated accusations from strangers haunted me. *The partnerships you choose are an assurance that nothing will come out of it.*

So what? I wanted to tell them, *Who says this isn't the right way? Who can prove that a single life is worse than a married one? Look around—how many couples are getting divorced and how many are cheating? Am I better off suffering in a relationship accepted by the norm or in one that is unaccepted?*

My secretary interrupted my thoughts. "Sloan is here."

"Hey there. You're early," I said as he entered my office.

"What's this?" he looked at the canary as if he refused to believe.

"Well, it's a canary."

"He's gorgeous. Who does he belong to?"

"Me."

"You?"

"As a matter of fact, me and you." I handed him the letter from Alon.

"This is crazy. He's nuts. Did you know it was coming?" His voice held a mixture of anger and jealousy.

"Hell no. Why are so upset? What's your problem?"

"I'm not upset. But he's nuts."

"Calm down."

"I'm fed up with all the men who are after you." He took his coat off, threw it on the chair, and leaned against the desk.

"So, that's the problem? There's nothing for you to worry about. You should know that they aren't competition." I stopped and asked myself if he didn't know by now that I wasn't going anywhere? Sloan had never shown any insecurity before. "However, jealousy is good!" I added with a smile. "That means you love me."

Thinking of it, I actually enjoyed seeing him jealous and distressed over other males who were hanging around. It made me feel needed and loved. I found it very sensual.

"Okay, I'm leaving. What time will you make it home?"

"Two hours maybe," I said while he put his coat back on and walked toward me.

Sloan grabbed me in his arms and squeezed me to his chest. "I'll see you later," he said.

"Do you mind taking this cage home?" I asked him right before he took his arms off me.

"Are you out of your mind, or what?" he sounded hysterical.

"No, I'm not. What's the big deal? I'm only asking you to take this little bird home." I knew it was a lot to ask—it could put him at risk if someone confronted him. Truly, I knew I was being mean, but he could say no. And he did.

"I'm not going through the main lobby with a canary and a cage."

"Of course not. What would people think of you, in particular those who don't know you? That you are a vet and not an OBGYN?" I didn't let him off the hook.

"You win. If you carry it to the car, then I'll bring it home."

"Fine." I rushed to pack the cage back into its box.

"Listen," I told him while putting my coat on, "Alon says canaries are very sensitive to cold. You have to be careful and make sure he doesn't get exposed to the wind. Keep the cage in the box but don't seal it, he needs to breathe. And when you get home, take the cage out of the box and fill up the water tray."

"I will listen to him with my stethoscope and make sure he is not catching pneumonia, how about that?"

"Whatever. Just make sure he survives," I said.

"Here, let me take it." He reached for the box.

"I thought you didn't want to be seen with this box." I pulled back on the box.

"I guess I changed my mind." He grabbed the box away from me.

"I see." I let him have the box before the little bird sustained a concussion.

The journey from my office to Sloan's car didn't draw attention from anyone. We placed the box securely in the front seat next to Sloan.

I gave Sloan a quick kiss on his freezing lips and left to return to work.

It was not much longer before I wrapped up my things and left the office.

It was almost four p.m. when I walked into my bedroom. The wind whistled through the tiny openings that the windows could not seal. The rain lashed at the shutters and a neglected cat wailed in the wet, cold yard. Sloan was sleeping under a warm blanket and looked peaceful, as if nothing bothered him. There was nothing more tempting than snuggling with him in bed.

I got into the bed quietly, trying not to wake him. But once his hand reached my butt it was clear that he was no longer asleep.

"I'm glad you're here," he whispered over my neck.

I turned around so I could look at his face. Sloan was impatient. He was ready to let our bodies dance but first he had something to share. "Last night, after I left here," he paused, "right as I walked into the house, Sharon jumped all over me."

I listened to his story and paid attention to all the details. When he referred to his wife by name—Sharon, I was gratified. The fact that he didn't call her "my wife" meant a lot to me. I wondered if he did that so as not to hurt me, or if he didn't really count on her as a wife.

"And?" I asked in a curious voice.

"She looked straight in my eyes and asked, 'What are you so happy about? You have a smile on your face as if you just left your mistress after a remarkable fuck.'"

What I'd heard so far was enough to make me angry. Her rude words made me sick. Rage overcame me. I was ready to kill her—or at least to call the bitch and advise her that she could refer to me by name rather than an insignificant label. I wanted to make sure that she understood that I was way more than just a fuck. But I held it all in as I waited to hear how he'd answered her.

"I was so pissed and irritated by her that I told her, 'This time, it was not a fuck—it was a blowjob.'"

I was beyond insulted. I was ready to get in a real fight with him and to take the risk that the neighbors would hear us. And I did.

"Well, so that's what I am to you right now—somewhere between a fuck and a blowjob. Did you remember to give your wife some juicy details about how far I can spread my legs?"

"Almost, but no," he answered with a loud laugh. "You are hilarious."

"It was not meant to be funny." I looked at the ceiling and fixed my sight on the light bulb. I felt tears at the back of my throat and could not hold in the ones that rolled from the corner of my eyes and into my ears.

"Hey, are you crying?" Sloan asked and turned on his side facing me. "Stop crying." He wiped my tears away.

"Why do you bring your wife to my bed?" I asked him while wailing.

"You mean our bed," he said.

"Right now, it's my bed," I said stubbornly.

"And later on?" I knew he was trying to lighten the mood. But I wasn't ready to go there yet.

"Later? I don't know. Maybe I'll consider bringing you back into my bed and maybe not. Depends."

"Depends on what?"

"I don't know. Maybe if you tell your wife more details from our life..."

"Since when can't I tell you what's happening in my home?" he asked calmly.

"Oh my God. I hate you so much. It's hard to believe how good you are at turning around the whole situation and positioning it in your favor. Why is it that we can never fight? Can you please explain it to me?" I was beyond frustrated.

"Why? Because I have no reason to fight with you. This kind of shit I can get at home." He sounded so rational.

"How do you know that she really didn't mean it? Maybe she knows," I said.

"I don't know and I don't care."

I stopped crying, although my tears had yet to dry. I wanted to tell him that I truly hated his wife and explain how much she irritated me. I needed him to know how much it aggravated me that he was married to her, or maybe just the fact that he was married. I was tired of it in every way. For the first time I was ready to claim my rights. And I did. But he had an answer.

"You will have to wait until my oldest son's Bar-Mitzvah."

I hurried to calculate how many years that would be—how many years left for me to live as a mistress? And when I realized that there were five more years, I kept it to myself—I assumed he had already done the math.

But where would that leave my desire to have a child? Was this the right time to bring it up? Fear kept me silent.

Sloan's finger gently caressed my shoulder in circles. He did not say a word, nor did he make any moves.

A few minutes later he turned his body over and got on top of me, asking to make love to me. He was hard and ready to engage our bodies. I, on the other hand, wanted to make out with him. I wanted to play. I was in the mood for something more erotic, like oral sex. I pushed him away so that I could possibly change our position, but he was stronger and quicker. Before I knew it he'd inserted himself inside me. He was hot and knew my body well, but not this time. This time he ejaculated right after his second long deep thrust. I was speechless and disappointed.

I didn't know what to think or what to do. My sexual hero shattered. I wasn't sure if it was a compliment or an insult, but way before I figured it out Sloan pulled out and dragged himself south.

Once his nose reached my belly button, he softly kissed my belly and continued down. I bent my knees and when his lips reached my clitoris, I placed my feet over his wide shoulders, offering him a second chance. Sloan gave me exactly what I needed, long moments of sexual indulgence, except he didn't let me come. I was ready to explode, but he pulled his tongue off me and traveled north. Once his lips touched mine he pressed his pelvis on mine.

"Are you ready?" he whispered in my ear and pushed back inside me.

He sure made up for his earlier slip. We stopped when our bodies could not take any more. By the time we were done I was satisfied and exhausted but still bothered by the first run, when he hadn't lasted. *Is it me? Is he still interested in me? Or is it just the stress of the situation and the fear of his wife?*

Twenty-Eight

Later on, early in evening, the Rosins stopped by.

"What's that?" Lori asked as they walked in.

"Isn't that a canary?" Jonathan said, stepping closer to the birdcage.

"Yes, it is," I said.

"They're hard to find. Where did you get it?" Jonathan asked.

"From a friend—or more precisely from one of Kaminski's friends." I wanted to tell them the entire tale but Sloan cut me off.

"Come on, tell them the truth. She got it from one of her fans."

"Well, that sounds kind of juicy," Jonathan said.

"Sounds to me more like someone is getting jealous," Lori said and kept looking at the mute bird.

"Whatever he is, let me tell you the story," I said and went on with the legend behind that bird.

"Sounds kind of kooky," Jonathan said.

"What's his name?" Lori asked.

"Alon," I said.

"Not the guy, the bird," she insisted.

"I haven't thought about it yet. I'll worry about it later," I said.

"Come on, we better give him a name. You don't want him to have an identity crisis or something." Lori made us all laugh. First she convinced us to name the canary after Sloan, and then she was the one that made it happen. She picked out the name Marco Polo because of the funny tale about his wife—the one who found that her husband's long travels were actually ending around the corner at his mistress' house.

Suddenly, the little bird spoke up for the first time. All four of us looked at him as he let out a few chirps—no, he had yet to sing for us—it was more as if he was insulted. At least we knew that he was not mute.

From that day on my canary's name was Marco Polo, or Marco, for short.

Still, it took Marco time to accept his name and new home. But when he did, he sang and performed acrobatics all day long. *Do you ever sleep, little man?*

I was driven to become the mother of the year, making every effort to ensure the tiny creature a long life. Since he resided in my house, I felt obligated for his overall well-being. I replaced the seeds in his cage regularly and refreshed the muddy water in his special dish daily. Once in awhile I added a few drops of the orange solution to the water. This secret mixture kept Marco's feathers a bright reddish orange shade. It was important to me that Marco remained a good-looking guy at all times.

For his singing performances, I included some poppy seeds in his diet once a week. I followed the advice of Alon, the bird expert, to the letter. I didn't deviate from the suggested protocol, and didn't dare to conduct any experiments that might put Marco's life at risk. However, often, I had mixed feelings regarding the poppy seeds. It was hard to decide if I was improving Marco's life or mistreating him, as those poppy seeds sexually stimulated my little Marco.

Whenever Marco consumed those poppy seeds he had a great desire to find a young female canary, and he would sing splendid courting songs. I goodheartedly thought to find him a female canary and move her in. But when Alon said that the horny male canary would literally kill the female bird, I was reminded how vicious nature can be. With this in mind, there was no way in the world that I could introduce a female to Marco—I had to keep Marco living on his own, horny and disappointed.

Sloan took charge of Marco's entertainment. Often, I witnessed them conversing with each other. Sloan would lecture Marco while Marco kept chirping. It was a special dialogue that wouldn't change—same words and same warnings.

"Hey, trouble, are you still here? Did you have a good day?" He would approach the bird once he entered the house. "Let's see, did anyone check your food and water today?" he would say. And upon leaving he would say goodbye to the bird. "Don't look at me like that. I get enough from her…. I'll be back, okay? And keep it a secret, are we clear? Whatever you hear or see stays at home. Got it?" he said while hugging me right in front of Marco. And Marco shook his head from right to left, and up and down, and chirped. And me? I wanted to remind my man that we were dealing with a canary and not a parrot, but since I thought that he would be better off venting to a canary than to a shrink, I bit my tongue and said nothing. Not less amusing were those moments when Sloan whistled and Marco lent a hand, contributing with his singing. It was quite impressive.

Soon Marco became part of my routine. The excitement over him waned. In fact, at times he turned out to be more of a bother than a joy. His singing at dawn served as my alarm clock, but on the weekends, early in the mornings, I kept his birdcage in my dark bathroom so he would sleep.

Sloan's upcoming birthday halted the monotony of my life.

I wanted to surprise him but needed a plan that would include a safe place to go and a noble alibi that would allow him to spend the night at my place. I called Lori, hoping to brainstorm ideas for Sloan's birthday with her. I was disappointed when she immediately cut me off. Her news was bigger than my plans.

"Listen, I'm late," she said.

"What do you mean you're late?"

"I mean, I'm late."

"How late?"

"Eight days."

"When was your last period?" I pulled out the due date wheel.

"On the twenty first of last month...."

"Let's see...." I paused, trying to manage the wheel. "Damn it, you are late."

"Can you draw my blood and send it out to the lab?" she asked in a calm tone.

Lori was composed while I lost my mind as if it was my own potential pregnancy. I had a truckload of questions for her, attempting to find a legitimate explanation for the delay of her period. I tried to blame the stress she had been under at work lately, the chaos in her house, and anything else that I could think of. But I couldn't ignore or argue with the facts. She was late.

"Of course. Why don't you stop by my work first thing in the morning," I said.

"No, let's do it today."

"I'll have to call Ruth and see if she has any tubes at home and if she can spin the blood."

"Okay. Let me know," she said and hung up.

I arrived at Lori's house forty-five minutes later. In seconds I drew eight ccs of blood from her and rushed back to Ruth so she could spin it. I was anxious for the test results.

The next day Ruth didn't call me—she paged me. βHCG positive, the screen displayed—I had no choice but to call Lori.

"Hey."

"Do you have it?" Lori asked.

"I do."

"And…"

"You're pregnant."

"I am, ha?"

"Yes, you are. Do you have a plan?" I asked her straightforward and considered that she might get upset.

Lori shared the pros and cons and said that she was determined to keep the pregnancy. I gave her my blessing and prayed to God that she was doing the right thing. I wondered what her life would be like with four kids, what the pregnancy would impose on her marriage, and whether it would affect her job.

That evening, instead of planning Sloan's birthday, we all went out to celebrate Lori's conception. Even Sloan changed his plans and joined us at Lori's favorite place at the Port of Tel-Aviv on a bright night with a full moon and endless stars. It was one of the better places where you could get fresh seafood.

Only a few feet from the water, around a square table, covered with two layers of tablecloth, red over white, we looked at the menu and placed our order.

Lori didn't believe much in conservative theories and allowed herself a glass of wine.

"*L'chaim*," she said and we all raised our glasses.

"Well, Sharon," she said, "what are you waiting for? What about the future generation?"

Jonathan's jaw dropped. He didn't say a word, nor did he move.

Sloan covered his shock with a foolish laugh and blushed as if the Rosins didn't know that we were having sex.

I almost aspirated on the wine but recovered with only a few coughs. "I have plenty of time," I said in effort to save the entire table from getting into a drama.

"No, you don't," Lori said.

"Yes, I do. You're just looking for a girlfriend to join you on this journey." I tried to cover up what Lori had just broadcast—I wanted to be the first one to tell Sloan about my desire for a child. Lori sure did upset my plan—now was not the time. "Maybe, when Sloan leaves his home," I said.

"By then you'll be in menopause," Lori said.

"I'm sure my private OBGYN will keep me fertile." I looked at Sloan with a smile.

"Well, I don't have the magic wand, or the magic sperm." He rushed to speak.

Sloan's sense of humor subdued my anger and turned the painful subject into a joke. Then he quickly changed the subject, reminding everyone of his leave of absence and the board exam. "We probably won't see one another much while I'm off."

I felt as if he gave me the kiss of death. "I thought you would be studying at my place." I couldn't hide the disappointment from my voice.

"Are you kidding? I can't do that."

"Why not? Can't you tell her that you're going to the library and come here instead? I bet she won't check on you."

"There's no way that I can study with you around."

"Why not?"

"Because."

"Because what?" I didn't give him a way out.

"I won't be able to focus on anything serious," he said.

My thoughts went into a tailspin. *Really? Why's that?* I wanted to ask him but instead I reassessed my relationship with that married man who was sitting in front of me. I wondered if there was more then just sexual lust between us. Could we not do other things together without sex entering the picture? *What does he mean by not being able to do anything serious when I am around? Should I be flattered or hurt? Why can't he admit that he's afraid of his wife and that he's unable to dodge her questions? Why can't he be creative and find a way to get out of the house? Maybe he isn't planning his future life with me. What are the qualities of this relationship? Do they even exist, or are they nothing but pretention through his betrayal?* I went through the motions for the rest of our dinner, staring at the water, trying to distract myself from my troubling thoughts.

Time flew by, leaving only two days until Sloan's birthday and five days before the start of his leave of absence.

Sloan walked in. He seemed different. Something in his step, as well as the expression on his face, voiced a problem. I expected to hear something out of the ordinary.

Only later, at the table he finally spat it out. "I had a nasty run-in with Sharon last night."

"What about? Your mistress again?"

"Not only...."

"Then what was it about?"

"Different things—but that's beside the point."

"So what was the point?"

"Lately, every little thing turns into a battle with her. Besides, this time I turned my back, packed a suitcase, and told her that I was leaving, that I was done…"

"And…?" My heart raced.

"Basically, that's it. I packed, left the house, planning to come here. I was sure that this was the end—that I would look for a lawyer, file for divorce, and move on."

I looked straight into his eyes, but couldn't find the right words. I hesitated whether to voice my opinion or to ask more questions. I was concerned that I might add salt to his open wounds. Moreover, I didn't want to take the chance of saying the wrong words that might push him away or delay the day in which we were to start our new life. I kept my lips sealed, waiting for him to volunteer more details.

Sloan was tuned into my emotions, trying not to hurt my feelings. He knew how happy I'd be when he retired from his family nest and moved in with me. Before he continued his tale, he looked into my eyes as if he had words on the tip of his tongue but didn't have the courage to voice them. He wouldn't dare manipulate me or insult my intelligence.

He added a slight smile to his face and finally continued. "As soon as I started to back out of the driveway, I heard my youngest son scream, 'Daddy, Daddy…' then I saw him running toward the car and I couldn't continue—I had to stop. I couldn't ignore him. So, I stopped and I rolled down the window. He looked into my eyes and asked, 'Daddy when will you be back?'"

My body shut down and my eyes were fixed on Sloan I could feel and touch his pain. His eyes were shining and I thought that he might shed a tear.

"Well," he continued, "he broke my heart and I couldn't turn my back on him. I had no answer for him. If I left, I wouldn't know when I'd be back. So, I told him, 'In a few minutes. Go back in the house.'"

That was more than enough. Any additional words would be pointless. I didn't want to hear any more about his dilemma and pain. I had no interest in hearing about abandoned children. My conscious was working overtime without his drama. I couldn't compete with his kids. Clearly it was a guaranteed loss. I truly had nothing to say to him. I asked myself whether he placed me ahead of his kids or at least at the same starting line. It was hard, but I had to admit that I would never gain the power they had. The thought of having my own child came back to me. Maybe it would be my ticket to gain more power and more of Sloan. A child could add decisive weight to the pan I was sitting in, on that balanced scale. I focused on two things—myself and the future with Sloan.

"I want a child." I took a long, deep breath and kept looking into his eyes. "I'm not getting any younger. Every day that passes never comes back. If I'm the woman you wish to be with, then I'm ready to have a child without the formality of marriage."

Wow, I thought, *that's a lot to say.* I was breathless after my outburst. It was his turn to respond to my confession. Or, he could pack himself up along with the few things that he had in my place and run away from the sinful site where he maintained a double life. But he didn't. He didn't reveal a hint of hysteria, panic, or madness. He didn't even seem surprised. He kept silent for a few moments, and then he said, "I'll have to think about it. This is not so simple. I'm sure you understand it comes with a long list of responsibilities. Having a child outside of marriage doesn't diminish my responsibilities—I would still be his father. It would be my child and sooner or later I would raise him with you."

"I understand. Take your time and think about it." There was no point in pressing the issue. I'd been thinking about this for a while but to him, it was new. As much as I wanted an answer, I had to give him time to consider it.

Twenty-Nine

I was patient enough not to bring up the sensitive subject again until Sloan took his board exam. There was no need to add to his stress. And until then, I would rather enjoy the few days we had left before he took off.

I was looking forward to celebrating his birthday—except that on the exact day of his birthday, the reality of being his second choice hit me again. Sloan had less than an hour for me. He had to be home on time to celebrate with his wife and family. He had already told me that she had been talking about his birthday, reminding him daily that he must be home on time. I could only think that she was planning a big surprise party for him or a night to remember on a private yacht. So, the little time that we had, we spent at a café, at a corner table, where we could hide away. A spot where we could be close enough to feel each other's breath, where I could wish him a happy birthday and dream of the next day, when he could stay longer.

When Sloan officially turned forty years and one day old, he arrived at my place as planned. I had a small, modest gift for him that could not make its way to his other home. In addition, I had prepared an epicurean meal to be served on a table for four with a festive setup.

I wanted to ask Sloan about his evening—how had he celebrated his birthday? I was curious to find out if he'd had sex with his wife, and if so, how good was it? Did she satisfy him? But I wasn't in the mood for a fight. Although, I must admit, I hoped that he would voluntarily tell me all about it. In the meantime, I remained quiet.

"Are you okay?" Sloan asked as if my silence disturbed him.

I ignored him and his question—who was to say that a mistress had to be nice at all times? Couldn't this relationship be just like the one with the wife—with ups and downs? Who put together all those mistress rules, and why hadn't anyone consulted with me before?

Sloan couldn't read my mind, and if he could, he really didn't care. All he wanted was to have his usual, happy mistress.

And me? Considering that it was his birthday, I gave in and put on the happy mistress mask.

When the Rosins walked in I was already at my best. Jonathan put the bottle of champagne that he'd brought on ice and Lori checked the menu. I placed four empty champagne glasses in the freezer for a few minutes so they would chill down a bit. But by the time that I was ready to pull them out, the phone rang.

"Sharon?" a familiar voice said.

"Yes," I answered, not sure if my guess was right.

"Is this a bad time?" she continued.

"Dalia?" I said in a loud voice so that everybody would pay attention. I gave a quick look at Sloan and could swear that his heart dropped a bit. He was pale and didn't move.

"Yes," she confirmed and continued. "Sorry to bother you, but do you have Dr. Blatsky's number, by any chance?"

"I think I do."

"Do you mind looking?"

"No, not at all. Hold on a second." I grabbed my phonebook from my purse and relayed the number to her.

As I hung up the phone, I looked at Sloan and asked him ironically, "Why do you look so worried? What's wrong? Do you think Dalia is doing CSI work for your wife?"

"Speaking of the devil," Lori cut in before Sloan answered, "what did she do for your birthday?"

"We went out with another couple for dinner at Dolphin Yam."

"That's all she could do?" Lori said.

"What did you expect her to do? It's just another birthday...."

"Come on, it was your fortieth. That's not just another birthday." Lori gave Sloan a nasty look.

"Okay," he said with a sigh, "I don't need you to remind me that my marriage sucks."

"What makes you think that life with Sharon would be any sweeter?" Jonathan said with a smile.

"Ha-ha-ha. At least he would have memorable birthday parties." I made everybody laugh.

Winter was nearing its end, getting ready to make way for spring. A few sunny days started to warm up this part of the globe and prepped it for a colorful spring. It was too early to replace winter clothes with spring ones, but it was certainly time to put aside the long, heavy coat.

It had been two and a half weeks since Sloan had left to study for his board exam. His absence disturbed me—I missed him greatly. I created an imaginary record to count how often we saw each other or spoke on the phone. Once he got stuck in his home, everything was dependent on him. I sensed that our relationship was imbalanced. He was the one to determine when we could talk on the phone and when we could meet. I had no freedom to reach him when I wanted to.

The last two weeks brought only five phone calls with Sloan, two reunions, and one quick sexual encounter. I promised myself, I would bring these findings to his attention. I was willing to give him an ultimatum and file for divorce, even though we had yet to be married. But when I was with him, close to his body and surrounded by his smell and wrapped within his love, I accepted him, along with his conditions and the quality of our relationship—even the quick sexual encounters.

My workplace turned into my savior, keeping me busy for long hours. It was an easy place to escape. My work hours extended into the weekends—all for the price of dimming Sloan's absence.

Sadly, nothing could make Kaminski happier than a situation where I was available for him 24/7. So when I reminded him that this was a temporary scenario—that this time I was the one who'd taken advantage of him and the job and not vice versa, he went ballistic.

The center had increased its business by five percent more than expected, so Kaminski scheduled four weeks off.

I felt relieved, as if God had done me a big favor by loosening the leash around my neck for a few weeks. I was mindful of my thoughts, but didn't like the vibes that came along with it. Was it time for me to look for another job?

I listened to Kaminski's thorough instructions. He didn't leave me room to breathe. It seemed as if I wouldn't get a break during his time off. There would definitely be no rest for me. I agreed to all of his tasks, including those affiliated with his politician friends. I wanted to believe that what he asked me to do was business related. I exhibited a positive attitude and assured him that he could trust me—I had no reason to interfere or damage his business or his public image.

But at the very last minute, Kaminski said that it was necessary for me to attend the debates. I thought that this was a lot to ask from someone who didn't want to be involved in politics. However, I didn't argue with him. I was too eager to see him gone. "Just leave—go away—disappear…" I wanted to tell him. Instead, I nodded, thinking that at the polling station, nobody would see me cast my vote behind the privacy screen.

"You know how Yaron is." Kaminski reinforced the importance of those assignments referring to the minister. "If he doesn't have assurances regarding his medical situation, he becomes unreasonable."

"No kidding—maybe he's always unreasonable." I hoped that would end the conversation.

"Make sure you're on time and that you have everything with you—aspirin, Xanax, a blood pressure cuff, and a stethoscope. You know what I mean, right?"

"I got it," I answered and wondered why Kaminski planned his vacation during the debates, just before the primaries. He was such a political freak that I couldn't see him missing that dirty game. I couldn't imagine him not being available for his hypochondriac friend during such a stressful period. It was odd that he trusted me to take care of his friend—did he really think that I was that good, or, was this a setup? Was his friend manipulating the situation so that he would have an excuse to interact with me?

I was uncomfortable. The thought of Yaron disturbed me. The idea of him trying to seduce me made me feel sick. Eluding his attempts became challenging. I simulated different situations, rehearsing responses, and designed a way out. Except, in a few weak moments, I gave it a second thought. *Why not—why shouldn't I live for the moment? Maybe if Sloan had to face the reality of competition he would hurry up, make up his mind, and move on. And, who knows—maybe the minister is a much better lover than Sloan. Perhaps it's worthwhile trying?* I let my thoughts run wild. But when my imagination put me together with the minister in my bedroom, I was nauseated to the point of throwing up. I didn't think that an episode like that would add anything positive to my life or my reputation.

Beyond the nausea, I believed that it was time to glance through my stable of men. Possibly even turn myself into the local meat market. My married lover was shackled in his own home and I was a prisoner in a virtual relationship. I wondered if I cast my fishing line out farther, would I reel in a bigger fish? I was ready to call Rachel and ask her to find a better fortune-teller, a really good one.

I wanted to be left alone, to float in my survival bubble. I thought about Melnick—I liked him and could relate to the qualities he exhibited. I recognized his broad knowledge and wisdom. He stimulated my intellect. I enjoyed his company and had an interest in his personality. I could not deny the intellectual excitement he brought into my life. The absence of any physical attraction between us allowed me to relax and be me. I tagged him as a friend. I trusted him and responded to his arbitrary invitations for breakfast or lunch in trendy places in town.

It was Friday, mid-morning. I met Melnick at Reviva and Silia, a favorite spot at the time. A place that was mentioned in the paper regularly. A place where things happened and shouldn't happen. It was the place where questions were asked, things were said, and answers were not given—where high society spent time and money, and where fashion was determined. It was a spot where you had to be at least once a week if you didn't want to be left in the dark—a melting pot where I spent lots of time.

Usually, my rendezvous with Melnick carried a personal tone. Melnick was comfortable offering me a piece of his mind. He shared his secrets easily and, in return, collected a few snapshots of my life as a mistress. But that day, Melnick was busy showering me with compliments that I didn't particularly deserve. The situation caught me off guard—was he acting on a whim? I didn't know what to say or think. I wondered if I'd been wrong and he wasn't a true friend. Maybe he had interests that I hadn't recognized before. I was edgy, worrying that the sudden tension between us might be visible—that someone would pick up a word or two from our chat, and turn it into the talk of the town. Beyond all else, I was nervous that I would be late to the debate, where I had to babysit the minister. I had to cut him off, but he was one step ahead of me.

"As much as I'm crazy about you," he said, "and love you in a very special way, I would never take my chances. You have nothing to worry about. I would never flirt with you."

I was relieved but speechless.

Melnick continued, "But as your friend, mind my words—Sloan will never leave his family nor his home."

Is that jealousy coming out of his mouth? I wondered. I was overwhelmed by the entire episode. I had no time to try and understand him or it. I was already running late. I had to keep moving and get to the political event so I could hold the minister's hand before and after his speech.

"I'm late. I really have to go," I said.

"You're right. I forgot. Don't worry, I'll wait for the check," he said, kindly.

As I expected, I arrived after the debate had started. I had no choice but to cross the entire hall, in front of the first row on my left and the stage on my right. The minister kept me in his sight as if he was my personal guard. I sat in a safe spot, where I could be away from the stage but close enough in case he needed my services.

While I was still recuperating from rushing, still catching my breath, and had yet to get my heart rate back to normal, someone from the minister's entourage landed next to me. He handed me a note folded in six—a secret message from the minister.

Notes like that were handed to me often and were disturbing in a way. For the most part they were personal and senseless. They could deliver an invitation for dinner or for a VIP event, sometimes they offered a ticket to a concert or to a basketball game—anything that might give Yaron a chance to be with me. Others were hysterical notes regarding his health. They could say things like—*My blood pressure this morning was 135/95. Do you think I might stroke? Should I take another pill?* Or, *Last night I had a headache. Do you think it's a tumor?* And then there were the emotional ones—*I wanted to call you this morning, should I have called?* Or, *I'm glad you're here, I already feel much better.* I never kept them. I automatically dropped them in my bag and trashed them later. But this note was somewhat different—very decisive in a way.

Will meet you at your place right after the debate—what's your address?

Wow, I took a few seconds to consider my response. Never-ending replies rushed through my mind. I twirled that pen that had come with the note, thinking to write down *That's not a good idea,* or *I already have another commitment,* or *Maybe some other time,* even an answer like *I'll meet you in my office* was on the tip of the pen. But I chose none of these. What I jotted down was my address.

While my response was on its way back, my head flooded with questions that I had no answers for. I was stressed from my own questions—*Why did I give my address?* Was I going to flirt with him or would I explain to him that I had no intention of getting involved with him in any manner—personal or sexual? I was on the edge of a panic attack.

I reached in my bag, looking for a pen and a piece of paper. All I found was a receipt from a gasoline station. *Who cares?* I used the back of it to let the minister know that I'd changed my mind. *Please cancel,* I wrote to him, and looked for that individual who exchanged our messages earlier. Seconds later, my note was on its way. I locked the courier in my sight, followed his steps, and watched him hand my note to the minister. My heart pounded inside my chest, my jugular arteries were exhausted from fighting the flow of blood that had to pass through them. I looked at the minister, preparing myself to deal with his offensive response. He spent a lengthy time reading my two-worded message. He smiled, lifted his eyes, and gave me a quick look. I was surprised and disappointed, anticipating that at the end of the evening he would not try to rehash this nonsense with me. I prayed that he would rush to his vehicle and order his driver to disappear. I pulled out my calendar and verified that the next debate was not before next Wednesday. I promised myself to instruct my secretary not to transfer any calls from him or from his office. I was willing to provide her with a list of lies and alibis, just to make sure she kept me away from him. I prayed to the Lord that my boss would not call me with a new assignment that would require me to contact the minister or his office.

Yaron made his way out without passing by me. He was escorted by his bodyguards and vanished. I was relieved and quickly found my way out. Minutes later I was on my way home. It was early in the afternoon, and I was ready for the weekend. All I had to do was to pick up some groceries and go home and crash.

Thirty

I t was only an hour after I arrived home when the intercom buzzed.

"Yes?" I answered.

"I doubt you'll send me away if I'm already here." Yaron's voice stunned me.

"I guess I won't. Just give me one second." I put the receiver back in place and hurried to grab a pair of pants. As I dressed, I finally pieced together that unexplained smile he'd had when he'd read my note. *Holy shit, what the hell is this wacko doing here? He's ridiculous. What am I going to do? Evaporate?*

I was terrified by my own mistake. I couldn't evade him or change my state of matter to gas. I had to get back out there and answer him. I reached back to the intercom and pushed the button to release the gate. I stuck my hands in my front pockets and clenched them tight. I watched him through the living room French window as he stepped into my yard. I wanted to kick him out but didn't dare. I clenched my jaw even harder than my fists.

"Come on in," I said as I heard the knock at the door.

"Well, it looks like I'm the one who has the last word after all," he said with a juvenile smile and handed me a box of Lady Godiva. "Here, this is for you—I thought you might like these."

"Thank you, but I really can't afford to eat them—too many calories."

"Come on, you can eat anything. You have a perfect figure," he said.

"You'd soon change your mind if you saw me naked." The words tumbled out of my mouth before I could stop them.

"I cannot wait." He rushed to answer.

"That's not what I meant," I corrected myself as I felt the heat creep up my neck.

"So, what did you mean?" He walked into my living room.

"Would you like something to drink?" I changed the subject.

"I'll have some tea with milk if you don't mind."

"Sure," I said and stepped into the kitchen, questioning why I let him in and why I accepted that box of imported, high-calorie candies he brought with him. But, I had to confess to myself that I was young and stupid enough to enjoy the glory of hosting a minister in my house.

As I served him his tea, I realized how much I missed the aroma of the fresh coffee that I used to have with Sloan. I entered into an ordinary chat with Yaron, letting wild memories of Sloan cross my mind. Our interaction was interrupted twice by phone calls.

"May I speak with the minister please?" a strange voice asked.

"Sure. Please hold." I handed him the cordless phone.

I was flustered by the public exposure and planned to advise him that he should ask me before fertilizing the environment with my phone number and with his visit.

It was only after the second call that I suspected that his security guards were waiting in front of my house. "Is your driver and security out there?"

"Yes," he said.

"Hum…." I was amazed how big his balls were. I was furious with the idea that I had become an integral part of the gossip column. I wanted to ask him if he kept anything to himself or if he shared it all with his support staff. I thought, *What if I had sex with him—how quickly would that be reported to his entourage?*

I kept a physical distance from Yaron, and quietly said, "You should leave now."

"I understand," he said and stood up. "When can I see you again?"

"I thought you just said you understood." I stepped toward the door, hoping that he would follow me.

"I did. Thank you for the tea."

"You're welcome. And thanks for the Godiva." I couldn't wait for him to leave.

"I'll call you sometime tomorrow."

"That's fine." *Did I just say tell him that it was okay to call me? What the hell is wrong with me? He probably thinks that I've changed my mind or that I'm bipolar.*

I walked him all the way to the gate, making sure that he was out of my territory. I locked the gate and stepped back in the house. I locked the door and the windows, and crawled into my bed as if I'd lost my privacy. I felt insecure.

Kaminski and the mission he left me to complete were no longer a priority. I put aside the trust he had in me. I would not show up at the next political event and planned on being late to the final one. I was done and ready to move on. I swore to never talk with that dirt bag again.

Two days prior to the final debate a hysterical voice from the minister's chamber ruined my plan—informing me that the minister had lost his voice. Again, I was being requested to provide medical advice. To my frustration, I couldn't avoid him or the big event.

"I'll get back to you within the hour," I said to his assistant and pulled out my telephone book. I went through a list of ENT physicians, looking for someone who would be helpful, wouldn't ask for a fee, and would not advise me that he must see the patient prior to prescribing a drug of choice like a steroid inhaler. Not less important, it had to be someone that would not ask me to repay the favor he was about to do.

My choice was right. The one I picked was nice enough to offer me a sample from his office, saving me a trip to the pharmacy. I thanked him for his help and for his personal contribution to the politics. Also, I thanked the pharmaceutical companies for the brilliant invention of samples.

"This is Sharon Lapidot. I need to speak with the minister please," I said to the voice in his chamber that answered the phone.

"Sure, hold on please," she answered immediately without asking a thing.

"I'll stop by your office around two," Yaron said in his hoarse voice, after I explained that I had some medication for him.

"That will be fine," I said.

His voice faded and was replaced with a whisper. "Maybe lunch?"

"We'll see. I need to run," I said and put a quick end to the conversation.

The next forty-eight hours passed quickly. I was busy holding Yaron's hand, assuring him that his voice would come back, that it was just a matter of time.

Kaminski returned to work in a whirlwind. He was full of energy but could not remain civil for more than a few hours. It didn't take long before he lost it and jumped all over me.

"What's going on in the restrooms?" he yelled at me.

"I saw that. I already called housekeeping and asked them to clean it up."

"Who did it?"

"I have no idea."

"How come?"

"How come what?" I asked.

"How come you don't know who did this shit?"

"I'm not exactly guarding the restroom or keeping a log of the people who are using it."

"Watch the way you talk to me—do you understand? Go and clean it up right away," he ordered me.

"Excuse me?"

"You heard me. Go and clean the bathroom. Now," he said.

"Can I see you in your office?" I gave him a way out of the drama he had just started.

"No, you cannot." He continued on his way. "Go and clean the toilet," he repeated and left the building.

"Shame on you, my dear boss. You're moving in the wrong direction. I don't give a shit about you or about how much you pay me. I'm out of here. Go to hell," I said to the walls, as nobody else was around.

I was not sure if I was pissed or insulted, but clearly I was not planning to approach the cleaning experience. I picked up my stuff and was on my way out.

"I'm not coming back. Please don't try to reach me. I'm no longer available," I said to my secretary on my way out.

"Today or ever?" she asked and I left her with no answer.

I drove to Lori's office and interrupted her. "Hey, can you cut your day short?" I asked as I walked into her office.

"What's going on? Are you okay?"

"I had a huge fight with Kaminski. I think I'm done with him." I paced back and forth in front of her desk. "Let's get out of here."

"Another of your boss' daycare issues? Give me a minute." She cleaned up her desk and grabbed her bag.

"I'm hungry. Let's go to Reviva and Silia," I said.

"Good idea. I'll be right behind you."

At that trendy café, Lori shared her opinion. "You know I can't stand your boss, but I don't want to see you without a job again."

"I agree. I need my job. But I don't see you cleaning the bathroom at your workplace—would you?"

"No, I wouldn't, but I wouldn't work for someone like Kaminski either. I'm not suggesting that you accept this working condition. All that I'm saying is that you shouldn't quit before you find another job."

I couldn't disagree with Lori. She was looking out for my best interests. There was nothing to argue about and nothing further to discuss. I needed to start looking for a new job.

Lori's appetite was insatiable. I had never seen her consume so much food. She was extremely obsessed with her condition and rehashed the topic often. Sometimes it felt as if there was nothing left to talk about but her pregnancy. Except this time, once I realized that I was late myself, the conversation took a different direction.

"Let's go see your friend, Ruth," Lori suggested.

"She's out of town. I'll have to go elsewhere tomorrow morning."

"Where?"

"I'm not sure. Maybe it's nothing. Just stress."

"And maybe not." Lori smiled.

"You sure need a pal for this journey—don't you?" I said and asked for the check.

I elected to have my blood drawn at my doctor's office—where I'd received most of my health care since I was a child.

I walked into the nurses' office and handed the nurse the physician order for my blood work.

"Let see," she said and looked at the clock on the wall. "I guess we can still send it out today—I still have enough time to spin the blood before the pick-up."

I sat in the chair and extended my arm to the nurse who had been my elementary school nurse twenty years earlier.

"I didn't know you got married," she said, while placing a tourniquet over my upper arm above my elbow.

"I didn't."

"Huh—I see." She looked at me for a second and then cleaned my antecubital area with alcohol pads. "So, am I to believe that you are hoping for a negative result?" she asked as she attached the syringe to the needle.

"When will you have the results?" I asked, avoiding her question.

"Tomorrow, sometime around noon." She stuck the needle in my vein.

"Should I call for the results?" I watched the syringe fill up with ten ccs of my warm red blood.

"We'll call you," she said while releasing the tourniquet, pulling the needle out, and placing a folded two-by-two and a piece of tape to the puncture site.

"Thank you," I said and left.

While I survived the blood drawing as well as all the direct and indirect questions, there was nothing more for me to do but hunt for other evidence that might support pregnancy. Still, I couldn't pinpoint a thing. No nausea, no hunger, no special craving for sour foods or salt, no fatigue and not even engorged breasts. *Maybe I'm not pregnant—maybe it's just stress.* I thought while I walked to my car.

I drove to work, hoping that Kaminski had moved on and put the drama from the previous day behind him.

"Good morning. Did the bathroom get cleaned?" I asked my secretary.

"Yes, it did." She laughed.

"Did Kaminski look for me?"

"No. But Sloan did. He said he would be here by eleven." She smiled.

"Did he really?" I was surprised.

"Yes. Why? Is something wrong?"

"No. Not at all."

I walked into my office, pondering how to share my morning doctor's visit with Sloan. I sat at my desk but couldn't focus on my work. It was almost nine. There were only two hours before Sloan would show up. *Should I tell him about it or should I wait to hear back from the nurse first?* I'd never lied to him or hidden anything from him. *Oh my Lord,* I begged, *if he could just wait one more day to visit—let him come tomorrow instead of today. The intense details suffocated me—there was a lot I had to deal with.*

My thoughts and wishes did not postpone Sloan's visit, nor did they take away my fears and frustration.

I was nervous when he walked in and shut the door behind him. My heart skipped at least two beats and restarted at full speed. My knees shivered and I felt as if someone had punched me in my stomach. Before I recouped, Sloan's face was already less than an inch from mine. I looked into his eyes and let him take me into his arms.

"Why are you shivering? Are you alright?" he asked.

"Yes, I am." My voice quivered and I could not hold back the tears. I buried my face in his shoulder, hoping that my sobbing and sadness would vanish.

"What's wrong with you?" he insisted.

"Nothing…I just missed you." I aimed to sound reasonable, suppressing my need to tell him that I had lots of reasons to cry—the man I loved belonged to another woman and lived a double life, I was almost two weeks late, alone and had no one to lean on. And on top of all this, I was frustrated with my job and hated my boss. But I shouldn't bother Sloan right before the board exam. And for that reason only, I kept my pain and stress to myself. The short hour with Sloan didn't make up for the pain I buried, nor did it secure my future. We walked to his car and after a loving but painful hug, we separated. I stood there as if someone had anchored me to the ground, watching him drive away until I could no longer see him or his vehicle.

The next day at noon I answered a call on my direct line.

"Sharon?"

"Speaking."

"Hey, it's Shula, from your doctor's office."

My hands got cold and sweaty and my adrenaline level probably reached a new record. I held the phone so tight that my nails left deep marks in my palm.

"Your pregnancy test came back negative." She was stark and clinical about it.

"Really. Thank you for letting me know."

Disappointedly, five days later, I started my period.

There were two weeks left until Sloan's board exam. The days got longer. I waited for each day to come to its end. Being alone turned into the blues—I greatly missed Sloan. The silence he imposed on me often made me think that he'd forgotten about me and us—that he'd grown accustomed to his life with his wife at home—that his marriage had solidified. I considered entering my mourning phase but held on to the hope that better days would come.

The old saying, out of sight out of mind, hit me hard—I could feel it in my stomach. I wanted to remind him that I was still alive. My frustration was replaced with fear. I wondered why he hadn't called. My mind wrestled with thoughts of separation from Sloan and my entire body grew weak.

I called Dalia and asked her if she wanted to meet somewhere. Despite my urge, I didn't have the courage to disclose to her who was the married man I was messing around with.

"Sure. Where would you like to meet?" Dalia sounded thrilled.

I met Dalia at a coffee shop in Tel-Aviv. I was careful not to divulge Sloan's identity, nor to give her any clues. As a matter of fact, she appeared as if she didn't care who he was. Nevertheless, something didn't seem right—Dalia's reactions seemed a bit suspicious. The thought that she might know my lover's identity bothered me, and the odds of her serving as a double agent hit me. My mind searched Dalia's contacts and cross-referenced them with mine, wondering if I, or someone else, might have let something slip.

Thirty-One

Lori and Jonathan made the effort to cheer me up as if something better waited for me after the exam. I valued their support but wasn't convinced that better times were ahead.

They were clueless. They had no idea that Sloan's working hours at the hospital would decrease. They had no idea that opportunities like staying late at work, going to the library, attending continuing education classes, emergencies—they were all about to vanish—or at least become limited. They could not figure out that I was about to enter a very gloomy time. It seemed as if the truth was laughing at the rosy brush strokes created by the Rosins.

With only a few days left to the exam, I played by Sloan's rules and kept it quiet.

I was confident that Sloan would successfully pass the exam and become board certified, but still the stress was there.

I talked with Lori, brainstorming what gift I should pick out for Sloan. I looked for something that he could take home with him, something that would remind him of me.

"I agree, business cards are a great idea," Lori said.

Every doctor wanted to have these. They would display his information in both languages, Hebrew and English, and he would use them for his private practice.

All I needed was the correct spelling of his name and address in English. For that I needed a cunning plan. And when I arrived at my office I came up with one.

"Hey, I need you to call Sloan's wife," I asked my secretary over the intercom.

"Yeah, really?" she asked.

"I'm serious. Come here, I'll give you the scoop."

My secretary walked into my office with a hesitant look on her face. "You're kidding me, right?"

"Here's the deal," I said as I leaned back in my chair. "I want to surprise Sloan with business cards and I need his information in English."

"Now I get it...I think it's a great idea." She sat in the chair across from my desk. "You know what? You are one of a kind. I admire you."

"You don't have to admire me, just get his wife on the phone." I was anxious but excited.

"Are you sure?" she asked again.

"Yes, I'm sure. Come on," I said.

My secretary got ready. She stood up, looked around, pressed the "do not disturb" button on my phone, shut the door, cleared her throat, and sat back in the chair.

"Did you think of working for the Mossad? God, what preparation! It's only a phone call, relax!"

"Fine, just give me a minute," she said and reached for the phone, turning on the speaker and dialed Sloan's home phone number. It took three rings before someone answered.

"Hello," a screaming female voice answered.

"May I speak with Mrs. Sloan please?" my secretary asked, professionally.

"Speaking," the voice barked back.

"I'm calling from CheckMed. I have Ms. Lapidot on the line for you. Will you please hold?"

"Sure," Mrs. Sloan said and my secretary placed the call on hold.

We looked at each other. My heart rhythm switched from a waltz to a samba. I considered bailing out of the deal and asking my secretary to save me. But when I looked at her, I knew that I was on my own. She was extremely pale and looked as if she was about to pass out. I had to fight the fear that threatened me and pull myself together. My knees were shaking and I felt uneasy. I doubted I'd be able to say the right thing and questioned my ability to manage the stage that I had just crafted.

"Mrs. Sloan?" I asked.

"Speaking," she barked.

"This is Sharon Lapidot. I'm the manager of CheckMed. As you probably know, Dr. Sloan will be working in our facility," I said.

"Yes," she said.

"The center is customarily welcoming its new members with business cards."

"Cool," she said.

Did she just say cool? I couldn't believe I was talking to a grown person in her late thirties. *Hello, get a life, grow up lady*, I wanted to tell her. *Is this the woman my boyfriend lives with? No wonder he's screwing around....*

"Do you mind giving me your exact home address and the correct spelling in English?" I stayed focused.

"Are you ready?" she asked.

"Sure," I said and carefully wrote down the information. "Thank you very much," I said. "By the way, Dr. Kaminski would rather keep it quiet, as he likes to hand those to physicians himself."

"Of course," she said.

Her voice as well as the entire conversation pissed me off. I hated her, hated myself, and hated Sloan. I barely thanked her, rushing to end the call.

I looked back at my secretary and was happy to see that she was alive and back in business.

"Hello, hello, hello...." She imitated Mrs. Sloan and laughed loudly.

I called the graphic designer and faxed him the updated information for the business cards. I had to have these ready in forty-eight hours. I planned to give them to Sloan while celebrating with him on the day after the exam.

The day of the exam arrived. I woke up earlier than usual, feeling anxious as if I was the one who was about to take the test.

I assumed Sloan wouldn't stop by after the exam but would go straight home to his family. I entered into a monologue with him, anticipating his answers. "I had to get back home right after the exam," his voice echoed in my mind. "I'm sorry—it was not my choice. Sharon is not stupid. I wanted to call you but I couldn't—after all these years she wanted to celebrate as well...."

Once I finished monologuing with him, I tackled his wife. I accused her and women like her. I jumped all over her and the entire community of doctors' wives. I blamed them for their beliefs that, without them, their husbands would not get through medical school. I laughed at them for believing that their spiritual, emotional, and financial support was essential for their husband's graduation from medical school. Furthermore, I questioned them for linking their own identity with their husbands' credentials. Come on ladies, who said that you have eternity rights to your husband or his income? Get your own life. There is more to life than being a doctor's wife. It was time for

Sloan's wife to understand that nothing in life is permanent—she shouldn't keep a leash on him.

Monologuing with Sloan and his wife did not promote a thing—it just served as an outlet to vent.

There was nothing on my agenda that day except one conference call and a short meeting. I glanced at the clock every few minutes and jumped at each telephone ring. By lunch I was stretched to the limit, and called it a day. I had to get out of there and get some fresh air.

Going home and sitting in my own living room alone wouldn't do any good. But when I ran out of errands, shopping, and friends' visits, I went back home, hoping to find a message from Sloan. Disappointedly, the only message on my machine was from the office.

"Please call the office ASAP," my secretary's voice advised me.

I bet Kaminski was asking for an explanation as to my absence, but I was not ready to listen to his lecture about work ethics and morals.

I headed to the kitchen but was distracted by a solitary white note on the dining table. I diverted my steps and gave a second look. As I recognized the handwriting, my diaphragm spasmed and pushed my stomach into my throat. The familiar handwriting left me with so few words but substantial comfort.

Hey butterfly, I was on my way to nowhere.
I couldn't find you at work or home.
Where are you?
Love you, Sloan.

I inhaled deeply through my nose, looking for the familiar scent of Sloan, searching for evidence of his unexpected visit. Tears in the back of my throat offered a sharp, cruel pain. I couldn't forgive myself for not being at home, for running around and not being at work. I was stunned that Sloan had made his way here right after the exam instead of rushing to his wife, who thought she'd worked so hard to get him to this desired moment. I called the office, hoping that Sloan had left a more precise message for me there.

"Hey, did you call me?" I asked my secretary.

"Yes. Sloan was looking for you," she said.

"And?"

"And that's it. He didn't say much—just asked if you were in."

"I guess I missed him—I'll see you tomorrow," I said, disappointed.

I looked at the phone and paged Sloan, hoping that he was still someplace where he could turn around and come back. I needed to find him. I was angry and miserable, even willing to get into my car and drive by his house.

But it was too late to reach Sloan and too risky to drive by his house.

Again, I looked at the note from Sloan, reading it over and over until finally I placed it in a small drawer with many other notes—a hidden drawer in my antique desk that safely kept all kinds of words from him—a drawer that nobody else knew about.

Thirty-Two

y drive to work on that early spring day was brief. The traffic was light and the weather was nice. I couldn't wait to see the business cards that I'd ordered.

Finally, at eleven-fifteen they were delivered in a small package by courier. I opened the box to see them. They were nicely done, and definitely suited my style and my man. I couldn't wait to give them to Sloan that night.

In early afternoon Sloan showed up at my office. He was relaxed, cloaked in pride and happiness. His gratification made me smile. I glanced at him—nothing had changed. He was the same man who I had known. His new credentials hadn't influenced his personality or his attitude. The long period of time where I had been left alone was coming to an end. In one second all my bitter memories and suffering were history, like they had never happened. My life was back on track as if it had never paused.

I was ready to restart the routine that I'd ironically both missed and complained about. I was quick to share how much I'd dearly missed him—I let my confession spell out my love for him. In return, he spoke about his time at home, during the pre-exam period.

"Thank God it's over. One more day at home and I would have died."

"That bad, huh?"

"It was a nightmare. Nothing but fights and arguments—everyday—all day. If you only knew how many times I thought of just packing up and leaving for good…."

While I tried to show sympathy for him, inside I truly enjoyed hearing about the constant drama from his married life. I couldn't tell if his intention was to vent or to give me hope. But me? I played by the rules of a mistress—rules that were difficult to follow.

"I guess thinking is not enough." I ended up breaking the rules.

"Are you ready to leave?" he quickly changed the subject.

"Where are we going?"

"We can go straight home or we could go grab something to eat first."

"Are you hungry?" I asked.

"Not really. Besides, I thought we were going out with the Rosins tonight."

"We are."

"Then let's just go home."

While driving, my excitement overflowed. I wanted so much to catch up with him in private. I felt weird, as if I was about to lose my virginity, or as if I was about to hook up with a new lover for the first time.

And at home, in our court, on our stage, when no one could disturb or watch, we reconstructed all that we had missed—we settled back into our very special nest full of love and tenderness. "We cannot interrupt this love ever again," I whispered to him.

A few hours later, we had to leave and meet with the Rosins. I was saturated with sex, emotions, words, and wonders. I could no longer talk or listen, love or be loved, or be with him or without him. Nevertheless, I had yet to fulfill my needs and goals.

"Are you all right?" he asked right before we left.

"I am."

"Shall we?" he said as he grabbed his keys and offered his arm.

"Of course," I said and could not resist the confidence he offered.

"You look beautiful." He smiled and we left the house.

As I got into his car a flash of light caught my eye. But when I looked around, there was nothing there. *Was it a flickering streetlight?* I thought and didn't bother to mention it to Sloan.

The ride passed by quickly. Sloan and I were comfortable and had a lot to talk about. There was no tension or worries. No hostility and no hard feelings from the past months that we had been apart from each other.

"What time did they say?" he asked while parking in the first available open space, about a block away from the restaurant.

"Eight."

"We're early—do you want to go in or wait here?"

"Let's go in," I said and got out of the car.

Sloan locked the car and rushed his first few steps. As he caught up with me, he coiled his arm around my shoulder—so simple and so close to each other.

It was still chilly on that evening on Rothschild Avenue, in Tel-Aviv. The winter was nearing its end. I didn't need a coat, but I appreciated his arm around me.

Sloan and I, walking as a couple, on an early evening in Tel-Aviv, down Rothschild Avenue, between two columns of trees—what more could I ask?

The streetlights were already on and revealed the avenue's distinct evening ambiance. Homeless people prepared themselves to spend the night on a bench while elderly folks sat around, staring at nothing. And younger ones hurried to get home to their families after a long day at work. It was a typical weekday evening in the city.

I wished that our walk would never end—that we could walk and walk until we entered our own new life.

Minutes later we entered the small cozy restaurant where we'd agreed to meet the Rosins for dinner.

"Good evening." A well-groomed host welcomed us.

"We have a reservation for dinner, a party of four," Sloan said.

"Under what name, please?"

"Probably Rosin," Sloan answered.

"Sure, follow me please."

Sloan and I were seated next to each other, at a table for four. The Rosins had yet to arrive. In the meantime, Sloan perused the wine list, while I excused myself and went to the ladies' room. By the time I returned, Lori and Jonathan were at the table.

"*L'chaim*," we said once we raised our glasses.

"Well, how does it feel?" Lori asked Sloan.

"Relieved." Sloan smiled.

"Any plans to start a private practice?" she continued.

"I guess."

"I'll be your first patient," she said.

"I thought you already were."

"I really mean it. I want you to deliver my baby."

"I'd love to."

"This is for you," Lori said and handed a small gift to Sloan.

"You didn't have to do this, but thank you."

"You're welcome—I hope you'll get the hint," she said quickly, making me curious as to what the package held.

We watched Sloan as he ripped the wrapping paper.

"*There is No Place Too Far.*" Sloan read the title out loud and smiled. He took the time and read the short book of less than twenty pages—a book with only a few words, big letters, and simplistic line drawings. It was the type of book that said so much in very few words—another gift that wouldn't make it to his other home.

"Thank you," he said again and nodded as if he understood the message that came along with the gift.

"And this is from me," I said and handed him my gift.

"Thank you, darling." He looked surprised.

As Sloan reached for my gift, another flash got my attention. I was disturbed by the two incidents of flashing during the last few hours. *It can't be another flickering streetlight,* I thought. I wondered if I was experiencing a medical problem—something neurological, maybe even a stroke. I started to review my entire system—I went by the textbook, asking myself if I'd had any headaches lately, maybe numbness, tingling, or weakness in my hands. I visited my vision and anything else I could think of. But I couldn't find anything. I was completely fine. But the fact that no one else said a thing about those flashes worried me.

Finally it hit me—I should have considered that someone was photographing me. But I had no proof—no one around looked suspicious.

If earlier I had thought that this night was when my life began, it wasn't. It may even have been the moment when my life stopped.

"Are you alright?" Sloan asked once he noticed that I was in my own world.

"Sure—go ahead, open it," I said.

"Wow, this is perfect. You are smart." He smiled.

"Do you like them?" I asked.

"I love them." He turned toward me and reached my lips as another flash caught my eye.

Now I was convinced—someone was taking pictures of me or of us. *Am I the only one seeing it, or what?* I could no longer keep this to myself.

"Sloan, I think you need to get out of here," I said.

"What's wrong with you?"

"I keep seeing flashes—don't you? I think someone is taking pictures of us."

"You're out of your mind. What do you think—now that I've passed the boards I'm a celebrity?" He laughed.

"No, I just think that maybe your wife is having you followed."

"You have nothing to worry about. She wouldn't spend the money."

"That's right—his wife is cheap, how could you forget?" Lori said.

"Seriously, I haven't seen anything," Jonathan said while glancing around.

"Here, you should be the first to have my business card." Sloan took the first card from the box seemingly unconcerned and handed it to me.

Thirty-Three

Nature continued its cycle, giving its clues for spring to take over—reminding people to wake up and leave their winter caves. It was time to rejuvenate.

My relationship with Sloan metastasized into every aspect of my life. Across from the imaginary future with him rose an excruciating reality of the present that held a punishing and harsh routine, molded from phone calls, short dates, sex, love, hate, pain, and stolen moments. While new elements brought an appealing diversity to the predictable schedule, I was still the mistress and he still lived a double life. And as such, our relationship started to display some rust and bitterness. Clues pointed to the impossibility of the affair.

Passover was fast approaching and, along with it, a threatening reminder of the solitude of the life of a mistress—one more holiday to pretend that I was happy and content with my life.

Time hurried by—Passovers' eve arrived. It was early afternoon—I was ready to lie down for a bit before leaving for a festive dinner at the Rosins. They would set up the table with a seat for Sloan, knowing he would never show up. They would excuse his absence, telling everyone he was on call and was at the hospital because of an emergency. The Rosins knew how to turn any scenario in my favor.

The unexpected sound of the gate shutting pulled me from my thoughts and piqued my curiosity. I was not expecting anyone, definitely not someone who had a key to access my property. Had I left the gate unlocked?

"I'm here," Sloan called as he walked in with a big, colorful bouquet of anemones—a mixture of colors and love—something he put together especially for me.

Moments of joy were mitigated with moments of agony. Words could not add anything to the moment. I didn't have to ask what he had planned for the evening, or find out what he might have bought his wife for the holiday. What I knew was enough. And what I did not know didn't hurt. I wanted to ask him to stay for the night but could not endure the rejection in his answer.

Another holiday passed without Sloan. It was the same dinner, with the same people and the same empty chair to my right. Being apart left us with nothing but aching hearts.

And after that holiday? There was another day, another holiday, another season and another spring. Extreme fatigue drained away every bit of my energy. My tedious day-to-day life became annoying. I was tired of the snobbish center where I worked. I had no more patience for Kaminski or his showoff lifestyle.

I missed the hospital environment, the culture of the ICU, and the complexity of patient care. The unique stress of the operating room was my biggest longing. I reconsidered my options and found them very limited. The unemployment rate was high and hospitals were downsizing daily. None of this enhanced my odds of finding a new job. The cost of living increased weekly but, as experts predicted, had yet to reach its peak. Israel is a small country and there were only so many hospitals and medical centers. It was true that everybody knew everybody, but most of the time, this hurt rather than helped. Society was characterized by jealousy and it was best not to stand out. Low key was a fail-safe way to survive.

Like before, I was trapped in a dance with the devil. My mind was tangled with thoughts of *what if?* Sloan did nothing to interrupt my fantasy. On the contrary, he led me in an imaginary dance of a pregnancy and a child. I was intoxicated by the situation, trying to determine if this was a demon dance or maybe a tango with my lover.

In conversation with Sloan, like in the dance, we were strong-minded about our lives. By mutual agreement we didn't stage the future and let life navigate us—we let things happen and lived our lives. We no longer put the effort into conceiving a child, though neither of us avoided a possible pregnancy.

Spring threatened to let summer in. My birthday was fast approaching and I hoped for something special. I thought maybe God would surprise me with a pregnancy, but he didn't. It was just another birthday. Sloan spoiled me with a gift of love and two consecutive overnight stays.

And when my birthday passed, my life hadn't changed and my relationship with Sloan was in the same place it had been the previous year—only I was one year older.

A few weeks later, Dalia called eager to share some news about one of her acquaintances. "He is about to start work at CheckMed," she said. I could only assume that she was talking about Sloan, but I didn't volunteer any thoughts.

"What's his name?" I asked.

"Dr. Sloan—a good looking OBGYN from Tel-Hashomer hospital."

I wondered which part of the information I should respond to first, the OBGYN specialty part, the hospital where he worked, or the more juicy part, his looks. I quickly made up my mind—I ignored it all. I changed the direction of the conversation so it would benefit me. "Oh yes, I heard about him. He just took his boards, right?"

"Yes."

"I think he's going to start next month. I'm not sure."

"When I heard about it, I just had to call you...."

"So, how well do you know him? Are you two close friends?"

"Not that close, but you know how it is here. It's a small township. Everybody knows each other. Last Friday we were invited to visit with some friends and he and his wife were there. We were talking, nothing in particular, just small talk. Then he told me about a private medical center where he is going to work. So, of course I cut him off, telling him that I know the manager, Sharon Lapidot, very well. He said that he heard that you're running the entire place—that you're the big boss over there."

"Thanks for the compliment, but that's not the case. Kaminski is the big boss. Anyway, it seems like only good-looking people reside in your neighborhood. Is that an admission requirement?" I made Dalia laugh.

"Are you kidding me or what? You should see Dr. Sloan's wife. You would have something different to say."

"Isn't she hot?"

"Hot? You have no idea what you're talking about. First of all, she is a heifer—I mean she is huge—and secondly, she is vulgar—an absolutely awful person. She's always bitter. She fights and argues with everybody. I don't think many people here like her."

"Seriously—I would think that someone like him would have a good-looking woman. Not that I saw him, but I heard quite a lot about him," I said.

The new piece of information about Sloan's wife was exciting, even encouraging. Now that I knew what my competition looked like and that Dalia didn't like her, I was willing to tell Dalia that her neighbor was more than just good-looking, that he was a great lover. I was ready to make her a close friend of mine, but it was still too risky—I didn't know enough about her circle of friends. So, I bit my tongue and sealed my lips. I clenched my teeth, trying not to let something slip. It was too much. I had to end the call. "I don't want to sound rude or anything, but I have to run. Can we catch up later?"

That evening, I joined Kaminski at an important business function—the kind of event that the entire town talked about beforehand and that at least one column in the paper would mention the day after. I stayed close to Kaminski, following his small talk and PR show—he knew all the tricks.

"Sharon, I'm glad to see you here." Melnick, my friend from VISA, interrupted Kaminski's horse and pony show.

"Long time no see," Kaminski said to Melnick.

"It has been. We need to catch up sometime."

"Yes, how about lunch sometime next week?" Kaminski was eager to secure a meeting.

"I'll call Sharon and set something up," Melnick said.

"Oh, I didn't know you wanted to include Sharon." Kaminski's jealousy poured out.

"Sharon, let me get you a drink," Melnick said and pulled me away.

Aside from the big crowd, I divulged to Melnick details from the conversation I'd had with Dalia. The visual description of my competition didn't make him smile—Dalia's opinion about Sloan's wife didn't faze him. He didn't even bat an eyelid. I doubted the quality of his emotional world. I looked at that person standing in front of me and tried to understand exactly how his mind worked—if his emotions correlated with his rationale. I was clueless as to why he didn't take any interest in my news—was he for me or against me, was he happy for me, or laughing at me?

"You don't get it," he said right after he got me a drink. "It makes no difference what she looks like, if she's smart or not, or if people like her. In this competition you are by far the winner. There's only one thing that makes a difference—she is his wife and you are not. She is the one who wakes up in the same bed with him. She is the one he spends time with on the weekends and during holidays, and you're not. She is the one who will get his loyalty no matter what. You are the one who is alone. You are the loser."

I wanted to strangle him and tell him that I didn't have any desire to hear his opinion. He knew that he'd poured salt over my open wounds, wounds that might never heal. But he continued. "Friends aren't here to tell you what you want to hear. Sometimes the truth hurts. Sorry, kiddo."

That summer night, Melnick's voice replayed in my mind. I agreed with his words but wasn't willing to accept them. I knew he was right. My affair with a married man would lead to nothing but problems. The ocean breeze wafted in through the open window. The bright stars illuminated my way home, but did nothing to lift my mood.

I guess no one could force me to put sense before my emotions—not even Melnick. His words fell on deaf ears. It didn't take long before I forgot his lecture and fell back into my bad habits. The next day put me exactly where I'd been twenty-four hours before.

"Hey," Lori said.

"Hey, what's up?"

"I need you to find Sloan for me. My water just broke. I'm on my way to the hospital."

"Are you sure?"

"What are you suggesting, that I might be peeing? Yes, I'm sure. Come on, it's my fourth pregnancy."

"Okay, I'll find him," I said and thought, *Who will find him for me when my water breaks? Will he still be with his wife?* I was disgusted with the thought that he might not be there for me. *Do I really want to have a child with a man who is not mine?*

"Can you check on the kids for me?" Lori asked.

"Sure. Do you want me to bring them to the hospital?"

"Not right now. Just find Sloan."

"Sure. Don't worry. I'll take care of it."

I couldn't tell Lori that Melnick's lecture was still replaying in my mind—that I probably should consider cooling off my relationship with Sloan. I had to place all of that on the back burner. I had to find Sloan for her.

Sloan didn't seem too excited. He was short. "I'll let you know after she checks in."

"You might not have time. It's her fourth baby," I said.

"Calm down, Dr. Sharon—I said I'd call you."

An hour later Sloan confirmed that indeed Lori's water had broken, but her contractions were weak and her cervix was only two centimeters dilated. "It's going to take some time," he said.

"You think so?"

"I know so."

"Okay. Keep me posted."

I left the office, walking from a comfortable air-conditioned building into another hot summer day. My car felt like an incinerator. I had to open the windows and let some air circulate before getting in. Even then, I had to place a towel on the burning seat before sitting.

Finally, I was on my way to the Rosins' house. Shortly after, I left their children with the nanny and went to see Lori at the hospital. I was impatient, but Sloan didn't pull any strings. I had to wait outside of L&D—it took forever, and she still hadn't delivered.

Lori's labor was taking longer than I could wait, and probably longer than she'd hoped for. I couldn't stand being a visitor in a gloomy waiting room. I looked for Sloan, told him I was leaving and asked him to keep me posted. I went home and rushed to the shower, hoping to cool down and survive the heat. A ringing phone cut my peace short. I heard Kaminski's voice, leaving me a message on the answering machine. I couldn't ignore my boss—I stepped out and grabbed the phone.

"Hey," I said.

"What's going on?" Kaminski sounded more annoyed than concerned.

"Nothing," I said in a tone that I knew would make him angrier.

"I haven't seen or heard from you for the last two days. Are you planning on coming back?" he asked.

"Today? I don't think so." I didn't give him any explanation. I could have told him about Lori and make my absence from work excusable, but I didn't—I wanted to piss him off.

"Did you lose your watch or maybe you're working on New York time?" he asked in a raised voice.

"You mean more like Tokyo time." I wanted to show him how stupid he was for not knowing the local times around the world.

"Don't be a smart ass. You know exactly what I meant—did you work a short day, or what? It would be nice if you asked or at least let me know."

"FYI, I was in the office at six-thirty this morning, not to mention that last Saturday I worked twelve hours," I said and bit my tongue so as not to suggest he start paying me by the hour. What I should have told him was that I was sick and tired of his audacity and that he was abusing me.

"I see. But still...." He tried to argue but I cut him off.

"There is no but. I need to go—Lori is in labor and your call pulled me out of the shower."

Even after getting rid of Kaminski, I couldn't get a decent shower—the interruptions continued. I ignored the ringing phone but was attentive when Sloan's voice came over the answering machine.

"Hey, it's me. Pick up the phone," he said. "Are you there?"

"I'm here." I rushed to answer.

"What took you so long?"

"You pulled me out of the shower."

"Sorry. Anyway, Lori just had a baby girl. Everybody is doing fine—no problems."

"Really? Finally. I bet she's exhausted." I felt a twinge in my stomach, as I wanted to be in her shoes—at least for a few hours—to feel what it was to be a mother.

"Are you coming back to the hospital?"

"Yes, I'll be there in an hour."

Six weeks later, when the summer reached its peak, I was in my office working.

"May I come in?" Dr. Lerner disturbed my work.

"Sure, come on in," I said, thinking that this shouldn't take long. He was just another doctor, not a friend, but not an enemy—we'd never had any confrontations.

"How can I help you?" I asked.

"I wanted to talk with you about that patient I saw last week."

Our conversation carried a professional tone until he redirected the subject. "By the way, I heard there's an opening in the Recovery Room at Tel-Hashomer."

Why would he bring this news to my attention? It seemed odd that he would blurt this out.

"It sounds interesting. That may be worth looking into," I said.

"Are you thinking of leaving? I would never have thought that you would be interested in a change."

"I'm not saying I am, but, as I said, it might be worth looking into it."

"Can I ask you something?"

"You can ask. I can't guarantee I'll answer."

"Just out of curiosity, do you have something going on with Dr. Sloan?" He blurted it out, so bold and direct.

"Tell me something, just out of curiosity, how is your sex life with your wife?" I still couldn't believe his nerve.

"Excuse me?" he opened his eyes wide.

"No. Excuse me. I don't think it's any of your business what I have or don't have going on with Dr. Sloan, or any other man for that matter. And why not ask Dr. Sloan? Correct me if I'm wrong, but I thought you were closer to him than to me. Aren't the two of you working together?"

"Come on. Don't take it the wrong way. I didn't mean to rub salt into your open wound."

Really? Talk about presumptuous. "What makes you think that my relationship with Sloan is an open wound?" I held up my hand so that he wouldn't answer. "Wait, no, I don't really want you to answer that. Please excuse me." I got out of my chair, implying that I wanted him to leave.

As soon as that ass left, I grabbed some files and rushed to a meeting on the business floor. By the time I returned I was still bothered by that nosey visitor, though I was amused by the fact that my affair with Sloan turned out to be the talk of the city. I sat at my desk mulling over the open position I'd just heard about.

Seriously? I thought. I was ready to jump and tell Kaminski that I was resigning from my job without any notice. I was willing to accept the new job without applying or hearing about the pay and benefits. *Just let me work there.* I let my thoughts take me to a dangerous place.

I picked up the phone and called the hospital's HR department, inquiring about openings. Within minutes I was tentatively scheduled for an interview. The next day, I faxed my resume, and waited for HR to call and confirm the interview date and time.

Four days after my interview, I was offered the job—but was given only forty-eight hours to get back to them with my decision. Under the circumstances, that was not enough time—working at the same hospital with my married lover could be a dream or a nightmare. Indeed it was not easy to take a substantial pay cut, step down, drop the management title and work as a staff nurse. It was a high price to pay for a few more hours next to Sloan.

I entered into my familiar marathon of pros and cons. I ran frantically between Sloan and the Rosins with my questions—the same questions and the same answers. I annoyed Sloan, calling him every hour, disturbing him at work. I simulated every possible scenario and was close to driving my advisors crazy. I tortured myself to the point that I couldn't stand myself. My inability to make a decision aggravated everybody.

"Just take it already," Sloan said.

"Are you saying it because you think it would benefit me or because you're getting tired of hearing about it?" I asked.

"I said take it," he said.

Well, that didn't sound friendly, I thought. His hostile tone was loud. I guess he had a reason to be grumpy. I knew I was being annoying. But his exasperation only made me question the decision more.

The next morning, with some hesitation, I called the hospital and accepted the position.

I had two weeks before starting the new job, but only a few hours to break the news to Kaminski—telling him that I was resigning with only two weeks' notice. Ouch—that wouldn't be an easy task.

Technically, I didn't have to give him any notice whatsoever—I had no written agreement or contract with him. But that wasn't my style. Besides, I had no reason to hurt him or his business. I took the professional way and kindly approached him, giving him the news.

He on the other hand, lost it and turned into the devil. "You're what?" His eyes opened wide.

"I'm giving my two weeks' notice."

"This is unacceptable. You are committing suicide."

"I don't think so."

"Do you think that I invested in you for nothing—so that you'd leave one day just like that? That's not how it works in the real world and it will not work here, young lady," he said with a raised voice and tapped his pen on the notepad on his desk.

"I'm not sure what investment you're referring to. It's time for me to move on—there's no future for me here."

"Are you saying that my business is not good enough for you?" His face turned beet red. He stood and pointed his finger at me. "You'll be sorry for this. I'll be waiting for you around the corner. I'll destroy you."

"Wow—is that a threat?"

"No. Actually, it's a promise." He exposed his teeth and nails.

Hey, I wanted to tell him, *calm down. I'm not your wife. I'm your employee—soon to be your ex-employee. I'm no longer interested in overtime, crazy schedules, or irrational tasks. I'm tired of the political work that you impose on me and am even ready to give up the rub with the VIPs. It was nice meeting you, but it's better leaving.* Instead I looked at him and said, "I'm sorry, I already accepted another position. I'll work my notice, or I can leave now if you prefer. It's your call."

Kaminski didn't give up the notice I'd offered. He squeezed every bit he could possibly get from me during my last two weeks with him. I had to survive his disappointment and stress along with my own hesitation about the new job.

As soon as I finished my two weeks' notice, I collected my belongings and left. There was no one to say goodbye to and no one to thank. My secretary was home sick, and Kaminski had planned his day so that he would not have to be in the office while I packed up—typical Kaminski, but that was fine with me. Still, I left a note on my secretary's desk, saying, *Thank you, take care. Sharon.* I looked around and walked out with no regrets or second thoughts.

I rode the elevator alone and crossed a quiet lobby on my way out. I reached my car and began my ride into a new chapter in my life.

At home, with only one day left before starting the new job, I repeated my orders to Sloan.

"I'm begging you," I told him, "please don't come visit me in the Recovery Room on my first day—maybe not even during the first week. And, if you need to be there, please ignore me—ask a different nurse."

"What's wrong with you? Have you lost your mind? I don't give a shit about these people. They can kiss my ass. You need to slow down. Take a deep breath. What you really need is some Xanax or a drink."

"Since when don't you give a shit about them?"

"I never did. Who cares?"

"It's your workplace."

"So what? This, here, you and I—this is my life. Come on, let's go out for dinner."

Sloan made his point very clear. It was senseless to continue my speech. He didn't appear to be in a good mood and I didn't want to make matters worse.

Going out with Sloan didn't ease my worries. My mind was still preoccupied with the unknowns at my new job. I was busy preparing myself for the journey that would force me to lie to those I would encounter. Would they cross-interrogate me with no mercy? I guessed it was part of the deal. Besides, I'd brought it upon myself.

Finally, the wine did its job and I was over the subject and the stress. Now all I wanted was sex.

"Will you stay the night?" I asked Sloan while he sipped his wine. "Will you? Please."

"Are you asking me or seducing me?" he said in a soft voice with a gentle grin.

"Both."

"Let me make some phone calls," he said and left the table.

"Are you ready to go?" he asked as he returned.

"Is that yes or no for the night?" I asked.

"I wouldn't rush to leave if not for the seduction you mentioned a few minutes ago." He laughed.

"I guess I'll see you tomorrow at work," he said the next morning on his way out.

"You said that you wouldn't come to the Recovery Room."

"No. What I said is that I don't give a shit." He smiled and pulled me into his arms.

Sloan did honor my request for three days, though I wasn't really sure whether it was him or my orientation that kept us apart.

But after that, it didn't take long before Sloan followed his heart, gradually increasing his visits to the Recovery Room. But since the Recovery Room was the hot spot for many physicians, nothing seemed that suspicious. He turned the Recovery Room into his comfort zone.

With time, he gave up his bed in the on-call physician room and slept on a stretcher in the Recovery Room as if he was better off being within my sight. And me? I watched him while he slept—I could hear his breath and often heard his tiny snores. I watched his chest rise and fall in correlation with his breathing. I could see his eyelids fluttering in response to a dream. And when the summer started to turn its back and temperatures dropped at night, I made sure to cover him with a blanket. And if, in the early morning, he happened to still be on the stretcher, I would gently wake him with a whisper and hand him a cup of fresh coffee.

It was late one autumn night. The nurse supervisor entered the Recovery Room during her rounds.

"Is that Dr. Sloan on the stretcher?" she asked.

"It is." I continued my work.

"Why is he sleeping here? Is there a problem with any of the patients?" She searched the room, seeking a reason why a physician would sleep there.

"No, not at all."

"So, why is he here?"

"I have no idea."

"I heard his marriage is on the rocks. Did he say anything?"

"Not to me. I have no clue what you're talking about."

"I thought the two of you were pretty close."

"I wouldn't say we are close. He's a nice guy, and he's easy to work with. I don't really know much about his marriage." I held to my story and finished up drawing blood from the patient.

"I'm surprised he didn't say anything." She sat at the nurses' station.

"Do you mind taking these to the lab for me?" I asked her as I completed the necessary paperwork.

"Oh, sure, no problem. Anything else?"

"No, everything is as usual," I said, while giving her the blood specimen. "Will you please tell them to call me as soon as they run it?"

"Of course."

"Thanks," I said and couldn't wait to see her turn and leave the unit.

"You bet," she said on her way out.

"I heard his marriage is on the rocks." Sloan's voice imitated the nurse supervisor as soon as the door closed behind her.

"I thought you were asleep."

"How can you sleep next to drama like that? What a bitch. I'm surprised the patients didn't wake up."

"They are loaded with narcotics." I watched him getting off the stretcher. "She is kind of loud, isn't she?"

"By all means. Why didn't you tell her that my marriage is down the tubes, that actually I am getting divorced. That would make her day."

"Are you really?" I said and didn't make eye contact with him.

"Eventually," he said and stepped into the bathroom.

If you would just give me a specific date, you would make my day, I thought.

"I'm going to check the L and D. I'll be back shortly," he said on his way out.

Sloan's few minutes turned into almost two hours. By the time he came back, my shift was almost over. He seemed aggravated and worn out. He pulled the chart cart to the desk and completed charting for his three post-op patients. By the time he was finished, the morning shift nurses had already arrived, gathering at the nurses' station.

"Hey, give me your hand." He grabbed my hand and drew a big smiley face on top of it with his pen. Then he turned my hand over and scribbled, *I'll see you at home*, and folded my fingers over it and left.

Three hours later, away from the nosey people, we sank into our love and passion. The endless lust and hunger we had for each other tied us together. But nothing was enough for the relationship that already had turned into a life that we could not resist.

My new job turned out to be boring and pale. Nothing could excite me at work. My colleagues seemed dull and mean. My interest in obstetrics or gynecology was nonexistent. This job didn't really benefit my intellect, my physical needs, my emotional world or my lifestyle.

Sloan on the other hand was happier, as if seeing me more hours energized him. With each day at work Sloan became more comfortable with our relationship—maybe too comfortable. I found myself redefining our boundaries over and over again. I was the one who watched out for my lover's reputation.

Still, it wasn't long before my excuses and lies couldn't cover the truth. I couldn't deny what my co-workers witnessed. My relationship with Sloan was obvious.

Thirty-Four

I t was Rosh-Hashanah Eve, the Jewish New Year. The homeland's backdrop changed from work-oriented mode to a festive one. The hectic business ambiance was replaced with celebration, shopping, and indulgence. The roads were congested with traffic. Endless steps of pedestrians rushed, beating the wide sidewalks and the clock. The mixed crowd of kids, adults, and elderly wrapped up their preparation for the holiday.

I was no different. Though I had no guests to host and no complex dishes to prepare, I was part of the herd—running with no reason, buying clothes and gifts, and loading carts at the grocery stores as if someone had announced a war, or at least a siege.

There had been weeks where I hadn't bothered to stop at the supermarket, fulfilling my nutritional needs at the tiny neighborhood grocery store—but not on New Year's Eve. That day, I insisted on being part of the density at the stores. I couldn't miss the aggravation of long lines at the checkout and the fully packed parking lots.

I drove to the local pita bread bakery and joined the long column of people. Finally, I bought twenty fresh, warm pita breads as if I was expecting a big crowd for a cookout. How pathetic. I didn't even have a grill in my yard, but at least I had twenty fresh pita breads and meat in the freezer.

To make the holiday perfect, I purchased fresh flowers and four New Year's Eve edition newspapers—*Maariv*, *Yediot Achronot*, *Chadashot*, and *Haear*—making sure I wouldn't miss any political reports, scandals, gossip, crossword puzzles, obituaries, or horoscopes.

Back home, I unloaded my groceries and climbed into my bed. I used Sloan's side for all the papers and a bag of cookies.

The Jewish New Year entered at sunset. I was about to share this festive time with the Rosins. And, like before, they would pretend that Sloan had accepted their invitation but had been called to the hospital. How nice was it for them to pretend that I was sharing my life with a successful OBGYN who was on call? And I played right along with their game of illusion.

If not for the phone call at six p.m., I was confident that I was immune to any possible development that life threw at me.

"Hello," I answered.

"May I speak with Sharon Lapidot?" an unfamiliar female voice asked.

"Speaking."

"Listen young lady, you're wasting your time. You shouldn't wait on him. Mind my words, Dr. Sloan will never get divorced. He's pathetic. Trust me, his wife will never sign divorce papers."

"Anything else?" I tried to sound calm.

The stranger didn't bother to answer me. She hung up.

This kind of drama wasn't what I had planned for New Year's Eve. But being part of such an affair didn't give me the liberty to schedule its consequences. My feelings ran the gauntlet from confusion to shock to worry and stress. I doubted I could cope with this aspect of the affair. I had to choose which path to take. Would I let my morals take over and end this relationship, or would I be selfish and lie in the bed I made? I felt like I was running a marathon, nearing the end, but was unable to reach the finish line. I was weak, hoping that the three-day holiday would allow me to recover from that ugly call and decide on my strategy.

But first, I had to talk with Lori—see what she thought. But Lori was way ahead of me. She was ready to start my fight. She took my chances in her hands and called Sloan at home right after sunset—when the holiday was over. She trusted her power, except she didn't take under consideration his response.

"Hey Sloan, I think you should come here," she said to him.

"I can't," he said with no reservation. He sounded pathetic, just like that stranger had described him.

"Say I'm bleeding—that you need to meet me in the ER."

"I can't," he said.

And with this kind of slap in the face, there was not much choice left. I waited until the next day, a working day—when he was free.

Sloan called the following morning and listened to my story about the anonymous call. He didn't show a hint of stress or concern. His lackadaisical attitude bothered me but I avoided reading too much into it. But when he wouldn't see me for two days, I got nervous—why hadn't he rushed to see me right after the three-day holiday? Was he trying to tell me something? Was he thinking about ending this relationship? How could he not be worried about the situation?

Neither my morals nor my strength prevailed. I took the easy path and let my concerns die. I allowed myself more time and waited to see him.

Although Sloan didn't reveal his emotions, he spent time thinking about who could be behind that call. "You don't think it's Sharon, do you? You know she would never act that low."

Of course I think it's your wife. How could he possibly defend her? She probably had started to fight for her husband and for her damaged marriage. Why wouldn't she?

The idea that Sloan's wife knew about me and about my affair with her dear husband gnawed at me. I resented the thought that someone was spying on me. I became paranoid, trying to protect my privacy—spending much of my time looking over my shoulder, to see who might be watching me.

A week later, Yom Kippur Eve was on my doorstep. It was Sunday at sunset when Israel shut down and entered the highest holiday for the Jews. It was one holiday when the entire country was paralyzed for twenty-four hours, when all businesses were closed—no public transportation, no vehicles on the road, except for emergency ones. It was a whole day when entertainment was absent, when the TV offered only a blank screen and radio stations were silent. Twenty-four hours when I could do nothing but converse with God—a time to confess.

The voices of silence echoed from each corner. Jews were busy praying to God, asking for his mercy and forgiveness. Many spent the entire day in synagogues, and most of the nation fasted. It was the one day a year when the entire country was dictated by religion.

Late that evening, the stillness was interrupted.

"Hello." I answered the phone, thinking that it was the hospital, asking me to come in since I was on call.

"You're nothing but a slut," a stranger said and immediately hung up.

Wow. The tone of that voice, along with the statement, pissed me off. *What an ass.* "Don't you have something better to do?" I screamed. I had to get it off my chest. Who in the world would be so bold as to call me on Yom Kippur? It was stupid to think that this was a one-time event. Undoubtedly, I had entered a war that I might lose. "Don't give up," I whispered to myself.

But that person didn't leave me alone. He kept calling, didn't say much, and then hung up.

The holiday became unbearable. I thought I'd go crazy. I wanted to unplug the phone but couldn't since I was on call.

Yom Kippur was just the beginning. The calls kept coming day and night. My nerves were on edge with each ring. And like before, my concerns fell on deaf ears. Sloan didn't seem bothered and didn't ask much about it.

I let the answering machine deal with my new reality and handle those calls. It was obvious that these calls weren't from random people who weren't comfortable talking to a machine. Evidently, someone didn't like my affair with Dr. Sloan. And who would be the person most against our relationship? But no, Sloan's wife would never stoop that low. The stress was getting to me. Could it possibly be you, my lover, who is behind this evil trick? Why would he want to drive me crazy? Was he looking for a way to end this affair without being the bad guy? *That can't be—I know that much about my lover.* Shaking off a feeling of dread, I continued my life as though on autopilot.

It was eight-ten in the morning. I stepped into the shower and washed away the hospital junk and the night shift that I had just finished. The morning paper didn't disclose anything interesting. All the articles were dull compared to what was happening in my own life. I made myself comfortable in bed and tried to get some much needed rest. My thoughts drifted back to the anonymous phone calls and the person who intended to wear me down. I floated between misery and anger. I honestly believed that Sloan's wife was orchestrating this. I had the urge to get more information about her.

I had to study my enemy. I could only assume that Sloan kept some things from me.

Curiosity pushed morals. My imagination lost its boundaries and rehearsed scenes where I followed Sloan's wife in a grocery store, or visited her at work, pretending to be someone else. I could even see myself stalking her. But my common sense intervened, reminding me that she might already know what I looked like, and maybe more. *There must be a different way,* I thought.

Then it came to me. I picked up the phone and dialed.

"Hello," she answered.

"Dalia?" I asked.

"Yes…"

"Hey, it's Sharon Lapidot."

"Hey, what's going on? Funny you're calling, I've been thinking about you in the last few days."

"Why? What happened?"

"Nothing really—I was thinking about that man you're messing around with and wondering who he is. It must be pretty serious if he's been living a double life for this long?"

"You never asked before."

"It's only recently that I realized that you have been in this relationship for so long."

"Actually, that's kind of why I'm calling."

"Seriously? What happened? Did you guys break up?"

"No, not at all." It was now or never. Did I actually have the guts to do this? How badly did I need to know more about Sloan's wife? Was I actually ready to risk exposure for it? The thoughts whirled through my head. I swallowed back the anxiety and pressed on. "Actually, you know him."

"What do you mean I know him?"

"I mean you know him. I'd bet you also know his wife." The pain of where I stood in Sloan's life hit me again, mixing with the fear that I was mistaken, sharing so much information with Dalia.

Dalia delayed her response. "Should I guess?"

"Sure, go ahead." I let her play, thinking that in a brief moment, I would make her a partner to my sin and maybe even position her as an undercover spy.

"Don't tell me, it's Dr. Sloan," she said boldly.

"It is. How did you know?" *Does she know something I don't?*

"I'm stunned. Give me a second to recover." She paused for a brief second and continued, "What do you mean how do I know? Who else could it be? The two of you really suit one another."

"That's funny."

"No. Seriously. Now that I think about it, I don't understand what he's waiting for, why he's still here?"

"So, you don't think I'm wasting my time?"

"I don't know about that, but I see you guys together. We have to meet—do you have any plans this morning?"

"Not really. I just got home from a night shift."

"Why don't you come over here? Do you know where I live?"

"Sort of, but I'll find my way."

"Let me give you directions."

I wrote down the directions and got out of bed, rewinding the last hour—clothes, hair, and makeup. I looked in the mirror—I was tired and needed sleep—was it the right moment to venture into the nest of my enemy?

Thirty-Five

The drive to Dalia's was shorter than I'd expected. Once I went off the main road, turning into that small settlement where she and Sloan resided, panic squeezed my chest. My imagination pulled me in a terrifying journey were I was passing Sloan's house and seeing his wife, sitting on the porch or taking a walk. I pushed through the anxiety and found myself hyperventilating. My blood was saturated with catecholamines. I fought my accelerated heartbeat, trying to break the fight-or-flight response.

I continued to follow Dalia's directions. The fact that she and Sloan didn't reside on the same street offered me some relief. Still, it wasn't enough to push away my worries over the unexpected.

I stopped at each turn and carefully read the street signs. Once I reached Sloan's street address, I was close to having a stroke. My heart lodged in my throat until I looked again at the directions, realizing that all I needed to do was cross the street. It wouldn't be good to end up lost in front of his house. Though, deep in my heart, I did want to see his wife and even wanted to run into the two of them together. I was ready for the drama but was on someone else's clock.

The beauty of the subdivision overwhelmed me. It was situated on a hill, unfolding a panoramic picture of the local vineyards planted on a sloping landscape. It was a sight to behold. No two houses were alike—each had its own unique architectural design. Many of the cozy, narrow streets had yet to have a walkway poured. It looked high end, living up to its reputation.

I reached Dalia's house, parked, and stepped out of my car. I surveyed my surroundings as if I was a thief. I could see Dalia, from a distance, standing in the open doorway.

Dalia left the formality aside and skipped the social rules. In seconds she invited me into her kitchen, making me feel at home.

"Remember that day when I called you and told you that Sloan was about to start working at the medical center?" she asked.

"Yes...."

"You guys were already together, right?" she asked and immediately answered herself, "Of course you were. How did I miss it?"

"You probably didn't want to be nosey."

"I must say, you concealed it pretty well. You know what? I'm still stunned." She paused and then said, "The two of you are a perfect match. It doesn't even look odd." She stepped away to get us something to drink. If you knew anything about the cow he is married to, you would understand what I'm talking about."

"What's wrong with her?"

"Nothing is wrong with her. She's a bitch, that's all. I really don't blame him." Dalia slowed down as she drifted with her thoughts. "Anyway, he is really something. What can I say? You sure have good taste."

"Tell me about his wife and the kids."

"What do you want to hear?"

"Everything."

"Remember, we're not that close. We don't socialize with them often. But I think what I know is enough." Dalia generously volunteered the exact information I wanted. Again she mentioned

Sloan's wife, describing her size and look, using words like gross, vulgar, and rude. Time passed quickly—before I knew it, almost three hours had gone by.

Now that I knew what my competitor-slash-enemy looked like, I felt pretty good—I was a beauty queen compared to his wife.

And when it was my turn, Dalia's curiosity had no boundaries. She asked for details that she had never bothered about before. What I'd kept secret from her a few hours earlier was now easy for me to reveal—details that completed a mind-blowing mosaic.

As soon as Dalia had put the picture together, she cut me off. "Okay. You're going to love this," she said. "About six months ago, on a Friday afternoon, maybe around four o'clock, I was on my way back from the grocery store. I saw Sloan's wife, sitting on her front stoop. I stopped by—you know, nothing special, just to chitchat. She was agitated, venting about her husband who had been on reserve military duty for the last two weeks. She complained that this time, like never before, he hadn't been home much. In the same breath, she looked at her watch and added, 'Look, it's almost four-thirty and he has yet to come home or call.'" Dalia continued drawing the entire picture from that day. And then, she had an outburst of laughter. "I'm sorry," she said, "but now, when I know why he was late, I can't help but laugh."

And so did I—I had to laugh. But once I told her in detail about the anonymous calls that offered nothing but silence and hang-ups, she slowed down, narrowed her eyes, and frowned.

She believed that Sloan's wife was behind it. "It suits her," she said. "You're better off staying away from her. Don't play her game. She's nuts. The best thing would be to ignore it."

"It's easy to say, but hard to do," I said as if I refused to step back from the war I was already in.

"I can only imagine. But listen to what I'm telling you. It takes two to fight. If you don't react, she won't fight."

Dalia's advice was probably wise but not practical. In reality things were different, not like in her kitchen. My day-to-day life was tiring and, at times, tested my sanity. I was a soldier in a never-ending battle. The artillery used by my enemy was beyond my imagination. My young age and lack of experience were not in my favor.

I couldn't follow Dalia's advice. I had to respond to each and every crazy episode that came my way. I faced malicious calls, surprising mail, and the unexpected reactions from the man I loved.

Life sped up as if someone had pressed the fast forward button and wouldn't let go. It all happened faster than I could react. The number of phone calls increased and soon the caller found me at work. I had no time to speculate about what would come next. I manipulated the calls, avoiding direct interactions with the caller—all for the sake of keeping my colleagues out of my private life.

It was at the end of my shift. I was in the parking lot, only a few steps away from my car, when I noticed a white piece of paper under the wiper blade. *Solicitation? In the hospital parking lot?* I thought and grabbed the note.

Leave him alone! A black pen conveyed someone's mind.

Dammit, this must be his wife. I got in the car and left. Maybe if his wife knew that I suspected her of being the one behind this, she would stop. I had to put a new plan in place. I was willing to lose the battle, but not the war. I was ready to fight Mrs. Sloan and leave her husband behind to wait on my return. Honestly, leaving him in the dark was my best option. I didn't want to count on anybody—not on him or anyone else who would try to analyze me and the entire affair. I wasn't the crazy one—couldn't they see that?

Everyone preached to me, fertilizing me with unsolicited advice. I felt as if the entire world danced around me in a loud, intense Indian ceremonial dance. I could hear the never-ending, constricting steps circling around me. And all they offered was a band-aid—a temporary fix that would not last.

I was weak and failed to break the heavy chains around me—people, occurrences, and consequences. It was all spinning at such a fast pace, creating a fear-inspiring noose around my neck.

I wanted to run away. But instead, I stepped forward and dealt with the note that I'd found the other night.

"I'm going to mail this back to his wife," I said to Lori.

"Did Sloan see it?"

"No."

"Does he know about it?"

"No. And I'm not planning on telling him."

"What's wrong? Why you are so decisive?"

"Because everybody, including you, has an opinion. I'm fed up with everything. I can make my own decisions and I'll handle this bitch by myself."

"People just want to help you and be there for you."

"Oh, really, where exactly did these advisors get their credentials—would you remind me please? What university was it, or was it their personal experience that made them certified? Come on, Lori, do you really think that I'm not smart enough to fight this?"

"I didn't say that."

"Well, are you coming with me to the post office or not?" I asked her while inserting the note in an envelope.

"Are you really going to do this?"

"Yes, I am. And, I want her to know it's coming from me. I'll use my own handwriting and will send it from the local post office—making sure that she sees where it's coming from— Ramat'Sharon."

"What if she's not the one behind this?"

"Don't be ridiculous. Who else could it be? His other mistress?"

Once at the post office, with Lori, butterflies attacked my stomach. I didn't say anything. I could feel my elevated adrenaline reminding my body of its power. My jugular veins extended, empowering my blood to rush through them—my pulse pounded in my neck. I had second thoughts and considered telling Lori that she was right—that I shouldn't mail it. But it was too late—I couldn't stop the line behind me.

"Go ahead," Lori said, when I didn't respond to my turn.

My relationship with Sloan adopted awkward characteristics—we now remained alert to the idea that someone was eavesdropping on us. Our phone conversations carried tension and became shorter. We were more careful than we'd been before. Whenever we appeared in public, we looked out for anyone who might be watching us. Sloan didn't say much, insisting that his wife wasn't behind those malicious calls. He strongly believed that everything was normal in his house and his marriage, that there were no clues that there was something to worry about. I found him somewhat indifferent. I was disappointed with his reactions.

"I'm telling you, it's not Sharon. I know my wife," he insisted.

I couldn't agree with him nor did I get the vibe that he was telling me the truth.

Had the anonymous caller really fooled both of us, or was I the only fool? I had to ask myself again, was it possible that Sloan himself was behind this or was I losing my mind?

While Sloan attempted to remain calm, I struggled to keep my sanity. It was hurtful when he limited our time together. I believed that his wife or whoever was behind this harassment platform was already winning, maybe even celebrating the victory of keeping Sloan and me apart—making fools out of us.

My life turned lurid. I suffered significant lack of sleep—my nights became longer while my sleep shortened. I followed my work schedule without missing one day, not even one hour. I clocked in on time, did my best, and left as soon as my shifts were over. I looked just as I felt—tired, stressed, and worried. It all went quite smoothly until the anonymous person found me again at work.

"Recovery Room," I answered the phone.

"May I speak with Sharon Lapidot?"

"Speaking."

"It's me," he said.

"Me, who?" I asked. And the person hung up.

My stomach twisted and I felt nauseated. It was hard to accept that my private life was interfering with my job. I couldn't afford to let this matter unravel in public.

Twenty minutes later, I called Dalia.

"Hey, what's going on?" she asked.

"Do you have any plans for tonight?"

"No. Why?"

"I need to talk with you. Can I stop by?"

"Sure. How about eightish?"

"Great. I'll see you then."

A few minutes later Sloan entered the Recovery Room with firm steps and a big, wide smile spread across his face. I made direct eye contact with him and stepped toward the door. He followed me, forgetting that someone might be watching us.

Outside of the Recovery Room, in the long, wide corridor, I told him about the earlier call.

His smile irritated me. I didn't go through the trouble to try to understand him or his stupid grin. I didn't care if his expression was meant to cover his stress. My stress and pain were written all over my face. For once and for all, it was all about me. I wanted to wipe that smile off his face and tell him that I needed him—that this was the real test—that I no longer had the strength to fight the unknown. But I spat out something different.

"It must be your wife. Who else would care? The only other option is that it's one of your previous mistresses."

"I never had a mistress."

"Oh, excuse me, I meant one of your previous sex objects."

"What the hell is going on with you?" he said with a glowering expression.

"What is going on with me? Let me explain something. I'm tired of being number two. I want a child. I hate competing with your wife. There's someone in this world that knows about us and doesn't like it. And, the only light that I see at the end of this tunnel is the light of the oncoming train. So you tell me, what the hell is going on with me?"

"You need to calm down. We can talk about it later on at home," he said.

"I'm done talking. I'm going to meet with a private investigator."

"It will cost you a fortune."

"You can't put a price on my freedom or privacy."

"Fine. I'll see you at home around five." He ended the conversation with a taut voice and went back to his work.

"That's it?" I talked to his back.

"Yes. That's it. You're irrational—I can't talk to you when you're like that." He continued on his way, without turning back to face me. I watched him walk down the corridor until he turned and stepped into the staircase. I pulled myself together and went back into the Recovery Room.

My shift seemed longer than usual. Neither the routine nor the excitement of the Recovery Room could take my mind off my private life. I functioned, but my brain was elsewhere. I hated working in the same hospital as Sloan.

Each hour seemed to last forever. I kept looking at the clock, calculating and recalculating how many minutes remained before my shift ended.

At two-fifty I rushed into the locker room to get out of my scrubs and put on my street clothes. I had two hours before Sloan would come home. It wasn't enough time for all my plans. Still, I took my chances and dropped in on an old friend—Oded, a private investigator. I didn't go through the trouble of calling him first or scheduling an appointment. I couldn't spare the time. Every minute was important. I trusted he would see me, if only for a few minutes.

Thirty-Six

Oded was in the office but not accessible. I had to struggle with his personal protective device, his secretary, convincing her to tell him that I was there.

Before I knew it she returned with a defeated look on her face, admitting that I'd won. "Please come in." She gestured toward the door.

In less than ten minutes, I'd relayed the entire, ugly story to Oded.

"So?" His reaction drained my emotions and left me disappointed.

"What do you mean so?"

"This is nonsense, kiddo. Don't waste your time and money." He sounded as if he had no interest in my story. I could only assume he heard stories like mine daily—after all, it was his job.

"I'm not giving in. I want to know who this person is."

"Who do you think it is? Come on, grow up, girl."

"I need proof."

I listened to him carefully. Every item on his menu had its own price. They were all expensive—just as Sloan had warned me. I couldn't believe the price I had to pay to fight with someone I didn't even know. Oded's suggestions sounded attractive but didn't fit my budget. The only thing I could consider was upgrading my telephone service to include a detailed telephone bill.

"I think this is a good start," he said. "Give me a call when you get the first telephone bill with the report. Let's go from there."

"I will."

"You know what? Let's take care of it now." He picked up the phone, helping me arrange for the services I needed.

I left Oded's office and headed home. Traffic was in my favor and I made it home with just a few minutes to spare. "I stopped by my friend's office," I told Sloan as soon as he arrived.

"And?"

"Like you said, it's expensive."

"And?"

"I don't know, but we have to do something. I cannot continue this way."

"So, what do you want to do?" he asked while unbuttoning his shirt.

"I don't know. But, I took his advice and added a detailed call log to my telephone service."

"Interesting. I can't wait to see where these calls are coming from." He took off his shirt, leaving on his white undershirt.

"Coffee?"

"No, I'll have a beer." He grabbed a bottle of Goldstar from the refrigerator.

Though he looked calm, I could see his stress beneath the outside layer. It was hard to say if he was struggling with his pain or with mine. He got comfortable in a chair at the dining table, sipped his cold beer, and placed the bottle on a notebook that was lying on the table. He looked too tired and too lazy to get a coaster.

"Come here." He grabbed me around my waist and pulled out his chair as if he was inviting me to join him. I sat on his lap, facing him.

"I don't know, so don't ask," he said, as if he knew that I hoped to rehash the subject.

He put out his cigarette and sipped his beer. I didn't like the combined sour tang of the two, but I kept it to myself. Sloan was in his own world and didn't say a thing. Needless to say, he was still attractive and sensual. Something in this man acted as a magnet for me, more like an addiction. He pulled off his white undershirt and got busy with mine.

I looked at his perfectly built, tanned upper body, displaying a six-pack that I could not resist. It wasn't long before he had me naked and sitting on the dining table in front of him. My pedicured feet were on his lap and my toes were gently rubbing him. He put his hand around my hips and got closer to me. His lips reached my belly button and my G spot went on high alert. Sloan didn't wait for my permission, nor did he take the time to play. He recognized my body language and let his lips and tongue travel in one direction—south. I got wet way before his lips reached my clitoris. I didn't want him to stop, but didn't want to miss the feeling of his impeccable instrument sliding in me. I held his head in my hands, pressing his face into me as if I was afraid that he would change his mind—except Sloan wasn't about to change his mind. He was wild and acted as if the dining table was our bed.

There was nothing that I loved more in our sexual encounters than reaching the climax at the same time with him, but this time I was ready to explode regardless of his needs. Sloan buried himself between my thighs. "Let it go," he whispered. The vibration of these three words traveled through my entire body and made my pelvis move forward until it engaged completely with Sloan. And once that happened there was nothing else that I needed to do. Sloan and my body played their own duet. I wondered if this was about me or us. I wanted to ask him if he was having fun, but I was too busy with myself. My breathing accelerated and my pelvis rocked on the dining table, moving my clitoris in and out of Sloan's lips. Sloan adjusted his pace to mine until I really let it go, and exploded.

A unique mixture of body fluids covered my entire body. The hormonal aroma overtook the sweaty odor. I still shivered, trying to put my body parts back together. I was exhausted but not enough to refuse Sloan's erection—we started all over again. The phone interrupted our passion. I froze as if the caller might appear at the door.

"What are you afraid of? There is no camera in the phone, relax," Sloan said.

"I can't. It drives me crazy," I said, while the answering machine picked up and the familiar silence was followed by a hang up.

"Well, here it goes again," I said. "At least you see that my story is true and I can eliminate the possibility that you are behind it." I pulled myself off him.

"Seriously? That was unexpected," he said.

"Said who?"

"Said me. Did you really think that I was the one behind this?"

"Not really, but it's nice to *know* that you're not."

The phone rang four more times. The machine picked up and handled the silence and the slams. I didn't say a word. I let Sloan get the idea by himself. The room was charged with tension. Sloan and I stayed away from each other. And when he stepped into the shower alone, I knew that I had no partner to this drama. Right after, he gathered his stuff, along with another bottle of beer. "I'm heading home. I'll see you tomorrow morning on my way to work."

"I'll be here," I said and let him reach my lips for a small kiss.

Sloan left, and I followed just behind him on my way to see Dalia.

I hated myself for keeping my friendship with Dalia from him, but couldn't bring more pressure into our lives. There was enough at the moment. I sensed that Sloan was weakening, but had no idea how to help him. I was fragile and needed some support myself. I hoped that the upcoming detailed call log would relieve some stress and wake him up to the truth.

"Let's go," Dalia said.

"Where are we going?"

"I'll tell you in minute. Leave everything here—we need to take a quick ride," she said with a quirky smile.

I followed Dalia into her garage and got into her car.

"Where are we going?" I asked again.

"You'll see."

"Hey," I said as she was about to turn onto Sloan's street, "I can't do this."

"Of course you can. It's dark and nobody knows you. Let me get you closer to your man so you can see what waits on him when he gets home," she said in a very content voice and turned onto the street.

Fear tightened my chest. Dalia didn't seem apprehensive. She parked two houses away from Sloan's, in a spot where we could see his house. The entire kitchen and living room were clear. My heart reminded me of its place, beating hard from the thought that I might see his wife alive in her own house. I wanted to see her, but was afraid.

I looked around into the darkness. The moon appeared in the shape of crescent, not enough to light the earth. The brightness of the stars was shielded behind the clouds.

Sloan's house was lit up, giving a clear picture of the inside. Its wide, spacious kitchen was open to the living room. The only person I could see was Sloan. His wife wasn't around. I wondered if she wasn't home or if she was lying on the couch, ordering him around.

I watched Sloan in his own home, where he claimed that his life was annoying, but he didn't look like he was suffering. I wanted to see his expression—was he happy, or sad? But the distance blurred the picture. His complaints about his wife replayed in my mind, but I couldn't feel sorry for him. *It can't be that bad*, I thought, *otherwise he would spend the evening with me.*

My mind was filled with imaginary pictures from his sex life with his wife. I had to accept that he must still have sex with her. But how often? Once would be too often in my book.

"Look, I bet he's making her a hot chocolate," I said.

"Why do you think it's hot chocolate?" Dalia asked.

"Didn't you see how much milk he poured? It can't be coffee."

"And why do you think it's for her?"

"Because I know that he doesn't drink hot chocolate."

"Maybe it's for one of the kids," she said.

"Come on, trust me. I'm telling you it's for her. Who else would get a drink that rich in fat and calories but a heifer?" I made Dalia laugh. "Besides, let's not bring kids into this setting." I could only imagine how I would feel if I saw my man in his fatherhood mode.

Sloan picked up the cup and walked toward the living room. Then he bent over and set that cup on the table. There was nobody else that we could see, but not all of the living room was in our sight. *It must be for his wife.* Sloan walked away and vanished. Had he found himself a seat right there or had he left the room?

Nothing more happened in Sloan's house. Dalia suggested that we leave and go back to her place.

"Good idea," I said. "If I see a few more idyllic pictures from his house, I might say that the Sloans make a nice family, or alternatively, I could puke." I wondered why she'd brought me here in the first place.

Thirty-Seven

Two weeks later, only minutes after I started a night shift, the phone rang.

"Recovery," I answered.

"Hello?" I tried again.

I wanted to fuss and cuss to that mute person that was harassing me. But how could I? At work? In front of co-workers and patients? No—I couldn't.

"May I speak with Sharon Lapidot?" Finally a female voice asked.

"Speaking." *Doesn't she recognize my voice by now?*

"Keep in mind that this affair is about to end," she said and hung up the phone.

I ignored the message, focusing on the voice—was it his wife or that woman who had called me on New Year's Eve? I was raging and swiftly dialed zero for the operator.

"I need you to page Dr. Sloan STAT!" I said in a panicked voice while facing the wall, hoping that no one could hear me. I couldn't believe I used the word STAT. During real emergencies I would think twice before using this term—*What's wrong with me? Am I losing it?* Well, I guess I felt that my situation was becoming more urgent.

"Right away," the operator said and hung up.

In seconds the telephone rang back.

"Recovery," I answered.

"Sloan here," I heard him say in an authoritative voice that was ready to take charge over a true emergency.

"I need you to come here now," I said.

"What's going on?"

"I need to talk to you."

"For that you're paging me STAT? Are you out of your mind? I'm on my way to L and D. There's a fetal distress that I need to see."

"The only distress I can see right now is mine. You should come here first—at least for a minute."

But Sloan prioritized his own list, leaving me second.

He came to the Recovery Room only after he finished in L&D— where real problems existed.

"Are you out of your mind, or what? What the hell is going on with you?" he said once he reached the nurses' station.

"I don't know. You tell me." I looked at him and then continued with the details of the earlier call.

After hearing the details he said, "You're overreacting."

"I don't think I am. I think that you're ignoring the situation."

"You need to stop it. You need to calm down."

"Stop what?"

"Stop fuming at each of these calls."

"I see—that's a good solution." I nodded.

"I need to go back to L and D," he said, at which time one of the nurses returned from her break. "Hey," Sloan said to her.

"Hey, I haven't seen you in a while," she said in a friendly manner.

"That's right. You might want to work Sharon's schedule. She sees me all the time." He smiled and left.

It was after three in the morning when Sloan returned. He walked in and helped himself at the coffee bar.

"Hey, Feldman," he said to the other OBGYN, "it looks like all we have is that lady in L and D. I left her on a monitor. I think I'll go and get some sleep. If you need me, page me or call the Recovery Room." He finished his coffee, grabbed a blanket, and made himself comfortable on the first stretcher he found.

It took Sloan a few minutes to fall asleep, leaving me to those intimidating pairs of eyes. I felt uncomfortable and sensed some tension in the room.

My stress reached its peak a week later. It grew exponentially, spreading to every facet of my life. My paranoia increased along with it. Wherever I went, I felt someone was following me. When I was on the phone, I measured each word as if someone was listening. And at work, I was convinced that everybody was whispering behind by back. Then I became uncomfortable walking into my own house. I found myself sitting in my car, waiting for Sloan to arrive. I was terrified, fearing that someone might be watching me from a distance or from a nearby corner. I thought that if Sloan was next to me I wouldn't be afraid, except the reality didn't play out that way.

When Sloan showed up, I opened my window, seeking his attention.

"What's going on?" he asked once he got close to my car.

"I'm afraid to go into the house."

"Afraid? What are you afraid of? Come on, stop it. Nobody is going to hurt you. You're losing your mind." He opened my door. "Let's go."

Sloan entered the house as if he was the homeowner and I was the guest. I felt like a stranger in my own home. Things were different that day.

Sloan and I were categorically worn out. He unplugged the phone and we both crashed in bed.

It was almost four in the afternoon when we woke up. Sloan didn't say much. He kept to himself and looked worried.

"I'm going back to the hospital."

"Why?"

"I'm going to call home, tell Sharon that I have to cover for the on-call physician. I'll leave my car there and spend the night here."

"What?"

"You heard me. You're a basket case. I don't think you should be by yourself. Call Lori and ask her to pick you up out back."

"And?"

"Come to the hospital and pick me up."

"Why do I need Lori? I can come pick you up by myself."

"No you can't. See? You're not thinking. I have the feeling that someone is watching the house from the street." He started to get ready.

"I don't get it." I followed him around the house as if I was his shadow.

"What's so complicated? I want to move my car from here so nobody thinks that I'm here. And if you leave your car here and get out using the back gate, then it appears that you're home."

"Oh, now I get it? Did you think of a career change, maybe a PI?" I laughed.

"Speaking of which, don't call Lori—don't make any calls from home. Leave the phone unplugged."

"Do you think that the phone is bugged?"

"It wouldn't surprise me." His one-eighty caught me off guard.

"So, how will I get in touch with Lori?"

"I'll call her on my way from a pay phone."

"And what if she isn't home?" I looked at Sloan and saw a worried look on his face, though he came across as relaxed and in charge. I was flattered that he chose me over his wife and family. I could trust him more than at any other time. I felt as if we were the closest we had ever been.

"I'll find her. If not, I'll call Jonathan." He paused and then added, "Don't switch off the light when you leave—leave the house as if you're home."

"Okay, and don't forget to tell Lori not to call here, that the phone is unplugged."

"I will." He enveloped me tightly in his arms. "Stop shaking," he whispered.

Thirty-Eight

I left the house using the back door and ran to the back gate. I wanted to run faster but my legs felt heavy and slowed me down. Tears at the back of my throat felt like razor blades. My jaw was locked, leaving me with a sharp, bilateral burning pain, shooting from the front of my ears down to the lobes and all the way under my jaw.

"What's going on?" Lori asked as soon as I got in her car.

"Just drive," I said. "Get out of here—use the back roads."

"Okay. But will you please tell me what's happening?"

"I will. Just give me a minute. Let's get on the main road first."

After filling Lori in with the breaking news, she asked, "Why didn't Sloan say anything?"

"He probably wanted to save time."

"So what's next?"

"I guess we'll pick him up at the hospital."

"It looks to me like he already made up his mind and that he's moving on," she said.

"I'm not so sure."

"Will you stop it? Why are you always so negative? If you believe in it, it will happen."

"Because, I'm more realistic than you. I want to be optimistic, but it's just not in me right now. It feels like my life is spiraling out of control."

"You might be right on that part, but you can't overlook what he's doing. Don't you think he's telling you something?"

"No, I don't."

Lori didn't argue with me. She sped down the highway and got us to the hospital in no time.

"What should I tell him?" she asked while paging him from her car phone.

"Tell him that we're here."

"How will he know where to find us?"

"Say 'chocolate covered banana ice cream bar.'"

"Huh?"

"Just tell him. Trust me."

"What exactly is that?" She asked right after she left the message on his pager.

"You see that bench, next to the kiosk?" I pointed toward the entrance of the hospital. "That's where we meet every shift and have the same thing—a chocolate covered banana ice cream bar."

"So romantic—what do I know? You think he'll understand?"

"I know he will. Look there." I saw Sloan passing through the hospital's gate. He looked confident.

"So what now?" Lori asked as Sloan got in the back seat.

"I'm not sure," he said.

"What the hell is going on with the two of you? Could you be more specific? Why are you being so cryptic?" Lori jumped all over him.

"I'm not. Will you calm down? It's too hectic. We have enough stress without you. Where's Jonathan?"

"Still at work," Lori said.

"Maybe you should call him and see if we could meet him somewhere for dinner?" Sloan asked.

"Why don't we go to our place?" Lori suggested. "We can have a nice dinner and talk without being worried about who's watching or listening to us."

"Sounds good to me. Let's hope it's safe," he said.

"Come on, don't be ridiculous," Lori said.

"What time will Jonathan be home?" Sloan asked.

"Probably around seven," Lori said and hit the road.

Jonathan was ahead of us. We found him already at home. His jacket was discarded and his tie was loose around his shirt collar.

"What's going on? You guys look frazzled." He approached us.

"What about dinner, are we ordering takeout or are we cooking something?" Lori asked.

"You tell me," Jonathan said. "I have no clue what's going on."

"Just more drama," I said.

"Can you be more specific?"

"Why don't you start dinner first and then we'll fill you in," Lori said to Jonathan.

There was nothing that could shake Jonathan's sanity. He always had that radiance of confidence and reliance. But this time, the evening with the Rosins didn't dim my paranoia. I was occupied with those who interrupted my life—collecting evidence of my affair. I no longer enjoyed the sin I was living.

There were only three days left before the telephone billing cycle ended, and probably another week before the statement would arrive.

I was anxious to see the call log, hoping to get my answers and put an end to the mystery and the misery I was living. In the meantime I survived the game, while Sloan had his ups and downs—he appeared in different costumes. It was hard to tell if he was ambivalent or spineless. Our physical intercourse couldn't make up for our pain. The sadness in our hearts started to reveal itself in bed. With each climax I reached, my heart ached and tears rolled down my face. I couldn't pick and choose the measures—I had to accept it all. It was a package deal. I was devastated and hurt. My feelings toward Sloan were mixed, but not defeated.

The telephone bill arrived in the mail a day earlier than I expected. I was excited and nervous at the same time. I wanted to find information that might lead me to some answers. I hurried to open the envelope. I pulled the bill out and sat on the couch. My jaw fell open—239 incoming calls in thirty days. *God, someone is nuts.*

I sank into the log, figuring out how it was laid out and then reviewing it thoroughly. I was systematic, taking my time. In a few minutes, I corroborated that the unknown person was calling from different phones. But how could that person call from different area codes on the same day and sometimes even during the same hour—maybe there was more than one person involved in this conspiracy. I went through each line and identified only two calls that where dialed directly from Sloan's house—both on days when he was on call at the hospital. Clearly his wife was the person behind this game. But I still needed proof.

I identified times when calls that came to my home were followed with calls to my work. Interestingly, these happened only when Sloan's schedule overlapped with mine.

I trusted that once I relayed this information to Sloan he would confront his wife. I hoped that it would be enough to trigger his divorce. Now, when my affair was already exposed I didn't care if someone was eavesdropping on my calls. I rushed to call Lori. Then, I went to Dalia's.

Thirty-Nine

The evening at Dalia's was helpful. I counted on what she said and loved to tell her all about her neighbor and my affair with him. She was funny and intriguing. Her joy from my stories was evident on her face and in her voice. Her advice covered all of my concerns.

"Please don't underestimate his wife. I'm telling you she's a bitch and she's batshit crazy. I don't see her signing divorce papers so easily. I know how her brain works—first she would find out everything possible about you and the affair. She would use all of her connections—and trust me, she has quite a lot. Then, I can assure you that she won't let him go. She's all about titles and she won't give away the status of being a doctor's wife easily. You have a formidable opponent. If you're planning on staying in this game, you'll need to be ready for a battle. And more likely she'll be the one to make the rules. You have to just hope that Sloan won't give in to her. You never know."

"Why would he give in? Our relationship passed the point of an affair a long time ago."

"Wait and see. You don't know what cards she might hold over him."

"Like what?" I asked.

"I don't know, but I know her. I wouldn't be surprised if he changes his mind completely. I guarantee you that he's afraid of her."

"Well, that's not very encouraging."

"But it's the truth."

"Do you think I'm better off not sharing the call log with him?"

"Of course you should show it to him. He needs to be prepared for her unexpected actions."

The next day, following Dalia's advice, I told Sloan that the telephone bill had arrived.

"And what did you find out?" he asked.

"Just as I thought, it is your wife."

"What do you mean it's my wife?"

"What I mean is that your wife is the one behind all of these calls."

"All of them?"

"No, not all of them, only two—interestingly both on days when you were on call at the hospital. But still, it's clear that she's behind all of this."

"I can't wait to see it."

"And I can't wait to show it to you. Maybe you will recognize some of the other numbers that are there."

"Maybe."

"You can look at it tomorrow when you come over."

"I will."

Our plan to see each other the next day was interrupted. Sloan's schedule was thrown off when he was bumped twice in the OR.

"I just finished now. I won't be able to make it—it's too late. I have to run home," he said over the phone around seven p.m.

"I understand." I lied to him as disappointment drained all my energy.

Two days later, on a morning shift, I saw Sloan. It was in the Recovery Room. He had a different look on his face. He seemed confused and tired, as if he had missed hours of sleep.

"Hey, what time is your lunch break?" he asked in front of everybody.

His carelessness surprised everyone but me. I could only assume that his drama at home had already started—that his wife probably knew everything by now. And if she already knew, then why keep it a secret?

"Probably twelve forty-five," I said.

"I'll meet you at the bench by the kiosk," he said.

"I'll be there," I said and watched him leave the Recovery Room.

"Is he okay?" one of the nurses asked.

"I'm not sure."

"He looks like shit," a different nurse commented.

"You're right," I said.

At noon some of the nurses left for their lunch break. The Recovery Room was busy with nine post-op patients and only three RNs to do the work. Time went by fast. I had no time to think about Sloan, his look, or his mood. At twelve thirty-five I gave a report to the relief nurses. I went to the locker room, pulled the telephone bill from my purse, and hurried to the kiosk. I could see Sloan from a distance. He was sitting on the bench, leaning forward—his elbows on his lap and his head between his two palms. He stared at the ground as if he was completely lost in thought.

"Hey," I said and sat next to him.

"Here, I got you your ice cream." He handed me a chocolate covered banana ice cream bar.

"Thanks."

"Listen, Sharon knows all about us—days, times, places—you name it. We have to stop seeing each other for now. You need to give me some time." He looked straight into my eyes, asking for some mercy.

I was speechless. There was nothing I could say or think—I couldn't even cry. My diaphragm spasmed and a sharp pain hit me in my upper stomach. A severe headache attacked me as my entire life and world dissolved, right there, on the bench. There was nothing that I could say. Suddenly he was a stranger—a borderline enemy.

I stood and looked at the melting ice cream I left on the bench. It dripped on the ground, mirroring my own life. I walked away, leaving Sloan behind me. I didn't think he felt any relief from my involuntary acceptance. I walked back to the floor with short, heavy steps. I didn't rush and allowed myself time to start grieving. I heard Sloan's last words asking me for some time, but couldn't see him breaking his chains and coming back. Life without Sloan seemed like a death sentence to me. My heart ached for my loss that I had yet to admit.

I pulled myself together, committing myself to continue working at my best. I was determined not to let my personal crisis get in the way of my work. I promised myself to keep my appearance at its best—not giving anyone the satisfaction of seeing my pain. I pledged to truthfully answer each question that might be thrown at me—no more lies. I was ready to say, "Yes, I did," to anyone who asked me if I'd had an affair with Dr. Sloan.

As soon as I walked back into the Recovery Room I was told I had a call from the Chief of Nursing office.

I picked up the phone and dialed the CON's office.

"This is Sharon Lapidot calling. I have a message here that someone is looking for me."

"Yes. Mrs. Robinson would like to see you. Could you please stop by?" the secretary said.

"What time?" I asked.

"Can you come now?"

"Sure. I'll be right there."

I wasn't disturbed by the request to appear in front of Mrs. Robinson, the chief of nursing. I really couldn't care less about anything that life threw at me. I didn't rush and didn't think about the reason for the call.

I walked into Mrs. Robinson's office. She greeted me abruptly and said, "I received an odd call this morning, asking me to fire you. It was Dr. Sloan's wife. She claims that your affair with her husband should be grounds for termination. And not to mention the strong vocabulary she used — something that I wouldn't repeat." She looked straight into my eyes.

I took a deep breath, trying to process what had just caught me off guard. "What do you expect me to say?" I asked, not wanting to share my personal life with her. "Are you calling me to hear my side of the story, or to let me go?" I asked quietly.

"Neither," she said and got out of her chair. She was a tall, pretty, and well-mannered woman, who was respected by the entire staff. She walked around and leaned on the edge of her desk in front of me, crossing her arms and her legs. "Your personal life is not my business, or anybody else's for that matter. As long as it doesn't affect your work, I have no problem with whatever affair you may or may not be having. And these are the same words I used to express myself to Mrs. Sloan this morning." She stepped forward and sat in the vacant chair, next to me. She placed her hand on mine and smiled warmly. "I thought it was important to tell you about it. You have to be strong now. You are not the one to blame, or at least not the only one—it takes two to tango."

"Thank you," I said in a quivering voice and wondered what she really wanted me to know—that my job was secure or that Sloan's wife had no boundaries to her actions.

"You can go home early if you want."

"Thank you, but I'd prefer to go back to work. Sooner or later I'll have to face it all," I said and stepped away from her office.

My slow pace didn't catch up with the speed of my life. From the moment I left Sloan sitting on the bench, everything happened fast—too fast.

By the time I left the hospital, the entire staff knew about me, Sloan, his wife, and the whole scandal. Everyone became a partner to my sin, but only a few became a partner to my pain. Those who were closer to me asked direct questions and were obliged to accept my direct answers—answers that turned the gossip into the truth. Those who weren't close to me didn't dare approach me, but didn't bury their feelings and curiosity. They looked at me with wide eyes and gave me nasty looks.

As soon as my shift was over, I left the hospital and drove home. I wasn't yet ready to share the latest development with anyone, not even Lori or Dalia. I needed to be left alone. I had to process everything. Sympathy wouldn't help me at that moment. I had to get back on my feet.

Suddenly my home felt secure and comfortable. I assumed that Sloan's wife wouldn't spend any more time or money collecting more evidence from my life. It seemed like she had enough proof. I could go back to my routine or actually start building a new one.

I looked at the mail, giving priority to an oversized brown envelope that attracted my attention. My name and address were printed on a white label while the sender's information was missing. I wanted to think that it was only junk mail, but my instincts told me not to put the envelope aside. I turned the envelope over and looked at its back, hoping to see if the sender had bothered to reveal their identity, but the back of the envelope was blank.

I opened the envelope and pulled out a stack of photographs, clipped together. *Unbelievable!* I thought as I went through the photos. "Wow, Mrs. Sloan did spend some time and money," I said to myself, thinking how Sloan thought his wife was cheap and wouldn't spend the money to spy on him. I went through the evidence over and over again. Some pictures I looked at longer than others and some I turned faster. *Nice souvenir.* I picked up the phone to call Lori.

"Hey, remember that night when we went to out to celebrate Sloan's board exam?"

"Yes."

"Remember how you guys thought that I was crazy for thinking that someone was photographing us?"

"Yes—when you thought that Sloan's wife hired a PI," she said.

"Right. You won't believe what I just got in the mail."

"What did you get?"

I leaned forward in the chair and examined the photos laid out before me. "A lot. Too much to go over on the phone."

"What is it?"

"Photos. All kinds of photos. Maybe Sloan's wife isn't as cheap as he thought."

"I have to see that to believe it. I'll be at your place right after work, probably around six."

"I won't be here. I have to go and meet with Oded, the PI."

"What the heck is going on?" she asked. "Why don't you wait and I'll meet you there?"

"No. I have to go now. Maybe it would be better if I went from there to your house."

"Okay." She sounded reluctant to let me go, but she left it at that and hung up.

I rushed back to the car, drove to Oded's office, and shared the photos with him along with the call log.

"So, what do you want to do?" he asked while glancing through the photos.

"I don't know. What do you think I should do?"

"What exactly bothers you?"

"Everything."

"Like what?"

"Who is behind these photos? Did she hire a PI or was she asking her friends for help? Was anyone listening to or recording my calls? Are there any listening devices in my house?"

Oded leaned back in his chair and looked me in the eye. "I can give you the answers—his wife is the one behind it—and, from the looks of the photos, yes, she hired a PI—and, more than likely there are a few listening devices in your house."

"How do you know?" I started shaking.

"This is what I do for a living. And, I'm good at it, probably the best you can find. Besides, you don't have to be a genius to figure this out."

"So what's next?"

"I'll have to dig into this a little bit, find out more information and probably look for any devices that might be installed in your home."

"How much will this cost me?"

"Don't worry about it right now."

"I can't afford worrying about it later. I may not be able to pay you."

"I'm not going to charge you for my time. If there are any expenses involved with the job, I'll let you know."

"Thank you. That's really nice of you." My body sank into the chair, as I felt relieved and somewhat secure. "Let me know when you find something, and please don't lose the photos, I need them back."

The next day at ten a.m. my phone rang.

"She's not done with you yet," Oded said with no preamble.

"What are you talking about?" I asked.

"She's still after you and him. Most likely she doesn't trust him and thinks that the two of you are still seeing each other."

"Meaning?"

"Meaning that you have to remember that wherever you go, someone may be following you."

"Should I get a bodyguard?"

"No." He laughed.

"Why?"

"Because you don't need one and you can't afford one."

"So, I'm not that important, huh?"

"You are important, but not at risk to be assassinated."

"That's one way to look at it," I said.

"Come on, be realistic. You're screwing a married man who has been living a double life for years. What would you expect? If you were in her shoes, what would you do? She just wants to make sure that he's not seeing you."

Sloan was cut from my life, but I had yet to feel the freedom. The few days without him seemed like an eternity. I was challenged with a reality that I didn't know how to handle. There were moments when I was ready to drive to his house, help him pack and walk him out of there, while at other times I was a hostage to my pain, loss, and sadness. My heart was broken and my future didn't exist.

The malicious calls continued, just as Oded had promised. Often I felt as if someone was calling me back into the fighting ring, except I was drained and didn't have the strength to make it back to the ring let alone fight. The pain that swelled inside me quickly mixed with ambivalent feelings for Sloan. I wondered if the friend I had for the last few years was a worm or a man. He couldn't have done more to convince me that I'd wasted years of my life waiting for him.

Relief didn't come in the form of work. My workplace became a threat. Coworkers pretended to have empathy for me, but sold it for the high price of juicy information of my affair with Dr. Sloan. Quite frankly, I didn't mind giving the entire world a comprehensive speech about Sloan and me—just not right now. All I asked for was some time to digest what I had just gone through.

Fate had its own way, trying to throw us together. But, Sloan did everything in his power to avoid me. He wouldn't show his face in places where I might be. He managed his patient's care over the phone or sent a colleague.

The new form of our relationship was noticeable. Those who had previously witnessed our love and secrets now watched our agony. Some even knew that Sloan's life was shattered, just like mine. The tale was enough to feed the gossipmongers—their comments followed me everywhere.

Forty

Sloan's return to his wife didn't stop the harassing calls I received. We were both under his wife's gun—he on a tight leash at home, and me with no privacy.

Another week of misery brought Oded to my house to remove three recording devices—one wiretap from my phone, one bug under the dining table, and one in my bedroom.

The thought that some abominable creatures stepped into my house and invaded my privacy was devastating. *Is that even legal?* I wondered.

It was after midnight. I was in bed, closing the day behind me. All I wanted was to get to the next day.

An unexpected and sudden ring interrupted the silence. I jumped in bed and looked at the clock—twelve forty. I reached for the phone and answered.

"Hello."

"This is Dr. Sloan calling." I heard the voice of the man I no longer knew.

"Yes," I answered in my stupidity, instead of hanging up on him.

"Listen, everything between us is over…." His words lashed out at me. I didn't allow him to finish saying what he'd planned. I hung up.

I was shaking and cold. My palms were sweating. *Am I going to make it or is my body giving up on me?* I couldn't think of an answer. I would have considered taking 5mg of Valium or 0.5mg of Xanax if I had it at home. Instead, I tried to control myself and took a long deep breath in, and let it out—and again—just as if I was my own patient in the Recovery Room after general anesthesia. But I was a bad patient—I didn't listen to myself. My breathing accelerated, saturating me with carbon dioxide. My head was pounding from a severe headache.

I was overwhelmed with mixed feelings. I sensed hate and disappointment, fear and humiliation, discouragement and embarrassment. It was pointless to say how painful it was to turn the man I loved, my friend and lover, into my enemy.

"I need to come see you guys right now," I said to Lori as soon as she picked up the phone.

"It's almost one o'clock. Everyone is asleep. What happened?"

"Sloan called me from his home. I'll tell you all about it when I see you."

I rushed out of the house, jumped in the car, and flew to the Rosins'. The streets were dark, quiet, and desolate. I ran red lights and exceeded speed limits. I focused on getting to the Rosins—the faster the better.

Lori and Jonathan waited on me in the TV room. Their faces displayed their irritation from the latest drama in my life—I could feel their disappointment.

"I never would have thought that he would do such a thing," Lori said.

"I gave him more credit than that," Jonathan added.

"Sounds like he's afraid of her," Lori said.

"Maybe there's more to it," Jonathan said.

"I guess I lost the war."

"No you didn't. You need to fight. Maybe even hurt him a bit," Lori said.

"There is nothing I could hurt him with."

"Really? Of course there is. It's not that hard," she said.

"Why waste more of your time? Do you really think you'll win him back?" Jonathan asked.

"She shouldn't give in so easy. The man loves her—you know that. She just needs to remind him of that."

"Guys, stop it. It's over," I said.

"You don't know that. Call him," she said.

"Call him?" I said.

"You need to talk to him."

Lori sounded convincing, but not enough for me to believe in it. But deep in my heart, my yearning to speak with Sloan empowered me to make the call.

My intention to hurt Sloan was never executed. My call turned into a sword fight with his wife, Sharon Sloan.

"Listen to me, you stupid bitch," she said. "You are nothing but a slut. Didn't you hear what my husband told you? It's over. Move on."

"You might think it's over but it's not. This will never end." I lashed out at her.

"Look at yourself, an injured animal, licking your wounds."

"But they will heal," I said to her.

I hated her and couldn't forgive Lori for talking me into this call that totally defeated its purpose. I had to sharpen my sword and moved forward. I had to survive if not to win.

It was Sharon Sloan versus Sharon Lapidot—two professional fencers, squaring off against each other. But I was the better fencer. I stabbed her and twisted the sword to the right, paused, and then made one more twist to the left.

"You, on the other hand, might die from the pain—how long will you survive hearing your name, not knowing who is actually in your husband's heart, me or you—just like it has been during the last three years."

Silence replaced Sloan's wife's answer—*Did I leave her speechless or did she choke on her painful tears?*

I knew I'd won. Oh yes, I did hurt her and maybe I even hurt him too.

The confrontation with Sloan's wife assured me that he was chained to her. I debated if he was a willing hostage or a prisoner.

My night was long. I ended up with only a few hours of sleep.

As early as eight a.m., I was on my way to Dalia.

"I have a lot to tell you," I said as soon as she opened the door.

"No, let me go first." She pulled me into the kitchen. "You better sit down," she said. "I think half the neighborhood was up last night. Your boyfriend and his wife were in the spotlight. The lights in his house never went out. The yelling was unbelievable. The dogs in the street were barking like crazy. I wouldn't be surprised if that's the end. I bet you he's leaving her."

"If I'd known, I would have extended the drama on my part and volunteered more intimate evidence from my affair with her husband."

"What are you talking about?"

"Let me tell you what happened last night," I said, while emptying the bag with the groceries I'd picked up on the way. "Where do you want me to start?"

"Just tell me." She set the table for breakfast.

There was a lot to tell Dalia. Starting with the PI's news and the recording devices, through the endless anonymous calls, Sloan's call and finishing up with the cream—my unbelievable conversation with Mrs. Sharon Sloan.

Dalia absorbed all the details. She didn't say much while I was talking. But then she cut me off. "Stop eating. What's wrong with you?"

I ignored her comment about the food. "What do you think? Is he going to leave her?"

"If he hasn't left by now, I'm not sure he will."

"What do you mean?"

"If he stayed there through the night, after all this drama, I think there's more to it."

"Are you saying that I'm already out of his life?"

"Stop eating. You're going to look just like his wife. What's wrong with you?" she said and took the food away from the table.

Dalia never answered my question nor discussed the subject. Was she trying to stay out of this or was she trying to keep my mind off it?

Later that afternoon, I nibbled on a large bag of shaved chocolate. Dalia's worries about me gaining weight were no longer a concern. She had something else in mind. "Is it possible you're pregnant?"

"Pregnant? Are you out of your mind? Who could get pregnant under this much stress?"

"Do you realize how much you're eating? I've never seen you like this—from sour to sweet, from sweet to salty." She laughed at her own description.

"I guess it's from the pressure," I said.

"Are you sure?"

Thank God the phone rang, taking Dalia's attention away from my eating habits—I didn't have to listen to her anymore.

"You're not the one breaking the news," I heard Dalia say to the caller. "I might be the one with some news for you.... It's not something new...it's been going on for the last few years. Also, just so you know, the young lady you're talking about is sitting right here, next to me, at my kitchen table…and in my opinion, he's an idiot—nothing but a loser. She'll be fine. I'm not worried about her."

Apparently, Dalia's neighbors were now busy talking. People knew more than I thought.

Three days later, again in Dalia's kitchen, I lit a cigarette, inhaled one puff, and put it out. "Yuck," I heard myself saying.

"Are you sure you're not pregnant?" Dalia started again.

"Why would I be pregnant? I don't feel pregnant. Besides, let me remind you that for the last year, I didn't do anything to avoid pregnancy and didn't get pregnant, so why now—that's the last thing I need."

And two days later, when I told Dalia that I felt tired, she insisted, "Listen to what I'm telling you. You're pregnant!"

I heard what she said but didn't want to listen. I ran through the calendar in my head, not sharing my thoughts with her. I counted the days of my cycle and then asked her for a calendar. I restarted the count and ended up with the same numbers. I counted in every possible way—from that day back, from the first day of my last period, from the last day of my last period. I added fourteen days, deducted days, but no matter what, it all ended up with the same conclusion. I truly was forty-nine days from the first day of my last period.

Wow. This is bad, I thought. I'd wanted a baby for so long and now, it didn't hold the same appeal. Now it came across as a threat. My knees grew weak from the thought.

"I think you need to check what's going on. Let's go to the drug store and get a pregnancy test," Dalia said.

"No. I'm not doing this over the counter thing. I rather do a blood test. It's more accurate. It detects pregnancy as early as ten days, not like that urine test."

"How late are you?"

"Twenty-one days."

"That means you are three weeks pregnant."

"No—actually it's seven weeks. You count from the first day of the last period."

From the moment I left the lab until the second I called back to receive the results of my blood work, my mind was spinning between reality and imagination. *What if I'm pregnant? Would I keep the baby? Could I have an abortion and live with myself?*

Lori was the first one I shared the results of my pregnancy test with. Then, I paged Sloan, leaving him a very short message, an incomplete one—*Last period on October 8.*

Sloan's lack of response hurt me more than ever. My body shut down—I couldn't move or talk, or even think. I was deaf to the call that came only an hour later. I was afraid to deal with another cold shoulder and let the answering machine pick up the call. It was Sloan.

I heard his voice, hoping that we could revive our relationship. But when I listened to what he had to say, I wasn't sure if we would ever speak again.

"It's me. Go ahead and draw blood for βHCG. Let me know when you get the results." He sounded cold and hostile—a complete stranger. I asked myself if I still knew the man behind that sad voice. I believed the devil would be nicer than him.

I called Lori back, hoping that she might be able to make a miracle happen. But she couldn't offer me anything except a shoulder to cry on, and a set of ears to listen.

"In an hour, he'll be in his private clinic," I said to Lori. "If I call him early enough, before he starts seeing patients, I might be able to talk with him and tell him that I already did the blood test—that I already have the results."

"Why call? Let's go there," Lori said.

"How far are you really going to push me? Maybe you want to go by yourself."

"It's not my pregnancy. Why would I go by myself?"

"That's right, why would you go at all?"

"I'm on your side."

"So please, stop telling me what to do."

If I had known that the man who I had shared my life with for the last three years would hang up on me, I would never have called in the first place. Maybe Lori was right. Maybe I should have just shown up. He wouldn't dare kick me out of his office—or would he?

Two days later, I paged Sloan again, letting him know I had the results of the blood work.

A few minutes later the phone rang.

"The blood work came back," I said.

"I assume it's positive, otherwise you wouldn't page me."

"If you hadn't hung up on me four times you would already know that I'm pregnant."

"What are you planning on doing?" he asked.

"What am I planning on doing? What kind of question is that? Yesterday we were talking about having a child and today you're asking me what my plans are? I thought we had plans together. You're the one who turned his back, not me. You're the one who breached the rules. I'm playing by the rules we made together."

"Listen, this is very serious. We have to talk about it."

"Tell me about it. Are you on drugs or what? What the hell is going on with you? Are you the same man who used to be my friend?"

"I am. I'm still your friend."

"Look in the mirror. Do you like what you see? You are pathetic."

"I haven't changed. I told you that I can't leave my family now."

"Was I just a plaything to you for the last three years?"

"You know that's not true." His voice didn't convince me.

"I'm sorry but I cannot stand your grotesque behavior. Please, leave me alone."

Not only had Sloan turned his back on me, but also he was now showing a new side of himself. It was hard to think that this man was the partner to the eight-week pregnancy inside me.

The topic of my pregnancy took precedence. My friends were no longer analyzing Sloan's marriage. Not that they didn't care if I won him back or not, but they were more concerned about me, and the consequences of the affair. Everyone had his own opinion. Their words rolled off me. My emotions roiled—I was far from ready to make a decision.

Forty-One

F ar into the ninth week of my pregnancy, on an evening shift around five, I received a call from Sloan. He was still at the hospital.

"Hey, what's happening?" he asked.

"What exactly should be happening?"

"What have you decided?"

"I haven't."

"I think it would be better to end the pregnancy. It's not a good time right now." I debated if this was his opinion, or someone else's.

"To think that you have the audacity to say that. You're calling me at work, asking me to abort our pregnancy. Are you emotionally handicapped?"

"I'm sorry. I didn't mean to upset you. But for your own good, stop the pregnancy."

"My own good? What do you know about my own good? I don't think that you even care. Yes, it does hurt, but I don't need you anymore. Get back to your untruthful life where you are a wretched hostage."

"Please, be realistic. Use your brain. We have to talk and decide." He came off whiny.

"We have to talk—we have to decide. Seriously? I'll tell you what, I'll meet you downstairs in the outpatient OR. I'll check in while you go ahead and scrub in—I'll let you abort our child. How about that for doing things together?"

"Are you insane or what? You're crazy!"

"No. I think that you're crazy."

"We need to talk, face to face."

"We don't have to do a thing. The decision is mine. I would think that after three years, you would find a better time and place to talk with me, even if it's on your wife's or your family's time."

"I'll come upstairs to see you as soon as I'm done here," he said.

"No you won't."

"Why not? We need to talk."

"It's not a good time. I can't deal with all of this at work." I started to cry.

"I'll see you shortly."

"Don't you dare come anywhere near me at work. I'm telling you, you might be surprised to hear what I have to tell you in public." I hung up the phone.

"Are you okay?" one of the nurses asked.

"I am," I said and got back to work right away, sensing several pairs of eyes shadowing my steps.

The Recovery Room was busy with patients and physicians. The atmosphere was loud and dynamic—until Sloan walked in. His steps were uncertain and his eyes searched the room. Everyone froze in place and remained silent, waiting to see what would happen next.

I didn't have to ask for a break or to excuse myself. They all knew more than I wanted them to. I looped my stethoscope around my neck and passed Sloan on my way out. Sloan didn't waste time. He followed me right away, leaving behind inquisitive eyes and ears.

It took seconds for him to catch up and walk next to me. The sexual tension that we used to have was replaced with anger and hostility. We walked together, side-by-side, to the on-call physician room, as if we'd already agreed upon our destination.

Sloan sat on the bed and I leaned against the desk across from him. I looked around and remembered the long hours we'd spent in this place. I looked at the four walls that used to be the only true witness to our sin, but they looked different than I remembered. Now, the room appeared cold, threatening, and cruel. I felt as if even the walls had betrayed me.

"You know you have no respect for yourself. You shouldn't unfold our scandal in front of everybody," I said.

"It's not a scandal. And we need to talk."

"If not for this pregnancy you would never speak to me."

"You know I would."

"Stop lying. I don't think you really care about me or the pregnancy."

"Why would you say that?"

"Because. What you actually care about is to protect your family and to obey your wife."

"Don't you think that my family is important to me?"

"I do. But more important than me?"

"It's not something to compare."

"Of course not. How can you compare a child with a mistress to a child with a legal wife? Is she any better than me?"

"No. But she's my wife—the mother of my two children."

"And me? Am I going to be the mother of someone else's child? Just as a reminder, you wanted this pregnancy just like me."

"Now I don't."

"I appreciate your honesty. However, I still want this child."

"I do want us to have a child. But not now. You have to trust me on this."

"You'll have to live with the unknown. I'm sorry but I'm left alone in this battle." My voice quivered. "I gave you a lot of power during the time we were together. You stole my love. I won't make the same mistake twice—I'll hold on to my child."

Sloan stood up and didn't move. I looked at him and watched him suffer. I could see the pain and sorrow on his face. His body language was louder than his voice. He couldn't hold himself back—his eyes filled with tears. He got weaker by the second and couldn't resist the love we had for each other. He stepped toward me and took me in his arms. Did he want me to hold him or to help him out of this bad situation?

"I love you," I whispered to him and kept my eyes away from his. "But I'm not terminating this pregnancy." My voice quivered.

"I trust that you will decide what's best for you," he said and held me closer to him. Our bodies were so close. I could feel our hearts beating together—talking to each other. "You better remember that I'll die with this love and with you in my heart." His voice was weak and full of sorrow.

"That's exactly why I believe I should keep this pregnancy—it's the only thing I'll have from our love. I know you'll never be back," I said and cried.

My pregnancy was nearing the end of its tenth week. I didn't look or feel pregnant. My new physical condition evolved alongside my farewell from Sloan. The idea of having a child or the dilemma of terminating my pregnancy didn't cross my mind until the day of my first ultrasound.

Though my OBGYN respected my request and turned the screen away from me and turned off the volume, he was not careful or shy with his words.

"Everything looks normal. I don't see any problems," he said. "I'm not going to influence you one way or the other. I'll be here for you no matter what. But you don't have much time left. You have to make up your mind."

As my OBGYN said, I was sitting on a time bomb and was running out of time. I was left with only two weeks to make a decision. Beyond twelve weeks it was not recommended to have an abortion, not to mention the moral issues that I'd have to deliberate. The decision that I was about to make would have no point of return. It would be a commitment that I would have to live with until the very last day of my life, maybe even beyond that day. It was clear that either option would change my life.

I was occupied with myself and with the thing inside my uterus, the thing that had already started to form skin and tendons, something that now had a pulse. Pictures of Sloan crossed my mind. I wondered where this pregnancy was in his life. I couldn't think that he just put the subject aside.

I continued with my life, drowning in thoughts from the near and the far future. I tried to visualize myself raising a child on my own or with another man. My thoughts took me back to the dream of raising this child with Sloan, under the same roof.

Sloan's last words, along with his pain, were etched in my memory. I relived our last interaction in the physician room until week eleven was almost over.

Forty-Two

With only a few days left before I had to make up my mind, the ringing of the phone popped the bubble I was living in. "Hello," I answered.

"So, what have you decided?" Sloan was short—even intimidating in a way. The compassionate love from our last encounter was gone. His hostility was louder than ever. The cold, disconnected version was back. The stress was strong in his voice. I could picture his wife, standing next to him, pointing a gun to his head.

I couldn't count on him as a partner, and I certainly wasn't willing to make his wife a third party to my pregnancy. "You need to leave me alone. My life is no longer your business."

"Enough with your nonsense. This pregnancy is just as much mine as it is yours. And I'm telling you to terminate it."

Dealing with the hostility, the hate, and the confusion that this spineless man offered put me in a new position. I was left with one option—standing up for myself. I wasn't too sure I wanted to be a single mom, but was determined not to let Sloan tell me what to do. "I didn't realize you'd already made my decision. I'm sorry to disappoint you. I won't terminate this pregnancy."

"Listen to me, young lady," he continued. "Sharon is adamant that if you don't terminate this pregnancy, we will raise the child." He sounded as if he was close to a nervous breakdown. But I had no mercy for him. I had to survive.

"You are insane. Are you listening to yourself? Or are you reading from your wife's notes? And who exactly is *we*? What right does your wife have to my pregnancy? Does she own your sperm?"

"She's my wife. Of course she has the right."

"What happened to your morals and ethics? Do yourself a favor—forget about me and move on." My voice choked with tears.

"I'm telling you, this child is mine," he said much louder.

"You know what? Imagine I had an abortion this morning. Let's pretend that it's all over and that we don't know each other. Say 'Thank you' and get the hell out of my life. Don't call here ever again."

"What do you mean?" He sounded confused.

"For God's sake. Are you stupid or what?"

"Did you really terminate the pregnancy?" He had some regret in his voice.

"Let's say I did. Are you happy now?" I started to cry, fearing that if I followed through with my lie, I would have to end the pregnancy.

"You should have told me. I would have gone with you." The Sloan I knew was back. His voice was warm and caring. It almost hurt more than if he'd remained cold and indifferent. *Are you senseless or deaf?* I wanted to ask him, but felt it would have been useless to start another argument.

There was nothing left to say to him, so I hung up and left him with his wife and the unknown.

After misleading Sloan, I was prepared to mislead the entire world, announcing that I'd aborted the child I'd conceived with him.

I paged my friend, Dr. Gadi Lotan, dragging him into the real sin that I was about to commit.

"Hey, I need to see you. It's urgent."

"What's going on? Are you okay? You sound all worked up."

"I'm in trouble. I need your help."

"I'm on call. Do you want to come to the hospital? I'll meet you in the cafeteria."

"Sure."

"How about nine-thirty?" he asked.

·"I'll be there."

After breaking the news of my pregnancy to Gadi, I shared my plan with him, asking for his help. "I need you to help me stage an abortion."

Gadi frowned. He tried to understand what exactly I'd just asked. He stared at me for a long second and then said, "You're losing your mind. You need to decide what you're going to do with this pregnancy. Sloan is a by-product right now. This is all about you. Stop fighting over him—you already lost. You can go through your grief, but you have to move on and deal with the more serious thing, the pregnancy. You're almost twelve weeks pregnant—you need to wake up. You're asking everybody to leave you alone—fine. But you don't have to stage an abortion. All you need to do is deliver the message. Nobody is going to check your vagina or the hospital logs. Come on, get real—you need to grow up. Your belly isn't going to stay flat. Eventually, you'll show—and then what? You'll have a new announcement to make. Staging an abortion isn't the solution. Besides, I won't get involved with something like that."

"How did I get myself into this shit? This is so unfair," I said quietly and held back my tears.

"No, it's not. Actually it's pretty simple. Look at me—do you want to have a child under these circumstances or not? If you do, then go for it—if you don't, then abort it."

"That simple, huh?"

"That simple. You want to hear my opinion?" he asked but didn't bother to wait for my answer. "Sloan is history. He won't leave his wife. Do I think he loves you? Absolutely! Do I think you should keep this pregnancy? Absolutely not!"

I looked at him and broke into tears.

"I'm sorry if I sound too harsh. But, we're close enough friends that I can be honest with you," he said and continued after a brief pause, "Let's get out of here."

I let the seed I'd planted in Sloan grow. His belief in my fabricated abortion was something that everyone, but a few, had to believe. The only people who knew the truth were Lori and Jonathan, Dalia and her husband, and Gadi Lotan and his wife.

I was scared of the situation. Sloan's threats reverberated in my head. I met with an attorney, seeking legal advice. I wanted to know if Sloan or his wife could sue me or interrupt my plans.

"What would they sue you for, stealing a sperm? I'll be happy to take a case like that and represent you." He smiled.

Sloan's next move happened when my pregnancy was at the beginning of its twelfth week. It was an early evening. I was at the Rosins. The phone rang. Lori pressed the speaker button to answer the call.

"Lori?" Sloan's voice was clear over the speaker.

My heart stopped. Jonathan lifted his eyes from the paper while Lori let her eyes travel between Jonathan and me.

"Speaking," she answered.

"It's me, Sloan."

"Long time, no talk."

"I'm calling about Sharon."

"I can only imagine."

"You have a family. You're a mother of four. You know children are a serious matter. I need to know if Sharon is still pregnant or if she had the abortion. I need you to tell me the truth." His voice was robotic as if he was reading from a script.

"Is there anyone else on the line?" Lori asked.

Sloan kept us on hold for a long second. Then, he admitted, "Yes."

"Wow, you really have big balls. Don't you think you're out of line? I don't recall being your wife's friend and I have no interest in her being a part of this heart-to-heart talk. However, as you insist on including her, I would assume that you're taking the risk that she may hear more than you want her to."

"I'll take my chances," he said.

"Fine, my answer is simple—you know where we live. I won't talk with you about your affair over the phone."

"Come on Lori, you should understand, I can't leave my house. Sharon must abort this pregnancy. Please tell me if she's still pregnant or not." He sounded agitated.

"Did you just say that she must abort it?"

"That's correct."

"I must say, you are something else—or maybe you've lost your soul. You've turned out to be quite the loser. Why don't you call Sharon and tell her that you want her to abort your child?"

"She wouldn't listen to me."

"I guess you have a problem then. You may not have a problem with being ordered around, but some people do. Obviously, you're staying with your wife and, quite frankly, the idea that you can't leave home to talk to us in person is laughable. I guess you're not the man I thought I knew. Regardless, I don't expect that Sharon would abort her child on your order. Why should I tell her what to do? I don't remember you asking me to step in when the two of you decided to conceive a child."

"I thought that you guys were my friends."

"We are. But you need to understand, we're first and foremost Sharon's friends."

I couldn't believe what I heard. I was impressed with Lori's speech and gave her credit for the way she handled it.

Three days later, I turned in my letter of resignation. It was a short and professional letter. I explained that my urgent resignation was related to family matters and therefore I could not offer any notice.

"I'm sorry," I told Mrs. Robinson. "I can't do it. My life is a mess right now. I have no time to deal with this scandal. I have to deal with its consequences. This isn't where I need to be right now. I need a better place—a safer one."

"I understand," she said and stood up.

"The letter doesn't reflect the exact reason for my resignation. I thought it would be better to keep it off my record."

"Certainly. Don't worry about it." She walked toward me.

"I want to thank you for your support and understanding. I truly appreciate it." I extended my hand to her, but she stepped toward me and put her hands on my arms, looked in my eyes and said, "I hate to lose you." Then she gave me a hug.

"Thank you."

"Good luck." She pulled back and looked at me.

I left her office and never stepped foot in that hospital again.

That afternoon, I was already holding a one-way ticket to the United States and was occupied with what I had to accomplish before leaving.

I was organized and worked through my list systematically. I packed two big suitcases. I went through books, papers, gifts, linen, towels, dishes, and furniture. I opened each of the cabinets and drawers. I boxed most of the stuff, threw some things away and gave some to my friends. What ended up in the suitcases was very limited.

The last piece of furniture that I had to deal with was the writing desk at the entrance of the house. While looking at it, I became nauseated and dizzy—was it my pregnancy or the mixed feelings I had toward the items that were buried there?

Deep inside that desk, evidence of the last three years of my life was waiting on me—things that I would never have thought I'd have to say goodbye to. They held meaning and history—they could breathe and feel—I could smell them. They were things that once were alive and were now about to die—things that could never find a second home.

I stared at that piece of furniture as if it was living my pain. I wanted to be left alone to deal with those things by myself—I had to go through the grieving process.

"I'll deal with it later," I told Lori who was packing my kitchen. "When I'm by myself."

"Are you sure?"

"I just need some time alone."

"You know what? It's getting late. Why don't I leave now and I'll take the day off tomorrow so I can help you," she said. "I'll be back around ten."

Forty-Three

I called Dalia, asking her if she could possibly keep my special writing desk at her house.

"Of course. When do you need it out?"

"Tomorrow will be fine."

I looked at the desk and wondered what went wrong. Why did my fairytale have to end as a nightmare?

With pain in my heart and tears in my eyes I studied each item that I found. Pop songs kept me company, playing in the background. The artist's voice filled the entire house and his words penetrated my heart.

I held pieces from the past—a puzzle that I would never be able to put back together. I collected each of the belongings of the man who no longer existed in my life, but had left his footprints in my heart and my uterus. I pulled out notes that he'd left me on different occasions, photos of him and of us. I looked around. There was much more of him and us around the house—two books with dedications from the Rosins, gifts that I bought for him, a toothbrush, a razor, aftershave, and some clothes. Wherever I looked and whatever I touched was him. I missed him terribly. My body ached as if I was withdrawing from street drugs. I held our two white terry robes close to my chest. I looked at the embroidery that I'd designed—one said *Happi,* the other said *ness,* and together they simply said, *Happiness*—the one thing that I'd believed no one could take away from us. I grabbed the tapes from the answering machine and broke down at the thought of what they held—they were the evidence of our love, lust, and pain. They could replay everything that was in Sloan's heart along with those malicious, anonymous calls.

I added these items to the desk and locked it, ending a long, exhausting chapter in my life—a chapter that was now in the form of voice and text, filed in a piece of antique furniture.

Gadi stopped by late that night on his way home from work. He offered his help with things that required more muscle. He really didn't say much until he was ready to leave. He stopped by the answering machine and replaced its outgoing message with his own voice—*No one can take your call. Please leave a message after the beep.* "That's it," he said. "Sharon Lapidot is no longer living in this house. It's over—it's history. You're about to start a new life. Go get some rest. I'll see you tomorrow evening."

"Thanks. I wish I would've done that earlier rather than just a few days before I leave," I said and gave him a hug.

"Are you taking Marco with you?" He stopped by the cage on his way out.

"I wish I could. I need to find him a warm, loving home. Everybody loves him but no one wants him."

"I would be happy to babysit him for you." He smiled.

"Really, you would do that?"

"Sure, why not? He's a nice little guy. I like him."

"That would be great. Thank you."

"Here, I can take him now." He was ready to pick up the cage.

"Maybe tomorrow? Do you mind leaving him with me for one more night?"

"Sure. Why not?"

The little rest that I got that night was enough to carry me through the next day.

Lori showed up a few minutes before ten a.m. when I'd already been working around the house for a good two hours.

I said goodbye to my belongings and was left with the writing desk, a few boxes and Marco. These were scheduled to go to their new homes with my friends.

That evening, seven of us gathered around the table—Lori and Jonathan, Dalia and Rami, Gadi Lotan next to his wife, and me. I looked around, searching for the empty seat that Lori was supposed to leave for Sloan. But she had stopped pretending—she finally lived the reality that I'd refused to accept. I, on the other hand, could still feel Sloan as if he was there with us. I could smell him and even hear his breathing. If I closed my eyes, I could swear he was standing right next to me.

"You should let him know that you're leaving the country pregnant." They echoed their consensus but were unable to convince me. I was still preoccupied with the writing desk and its contents. I revisited the items that it stored, wondering who might look through it in the future. I'd hoped that Sloan would give me a hand, but I could no longer see him around—just when I needed him, he'd vanished.

Two nights later at the Rosins', before leaving for the airport, I picked up the phone and dialed Sloan's house.

"It's me," I said right after he answered the phone.

"Yes?" he said and then rushed to converse with someone else—clearly telling his wife to get on the other line.

"I'm calling because I think you should know that I'm still pregnant and am leaving for the United States."

"You're not going anywhere—you're going to be surprised," his wife's voice cut in.

A picture of that enormous woman tackling me at the airport crossed my mind. I shook the image away and said, "Sloan, whatever was between us is over. I hope that you choose what's best for you. But just like you, I have to move on."

"You know you're crazy. I just hope that the baby won't be born crazy like the mother." His wife's voice was hysterical.

"Sloan," I said, "please don't let this conversation disintegrate. Let's keep the respect we had for each other."

"Keeping this pregnancy won't pull me from my family. I'm staying here, with them." His voice was stiff and devoid of emotion.

"And we will be the one to raise this child," his wife added, making me want to go back to my collection of tapes, looking for the most sensual, loving message that her husband had left me and play it for her. Instead I chose to ignore her and to direct my conversation to Sloan.

"Listen, wherever I go, this pregnancy goes with me. This child is mine from now to eternity. You chose to give up—I didn't."

"If you think that your VIP family or their money will help you, you're wrong," his wife screamed. She sounded deranged—completely out of her mind. "Let me tell you something, you're nothing but a host to this baby. You won't have the chance to see this child. I'm going to take it away from you as soon as it takes its first breath. I'll make sure that you are nothing but a surrogate mother."

Did she say "it"? How could she refer to my child as a thing? "I suggest that you calm down," I told her.

"This child will be raised here, in this house and will take the name Sloan. Do you understand? And don't fool yourself. You are not departing this country with this pregnancy."

"Seriously? I don't recall seeing you in my bed when this baby was conceived. Remind me please, what part do you have in this pregnancy?" I asked her.

"Make no mistake, my husband is not leaving this house. We are one unit."

"Yes, we are one unit." Sloan agreed with his wife as if he was a puppet on a string.

I laughed at the horror of it all. "Really? Funny, I didn't see her in our bed, in the dreams we shared, and in the nights that you called home, lying, so that we could spend more time together. Weren't the two of you one unit then? I couldn't care less that you claim to be one unit." I was out of breath, but still had more to say. "It's one thing that you lost me, but to lose us? To me it looks like you are a puppet and your wife is the puppeteer. Anyway, I didn't call to negotiate with either of you. I only called because I couldn't leave with you not knowing that you'll have a child somewhere out there in the world."

I truly felt how my words hurt them but I still wasn't satisfied. I had the need to stick the skewer into her one more time, but this time I had to make sure that it would be white-hot. I didn't wait for their response, but continued right away.

"I guess you guys will try to live your lie. But the truth is with me. I can only imagine how our sin will haunt you for the rest of your life. But your sin of betraying me might destroy you first."

Forty-Four

At three a.m. at the Ben-Gurion airport, I walked toward Delta's counter. My thoughts were locked on Sloan's wife's threats—would she really try to stop me from leaving? Would I be arrested at the immigration checkpoint? I doubted if I would be able to survive such a situation. My thoughts reached possible dialogues with the authorities and my attorney.

The previous conversation with a lawyer friend shook me up. I recalled his words to me. "Trust me. You have nothing to worry about. There is nothing they can do. Relax. What can they sue you for, stealing a sperm? He should kiss your ass and thank you for not suing him for paternity."

"Terminal two, gate three. Boarding at four-twenty." The airline representative handed me the boarding pass along with my other documents. "You've been upgraded."

"Thanks," I answered and didn't bother to ask what kind of upgrade.

It was time to say goodbye. I looked around, searching for familiar faces, but there was no one there. I wanted to ask for some mercy and prayed to the Lord, asking him to do something, to grant me a favor or even a miracle, but nothing happened.

I took a deep breath, inhaling the air of the Holy Land for the very last time—air from the place where I was born and where I belonged. I relived the past again, sailing between pictures and memories, deciding what I would take with me for the future and what I would leave behind.

Friends', coworkers', enemies', and gossipers' faces crossed my mind. I hoped they could now find a better topic for their venom.

I imagined Sloan's voice, whispering loving words, flying with me into tomorrow's dreams. I fancied seeing him, even smelling him. I wanted to run into his arms, but he wasn't there.

The memories became tainted and my feelings were mixed. The sweet memories of impossible love were not enough for me to forgive Sloan. I wanted to kill my love for him but, like a greenhorn solider, I couldn't pull the trigger.

The anonymous woman's voice from the call on New Year's Eve crossed my mind. I wondered if I should have used a different strategy. Would the roll of the dice have been any different?

My entire body was covered with goose bumps and I thought I could feel Sloan touching me. I wanted to run to a pay phone and call him so I could hear his distinctive voice one more time. I was willing to pay any price to God for changing it all, maybe even rewinding it to those days that I missed so much. But God was already rewiring my brain and pushing me to move on.

I had to concede that Sloan's wife had won the war, though her win was diluted with pain and insult. The only solace I found was that she ended up with her spineless husband. I wondered how I would have perceived him if he'd left her and chosen me—would he still be pathetic and spineless or would he be my hero?

I looked at Lori. Leaving her behind was hard. The silence spoke for itself. I let my tears convey what was in my heart.

I walked to the escalator, to the point of no return. I didn't turn back to look at Lori again. I kept looking straight ahead to where I had to be next.

I reached the immigration police counter. No one was waiting or looking for me. There were no legal documents to deal with or phone calls to make. It was just a stamp on my passport that sealed my exit. Who cared if I was Dr. Sloan's mistress? Why would the law be concerned if I was pregnant or not?

My steps on the portable stairs leading into the airplane were heavy. It was as if my feet refused to take me into tomorrow. I turned around and looked one more time at the view of my homeland, my country. Would I ever come back?

I stepped into the aircraft. A smiling flight attendant welcomed me, offering to escort me to my seat.

"Five A? Are you sure?" I asked. It finally dawned on me what kind of upgrade I'd received.

"I'm positive. Please follow me," she said and turned left toward the first class cabin.

"What would you like to drink?" she asked right after I took my seat.

"I'm fine. Thank you."

I looked around. No one looked familiar or suspicious. As a matter of fact, the first class cabin was pretty empty. I wondered who would sit next to me or if I would be lucky enough to finally be left alone and start it all from the beginning.

And actually I did. On that flight, I started a new chapter in my life—the one that happened to be the third phase of my life.

Forty-Five

There was one last page left for Leigh to read—the one in which she'd delayed reading. She had to deal with her emotions first. It wasn't just her mother's journal. It was the beyond—her genes and identity. How could she suddenly be someone else?

She looked at the last page. Its appearance resembled the very first one she'd read—fresh and new.

My dear daughter, Leigh,

I can only imagine what you are going through. You are probably confused and overloaded with doubts and questions. Though I am ultimately responsible for all the shocking information you have just read, I might not have answers for you.

My commitment to you started the minute I made up my mind not to abort you—way before you were born. It was a promise to love you unconditionally and to preserve you at any price—a pledge that I still stand behind each day of my life.

I couldn't possibly convince you to agree with my thoughts and feelings. Clearly I couldn't confer with you at the time.

Once you've looked at the circumstances in which you came into the world, I trust you'll understand why I didn't expose you to the truth earlier.

Life is a chain of endless, different loves. One love cannot resemble another. They each uniquely serve you in some way.

The love that transpired between your biological father and me left many scars. There are times when my heart still replays what it buried. There are minutes, hours, and even days that I still love him in the same way, as if nothing has changed. Again and again I recall the farewell that never materialized, standing at Ben-Gurion airport, carrying you inside me—my last few minutes in Israel—knowing that the fairytale had ended and I had to close the book. I looked around to see if your father had changed his mind. But he didn't. Sad to say how I still look for him each time I pass through that airport.

I have no doubt that you are the result of a supreme, impossible love. You are the testimony of your father's statement that our love would never die.

Maybe that's how things were meant to be. None of us could know what would have happened if we would have married.

Today, when you turn eighteen, I no longer have the right to keep you against your will.

Only you can decide whether to accept the decision I made. Use the information I provided you with. Go and meet your biological father and decide for yourself.

There are many late entries that I could add to my journal—I probably should have kept writing for you over the years. However, the only thing that I know about your father is that he is alive, residing in Israel and a father of three. I'm clueless about his feelings for you—I cannot guarantee you that he knows about you. You have to remember that I did challenge him and suggested that he abort you with his own two hands, but he refused—you should at least give him credit for that.

All that I have for you are assumptions—it's not enough for you to make decisions.

Whatever you decide or choose, I will always love and support you.
With all my heart,
Love, Mom.

Dear kiddo,
I realize that today you may decide to change your last name and
maybe even find a new or additional father.
In my world, you have always been and always will be my daughter.
Love, Steve.

The last page she read didn't resemble any of her mother's notes. It was just related to them.

It was not about accepting her mother's decisions. Obviously, she had been alive for the last eighteen years and, quite frankly, had nothing to complain about. It was about her not being sure if her mother really wanted a child or if she was looking for a tool for revenge. She questioned her mother's love for her. She wasn't certain of her mother's motive for sharing a secret that she had kept for eighteen years.

Reading her mother's journal hadn't changed Leigh's life but made her pause. The revelations from reading her mother's journal would force her to mature. How was she to feel about her mother and the man who raised her?

She sank into an emotional storm—love and hate, anger and acceptance, pain and sorrow, disappointment and hope, and beyond all, fear and confidence. She was confused—not understanding her yesterday and questioning her tomorrow.

Leigh couldn't comprehend how both, her mother and Steve could have lied to her all these years. She wondered what they'd been thinking—*Did they think that they'd done me a favor, or did they believe that they were protecting me? Was it right to raise me under a name that had nothing to do with my genes? Should they have told me all of this earlier, or should they have taken it with them to their graves? Did they really want me to forgive them or did they think that I would turn my back on them? Should I judge them or should I thank them?*

Her mother's confession wasn't enough to relieve Leigh's emotional storm. Her disappointment and anger took over.

She developed nothing but hate toward her biological father. She couldn't care less that he wasn't a part of her life. Though, she questioned his qualities that were revealed from what she'd read. She despised him for turning his back on her mom—for being a puppet as her mother had described him.

Although Leigh wasn't sure if her father knew about her or not, she felt as if he'd abandoned her. She wanted to see what he looked like, if she resembled him. She was curious to know why he hadn't left his wife and married her mom—why had he chosen his other kids over her—were they better than her, or maybe he had many more kids around the world. Suddenly, she had the need to cause pain to that man whose genes were a part of her genetic makeup.

And finally, she cried.

It didn't take long before Leigh made up her mind. Five weeks after her eighteenth birthday, Leigh landed in Ben-Gurion airport in Tel-Aviv. Dalia was waiting for her right after the baggage claim area.

"Here's the key and here is that writing desk you are looking for," Dalia said to Leigh.

The idea of going through the desk and seeing all the things that she'd read about was too much. Leigh couldn't deal with that at the moment and maybe she never would.

"I don't need it. I have enough. I want to see him."

"Do you have a plan in mind?" Dalia asked.

"I could knock on his door—he lives here somewhere, doesn't he?"

"He does. But do you want to take the chance of dealing with his wife?"

"What would you do?" Leigh asked.

"I would probably call his office and schedule an appointment and make sure I got the last appointment of the day. I'll go with you."

"That would be great."

"Have you thought about what you're going to tell him?" Dalia asked.

"There's only one thing that I want to know," Leigh looked in Dalia's eyes but never finished her sentence.

Dalia did not push the conversation further. She already knew what was on Leigh's mind.

Leigh was overwhelmed by the circumstances and tried to get over the jetlag. The five days that she had before meeting her biological father should have been enough to recoup.

She took the time to get ready for the meeting, paying attention to every little detail. She prepared all the documents she needed, securing them in an oversized envelope. Then she made sure she looked her best.

She sat in the passenger seat next to Dalia—her stomach in knots. She was afraid that her father might deny the whole story and walk her out of his office, or that he would call the police, or, worse yet, call his wife, the puppeteer, as her mother had described her.

"Do you think I need an attorney?" Leigh asked Dalia.

"Not yet. Maybe later. It depends on what you want to accomplish."

"What do you think he'll say?" Leigh asked.

"I have no idea." At least Dalia was being honest.

Dalia parked. Leigh was emotionally exhausted and she hadn't even met her father yet. She walked next to Dalia, holding the big white envelope against her chest. It was the only thing that could lead her to her biological father—a copy of her mother's notes.

Dalia checked Leigh in and sat next to her in the lobby. Leigh went by her stepfather's last name and didn't see any reason for her biological father to become suspicious. She rehearsed her questions in her mind, as if she was about to give a presentation at school. But there was no school and no presentation. It was simple—she was about to tell her father that he had a daughter.

"Ms. Stone," the secretary announced.

Leigh stood, remembering what Dalia had told her about private practices in Israel. *I should walk into his office first, where he'll be sitting behind his desk, waiting on me.*

And that's exactly how it transpired.

"Ms. Stone, it's nice to meet you," he said. "Can I call you by your first name?"

"Yes," she said softly.

"What brings you in?" Dr. Sloan asked.

"Well," she said and paused.

"Go ahead," he said and continued his chart review.

She couldn't say a word. Her body was glued to the chair as if she weighed three hundred pounds. She was speechless and afraid but not ready to run away.

"Leigh?" he said again and finally looked at her.

She looked back at him and studied his face. He looked exactly as her mother had described him only with the addition of the passing years.

"Is this your first visit with an OBGYN?" he asked, as if trying to understand why she was reluctant to tell him the reason for her appointment.

"Actually no, but it's my first visit with my father," she finally said. "Do you know about me?"

His face turned pale and he didn't answer. He leaned back into the chair, stretched, and took a deep breath.

"Well, I guess you don't. So here I am. I brought you a copy of my mother's notes. I'm sure you'll recognize the content." She placed the envelope on his desk.

He looked into her eyes and reached for the envelope. His hands were steady but he took his time opening it.

"Did you love her?" she asked.

He lifted his eyes and brought his hand to his chest as if he was not feeling well. "And I still do," he said in a weak voice.

"Are you okay?" she asked and saw his head hitting his desk.

Leigh jumped out of her chair, pushed the intercom button on the phone, and screamed, "I need help." She didn't hesitate—she rushed around the desk, pulled her father out of his chair, positioned him securely on the floor and immediately started to perform CPR. "Don't die on me now. This isn't fair," she told him while she delivered chest compressions. "Don't you do to me what you did to my mother—don't you turn your back on me." She talked to him as if he could hear her. "Don't die on my watch."

Almost fifteen minutes elapsed before the ambulance arrived. Leigh didn't revive her father but didn't give up. She stepped aside and watched the professional team do what she could not. Finally the straight line on the monitor came to life.

Leigh walked out of the building and saw the crowd of strangers. Shortly after, her father was lying on a stretcher and was rolled to the ambulance. He was unconscious, intubated, covered with a blanket, looking weak and pale. An IV line linked his arm to a fluid bag and his heartbeats were displayed on the portable monitor.

There was no telling how bad the situation was and if her father would survive. Although she had no strong emotional ties to him, she needed him to survive so she could get answers to the many questions that she still had.